DROP DEAD, LOSER

A Quirky Kind of Zombie Novel

JOE ARZAC

Front cover design by SelfPubBook-Covers.com/FrozenStar

To MB, C, and A

PART I

1

Morbid High got its name from Horatio Morbid, a Civil War colonel who fought for the South but returned to Illinois to seek his fortune after losing a leg to cannon fire. Legend has it that Colonel Morbid killed a thousand men in battle and that the ghosts of the violently departed followed him for the rest of his days, tormenting his soul until he blasted out his own heart with a shotgun. None of the high school kids believe a word of the legend, and most parents think it's a load of crap, but the fact remains that Colonel Morbid prospered in dry goods and used his fortune to found Pleasanton, making it the first town in the state with indoor plumbing. Why on earth isn't the town named Morbid then, you might ask? Well it was, originally. But back in 1971, about three years after the First Occurrence in Pennsylvania and right about the time most folks realized that the zombie problem was not going away, the town elders held a meeting and voted to change the name. They figured that a name like Morbid would send the wrong message to the rest of the country, in light of the facts, and scare away tourists. So Morbid, IL became Pleasanton, IL on December 21, 1971 – population twelve thousand. The elders saw fit to keep the name of the original high school though, I guess as a means of assuaging Colonel Morbid's ghost. You can never be too careful these days. There's always the chance the old colonel could come back from the grave, pissed as hell.

The bell just rang. I'm late again.

"Mr. Kantra, happy for you to grace us with your presence this fine morning," Twid, the Squid, sneers. Her name is Ms. Twid, high school English teacher, but we like the cephalopod moniker better, given her shapeless physique and inherent ability to suck the life out of you.

"Sorry," I say.

"Not good enough. Now please recite the opening stanza of William Blake's *The Tyger*."

"Uh, tyger, tyger burning bright, in the forests of the night. What immortal hand or eye could fear your fateful misery?"

"Sit down, Mr. Kantra."

"Did I get it wrong?"

"Marvin could have done a better job."

The class explodes into laughter, Amy Fairchild the loudest of all. Marvin Reynolds was our token zombie. Every class has one, the result of the integration laws of '96. He had to drop out last semester though to get a job. Works at Artie's now. Rumor has it that he gives out free curly fries to his friends.

"That's enough class."

"Now what about you, Miss Sky? I know I can rely on you."

Chastity shifts the weight of her body, and a glimpse of cleavage peaks through the V of her shirt. Milky white within a sea of black. "Tyger, tyger burning bright. In the forests of the night. What immortal hand or eye could frame thy fearful symmetry?"

"Very good, Miss Sky. Now what do you think this poem means? What is Mr. Blake trying to tell us with his beautiful and powerful use of words?"

"I'm not sure."

"Don't be shy. How could you be with those earrings sticking out of your face? Just tell the class what you think."

"Well, maybe he's just marveling at the wonder of nature. How powerful it can be. How fierce. How a creature like a tiger can on the one hand be this thing of beauty, and on the other hand rip out your throat with its fangs. It's like...well..."

"Go on."

"It's like the duality of nature or something."

"Freak," Amy quips from the back row, not bothering to whisper.

"That's enough, Miss Fairchild. Miss Sky's interpretation is perceptive beyond her years. Maybe you should try reading sometime, using that brain of yours for something other than cheerleading. I suspect that you can read. Although the D you received on your last composition doesn't really affirm my suspicion."

"Good one, Ms. Twid," I say, before realizing that my thought has taken audible form. I'm sure I'll reap the consequences. No one ridicules Amy Fairchild in public, not even the other cheerleaders. It's sort of this unwritten rule. A teacher might get away with the occasional sarcastic remark, like the Squid just did, but most of them just fall in line with the other adults, mesmerized by Amy's *Seventeen* smile and ability to make any sweater look good.

"Shut up, paste boy," Amy snaps, referencing the time she dared me to eat a jar of paste – and I obeyed like a hapless bee. Even in the first grade, she was already the hottest girl in class.

"That's enough," the Squid intervenes. "Passion is good, class. That is what poetry is all about – passion for love, passion for life or loss, passion for the little things that often go unnoticed. But I want you to express your passions in constructive ways, not in the base colloquialisms of the playground. Therefore, your assignment for this weekend is to write a poem, at least two stanzas long. It can be about anything you want, but make sure you write it from the heart. And don't use profanities. A good poet doesn't have to be lewd to get his point across. Now turn to page seventy-five of your textbook."

Dirty glances bombard me. There's nothing worse in class than a kid who generates more homework for everyone, especially on a weekend. I wish that Marvin were here. He was a natural target for ridicule, given his undead status. Without him around, I feel a heck of a lot more vulnerable. But the corpse found a job. I guess he had to. Zombies aren't typically hired for positions of authority. Sure, under the integration laws they're entitled to any job that I'm entitled to outside of law enforcement, healthcare, and preschool education; but law

3

and practice don't always converge. Most zombies I know of gravitate toward servile roles, like landscaping, fast food, and the custodial arts. Marvin's dad got a job at the DMV creating new queue patterns to help slow things down, but the money he earns isn't quite enough to pay the bills. That's why Marvin dropped out of school – to help his family. You see, Marvin, his parents, and his kid sister all died from the same can of spoiled tuna, and through some demented twist of fate all came back from the dead. Now they're stuck with making ends meet and paying top dollar for their injections. I hope for their sakes that the DMV has a good insurance plan. If not, there's always what's left of the Healthcare Exchange.

I glance over at Chastity. She sits next to me in class, not through random chance or some stroke of divine fortune, but through cold hard calculation. When we picked our seats on the first day of the year, I lingered by the door until Chastity sat down. Then I rushed over to the adjacent row as discreetly as possible, checking Katie Brennan into the wall when it looked like she might get the drop on my spot. And for six months now I've endured every one of the Squid's insults because I've had the strength of a greater goal: talk to Chastity Sky. Make contact. Do anything to win her affections without sacrificing my dignity the way I did with Amy in the first grade.

But guess what? In all of those six months, I haven't done squat. I've failed miserably. I'm a coward and a loser and will go to my grave a virgin. That's right. You heard it from me first. For all of my bombast and big talk, I've never danced the forbidden dance, never hidden the salami in anything that didn't have five fingers and double as a cup holder. My friend, Ernest, keeps talking about the zombie massage parlor by the bridge. I guess his older brother, Buck (IQ=?), frequents the place quite often. But I can't take Ernest seriously. He's big talk, just like me, and probably would wet his pants before he ever had the chance to take them off. If I'm going to do it, it's going to be with Chastity Sky. Or with Amy. Or with Wanda Lopez. Or with any of the other senior or junior or sophomore or freshman girls that roam the halls. But Chastity is my top choice. Has been since Mom told me to stop playing so much Blockbuilder and get into the sunlight more. I even have our first interlude planned out. Candlelight. Swigmont Cola. Vintage Madonna on the radio.

If I'm ever going to make first contact though, I've just got to get it over with. Tear off the Band-Aid. Leap into the pool. Prom is two months away, and I need to make up for lost time. The Squid's back is turned. She's writing on the chalkboard, reciting some grammar rule to herself. Almost singing it. Go ahead, tough guy. Do it now.

In my clearest whisper: "Chastity, I mean. Chastity...I mean. Like I said...I mean I don't think you're a freak."

She turns to me, as blank as the color of her skin. No smile. No sneer. No temperature reading whatsoever. And in my moment of victory, as I teeter on the precipice of what could be my finest hour, I commit a tactical flaw. I stare straight at her cleavage. Devour it actually.

She rolls her eyes, thick with black mascara. "Drop dead, loser."

Not exactly what I'd hoped for, but progress isn't always what it seems. You have to look for it sometimes – with a microscope. The point is, Chastity Sky talked to me. She actually talked to me. And she whispered, too, obviously concerned with the preservation of my dignity. Other girls would have screamed out loud to embarrass me in front of the entire class, but not Chastity. She whispered. That's what I call progress. I'm finally getting somewhere. Although dropping dead does seem a little extreme.

The bell finally rings, and America's future scrambles for the door. Doug Jerkins, Amy's boyfriend and starting quarterback, makes sure to sink his elbow into my ribs. "That's for getting smart, paste boy," he snickers.

What a moron. Doug and I used to be friends until the summer after eighth grade, when he grew tall, muscular, and handsome. And I stayed the same. Well, that's not entirely true. I got acne. Fortunately, it's all cleared up now, on account of the prescription Mom got me from the dermatologist my sophomore year. But I'm still average height, a little on the thin side, and let's just say the only people who have ever referred to me as handsome are Mom and her sister, Aunt Gertie. Aunt Gertie is built like a gun safe, forgets to pluck her unibrow, and usually reeks of garlic. But Mom swears she was hot stuff in her day, runner up for prom queen. I guess married life got to her though. Three idiot sons (technically my cousins) and four husbands later, she takes comfort in fried chicken, orange soda, and reality TV.

Chastity is shuffling over to her locker, five down from mine. I lag behind, wary of broadcasting a stalker vibe. She's dressed in black from head to toe – black leggings, black boots, black shirt, and black lipstick. Even her nails are painted black. It's so bizarre. She was blonde freshman year and giggly as all get out, best friends with Amy Fairchild. But now the two of them rarely speak, and the only time they interact is when Amy utters some aspersion to ignite laughter amongst her cronies. Chastity broods most of the time now, having replaced her giggles with a social statement. I guess she's declaring to the world that she will not conform or that she doesn't give a damn about what others think.

Either that or her fashion sense just stinks.

"Stop being a pervert," she says, glaring at me. "Stop standing there drooling at me."

My bad. Sometimes a little saliva does leak out, on account of my overbite. I dart to my locker in a feeble attempt to pretend that I have business with books and folders, and as I open the door, a wall of plastic containers tumbles out and crashes to the floor. One of them cracks me on the head. Amy, Wanda, and Doug are rolling in stitches by the water fountain. That's the third time this year they've filled my locker with jars of paste.

"Jerks," I whisper under my breath, loudly enough to generate an illusion of dignity, but not loudly enough for the Amy bandwagon to hear me. I feel the eyes of the entire hall bearing down on the back of my neck, laughing under their breath, searching for any strand of diversion to help their restless minds escape the dreariness of their own miserable futures. The whole world seems to be laughing. Mom is laughing. Dad is laughing. Jimmy, the little asswipe who steals my magazines, is laughing. But not Chastity. Not her. She picks up a jar of paste that has rolled to her feet and hands it to me. "Don't let them get to you," she says and marches off.

I feel the urge to eat that jar of paste.

Ernest walks up to me and takes a hit from his inhaler. "Again," he states, as if mentioning the weather.

"Looks that way."

"Too bad those jars of paste aren't incendiary grenades; then we could lob a few into enemy territory and blow them to smithereens. Use our gravity cloaks to shield ourselves from the shrapnel."

"Shut up."

"I'm just saying."

"Let's get out of here."

Ernest takes another hit and follows me outside through the blue steel doors. He's shorter and thinner than I am, and whereas my hair is brown, his hair is a mishmash of carrot peelings that only passes for red when he hasn't bathed for a week. It's smelling kind of red right now. His dad played football for Notre Dame, and his mother placed second in the NCAA 100-meter butterfly final her junior year, and to hear Ernest relay the story of their athletic achievements, you'd think he was there twenty years ago coaching them on to victory. So whenever I visit his house to play Blockbuilder, I'm always on the lookout for evidence of his adoption. I've come up empty-handed so far, but it hasn't gone unnoticed that both of his parents have jet black hair.

"Should we try to score some curly fries from Marvin?" Ernest asks, carrying a clarinet case covered in NASA stickers. He still thinks he's going to be an astronaut.

"Maybe later. I just defeated the Cinder Kitten without armor. I've got to get back to my laptop."

"Cool. Let's run."

"You know you're not supposed to."

So we walk. The walk to my house from the high school is approximately one mile and cuts a swath through downtown Pleasanton. The town has a sleepy, Midwestern feel to it, and if you weren't born and raised here, then every street would likely meld into the other. Colonials. Split-levels. White pickets fences. But to those of us in the know, the town is a smorgasbord of diversity. There's a Dunk-It Donuts on Main Street and a second-run movie theater on First. There's a bank, a library, a car wash, three churches – Presbyterian, Catholic, and Transcendental, twelve drive-thru restaurants, a Toughy Truck dealership, six pubs, a Buckstar Coffee, eight gun shops, a Good Buy, and a brand new Bathroom Depot. There's even a log cabin next to City Hall claiming to be the birthplace of Abraham Lincoln's second cousin.

And oh yeah, a dead zone.

Now the dead zone isn't really as ominous as it sounds. Pleasanton isn't the only town to have one, but we *were* one of the first. The dead zone is just a fancy way of describing the unpopulated areas surrounding our town where rogue zombies like to hide. Those are the zombies that for whatever reason have failed to receive their injections or have tasted human flesh. They've been marginalized by society as outcasts and sociopaths, and will attack unsuspecting humans if given the opportunity. But ever since the Cleansing of '87, the dead zone has posed no real threat to Pleasanton. Like most towns though, we still maintain a force of border guards who make routine sweeps, capturing and reprocessing any stray zombies who are too slow or too stupid to evade them. Those that respond to the injections and can be rehabilitated are reintroduced into society, and even serve jail time for any offenses they might have committed. Those that can't be rehabilitated are cremated. Every now and then you can see the smoke from the crematorium rising over the trees. Mom says it makes for pretty sunsets.

Don't get me wrong. I've never had anything against zombies. You might even say I'm friends with them. Marvin and I used to trade baseball cards, and I'll definitely try to score free curly fries from him. I'm on speaking terms with several of the neighborhood zombies, too. As far as I'm concerned, most of them are hardworking posthumans, just trying to do the best they can with whatever they have left – literally. Some of the poor souls are missing arms, legs, eyes, or all of the above. It depends on how they died. Mrs. Rothschild over on Stevens Avenue, for example, used to be a secretary in an office building before she lost an arm in a freak copy machine accident and bled to death. Now the poor woman has to scrub toilets for a living because no one wants to a hire a one-armed typist. If you ask me, death can have a pretty screwed up sense of humor.

Not everyone is as sympathetic toward zombies as I am though. A lot of folks treat them like trash and make no distinction between the law-abiding, taxpaying zombies and the rogue flesh-eating ones. Mayor Shight is one such person. He rose up through the ranks of the Border Patrol and got elected on a platform of reclamation. Dad says the word *reclamation* is nothing but a euphemism for wanting to disenfranchise the zombies. Just last year the mayor managed to get the City Council to add a 20% surcharge to zombie-owned property taxes, to offset costs associated with the Border Patrol and zombie-related clean up. Dad suspects that the surcharge is only the tip of the iceberg.

Mr. Jorgensen is one of the neighborhood zombies. He's tending to Mrs. Mayweather's garden right now in shorts and a tank top. They live next door to each other. They're both retired and widowed, and rumor has it that he had a crush on her when he was alive.

"Hi, Mr. J," I say.

"Oh, hi, Chris. How are you on this fine warm day?"

"It's forty degrees, Mr. J."

"Well, I really don't concern myself with that sort of thing anymore. Rain, snow, sunshine. It's all the same to me now. Just as long as I don't freeze into an ice cube."

"The roses are looking lovely."

Ernest shoots me a bewildered look, as though he's never heard the word *lovely* pronounced by a male before. He probably thinks I'm being a kiss-ass. But I'm not. I have nothing to gain from Mr. J. I'm just fond of the old guy. In life, he owned an ice cream parlor and used to hand out free samples to the kids. Rocky road was my favorite, covered in chocolate syrup. He used to give me extra sprinkles since I was so polite. Now that Mr. J is a zombie though none of the kids will go near him. It's probably all just the same. He doesn't own the ice cream parlor anymore.

"Thank you, Chris. They're just starting to bloom. The trick is to use good fertilizer. The crematorium was having a special on ash. It's the most fertile stuff I've ever used. When mixed with compost, it really draws out the red in the petals. I think Mrs. Mayweather is going to be pleased. I'm making her a bouquet right now." He points to a pile of flowers at his side – roses, tulips, and what looks like a bunch of green onions.

"What are those green ones?" I ask.

"Dinner."

A cloud of black dots is buzzing around his head. Like little dive bombers, they take turns landing on his face and neck, biting into what was once flesh before rejoining the formation.

Ernest swats away a few of the bloodsuckers. "We have to go now, Mr. J," he says, tugging at my shirt.

"Well, good seeing you boys again. Stay safe. And make sure to treat the girls right." He winks and grins, and for a moment, I think I see him blush.

Ernest and I press on, past two zombies in orange vests descending through a manhole into the sewer. Past a zombie in a delivery van, parked at the side of the road drinking coffee. Even past a group of tween zombies, who are beating the crap out of each other with hockey sticks as they rush back and forth on Rollerblades between two sets of orange cones. One of them loses a finger in the scuffle but doesn't seem to notice. A terrier runs off with the digit. It's a Norman Rockwell moment.

"Do you hear that?" I ask.

"What?"

"That siren."

Ernest shrugs his shoulders.

I stop to listen, holding my palm toward Ernest's mouth. It's a siren all right, coming straight toward us. Within thirty seconds the ear-rattling shriek crescendos on top of us and whooshes past. It's a patrol car, with cherry lights ablaze. Another follows. Then an ambulance. They're heading for Chestnut Street, two blocks from my house.

When we arrive on the scene, Ernest collapses to his knees and takes three hits from his inhaler. At least a dozen patrol cars are scattered along the street, lights flashing, doors open. A Border Patrol truck has driven right onto the lawn. A small army of border guards scrambles to form a line, guns drawn, inching toward the front door. A group of six run to the back of the house, shouting. The front window is streaked with blood – fresh bright blood that resembles paint more than the stuff coursing through my veins. It seems too red to be human, splattered across the glass like the psychotic graffiti of a Jackson Pollock wannabe. Chunks of flesh hang from the hedges, too, like the ones Mom buys for beef stew. On the lawn, six feet from the tires of the Border Patrol truck, the top half of a corpse is lying face up in the grass. The eyes are wide open, motionless, and what's left of the spine extends from the torso like a fossilized tail. A mess of intestines stretches from the vertebrae. They're tangled in the hedges, tethering the half-corpse in place.

Five or six shots are fired.

Talk on radios.

Footsteps.

The half dozen border guards who ran around the back of the house burst through the front door with a writhing body bag. It's moaning and gurgling, the contents muzzled and shackled within. They chain it to the bed of the Border Patrol truck and give it a good crack with a nightstick. That makes the bag writhe more.

The guards are winded. One opens a Thermos and pours a cup of coffee. Another just takes a swig from a bottle. A third lights up a cigarette and casts a glance my way. He wipes his forehead with the back of his cap and waves, smiling. I wave back.

The paramedics are busy winding the intestines into a loose spool, sort of like a garden hose. They lift the half-corpse onto a gurney and place the mass of human spaghetti on its chest. Another border guard, a petite woman no heavier than ninety pounds, emerges from the house with a leg. The foot still bears a black sock and slipper. She hands the leg to one of the paramedics. He stacks it on top of the intestines and asks where the other one is. She shrugs her shoulders and bums a smoke from her partner.

The half-corpse begins to twitch. Then its arms flail violently, knocking the mass of intestines back onto the grass. The paramedic tightens the restraints and this time places the casserole of body parts at the base of the gurney, where the corpse's feet should be.

It begins to whisper, then shout, turning its head from side to side. Then after sixty seconds of struggling, it relaxes and speaks in a surprisingly lucid tone. "What happened? What happened to me?"

"Zombie attack," the paramedic nearest the head says, hoisting the gurney into the back of the ambulance. "No worries though. We'll have you wheeling around in no time."

The only zombie attack I've ever witnessed before today was in the movies, and it wasn't until this moment that I realized how messy the whole affair could be – blood and gore everywhere. Of course I knew about the carnage already, learned about it in textbooks and lectures growing up. I've even watched a few news clips on late-night news reports. But those attacks usually occurred in far off places like New York or Washington DC, and usually (but not always) to some dumbass that wandered drunk into a dead zone. Rarely in suburbia, at least not since the Cleansing of '87 and the widespread distribution of injections. That said, there's no denying that an attack occurred today, practically in my own backyard.

I feel bad for Mr. J and the other zombies in town now. Folks will probably give them the cold shoulder for a month, crossing to the other side of the street when they see them coming. It happened last time an attack hit so close to home. It was back in '05, when I was still a kid. President Romero had just finished getting the 28th Amendment ratified, the jewel in the crown of a lifetime dedicated to fighting for zombie rights. He was making a champagne toast right in downtown Pleasanton, as part of his nationwide *thank-you-all* tour. People were cheering. Balloons were flying. And when the President leaned over to give the First Lady a kiss, she proceeded to rip out his throat.

There's still widespread speculation as to when she became a zombie and why she went for his throat. Many theories abound – forgotten injections, inadvertent exposure to human flesh, death from boredom in the Middle West. Personally though, I don't think any of that matters. What matters is that a great man died for his cause, and despite his final words of reconciliation, most people failed to see their meaning.

"She didn't mean it," he said, bleeding to death in front of the cameras. "It was an accident."

2

"Dinner time," Mom calls from upstairs.

Meatloaf and mashed potatoes. Again.

Dad's buried behind a newspaper, and Jimmy is chewing with his mouth open. He smirks at me, knowing full well I can't confront him at the table. He's pilfered one of my magazines, the kind I don't want Mom to find out about.

"So how was everyone's day?" Mom smiles, Tab soda in hand.

"I scored three goals today," Jimmy says.

"That's wonderful, sweetie. Great job."

"He has a good shot at winning MVP this year," Dad says, folding down the corner of the business section. "He's fast and agile and can switch between offense and defense without so much as losing a step. Remarkable for a seventh grader. Best natural athlete I've ever seen."

Jimmy blasts me with a finger tank.

"What about you, Chris. How was your day?"

"Fine."

"Anything interesting happen?"

"Not really."

I want to share my first contact with Chastity Sky, describe how months of determination and persistence have finally begun to pay off. But I know Mom will just respond with questions about Chastity's parents and our tentative wedding date, so I keep my victory to myself. Once I've persuaded Chastity to go to prom with me, then I'll mention something to Mom. It'll be an early Christmas present.

"A zombie ate Bill Jefferson over on Chestnut Street," Dad says. "The word at the office is that it slipped through the Border Patrol and went on a rampage. Also bit through a guy's leg on Brooks Avenue, near the perimeter before infiltrating deeper into the city."

"That's horrible," Mom mumbles, mouth brimming with meatloaf.

"Old Bill reanimated like lightning, within an hour of the attack. The poor guy got his legs chewed off. I doubt he'll keep his job, even with the ADA. You can't very well teach ballet with no lower half. He'll probably end up with one of those toll booth jobs."

"Until everyone converts to I-PASS. Then what will he do?"

Dad shrugs his shoulders. "It's a damn shame."

"I was there," I say. "I saw Bill Jefferson reanimate."

Mom shifts her glance to my hands, counting. "Did you watch your fingers and toes?"

"Yeah, Mom. I know the drill. Besides, there must have been a million border guards there. They pulled the zombie out of the house and chained him to the back of a monster truck. Rushed Bill Jefferson off to the hospital."

"What were you doing there?"

"I was walking home from school with Ernest and stopped to talk to Mr. Jorgensen for a while. That's when we heard all of the sirens and rushed over to see what was going on."

"Was there lots of blood?" Jimmy grins.

"Tons. All over the walls."

"Cool."

"That's enough," Mom says. "Let's try to talk about something more pleasant at the dinner table."

She attempts to rehash old news about last semester's report cards. She still can't understand why Jimmy receives straight A's while I squeak by on B's and C's. "You're smarter than that," she says. "You just need to apply yourself."

"Aren't you guys worried?" I say, interrupting. "A neighbor just got mauled by a rogue zombie, and you don't even seem alarmed. This kind of thing doesn't happen every day."

"Not now. But when your mother and I were your age, it happened more often. A couple dozen times a week before the Cleansing of '87. What concerns me is the fact that a rogue managed to slip through the perimeter. That just shouldn't happen, not with all the tax dollars that Mayor Shight has funneled to the Border Patrol."

"I feel sorry for the Jeffersons," Mom says. "I think I'll bake them a funnel cake."

"He doesn't need a cake," Dad mutters. "He needs a job. The poor guy reanimated ten times faster than normal, so the coroner didn't have the chance to enforce the cremation clause in his will. I'm sure he had one. Everyone does. Now the insurance company will invoke the reanimation exception and cheat him out of his death benefits."

Dad's an accountant, a partner over at Strafe and Subtle. He views the world in terms of dollars and cents and doesn't like to part with any of them.

"I'll still bake them a funnel cake."

"Do I have a cremation clause?" I ask, really wondering if Jimmy has one, hoping its use isn't limited to zombie attacks.

"Of course you do. We all have one. Your mother and I made sure to have wills drafted up for each one of you the day you were born. We had the lawyer visit us right there in the hospital room; signed the dotted line while you were at your mother's teat. It's good practice to formalize that kind of thing right out of the gate. You don't want to let it slip through the cracks and then wake up one morning wondering why you have no heartbeat. Rest assured, boys, in the unlikely event that you or your brother gets eaten by a zombie, Mom and Dad will have the remnants of your corpse cremated before you reanimate. Hell, we'll have you cremated no matter how you die, just to be safe."

"Thanks, Dad," Jimmy squeaks.

Brownnoser.

Mom smiles. Despite their squabbles over money, she's always viewed Dad as a good provider.

"What's so terrible about coming back as a zombie?" I ask. "Especially if you don't get eaten? I mean, isn't it like a second chance? Just look at Mr. Jorgensen. He died before his time in that ice cream parlor accident, and since he already had the zombie virus in his system, he rose from the dead. Now he's getting another shot at courting old Mrs. Mayweather."

Dad looks to Mom.

Mom looks to Dad.

They both turn to me.

"It's just not natural, sweetie," Mom says, smiling in that soft, understanding manner she used to use at story time when I was a kid. "Don't get me wrong. Your father and I are staunch supporters of zombie rights. My heart literally broke the day President Romero died. But our generation didn't grow up with friendly zombies. I mean, the First Occurrence happened when I was a baby, and by the time I was six, three of my neighbors had been eaten. We didn't learn much about the undead in school, the way you kids do now. Our experience was much more terrifying, with sirens blaring and body parts on the lawn. It wasn't until after the Cleansing of '87 that the world realized the zombie problem could be contained. Since then, people of my generation have learned to coexist, and the more enlightened ones have learned to accept. But no one encourages. It doesn't come as easily to us as it does to you kids. We're still tarnished by the carnage of our youth. Does that make any sense?"

"I guess."

"When you're eighteen, you can do whatever you want," Dad adds. "But until then and while you live under my roof it's cremation for you." He winks at Jimmy, and Jimmy gives him a high five.

"Can't we have Jimmy cremated now, just to be safe?" I half-joke.

"What a horrible thing to say," Mom gasps.

"Go to your room," Dad says, pointing. "Go to your room for a timeout."

And that about sums up the nature of my relationship with my parents. I'm probably the only kid in the history of the planet to receive timeouts at the age of seventeen. But I guess it isn't so bad. I can escape now to my room without excuse or pretext. Besides, I'm used to spending Friday nights in the basement.

There's no mistaking the fact that it's a basement either. Don't let the industrial carpet or paneled walls fool you. Lurking beneath the tenuous veneer are the concrete slabs and moldy two-by-fours that define the nature of my existence. In a way, the basement reminds me of the zombie lady that sells perfume at the mall – lots of makeup masking the death that lurks beneath. Dead flies. Dead spiders. I even saw a dead mouse the other day curled up like a sleeping baby behind the furnace.

Despite the questionable conditions, however, the basement is my domain. I can play Blockbuilder all night if I want to or read through my stash of magazines (the ones that Jimmy hasn't stolen). I can even try to do a couple of chin-ups on the bar that Dad not so subtly installed in the doorjamb last summer – you know, to buff up for Chastity. But Twid, the Squid, wants us to write a poem, probably because I screwed up that tiger burning bright one so badly. And I have to admit, I kind of want to pass her class, so this episode of downtime has a bit of a silver lining to it.

The Squid said two stanzas or more, so I'll shoot for two. And they need to rhyme. All good poems rhyme. Just ask any rapper with a microphone. Or that tiger guy.

For C

You are so cool and hot;
I want to touch your every spot.
I wish you'd pay me time of day;
And stop saying to go away.
You don't know how good I am,
With crafting worlds and cooking SPAM.
I'd treat you right and be your man;
If only you would lend a hand.

A fair attempt, if I don't say so myself. The last line conveys my sense that a healthy relationship must be grounded in mutual respect and reciprocity. Love can't be one-sided. I also want Chastity to know that I can cook. Women like that quality in men. It's the twenty-first century after all. The only problem is the subtlety factor. Chastity needs to get the message, to under-stand my feelings; but I certainly don't want all the snakes in class to get wind of it. They'd never let me live it down.

Let's try it again.

Hey, You

Every day you are a thought;
In my mind you are so hot.
Burning bright in the night;
Like a tiger running right.
The blackest hair, the whitest skin;
All I ask is to begin
The fate and fries we're meant to share;
If only you could be aware.

Not bad, Chris. Not bad at all for an aspiring man of letters. I'm not sure the *fries* part works, but I need to get food in there somehow. I'll let this one simmer on the back burner for a while, like a fine wine. The Squid says that all great writers revise their work and that although the writing process var-ies widely across authors, virtually every one of them writes a first draft from the heart and subsequent drafts from the mind. I guess it's that whole duality thing that Chastity was talking about in class today. The heart. The mind. Tearing each other's throats out. Besides, I'm getting kind of tired. My head hurts, and my arm is itching. My vision is also growing blurry. Hell, I hope I don't need glasses. Glasses would make my life even more miserable, giving Amy more to laugh at and something else for Doug Jerkins to break. Sleep. A little sleep is what I need. Right here on the couch. Right as rain. I can always revise tomorrow.

3

"Where were you this weekend?"

"Sick."

"What do you mean?"

"I had the worst headache imaginable. I couldn't crawl out of bed until Sunday afternoon."

Ernest leans away, shielding his nose. "You know I can't be around sick people, not with my asthma and all."

"Relax. I'm not catchy. I probably just got dehydrated."

The aspiring astronaut looks me up and down, like I'm some amoeba under a microscope. He focuses on my eyes a bit too long, a bad habit he developed in the third grade after taking a bad fall from the monkey bars. "It's probably West Nile Virus."

"What are you talking about?"

"The mosquitos are out in full force. My mom's been making me spray on repellent every morning before school. It tastes like crap."

"You get it in your mouth?"

"Just sometimes."

He wiggles away a couple of feet, taking the binoculars with him. If he doesn't stop moving, he's going to alert everyone to our position.

"Stop shaking the bush," I say.

"That's the least of your worries. You missed practice on Saturday. Clara was pissed."

"She'll live…at least a little while longer."

Two years ago, Ernest's mom and mine conspired together to enroll us in the New Curlers program over at the ice arena. They claimed it was to help us get some exercise and develop our hand-eye coordination, but I suspect all the sherry they were drinking at their Maggie K cosmetics party had something to do with it. Whatever their motivations, for the past ninety-two Saturdays, Ernest and I have spent our afternoons on the ice, perfecting our winter sport skills. We've been working on our sweeping technique as of late, and it's been a hell of lot tougher than you might think. You have to gauge the weight of the stone and the texture of the ice, sliding along without slipping while brushing the pebbles and avoiding the stones already in play. The local club skip, Clara MacGregor (née Lambeaux), is a veteran of the game, having first taken a brush back in '49, and even participated as an alternate on one of the Canadian Olympic teams. After emigrating to the States in the eighties, she started volunteering her time at the ice arena, teaching lessons to the local retirees who were struggling to rehabilitate after hip surgery. Clara sports two titanium prostheses herself, but you wouldn't think it the way she drives out of the hack like a well-oiled piston.

That said, looks aren't everything. At four foot eleven and eighty-five pounds, the great grandmother of twelve is nastier than that drill sergeant from *Full Metal Jacket*. I just know she's going to make me skate extra laps next Saturday until I puke on the ice, as penance for getting sick. Then she'll wave her broom in my face and make me clean up the mess.

"Did Eunice and Ethyl show?"

"Of course. They're training hard for the summer bonspiel. They don't want to get crushed by the Shady Meadows club again like last year. Apparently, Mavis and Helga are already driving out of the hack in top form. They both got hip replacements over the winter. Clara claims they're bionic or something."

"Crap."

"I think bionics violate the rules."

A blue jay flutters from our bush, sending Ernest and me into a dead silence. Ever since sophomore year we've spent

Monday afternoons watching cheerleading practice. Given our unfortunate social status though, we haven't had the liberty of watching from the bleachers like the jocks and other popular kids. Even when we tried to sneak a peek from the edge of the student parking lot, the football players chased us off. Not to be dissuaded though, we found a neat little observation post beside the groundskeeper's shed, about fifty yards from the goal post. On a clear day with Ernest's binoculars, we have a great view of the action. We like it when they do handstands the best.

Doug Jerkins, Amy's boyfriend, is looking in our direction.

"Do you think he saw us?" Ernest chirps, panicked.

"Shut up."

We lie as still as corpses for another five minutes, ready to run, but Coach Parsons yells at Doug to get his mind back on the drills. Even though it's basketball season, the coach likes to have his players train on the gridiron as much as possible. I guess football is the man's true passion. Amy and Wanda and the other cheerleaders practice outside as much as possible, too – to work on their tans. The two of them launch into a series of synchronized backflips, while Taylor and Katie shake a lot more than their pom-poms.

"Give me those," I blurt out, pulling on the binoculars. Ernest won't let go, clinging to the birdwatchers like a dead man clutching his billfold, so I punch him in the chest. He lets out a gasp and relinquishes the binoculars; then he starts wheezing up a storm.

"You jerk," he manages.

"It's my turn. You know I have dibs on Amy."

Two hits from his inhaler restore air to his lungs, meaning I won't have to explain his blue corpse to Principal Dawson. As far as I'm concerned though, it all evens out in the end. Last fall, for example, Ernest had the gall to bite my arm when Wanda changed her top on the fifty yard line and momentarily exposed her brassiere. He was pissed that I wouldn't share the binoculars and surrendered to his baser instincts. The little bastard even drew blood. I guess a bit of cleavage can have that effect on a desperate guy.

"What do we have to do to get one of those girls?" Ernest

mutters, more to himself than to me. It's the esoteric question that most defines our lives.

"Join the football team…or any team for that matter."

"But we're athletes."

I shoot him the *are-you-mentally-impaired* look and hand over the binoculars. "We're curlers. There's a big difference."

"I don't see why. Curling is a sport."

"So are darts and competitive eating."

He chews on that thought for a minute, and instead of distilling its intended meaning seems to conclude that we can become multi-sport athletes. "I've always liked darts," he mutters. "Sometimes I can even hit the board."

We watch in blissful silence for the next few minutes as the Morbid High cheerleading squad jumps and yells and flips and rolls. Their bodies seem to merge with the universe, shimmering under the grace and wonder of sunshine and gravity. Every cell of my being wants to go to them, to smile and relate and share the subtle nuances of my artistic eye. I'd like to tell Amy, for example, how her blue panties complement her eyes better than the red ones with white stripes. And Wanda might be inclined to learn that the diamond belly button ring she wears reflects the sun's rays in a much more scintillating manner than the ruby or sapphire one. But no. I'm not allowed to speak with them. I'm not allowed to commune. Some invisible barrier with barbed wire and an electrical charge separates us simply because the cheerleaders are popular and the curlers are not. It doesn't seem fair really, but there it is, plain as day. And the most demented part of the social apartheid is that I yearn to be with them even though they've always treated me like pond scum. It must be some kind of genetic defect. Either that or low self-esteem.

A loud banging knocks me from my musings. It's Frederick, the janitor (who is not a zombie by the way), hammering on the roof of the cafeteria. A load of shingles is sitting next to him.

"I didn't know janitors repaired roofs," Ernest says.

"I think it's related to the budget cuts, on account of our state bordering on insolvency."

"What?"

"Something my dad was complaining about the other night at dinner."

"Well, I wouldn't know about that, but I do know we better stay on high alert."

It takes me a couple of seconds to switch gears, but I realize what he's talking about. Another rogue zombie attack occurred over the weekend. It was all over the news. The nighttime clerk at the SlowMart, a foreign-exchange student from the community college, apparently tried to fight off the attacker with a frozen burrito and got cornered between the register and the slushee machine. The zombie let into him with a vengeance, clawing out every organ and flinging them across the aisles. Pancreas in the potato chips. Kidney on the corn nuts. Spleen and bowel on the cases of Suds Beer. No one discovered the clerk's corpse until the morning, after he'd already reanimated. When asked why he tried to fight off the zombie instead of fleeing, the clerk muttered in broken English that his boss would have held him responsible for any robberies, deducting losses from his paycheck. A bit of an uproar followed his sound bite, and a group of concerned housewives took it upon themselves to organize a boycott. The SlowMart's owner caved into their demands in less than two hours and agreed to pay for the clerk's injections. He also gave the poor guy a raise – ten cents over the state minimum. The contaminated food is now on sale for half price.

According to the clerk, the rogue was wearing a White Sox baseball cap.

"I still prefer curly fries," Ernest says, practically reading my mind. "It was a real drag washing the blood off the corn nut packages yesterday, although half off *is* half off."

"We'll swing by Artie's later."

"Hopefully Marvin is working."

Doug Jerkins and Chad Parker and the rest of the basketball team finish their five hundred push-ups, and Coach Parsons lets them breathe for about a minute before yelling at them to get to the gym. They fall in line and jog up the path to Morbid High's hardwood court. The cheerleaders blow them kisses and turn to shake their fannies. It's a heavenly sendoff. It's also the point in the afternoon that Ernest and I like the best. With the jocks out of the way, the risk of detection is a lot lower. We can breathe easier now and observe in peace.

Something catches the corner of my eye near the dumpster outside the cafeteria. Some poor soul is digging in it, searching for gold. It's kind of gross, especially given the industrial waste that our lunch lady serves up every day, but I won't judge the guy too harshly. I'm not a hypocrite. I've engaged in the same type of behavior once or twice out of necessity when Doug Jerkins stole my lunch money.

As the guy leans deeper into the dumpster, my artistic eye kicks into high gear. Something seems out of place, like chick peas in your spaghetti sauce. If I'm not mistaken, that backside is a bit too round to be a guy's. It's practically heart-shaped. I snatch the binoculars from Ernest and peer a little closer. The black jeans and the way they are presenting themselves are strangely familiar, the memory of a dream. I've seen that backside before, plenty of times on other reconnaissance missions.

"Gross!" Amy screams from the sidelines.

The girl in the dumpster snaps to attention, fists balled.

"Mind your own business," Chastity fires back.

"Scrounging through the dumpster. What's wrong with you? Double gross. I can't believe you were once a cheerleader."

"Neither can I."

The other cheerleaders want to laugh, but the expression of horror on their faces is wedged in too deeply. It's like they've been struck with palsy.

"I lost something," Chastity mutters, unconvincingly.

Amy smirks. "Yeah, right." She turns to the rest of her squad. "See what happens, ladies, when you get cut from cheerleading. It's not a pretty sight. So you'd better make damn sure to stay lean and obedient or you might find yourselves like poor Chastity over there, half a step away from a cardboard box."

Amy's comments strike a nerve, prompting Chastity to assume some kind of karate stance. "I wasn't cut, you idiot. I quit. Now why don't you come a little closer?"

"Cool, a cat fight," Marvin trembles, practically yodeling.

"Shut up."

Amy saunters toward the dumpster, wielding a silver baton in her left hand. Chastity stares down at the lethal rod but doesn't seem too concerned. Someone is going to bleed today. That much is a forgone conclusion.

Every synapse in my brain is telling me to intercede, to stop the madness before someone gets hurt. But a strange sensation, buried deep in an ancient place, commands me to watch and hope for carnage. It must be the primordial instinct that ancient Romans experienced at the Colosseum and that modern-day rednecks experience watching professional wrestling. I'm not proud of the urge, but I certainly can't deny it. I just hope it doesn't define me.

And I'm not alone. Ernest won't stop pulling on the strap of the binoculars; his chattering teeth are getting awfully close to my arm. Frederick is risking a three-story fall, stretched over the pile of shingles to get a better look. Even Wanda and the other cheerleaders have managed to recover from their palsy in time to grin like wolves. Every person within a two-hundred-yard radius can smell blood in the air and is responding in that trademark human fashion.

But I'm Chris Kantra, and I've always been something more or less than human (depending on who you talk to). I won't cave into the carnage. I won't condone needless violence. I certainly won't sit idly by while the two faces that have offered me so much comfort in the wee hours of the night commence with damaging one another. That would put a major crimp in my love life.

"Stop it," I yell, standing up in the middle of the bush. "Why don't we just talk about this?"

All eyes turn to me, even Frederick's. Their combined weight is about three thousand tons.

"You idiot," Ernest screams. "You gave away our position."

Amy clasps a hand to her mouth, practically in shock. "Paste boy? What a freaking pervert. Have you been spying on us this whole time?"

"I'm not spying."

"Then why are you hiding in a bush with a pair of binoculars around your neck?"

"Birdwatching?"

"Idiot," Ernest repeats, trying his damnedest to burrow into the soil.

Amy's shock transforms into the deep, guttural laughter of pure ridicule, the kind that only cheerleaders can muster. Wanda and the others quickly join her. Chastity though is staring at me with the blank expression of indifference...because she cares. She cares enough not to join in the ridicule.

Before I can make further inroads into our peace deal, however, a subtle change in air pressure sets the world into slow motion. Frederick is slipping.

Without hesitation, I come charging out of the bush. I'm no Olympic sprinter, but all those Saturdays on the ice have strengthened my determination if not my legs or lungs. With each step, I can see Frederick sliding closer to the edge. The shingles, too. One big mass of falling debris positioned directly above Chastity's head.

"Watch out!" I manage, but my steps are faster than my words, and as I thrust out my arms to push Chastity clear of the danger, her body twists into some kind of trebuchet. A foot catches me in the chest, and my momentum is stopped cold. Given Newton's laws though, she bounces back several yards... to safety. I can hear Frederick yell, and then the world goes completely black, and then a ringing in my ears insulates me from whatever insult Amy has composed for my benefit.

4

A bit of muffled, frenzied talk.

Sirens.

"You're going to be okay, kiddo," a voices murmurs, not too encouragingly.

Some kind of machine beeping, like what you hear on one of those nighttime dramas that depict young horny doctors screwing around.

Screeching tires.

An explosion.

Nothing.

* * *

The blessed aroma of curly fries.

Hands on my arms.

"I got you," he says. "Hold on."

The putter of an engine, maybe some kind of oversized lawn-mower.

The Moon in the sky.

A bright star...or maybe the planet Venus.

The moans of the same voice that told me everything was going to be okay.

* * *

Mom crying. Aunt Gertie chewing nervously on a chicken thigh. Dad tearing a piece of paper in half.

Jimmy pulling one of his darts from my leg.

And a face that I don't quite recognize at first. It's wearing a paper hat. It's young like me but doesn't look too healthy. A greenish hue supplants what should be skin tone. It places something on a table. A bag with grease stains. I can smell its contents with every corpuscle in my body. I must be in heaven.

* * *

Dr. Thurgood has been my doctor for as long as I can remember. Mom claims that he's a leader in his field, worthy of a Nobel Prize but still humble enough to turn his back on fame and fortune and devote his talents to healing the sick in the small town in which he was born. *A candidate for sainthood,* she once said. *His name should adorn at least one or two street signs.* I can't disagree with the woman. The man exemplifies everything that is good in the medical profession, not the least of which is his legendary bedside manner. Picture the epitome of the caring country doctor, capable of putting the most anxious-prone patient at ease.

"I'm sorry to tell you this, Chris, but you're dead."

"What?"

"Dead as a doornail."

"I don't understand."

"You died last night...ambulance crash...en route from the high school. For some reason, Frederick, the janitor, and a load of shingles fell on your head and broke your neck. But that's not what killed you. The large Dutch elm on Route 99 did, you know, the one that looks like it has two big eyes and a crooked mouth. It slowed the ambulance from eighty to zero in a fraction of a second."

"I'm dead?"

"Yeah...well...if you want to be a stickler about it, technically you're undead."

Undead. I let the word simmer for a moment, trying to grasp the full enormity of it.

"You mean I'm a zombie?"

Dr. Thurgood nods in concurrence.

"But why? My dad had a cremation clause drafted into my will. Why wasn't I burned to ash at the crematorium?"

"What was left of the ambulance spun into a ditch. It was a

good eight hours before anybody found you. Fortunately, Marvin Reynolds was on his way back home from a late shift at Artie's and came across the wreck. He loaded you, the driver, and the paramedic into the bed of his '76 Toyota pickup. Rushed you straight to the emergency room. By that time though all three of you had reanimated."

"What about Chastity?"

"Who?"

"Chastity Sky."

Dr. Thurgood pauses for a moment, ruminating. Oh... that Chastity. She's the little darling that called the ambulance. Apparently all of the other witnesses ran off...except for Frederick, of course. Principal Dawson made him clean up the mess. You broke his fall, son. You saved the poor man's life."

"I'm a zombie?"

Dr. Thurgood smiles and places a cupped hand beside his ear. "I think we might have an echo in here."

"I'm a zombie?"

His smile falls away, and he jams a light into my left ear. Then he jams it up my nose. Then he turns my neck gently. It's pretty damn stiff.

"Your brain is still intact, and it's still connected to your spinal column. I had to insert a steel rod into your neck to keep your head from slumping. But you should have full cognition. So why do you keep asking me the same question, son?" He flips through my chart but doesn't seem to find the piece of information he's looking for. "Remind me again, what did your IQ test at when you were alive?"

"Above average."

"Really?"

He continues with his examination and pounds my back with a fist. Then he tells me to breathe in and out. I break into a coughing fit.

"No worries. Your lungs don't need air anymore. I just wanted to make sure they weren't structurally compromised. We can't have you drooling blood or mucous in public."

"Great."

"Putrefaction levels are minimal."

"The news just keeps getting better."

"Heartbeat is fully arrested."

"Thanks, doc."

"Temperature is seventy degrees."

"Toasty."

"From what I can see, Chris, you're a perfectly healthy zombie. Your bones and musculature are sound, and your internal organs appear to be solid. As far as transforming into one of the undead goes, you're pretty fortunate. I see victims of car crashes and lawnmower accidents all the time, and believe you me, you got off pretty easily. Besides a stiff neck and a bit of a crack along the back of your skull, you're in relatively good shape. Not many little girls are going to throw dog poop at you."

"But why did I become a zombie? I wasn't bitten."

"You know as much about that as I do, Chris. You learned it in your third grade health curriculum. Modern medicine doesn't fully understand the gamut of vectors that introduce the virus into a person's system. It could have been bad air or water or an exchange of infected bodily fluids. It might have even been that mosquito bite that I noticed on your arm. It really doesn't matter now. The point is the virus managed to get into your system, and when you died, it reanimated you."

The more Dr. Thurgood talks about my fate, the more the point that I'm dead is striking home – like a Zulu spear. How do I deal with this? What am I going to do? Amy Fairchild and Doug Jerkins are going to have a field day. I can see it now. *Zombie boy. Road kill. Oh, I thought you were already a zombie.*

And what will Chastity think? How will she ever agree to go to prom with me now?

Despite the serious setback my love life just suffered, I can't help but notice the scent of blood in the air. It's weird, but Dr. Thurgood is starting to look pretty handsome in that slab of short ribs on the grill sort of way.

A needle plunges into my arm and strikes bone.

"It's starting," he mutters.

"What?"

"The Craving. It usually starts within twenty-four hours of reanimation. It's the characteristic of zombies that most defines them – the craving for human flesh."

"I don't want to eat anybody."

Dr. Thurgood shoots me a Twid, the Squid *you must be joking if you think I'm going to believe that load of crap* look. "Do you feel ravenous, ready to eat anything in sight...cooked, raw, spoiled, inanimate?"

"Not inanimate, at least I don't think."

"Have you been looking at people differently, having strange thoughts about their bodies and the meat on their bones?"

"Not really. I mean you're the only person I've seen since I woke up."

Dr. Thurgood narrows his brow, and the two puffs of cotton there practically stick together. "The truth, Chris. Remember, I'm your doctor."

"All right. You got me, doc. A minute ago I pictured you on the grill doused in barbecue sauce."

"Good. Good. That's perfectly normal for a boy in your condition. Everything appears to be progressing by the book. We'll have you back on the twenty yard line in a couple of minutes, as soon as the injection takes hold."

"Dexapalm 90?"

"That's right. It'll help curb your hunger and eliminate the desire for human flesh. It's a bit of a miracle drug really, much more reliable than its predecessor, Dexapalm 87. Only one-tenth of one percent of zombies are allergic to it."

"Allergic?"

"It simply doesn't work for them. They continue craving human flesh until they eat somebody and get put down. A few noble souls willingly self-eradicate. Larry at the crematorium offers a ten percent discount to those who want to do the right thing. He even puts their photos on the wall as sort of a memorial."

"He's all heart."

"But don't you worry one bit. The chance of the drug not taking hold is one in a thousand. We'll know for sure within a couple of minutes."

And sure enough, before Dr. Thurgood has time to finish scrawling notes in my file, the bottomless hunger that was tak-

ing over my stomach starts filling with dirt – deep, rich, cemetery dirt, with maggots and worms and wilted carnations. A
subtle hankering for the greasy bag on the table takes its place.

"I'm still hungry," I say, alarmed.

"For what?"

"That bag."

"Good. Good."

"What do you mean good?"

"You're a perfectly healthy teenage zombie, Chris, with all the
appropriate appetites. You can eat as many curly fries and Beef 'n
Cheeses as you want. Marvin left you a sack over there as sort of
a get well present. That young man is terribly considerate."

He passes me the bag, and I tear into it.

"You don't need to eat anything to exist, of course, but I recommend that you consume food products to stay social with
your family and friends. Dexapalm 90 will steer you toward appropriate edibles. Just make sure to empty your bowels regu-
larly, even if you don't experience the sensation. The food will
remain undigested, so don't be alarmed the first couple of trips
to the restroom. And use plenty of mouthwash. I recommend
Oralcline. We need to keep that halitosis in check. As for the
other thing that I'm sure you're wondering about, well, it will
still work. Just remember what I said about bodily fluids. Be safe
and take precautions. You don't want to infect anyone else with
the virus." He winks, and I swear to God I'm blushing. "Death is
not a total loss."

With one little phrase, Dr. Thurgood's bedside manner has
assumed its legendary status.

"It still works?"

"Like a charm."

The doctor chuckles to himself, then grows deathly serious.
"Just remember a few simple ground rules. One: don't go near
open flames. Dexapalm 90 contains napalm, Agent Orange, and
fenfluramine. The combination slows bacterial growth and
curbs the appetite, but it can combust without warning. Two:
don't forget to come to my office for your monthly injections.
My assistant, Gina, can put you on the calendar. If you miss an
injection, I will have to report you to the Border Patrol. Mayor

Shight has made the local ordinances very clear on this matter. And three: do not...and I can't stress this enough...do not in any way ingest human flesh. Not as a stunt or as a joke or even out of a perfectly natural sense of curiosity. Human flesh in your system will negate the effects of Dexapalm 90 – permanently. I've seen it happen before; the result is not pleasant. Blood. Entrails. Cremation. You get the picture. Not even Dolly cakes can curb the craving of a zombie who's tasted human flesh."

I'm starting to remember all of this now. I learned it in school. Dolly cakes – lumps of cloned human flesh that this scientist guy in Scotland claimed would satisfy the cravings of rogue zombies. He lost an arm during clinical trials and transformed into a zombie himself. But he's still researching away, locked in some dingy university basement, convinced that a few tweaks to the human genome might liberate his brethren and bring peace to our world.

"Saliva is okay. Even blood. But no solid tissues. Nothing with muscle or tendon."

"Why not blood?" I ask, remembering a thing or two from biology class. "Isn't blood a form of tissue?"

"You're quite right, Chris," Dr. Thurgood says, smiling. "It's a form of connective tissue. But again, as with many other questions concerning zombies, my answer is *we don't know*. The fact remains, however, that zombies who ingest human saliva and blood will not turn rogue. I guess the best explanation that I can give you is that zombies are zombies, not vampires. They crave flesh, not blood."

"Come on, doc. You know as well as I do that vampires are make-believe. I'm not a little kid anymore."

"I know," he says, chuckling. "I'm just injecting a little levity into our conversation. Here." He hands me a piece of paper. "Give this to your mother."

"What is it?"

"Your death certificate. A lot of new zombies like to hang it on the wall."

5

"I'm a zombie now."

"Cool."

"What do you mean cool?"

"Now you don't have to live up to such crushing expectations."

The clarinet player has a point. "Where were you when I got crushed?"

Ernest fidgets a bit, rearranging his briefs. "I had your back, but when I noticed that Chastity called 911, I stayed hidden in the bush until everyone left. I mean, there was nothing I could do at that point, and I couldn't let the cheerleaders think I was some sort of pervert voyeur, hiding in a bush like you."

"But you were."

"That's just semantics."

Ernest takes a hit from his inhaler and straightens his NASA shirt. The guy has always been a bit of a pragmatist.

A big crowd has gathered in front of the school, and from the look of it, something important has happened. Frederick, the janitor, is busy mopping a pool of gore from the concrete portico by the blue steel doors. A small cut along his forehead is the only evidence that he fell on top of my head. The bell rang five minutes ago, but the entire student body is transfixed by the gore, teachers included, paying more attention to the subtle machinations of the custodial arts than to the Pavlovian signals of the modern educational system. Poor Frederick is starting to buckle under the pressure. He keeps missing a patch of flesh by the ferns, and his mop is so saturated with blood that it's no longer absorbing anything. He's merely spreading the carnage out thinner, the way Jimmy pretends to eat peas.

The rumors have already started flying.

Sissy Slupchek, a mousy recluse with braces who sits in the back of earth science mumbling to herself about yetis and krakens all day, is warning the kids around her about the chupacabra. Her face is flush, and her eyes are wide, and her fellow students don't seem to appreciate the full implications of what's she saying; so instead of asking her to clarify her theory, they simply push her away amidst a deluge of aspersions. *'Tard, Moron,* and the like.

Lenny Stiles, who used to be a good friend of mine until he stole my magic wand in the fifth grade, is shouting at the top of his lungs: "An army of zombies attacked Twid, the Squid. They tore her limb from limb as she was begging for mercy. Then they chewed her into tiny little pieces and spit them in the toilet, on account of the bad flavor."

The Squid is standing right behind him, none too pleased. I think old Lenny can kiss that diploma goodbye.

Even Ernest is getting in on the action. "I think they got Principal Dawson."

Amidst this carnival of horror and wishful thinking, two faces in particular stand out – Amy Fairchild and Wanda Lopez. They're not crying or turning flush or looking to Principal Dawson for comfort and guidance like everyone else. They're just leaning against the bike rack grinning, as if they've won front-row tickets to *Twilight, the Musical.* They're as hot as habaneros, dressed in matching designer jeans and yellow midriff sweaters, and Amy's hair is in a double ponytail, the way I like it, while Wanda is wearing a sort of retro bun. It's as if their hotness shields them from the horrors of real life and protects them from the dirty nuances of blood and gore.

Chastity is glaring at them with a look of murder in her eyes, but they don't seem to notice her. They don't seem to notice me either, transfixed by something on Amy's phone. I try to navigate closer to Chastity, to thank her for calling 911, but the crowd is too dense. Principal Dawson raises her arms and commands everyone to stop talking.

"Mr. Brumley had a run-in with a rogue zombie last night," she says, standing in a pool of blood. "The dear man, so dedicated to the pursuit of academic excellence, was burning the midnight oil grading essays. Frederick didn't discover the corpse until this morning, and by that point, it had already begun to reanimate. He tried to beat it down with a broomstick, but Mr. Brumley regained coherence and asked him to stop. Don't worry though. Mr. Brumley only lost an arm to the zombie and an eye to Frederick's broom. He's expected to reanimate completely and return to class by the end of the week. He brings new meaning to the word tenured." She pauses, and sighs of relief trickle through the crowd. "The zombie got away, and the Border Patrol suspects it might be the same rogue that attacked the exchange student at the SlowMart last weekend. But there's no reason to be alarmed. We know what zombies are capable of. We've studied their methods in health science and watched films about them on the Preparation Channel. And for those of you who have never witnessed the carnage of a zombie attack in person before...well...now you have. Take a good look; breathe it in; file the image into your memory banks. This is part of the world we live in, girls and boys."

The educator lowers her head to let the gravity of her words sink in.

"But please don't fixate over today's tragedy. Don't lose sleep or hesitate for one moment to finish those homework assignments. That goes for you especially, Mr. Stiles." Laughter erupts. "Because to concede to this horrible event by sacrificing one iota of your precious freedom would be the same as embracing Death and his minions. No, my dear students. We shall do no such thing. Not in my school. What we *will* do is hold our heads up high and fight back to protect what is ours. And our weapon of choice will not be the ax or the chainsaw or the shotgun or the sword. Our weapon of choice will be the human spirit."

Cheers explode amidst a thunder of applause, and Principal

Dawson, a tiny woman of five feet and one hundred pounds, grins with the steely omniscience of a mid-twentieth century demagogue. For the spitting image of Veronica Mars at fifty, she's pretty damn intimidating. I guess you don't rise to the rank of high school principal without a bit of fire in the belly.

"Just as a precaution, however," she continues, less animated, "the Border Patrol has lent us one of its finest, Mr. Buck Pratt. He's an alumnus of Morbid High, lettered in football and baseball and set the record at the spring carnival's hot dog eating contest his senior year. Sixty-four, according to Mrs. Marshall, our esteemed lunch lady. Mr. Pratt will be joining us for the next couple of weeks, walking the halls and grounds and making sure that the threat of the rogue flesh eaters has abated. Please join me in welcoming him with a warm round of applause."

Buck (IQ=?) emerges from the shadows of the portico and waves his Border Patrol cap at the crowd. His tar-pit hair is thin on top, and he's compensated for it by growing a Village People moustache. He's tall and wiry, with a bloated lamb's bladder for a stomach and a dullness in his countenance that signals a lack of cerebral activity. But the crowd seems to love him, Ernest most of all, who's whistling like the quitting-time siren from *The Flintstones*. I guess he still admires his big brother.

"Now enough of this distraction," Principal Dawson says, directing Fredrick to a finger that's pinned beneath a Pepsi bottle. "Everyone return to class. We've wasted fifteen minutes already."

As the crowd disperses, Sissy Slupchek points at the red monkey art on the wall and repeats the word chupacabra a dozen times. Buck spots Ernest and me and walks over. The first thing he does is sock Ernest in the arm and call him a 'tard. Then he hones in on my face with lifeless shark eyes, and I swear to God, smoke starts billowing from his ears. I'm tempted to hand him a bottle of water, to douse the cognitive flame, but the rat bastard would probably just drink it instead. "Don't I know you?" he grunts.

"I'm Ernest's friend, Chris Kantra."

"Oh, that little Blockbuilder fairy."

"Not quite."

That throws him for a loop. He blinks about a hundred times, then sniffs my breath. For the first time since Mom weaned herself from that suppository infatuation, my sphincter clamps shut like a steel blast door.

"You're a zombie."

No fooling genius. "Yeah, since Monday."

"Where were you last night?"

"At home, studying."

"Can you prove it?"

"Ask my mom."

"He was at home, honest," Ernest tries, but Buck ignores him.

"You'd better watch your step, zombie boy. This mess could have been an inside job. I've got you and the other corpses on my radar now, and I don't play favorites." He saunters toward the blue steel doors, alternating the V of his index and middle fingers between my face and his eyes, only breaking contact when he passes Amy Fairchild and Wanda Lopez. He says something to them out of earshot, and they roll their eyes in disgust.

This isn't exactly how I envisioned my first day back at school as a zombie. My plan was to break the news to people subtly, responding in the affirmative only to direct inquiries and excusing myself at regular intervals for Oralcline breaks and foundation applications. I "borrowed" some of Maggie K's finest from Mom's stash in the medicine cabinet – summer squash – and rubbed it on the bags under my eyes, just to cut the edge off a little.

But my subtle subterfuge doesn't appear to be working. Buck's big mouth and razor sense of observation have undermined my plan, and at least a dozen kids now know that I'm a zombie. That doesn't sound like many, but in high school, a dozen kids can breed into a pandemic within minutes.

"Get to class, kids," Frederick finally snaps, waving his mop. He makes eye contact with me and nods his head. I return the gesture.

"You missed a spot, mop man," Wanda Lopez sneers, spitting a wad of gum by his shoe. "Don't step in it."

Ernest follows me to the lockers and hovers much longer than usual. We don't share many classes anymore, ever since he got moved to the *tap into your potential* studies curriculum, but something's on his mind. He takes a hit from his inhaler.

"You don't want to eat people, do you?"

"Not while I'm on the injections."

"Do you think Buck will catch the rogue that got Mr. Brumley?"

"Maybe, if it bites him on the ass."

"He's always been a smart guy. I hope that I can join the Border Patrol like him someday."

"I thought you wanted to be an astronaut...land on Mars and moon the camera when you set foot on the red soil."

"That, too. But first I'd like to defend our town and protect its citizens...you know, like that guy in those old westerns who walks with a limp and talks like a robot. He was tough. People respected him. They didn't call him 'tard or moron or rip his underwear off while he was still wearing them. If I could carry a gun like Buck and wear that uniform, people would step to the side when I walked by and say things like: *Hey, there goes Ernest, the border guard. He blasted fourteen zombies single-handedly the other day. Give him a free Beef 'n Cheese.* They wouldn't laugh behind my back or make me sit next to Humphrey Dingleton in class. He keeps a collection of boogers in a sandwich bag by the way – green ones, red ones, gray ones. It's pretty cool actually, except he doesn't know how to share."

"There's more to respect than carrying a gun."

"Tell that to Mr. Brumley. You should become a border guard with me. We could ride in our own monster truck. You could drive, and I could point the shotgun. Then we'd cruise around town hunting down zombies and talking to the cute girl that works the salad bar at Artie's. Marvin would score us free curly fries, and Randy, the manager, would reserve our table by the restroom. Even Buck would have to smile...might even shake our hands."

"I don't think the Border Patrol would let me join. I'm a zombie now, remember?"

"What?"

"You know...the integration laws. They exempt law enforcement agencies from hiring zombies. Besides, the thought of having to work with Buck all day makes me want to barf...no offense. I think I'd rather flip burgers."

"Would you score me a free one, with extra pickles?"

"Only if you'd let me drive your monster truck from time to time."

Without any warning, the first blow crushes my shoulder. "That's for the stupid poem you made us write last weekend."

The second blow pummels my intestines. "And that's for spying on cheerleading practice, paste boy."

Doug Jerkins high-fives his pal, Chad Parker, and they grope their respective girlfriends' backsides. Amy Fairchild and Wanda Lopez giggle on cue and saunter through the blue steel doors with the distinctive sway of matching pendulums. The tattoo at the small of Amy's back, the one that resembles the Rod of Asclepius (I Googled it one lonely night), appears to be slithering. Maybe she'll enter the healthcare profession someday. Her father *is* a plastic surgeon, after all.

Or maybe not. She's probably not the healing type.

Anyway, Doug Jerkins has inadvertently set a train in motion that will derail in a deluge of humiliation if I don't make it to the restroom fast. His blows have knocked me off balance, and even though the pain receptors in my skin are not what they used to be, I'm still susceptible to pressure – and it's third cousin: manually-induced peristalsis. I discovered this new condition yesterday when Jimmy threw the football as hard as he could at my gut, figuring I wouldn't mind. The force of the ball acted like fingers clamping down on a tube of toothpaste, sending the undigested food in my entrails down the path of least resistance. Well, it's happening again now. The breakfast of champions – rare pork chops, cheesecake, Hi Di Hos, pretzels, pickles, sardines, Every-Day vitamins, deviled ham, leftover fried chicken, scrambled eggs, and three-and-a-half clementines – is about to break loose.

I scramble to the restroom, and the only open stall is the one without a door, but my modesty isn't complaining right now. The horn of plenty rips open, and the guys next to me start screaming for a mercy flush. I oblige. They scream some more, and I oblige again. The third time I just ignore them. My strategy of doubling up my underwear has paid off. The inner lining has taken shrapnel, but the outer lining has emerged unscathed. I can wear the outer pair for the rest of the day and hopefully avoid any further blunt force trauma to the abdomen. It's not much, but it counts as a victory nonetheless.

6

"You're late, Mr. Kantra," the Squid snaps, eraser in hand. It's sticking to her palm, as if by suction.

"There was a zombie attack. They got Mr. Brumley."

"We know that, but everyone else made it back to his seat over ten minutes ago. Where were you these past few days?"

I don't think she realizes that I'm a zombie, so I hand her Mom's note.

"I see," she says, studying me. "How unfortunate for you and your family. You can take Marvin's old seat."

"But I don't want Marvin's old seat. I want *my* seat, next to Chastity."

The class erupts into laughter, and the quips I feared start flying. Not even in whispers. *I knew it. It doesn't surprise me one bit. He always looked kind of squirrelly. With that pasty skin. Yeah, and he still eats paste. And he's never had a girlfriend. Of course not. Maybe he attacked Mr. Brumley. Yeah, and ate his arm. Maybe you should check his mouth, you know, for evidence. No way. You do it. Are you kidding me? And what's with that cologne? It smells like piss and Oralcline. How gross. He was always kind of stupid. Maybe he was born a zombie. Could be.*

"That's enough, class," the Squid snaps. "You know you need to take Marvin's old seat, Mr. Kantra. That seat is especially reserved for the zombie student in class. It's right near the window where you can let in fresh air during the warmer spring months."

"But I like *my* seat," I say, looking to Chastity, who's a sheet of alabaster.

"Mr. Kantra, now."

My painstaking efforts to conceal my undead status have bought me a total of twenty-three seconds next to Chastity. I didn't figure on getting Marvin's old seat. I begged Mom not to write a note, to let me take my summer squash foundation as far as it would go, but being a former school nurse, she felt compelled to assure the school administration that I would do my best to brush my teeth and stay out of the meat locker. And zombie that I am, I assumed that teachers were bound by a duty of confidentiality to take my secret to their graves. What an ass I am. Right out of the starting gate, the Squid has relegated me to the zombie seat by the window, in case there was anyone in class who didn't already know that I'm undead.

The letters MR are scratched in the wood, for Marvin Reynolds. Beneath his initials are TJ, for Terrence Jacobs, the zombie two years ahead of me who became a private contractor to a demolition company. He's what they call a cluster-f specialist. When the demolition experts line a condemned building with C-4 and flip the switch and nothing happens, they send Terrence in to locate the faulty wire and replace it. It's dangerous work, but it pays well. Terrence used the money to buy a vintage conversion van. He thinks it will impress the ladies.

Terrence's initials are followed by another twenty, starting in '96, when the integration laws brought zombies to the classroom and George Beck (GB), the test case, had nothing better to do in civics class than destroy school property by carving into the wood. It's history frozen in time, a long and distinguished legacy, and I have to say there's comfort in knowing that I won't be the first to endure the humiliation of being asked by the Squid to open the window on a hot May afternoon to air out the reek of halitosis. It just happens to be *my* time now. I try to carve my initials above Marvin's, to add to the chain, but my fingernail breaks off.

"And I hope you have your assignment," the Squid says. "I was going to have you read your poem aloud on Tuesday, but you missed class."

"It's done."

"Good. I will get to you momentarily. But first, let's start with the other stragglers. Miss Monik, please take your place at the podium."

Susie Monik, tennis champion and Amazon descendant, stands up and marches to the podium. She must be six feet tall, dressed as usual in sweatpants and a short sleeve Adidas shirt. The color of the shirt varies from day to day, but the pit stains do not. Under the florescent lights, it's obvious that her moustache is filling in better than mine.

The Big Match

I serve the ball with force
Up and down the tennis course;
You run and dive, but cannot hide
From the volley that breaks your stride.

I'm the champ, will always be;
Don't visit my house pathetically;
If you try to take what's mine
I'll bust you up every time.

"Very good, Miss Monik," the Squid says. "That's quite an improvement from last time. What does this poem mean to you?"

"Mean?"

"Yes, deep in your heart, within the vibrant viscera that makes you the person that you are, what does this poem mean?"

Susie blinks a dozen times. "It's about tennis."

"Okay, good. Please take your seat." The Squid scans the room, and heads recoil into phantom tortoise shells. "What about you, Mr. Wooster? Dare you grace us with your lyrical rendition?"

Tad Wooster, motorhead and off-track drag racer, struts to the podium. His hair is greased back like Fonzie's, and the sleeves of his Mickey Mouse shirt are rolled up to his shoulders. He sports a tattoo of Count Chocula on his arm, and when he flexes his muscle, little drops of Hershey's syrup appear to drip from the fangs. Tad is the only kid that Doug Jerkins has steered clear of since the second grade, when Tad produced a monkey wrench from his back pocket and leveled Doug in the middle of *The Berenstain Bears*.

Cherry Glasspacks

Burning rubber in the air,
The glint of chrome everywhere;
The light turns green; the hotties scream;
I shift down fast and blow the scene.

Open wide and down the line,
Glasspacks humming oh so fine;
Getting paid at nine-point-eight,
A fifth of Jack to celebrate.

"Please sit down," the Squid says, reviewing her calendar.

"It's about street racing," Tad offers. "I just installed these new glasspacks on my Chevelle, and that bitch can sure scream now."

"Sit down, Mr. Wooster."

The Squid doesn't approve of drag racing, apparently. But I do. Dad says I can have a car once I get a job to pay for my own insurance. Grandma McGillicutty left me two thousand dollars in her will when she died of a heart attack in the retirement home. Dad says I can either use the money for college or for a car – it's my choice. Well that's a no-brainer now. I can't afford a Chevelle with glasspacks, but maybe a Dodge Dart is within my reach, or one of those old Chevettes. Something a little better than what those losers in *Wayne's World* drove.

"And what about you, Miss Fairchild? You haven't shared your work yet. Why don't you dazzle us with your eloquence?"

"I can't."

"And why not, pray tell?"

"My dog ate it."

"Don't be ridiculous."

"Seriously. I left the thing on my desk last night, and Rufus must have snatched it when I was taking a shower. He's as cute as a button, especially in his little red vest and booties, but he sure can be temperamental. He didn't like the fact that he had to get his shots and was probably holding a grudge."

The Squid is blinking, and for a moment it's as if she's been ripped from the comfortable depths of the abyss and thrust into the bright, blinding light. "You get an F for the day, Miss Fairchild, and likely an F for the entire semester. But I will grant you this. Your excuse gets a C+ for creativity. Your best grade all year."

Amy unleashes that sexy, gorgeous *I know if I pout like this you'll want to do whatever you can to rescue a damsel in distress* look, but the Squid doesn't fall for it. She's seen too many wondrous things in the depths and in the light, and the theatrics of a teenage prima donna just can't compare. Amy curls her toes into podiatric fists. "Whatever," she glares. "I don't need to pass this stupid class to graduate. My uncle is the mayor, remember? I'll still marry a Super Bowl MVP and drive an Escalade and splash a puddle onto your shopping cart full of cat food."

The Squid is livid, eyes beady, tentacles in a maelstrom, but before she launches an attack, she bites down on her beak and marks something in her ledger. Then she completely ignores the future prom queen. Her silence is the deadliest of weapons, honed no doubt by a life amidst bone-crushing pressure. Amy deflates into a pool of uncertainty, looking to the blank sheet of Wanda Lopez's face for guidance. Good luck there.

"Okay, it's your turn, Mr. Kantra. Please make it quick, so we can move onto the chapter on T.S. Eliot."

I slink up to the podium, and thirty pairs of eyes dissolve my flesh faster than any bucket of maggots could possibly do. I wipe my nose to make sure a night crawler isn't dangling from a nostril – it's been known to happen – and clear my throat of the Hi Di Ho wrapper that went down by mistake at breakfast. Chastity is sitting back in her chair, twisting a lock of coal-dust hair around a finger. She's staring toward me, but not at me, likely daydreaming about tigers and forests and weird Goth parties where kids drink hamster blood and play with Ouija boards. She's the most beautiful creature in the universe.

Kiss the Sky

As a child, I dreamed great dreams,
Of worlds far larger than they seemed;
Within my heart and within my soul,
Knowing their bosom held a role
For me to grasp and make my own,
Embrace with passion, build, and hone;
To leave my mark on this green earth,
Achieving more than death and birth.

I see this now as plain as day
Like sun-kissed drops of ocean spray,
Beside a shore of sand and brine
That nothing limits an able mind
From reaching for that ring of brass
Striving beyond the simple pass,
Throwing off the cloak of fear
And screaming finally that I'm here.

I know I'm dead with breath so ripe
And hungry bowels that lust for tripe;
But I'm still a boy who dares to dream
Of places far and places seen;
The crypts of hell can't hold me back
From tasting life's wondrous snacks
For now I know my purpose high
Is to someday simply kiss the sky.

The clock on the wall is ticking like a time bomb. Someone's mumbling the word chupacabra. Even the radiator is hissing, just to let me know that the sound of silence can tear out your guts faster than any rogue zombie with lockjaw.

"S-t-u-p-i-d," Amy quips.

"Zombie."

"Paste boy."

The Squid is blinking again. "That's enough of that, class. Enough. Very good, Mr. Kantra. Nice effort. I didn't think you had it in you, given your previous assignments, but that is a very fine attempt at poetry. Heartfelt and genuine, especially for one of the undead. A- work. May I ask what this poem means to you?"

I look to Chastity. She's staring back. "Everything."

I take my seat at the zombie desk by the window. A crumpled ball of paper hits me in the back of the head. Someone wretches a loogie from the depths of his bowels, and I brace for impact. Outside, Frederick finally wrings out his mop and picks a piece of flesh from his broom. Across the room, Chastity motions to me with a makeup brush, dabbing beneath one of her blue marbles. I guess a bit of my foundation has crumbled off.

7

Back in '79, eleven years after the First Occurrence in Pennsylvania and eight years after the town elders rebranded Morbid, IL to Pleasanton, IL, a gorgeous young woman named Gertrude McGillicutty garnered the second highest number of votes for high school prom queen. She didn't win a crown or wield a bouquet of roses; nor did she take center stage and blow tearful kisses to throngs of punch-drunk adolescents. Only the winner (whatever her name was) bore that honor. What Gertrude McGillicutty did do was shatter a stereotype. She demonstrated that royal ascension was possible for a normal person (i.e., non-cheerleader) and that popularity and smoking-hot looks didn't need to stem from fake smiles and springy pompoms. Gertrude McGillicutty came in second by simply being herself, and in doing so managed to accomplish what no other runner-up in the history of Morbid High has ever been able to match: she gave kids hope. Hope that being themselves was good enough. Hope that intelligence could be sexy. Hope that anybody, even the lowest-of-the-low third-string tuba player, was entitled to dream of greatness and someday achieve it. Or at least come close.

As Mom likes to point out, however, it was probably best that Gertrude McGillicutty didn't win the crown, for the senior prom of '79 occurred eight years before the Cleansing of '87, and when the prom king and prom queen (whatever their names were) took a ceremonial ride around the football field in the back of a '72 Coupe de Ville, a gang of rogue zombies ambushed them near the end zone and ripped out their throats.

"Want some more fried chicken?" Aunt Gertie says, thigh in mouth. "I brought over plenty of orange soda, too. None of that Swigmont garbage, but the real stuff. Orange Crush."

"Sure. I'm starving."

"I'm glad to see you've got an appetite now. You've always been a little on the thin side. I know you can't gain weight since you're dead – oh how I envy that quality – but that bottomless pit of a stomach helps your old Aunt Gertie feel less self-conscious when she goes for that fifth piece of Major Trough's finest. I know I'm just fooling myself with semantics and all, but when you get to be my age, it gets easier and easier."

She plops a juicy breast onto my plate and sucks the grease from her fingers. Then she doles out a thigh, using the same spit-laden hand.

"What are Jed, Fred, and Little Ted up to?" I ask, bound by familial courtesy.

"Your cousins are fine, sweetie. Thanks for asking. Ted is still in detention. Won't get out until five o'clock. His science teacher sent him up for a month-long stretch on account of a chemical explosion. Involved Mentos or what not. And Fred, well, Fred is probably at basketball practice smashing his skull into the bleachers. I keep telling him that head injury is the leading cause of brain damage, but he just won't listen. I think he figures the girls will like him better if he goes to class with bumps and bruises. And Jed, hallelujah, Jed is finally looking for a job. I know he just graduated three years ago, but I had to give him an ultimatum, for his own good. He has ninety days to rent his own apartment. He's working a few leads at the Wienerworld, and I put in a good word for him at the Chicken Trough. He'll land a job in time to make the rent. I'm sure of it."

"Aunt Gertie, are you ever sad you didn't win prom queen?"

She turns to me, head cocked, and a bit of grease trickles from the corner of her lip. "Has your mom been telling stories again?"

"A few."

"Well, let me tell it to you this way. Hell no. Winning prom queen that night meant death in the back of a '72 Coup de Ville. Lovely car, but no protection whatsoever from gnashing canines. In all honesty, I never really thought about becoming prom queen. Making runner-up just sort of fell in my lap. Ka-boom. And when it did, oh my, you should have seen the looks on those cheerleaders' faces, when for the briefest of moments they feared their dynasty had ended. Priceless, my boy. A real Kodak moment. Some say the cheerleaders *did* lose the election. Principal Rush oversaw three separate recounts, with kids crawling out of the woodwork claiming that they'd forgotten to vote. I suspect a few of them didn't even attend our school. That's high school politics for you. Anyway, Sandra Rothschild won two of the three recounts, and I won one, so she got to be prom queen."

Aunt Gertie drifts into silence, a statue of alabaster, worn and weathered by the wind and rain; and for a moment, I picture her in bell bottoms and a halter top, gliding down the halls of Morbid High atop platform shoes and a wave of fame, smiling deep within her heart because she knew that she meant something. You can still see that person beneath the dinner rolls and chicken thighs when the light is dim and Aunt Gertie's blue lasers find their range. The prom queen runner-up has never stopped dancing. She's a little slower now and a little out of vogue, but she's never stopped dancing. I'm beginning to understand why Mom talks so highly of her big sis.

"Why do you ask? Are you thinking of running for prom king?"

A chicken bone stabs my larynx. "Are you kidding me?"

"A strapping young man like yourself, with a good head on his shoulders and a healthy appetite, surely has a chance."

"I can't even get a date."

"Well, that'll come in time, when the fates decide you're ready for it."

"I'm *undead*, Aunt Gertie."

"You might be undead, but you're certainly not buried. Just keep the Oralcline regimen up and you shouldn't be any worse for wear. Hell, I've married a few husbands that were more zombie than you. Believe me, the effects of guzzling beer, humping the couch, and using the want ads as toilet paper can make any living man stink worse than a rotting corpse. No offense, sweetie. You know Aunt Gertie loves you."

"None taken."

"Besides, being a zombie hasn't stopped Ziggy Banks."

Ziggy Banks, for those of you who don't know, is the longest-running syndicated game show host in the history of television. He got his start on radio in the '30s, alongside Merton Boyle, and rode his penchant for quick one-liners into the big time. He starred in a *Father Knows Best* knockoff in the '50s with Bonnie Reed; hosted a variety show in the '60s in which wannabe comedians came on stage and revealed what jackasses they were to hordes of screaming fans; and then settled into a series of game shows in the '70s when his *Ziggy Zays* talk show lost the ratings battle to Phil Donahue. Ziggy's current gig is *The Wheel of Life*, in which contestants are randomly selected from the audience to spin a wheel and win whatever prize the ticker lands on. Cars. Cash. Hawaiian vacations. And of course, the gags. Half of the spots on the wheel are reserved for gags, and if the ticker lands on one of them, the contestant is obligated to perform the gag or risk losing the coveted consolation prizes. Some of the gags are mundane – farting with an armpit or reciting the Pledge of Allegiance without the teleprompter. But other gags are a bit more sinister, malicious even – flashing the audience, eating live bugs, taking a ninth-grade vocabulary test in front of millions of home viewers. It's always amazed me how eager people can be to embarrass themselves in front of the entire world just to win a few trinkets. I suspect it's the so-called fame that drives them, the desire to stand out and be special, even if the path to such distinction is self-deprecation. It's hilarious to watch. It's even sadder to think about. And it's made Ziggy Banks one of the wealthiest corpses in Hollywood.

"I guess there's hope."

"Sure there is, sweetie. Just take the bull by the horns and give it a hard kick to the meatballs...and never forget, your life is what you make of it."

The doorbell rings, and Mom yells from her bedroom for

someone to answer. Aunt Gertie is too busy washing dishes to notice, and Jimmy is probably downstairs in the basement stealing more of my stuff. That leaves me. I pause, unwilling to leave my chicken breast unattended.

Mom yells again, but still nobody moves. That's probably because no one important ever visits the Kantra household. The parcel delivery guy just leaves packages by the door and rings the bell out of courtesy, and little Sally Barton from down the street only rings when she's trying to unload those peanut butter cookies. At four bucks a box, it's best not to answer. And then of course there's Ernest, but he doesn't have any place else to go and usually rings the bell for ten minutes before coming around the back to knock on the sliding glass door. He still has nine minutes left.

Mom yells even louder, at the top of her lungs so that anyone at the door, including Mrs. Epstein across the street, can hear. Finally, she gets the hint and marches downstairs in a lavender headband and set of pink leg warmers, muttering something about deadbeats and dead bodies. She probably still thinks Ed McMahon will show up on our doorstep with a ten million dollar check in hand.

The door opens. The air pressure shifts. Mom begins mumbling something to somebody. She's getting short of breath the way she does when she debates with Dad over buying new furniture. The door closes. The air pressure shifts again. Aunt Gertie downs the last chicken thigh without sharing.

"You have a visitor," Mom says, hyperventilating.

"Tell Ernest he hasn't rung the doorbell long enough."

"It's not Ernest, sweetie. It's...it's..." She exhales loudly. "It's a girl."

I swing around, and standing next to Mom in black jeans and a black leather jacket is Chastity Sky. She's kind of smiling, but not really, wielding a backpack in her left hand. She tosses it on the table in front of me. "You left your backpack by the lockers. I didn't want Doug or Amy stealing it."

"That's mine," I mumble.

"I know."

"That's my backpack."

"I *know*."

Now you'd think that being dead and desensitized to pain would enable a young man to weather stress and adversity – charging the hill amidst machinegun fire or diving into the deep blue to save a swimmer from a shark. But despite the lack of adrenaline and the lack of a life to lose, zombies still experience fear. Fear of humiliation. Fear of retaliation. Even fear of crapping their pants. And although I've stalked Chastity for the better part of ten months (keeping tabs on her for much longer), the immediacy of her living, breathing presence in the middle of my kitchen with Mom looking on and Aunt Gertie listening is almost too much to fathom. I'm choking, choking on the useless words that rattle through my brain like the coins in Mr. Oinker.

"Say thank you," Mom helps.

"Thank you," I mutter.

"I was just going to drop this off, but your mom insisted that I come inside. Nice house."

"Thank you, sweetie," Mom says. "Now why don't you have a seat."

"I really should get going."

"Don't be silly. I insist." Mom grips Chastity by the shoulders and presses down with all of her weight, forcing Chastity into the chair next to me. "I can bake cookies."

"I like cookies."

"Of course you do, sweetie."

Communicating through telepathy and eye signals, Mom and Aunt Gertie get to work in the kitchen as if the very future of our family line depended on it. Pots and pans clanging. Plates clashing. Blenders and mixers roaring. I swear I can hear the cork of an '86 Dom Pérignon blow. And all the while, I'm sitting across from the third hottest girl in school paralyzed with fear. Fear of rejection. Fear of the unknown. Fear of bursting a dream. It's ludicrous really. I've embarrassed myself my entire life, pissed away whatever shreds of dignity I might have had long ago, but right now, at this particular moment, my biggest fear is to open my mouth and say something stupid.

"I liked your poem," she says.

"Thank you."

"Do you really feel that way? I mean, do you really think that people should throw off the chains of conformity and dare to dream?"

"Thank you."

"What?"

"Thank you."

Mom breaks the awkwardness by dumping a plate of rare pork chops onto the table in front of us. Pink blood pools around them. "You kids don't want forks, do you? Pork chops are nature's finger food, or so I've learned over the past couple of days. Dig in, sweetie. Don't be shy. The cookies will be ready in a couple of minutes."

Chastity shrugs her shoulders and takes a bite. A trickle of blood rounds the corner of her mouth and drips onto the cream of her cleavage.

"You would have made a great cheerleader," I say.

Chastity frowns. "Don't wish that on me. I wouldn't wish that on anyone. But thanks for saying so. I know what you mean."

Mom delivers a tray of chocolate chip cookies next. The aroma wafts into my nostrils and reminds me of simpler times. There's nothing like rare pork chops and cookies straight from the oven.

"These are good pork chops, Mrs. Kantra, fresh and gamey."

Mom straightens the bob of her hair. "Thank you, sweetie. I know how much you kids like rare meat. We keep plenty of pork chops on hand now. No need to worry about expiration dates anymore. You're just so pretty, did you know that? Of course you do. I could eat you all up. I can't imagine what happened to you though. If you don't mind my asking, how did you die?"

Aunt Gertie launches an elbow into Mom's ribs with such force that the woman falls into the oven door and singes the tip of her bob on the exposed rack. Of all the rotten, boneheaded things that Mom's ever done to me in her life – flashing Burt Mitchel at a Hemloch reunion, giving birth to Jimmy, marrying a tightwad – this has to be the worst. If my heart still pounded, it would burst from my chest and strangle her. She's ruined my only chance; she's flushed my winning lottery ticket down the toilet. I never thought I would say this, but my mom has killed me a second time.

"She didn't die, Mom!"

"What?"

Chastity eyes are wide open, probably from the shock of Mom's insult. She quickly regains her composure though and reaches for a third pork chop. "I'm not a zombie, Mrs. Kantra. I'm alive and well. Every now and then someone mistakes me for a zombie on account of the black eye shadow and pale skin. And I have to admit that I don't gargle as much as I used to. But I've gotten used to the faux pas. No harm, no foul. That's my motto. Do you have any milk?"

"What? Oh my." Mom practically faints, and only the strength of Aunt Gertie's chicken-wielding arms keeps her from crashing face-first into the linoleum. "You mean...you mean that's a real girl? A real living, breathing girl has come to visit Chris?"

* * *

It's not often that a guy's girl visitor gets called a zombie by his mom and stays for dessert. But Chastity did. And not only did she stay for dessert, but she helped me finish off the entire plate of pork chops and a gallon of milk; then she even succumbed to my pleas to check out the basement.

At the base of the stairs, I flip on the light switch, and right smack dab on the middle of the couch the March issue of *Big Smiles* is lying face up. Amber Strongsen graces the cover, a Minnesota farmer's daughter turned *Reality Island* finalist turned object of every man's desire. She's smiling at me, maybe empathizing with my predicament. My asswipe brother either left the magazine there for Mom to find, or worse, to sabotage any chance I'd have of impressing the first real girl to visit the basement. You might think I'm paranoid, but you don't know Jimmy the way I do. He's probably still here, hiding between the walls like the rat that he is, waiting for the gasp of disgust and the bonus slap across my face.

Before I can hide the magazine, Chastity turns it sideways and lets Amber Strongsen unfold in all of her glory. Straw hat.

Pitchfork. Best-white smile.

"Guys sure like a big smile on a girl, don't they?" she says, rhetorically I hope. She rearranges the mounds within her sweater. "I brush twice a day and floss once. That's enough for me. I can't imagine smiling any whiter just so guys can drool. This girl is kind of freakish, don't you think?"

"Thank you."

"What?"

"Yes."

She tosses the magazine back on the couch, face down this time, and begins to survey the basement. She must moonlight as a braille cartographer the way she's tracing her finger across every item in the room – Trinitron TV, stamps of the Middle East collection, HP laptop with Blockbuilder world still making sounds, poster of Madonna, assorted books, piggy bank (Mr. Oinker on his nametag), empty wallet on desk, crumpled ball of laundry in the corner, second poster of Madonna, twenty-five pound dumbbells, cobwebs on dumbbells, fly caught in cobwebs, spider eating fly, assorted baby food jars (don't ask), Tylenol, pop cans, crate of Oralcline, and a little garden gnome named Herbert with a clock ticking in his belly.

"You lived down here even before becoming a zombie?"

"Since I was fifteen. I had to get some breathing room."

"I know what you mean. My older brother, Benson, claimed the basement for a couple of years before joining the Marines. He did us all a favor by going subterranean. Your basement doesn't smell like armpit though."

"Thanks."

"Yours is a lot neater, too. Benson was a total slob. Pictures of naked women on the walls. Empty beer cans. DVDs and game cartridges everywhere, but not a single book. You have a nice collection. Poe. Hemingway. Vonnegut. If you don't mind my asking, how did you die? When the ambulance came to the school, the paramedic said you were going to make it."

"The ambulance crashed into the old Dutch elm on Route 99."

"Bummer."

"Yeah, I guess it happens."

"Thanks for trying to save me," she says. "I realize that's what you were trying to do. I'm sorry that I kicked you. It was instinct, on account of my martial arts training. I feel a little guilty for what happened to you."

"That's okay. It could have happened to anyone. I guess I shouldn't have been so clumsy in my rescue attempt. I wanted to tell you something though. I mean, something's been bothering me for the last few days. I mean, I don't want you thinking I'm some kind of pervert. I was only in that bush because of Ernest. He came up with the stupid idea, and I went along in a moment of weakness."

Chastity studies me skeptically.

"Maybe we did it twice."

"I don't care if you like spying on the cheerleaders, although I can't see why you'd want to do that. If you could only look inside of them, past the makeup and hair products, then you'd know what I mean. They're not as hot as you think."

Her words resonate on multiple levels, but the word that sticks in my brain the strongest is *hot*. "Did you ever find what you were looking for in the dumpster?"

Chastity breaks eye contact, and her blue orbs search for something to refocus on. They're unsuccessful. "No."

I must have hit some kind of nerve, blabbing too much with my big mouth; but I don't have a lot of practice talking to girls. At least not real ones. After about a minute, Chastity regains her smile and plops down on the couch, thumbing through the March issue of *Big Smiles* again. She pauses on Melanie Melonson, an oil worker from Texas with bone-white teeth and a PhD in chemical engineering.

"You could be in that magazine," I mumble, before my brain can stop me.

"Excuse me?"

"I mean... what I meant to say is...I mean...you know what I mean."

"Do I?"

"All I'm saying is that those women don't need to spend thousands of dollars on orthodontics to be attractive. If they're truly beautiful, with nice hearts and nice features, they could skip a day or two of brushing and still catch the right guy's attention.

A girl doesn't have to flaunt. A guy will still notice the little lapis lazuli dolphin with the ruby eye that's tied to the zipper of her backpack, or the scuff that runs along the left side of the left sole of her black leather combat boot, or the pot of lilacs that holds open the screen door on her front porch on account of the time her dad carried a La-Z-Boy into the house and knocked the pneumatic closer off its hinge. A girl just needs to be herself and she can compete with any magazine. Amy Fairchild and Wanda Lopez are dog butts compared to you."

"Nice save," she says, grinning. "If you weren't such a good writer, you'd creep me out with your eye for detail. But I'll cut you some slack, on account of my contributing to your death. Just don't mention Amy or Wanda anymore, okay?"

"Okay. And I'm really sorry for what my mom said. I think she's getting Alzheimer's...keeps forgetting to go on meds. She's past fifty, you know. A brain can't last forever."

"Oh, don't worry about that. She isn't the first person to make that mistake. Besides, I'm cool with zombies. Always have been. Even when I was a little girl, I made my mom buy me Zombie Darbie in addition to Cheerleader Darbie. I actually liked the zombie doll better. It seemed more grounded in reality."

Sitting here, exchanging words and feelings with this Goth bastion of beauty is unearthing urges that I didn't think I had. I'm not talking about lust or desire. I'm talking about a sensation of oneness, a connection beneath the surface forged in places that transcend time. I know this is going to sound corny, but I think that Chastity and I were meant for each other. Something about her persona just seems to be aligned with mine far more than I could have hoped for in my wildest dreams.

I want to kiss her. I want to lean in and kiss her right now. I mean, I'm dead and rotting, addicted to Oralcline with undigested pork clogging my bowels, but this Goth angel makes me feel alive.

But I'm afraid to...and not just because I've never kissed a girl before...and certainly not just because rejection would crush me worse than Frederick and his load of shingles. I'm afraid because I don't want to expose Chastity to the zombie virus. Exchanging spit with a live girl is simply not the cool thing to do.

So I sit here, trying to smile, resisting the urge to kiss her because that's the kind of person that I am, when the strangest thing happens. Chastity leans in to kiss me. I recoil in a last-ditch effort not to infect her, but she grabs the back of my head and presses her lips to mine.

"But the zombie virus," I mutter, when we come up for air.

"I know. And thank you for thinking of me. But I've already been exposed."

"You have?"

"Yeah. It's a long story. I'll tell you sometime."

8

I invited Marvin Reynolds over to play some Blockbuilder, as a way of thanking him for lugging my corpse to the emergency room. He's not much of a gamer though and just wants to watch TV. There's nothing really on, so he keeps channel surfing. The flickers of light and sound are driving Ernest and me crazy. Ernest pelts him in the head with a pillow, distracting him from the remote long enough for Kirk Karson, the local news anchor, to get a few words in – something about a chance of snow. Marvin had an early shift, so he brought over a bag of Beef 'n Cheeses, which Randy lets employees claim once they've shriveled under the heat lamp for more than four hours. Ernest has already downed two. I'm working on my fourth. And Marvin...well, let's just say he's been a zombie long enough to ingest six in one sitting. When I asked him why on earth Randy let him score a dozen free sandwiches, Marvin admitted to raiding the dumpster in the alley. *We throw out good stuff*, he said. *It's less than a day old.* Ernest is starting to turn a little green, but he'll get over it. I've seen him eat worse.

"Give me the remote," Ernest coughs, rather piqued. He takes a hit from his inhaler.

"Stop shouting orders," Marvin says "I hear orders all day at Artie's. Just let me relax and try to find something to watch."

"Put the Eastminster Dog Show back on."

"Are you kidding me?"

"No. That spaniel from last year might repeat."

Marvin looks to me, jaw limp. He's still wearing his paper hat. I shrug my shoulders. "Come on, Ernest," I say. "It's just the preliminary rounds. I'm sure USPN 6 will recap the highlights later tonight...you know, the action clips. Let's find something we can all tolerate."

Ernest tugs at his pumpkin hair. "Fine. Just as long as it's not that stupid *My Three Zombies*. I know you guys are rotting corpses and all, and I think that's cool, but I just don't see the humor in a bunch of zombies trying to learn life lessons from a custodial engineer. It's gross, really, if you ask my opinion."

"People throw out a lot of good stuff," Marvin says. "Our society is so damned wasteful. There's nothing wrong with three hungry zombies eating leftovers. It teaches kids the valuable lesson of recycling."

"He digs their dinners out of the trash."

"Where do you think those Beef 'n Cheeses came from?"

Ernest turns the greenest shade of green I've ever witnessed in a human and blends into the avocado slipcover Mom put over the couch. He's a veritable chameleon. Marvin leans to the side to avoid any *Exorcist* vomit, but Ernest, fierce competitor that he is, keeps the day-old roast beef down.

"Are you trying to kill me, Marvin? Just because you're dead doesn't mean that everyone else wants to be dead. Friends don't kill their friends. It's just not cool."

"I wasn't trying to kill you. If I wanted to kill you, I'd eat your brain and then go out for bratwurst since I'd still be starving."

"You couldn't eat my brain if you tried."

"You're right. I probably couldn't find it."

Marvin and Ernest go for their respective jugulars for quite some time, delivering one poignant salvo after another. Things like *ass muncher* and *zit popper*. Marvin even grows so bold as to accuse Ernest of stinking at chess, in spite of his seventeenth-place finish at last month's tournament. Ernest responds the best way he knows how: bragging about his plans to land on Mars and moon the camera. The living Chris would intervene and play the part of the even-tempered negotiator, explaining the merits of free curly fries and solidarity. But zombie Chris, the slowly festering corpse that persists because of a pharmaceutical derived from Vietnam-era incendiary ordnance and *Flashdance*-era diet pills, is not so quick to act. He detects a certain anthropological merit to their interaction. The clashing of cultures – life and death.

This is what happens when kids get tired of playing Blockbuilder and there's nothing on TV.

"Maybe we should go to the game," I suggest. "It *is* Friday night."

Marvin and Ernest stare at me like I'm mental. "The game?"

"Yeah, there's a basketball game in the gym tonight. We're hosting the Harrison Hominids."

"The game?" Ernest repeats.

"What's wrong with the game?"

"We never go to the game."

"I'm learning to try new things...like being dead, for example."

"And talking to girls," Marvin chuckles.

"How do you know about that? You don't even go to school anymore?"

"This is Pleasanton. Word spreads faster than rigor mortis."

And it has. People are talking. In the halls especially. *What's wrong with Chastity? Poor Chastity. She used to be so cool, and now she's slumped to this. That falling out with Amy and Wanda has sure taken its toll. The Goth thing and nose piercings – well – that was a phase. Other people go through it. But talking to a zombie! Eating meatloaf with him! Two servings! In front of the entire school! My God. She's going to get fat. And I don't know what's worse, the fact that she's hanging around a zombie or the fact that she's hanging around Chris Kantra. Double gross.*

"So did you give her the Beef 'n Cheese yet?" Marvin grins.

"They ate meatloaf," Ernest clarifies.

"That's none of your business," I say. "Besides, a gentleman never tells."

"Just be safe. You don't want to infect her."

"I know. What kind of guy do you think I am? Besides, we're just friends. So stop asking questions."

"All right, man, but you have nothing to be shy about. You're a rock star now amongst the undead community. No non-jock zombie has ever made it with a cheerleader. Marching band members and fry cooks, sure. But never a cheerleader."

"She's not a cheerleader."

"She used to be. Once a cheerleader, always a cheerleader."

Marvin has a point. I imagine that once a person ascends to the zenith of social relevance, the grandeur of the experience fuses to the genome, making it impossible to strip the consciousness of its newfound power. I'm only guessing here, since social relevance has never been my shtick, but I imagine a cheerleader not cheerleading would be akin to Chris Kantra not playing Blockbuilder...or Ernest Pratt surrendering his chessboard...or Marvin Reynolds removing his paper hat. Sheer torture, of the 15th-century religious variety.

"Leave that on," I say.

"What?"

"The news report."

"Come on. I'm missing the dog show."

"Leave it."

The camera zooms in on a man with peppered hair and a store-bought tan. He's sixty, but resembles a weathered forty-year-old, and he bears a smile that only years of oral isometrics could make possible. He's sitting behind a desk in a crisp suit with windows and trees in the background, and his teeth look like they've been capped. To his right, the flag of the United States of America looms gravely, and on the corner of his desk, cast in bronze, a small statue of a one-legged Confederate colonel grasps a shotgun in one hand while wielding a fist at the air. The caption at the bottom of the screen reads: *Special News Bulletin.*

"Come on," Ernest pleads. "Mayor Shight is boring."

"So is the dog show," Marvin says. "Why can't I find *Charlie's Angels*?"

"Good citizens of Pleasanton," the mayor starts, maintaining his smile, "I come to you tonight with open arms and with an open heart to ask for your help and understanding during these trying times. As I'm sure you've learned by now, a spate of zombie attacks has plagued our fair town, claiming five innocent victims in the prime of their lives. Fathers. Mothers. Neighbors. Tragic losses, all. Please join me in a moment of silence, as we remember these brave souls and the horrors they've endured."

He's referring to the zombie attacks that have occurred over the past few weeks, the worst of which struck two days ago at the Mr. Washy Laundromat. A couple of kids were playing a game of superwedgie by the dryers when a zombie crashed through the window and ate their mom. Bit right through her carotid artery and ripped her head off. When the zombie pounced on the carcass to feed, the boy had the presence of mind to sneak into an oversized dryer with his kid sister. They cowered there for twenty minutes beside a pair of thong under-wear while the zombie ingested their mom organ-by-organ. The rogue must have been ravenous because he stripped the bones clean, brain and all, then shuffled through the laundro-mat with a distended stomach searching for more. The kids bit down on their fingers to keep quiet, and the little girl squeezed so hard on her Homemaker Darbie that the doll's head popped off. The zombie moaned by their dryer for a minute or two, but didn't see them, and eventually wandered off. Hours later, Syl-vester Carnsworth, the blind guy who volunteers at the library, shuffled into the laundromat to wash his guide dog's sweater vests. Rover went straight for the mom's ribs without barking, and Sylvester completed two loads of laundry before opening the door to the oversized dryer. The moment he did, a nine-year-old boy jumped out kicking and screaming and beat him over the head with his own cane. Passers-by heard Rover howl-ing and alerted the authorities. Within minutes a reporter from the *Gazette* immortalized the scene for posterity. And now the boy is doomed to live down the image of a sweater-wearing guide dog chewing on his mother's femur and his kid sister sporting a pair of thong underwear on her head.

He was wearing a White Sox baseball cap was all the boy could mutter. *Like the one Mom bought me for my birthday.*

The mayor clears his throat, head still hung low. "Please let us take another moment. I'd like to pray to the Almighty for guid-ance during these trying times."

The Mr. Washy attack has got people talking, and I mean *really* talking. The previous attacks involved men whom society could do without (ballet instructor, SlowMart clerk, history teacher) and a soccer mom, who although disemboweled in the frozen food aisle at Pam's Club, still managed to reanimate in time to chair last Thursday's PTA meeting. The Mr. Washy attack, however, not only involved a young mom (who's kind of hot in the pics) but also represented the kind of attack from which a person cannot reanimate. Total consumption.

Mr. J says the tenor of the neighborhood is shifting as result, in a manner insidious to the 28th Amendment. The pictures of "Laundromom's" towheaded children all over the news have worked people into a frenzy, especially the conservatives, who are starting to blame the attacks on lax policies implemented by a liberal establishment. *It's going to be a witch hunt*, Mr. J mumbled to himself by his garden the other day, recalling the Chicago zombie riots of '74. And when a massive turd struck his tank top (hurled by a troop of Fudgies in a passing Suburban), he tried to take the offense in stride, mixing the feces into the topsoil for his roses. But I could tell that he was worried, terrified really that human decency might not prevail this time around.

The mayor finally raises his head, seemingly distraught, and the camera pans to the side of the room where a poster-sized photo of Laundromom rests on an easel. She's wearing a tank top and feathered hair and is squinting in the sun's glare with two children pressed against the mounds of her bosom. A White Sox baseball cap obscures the boy's eyes, while mud-pie swirls encircle his mouth. His left hand is held high in a gesture to the camera, the details of which have succumbed to the airbrush. The girl is as cute as a button with yellow pigtails and Pippi Longstocking freckles and eyes as deep as Blue Hawaiians. She, too, is making a gesture of her own with finger and nose, a little miner at heart. In the background, to the left of the trailer, a pit bull is off its chain, sniffing around an old tow truck that's sitting up on cinder blocks. It's a tender, family portrait – real salt-of-the-earth stuff – the kind of image that *real* people, not those phonies with jobs and straight teeth, can soak up and embrace. Even rally around.

Next to the poster of Laundromom, several Polaroids are taped to a sheet of construction paper – presumably the other victims who have since reanimated. It's hard to tell for sure though, since the photos are too small to make out.

Mayor Shight, on cue, regains an air of conviction and peers into the camera. "I want to assure you, good citizens of Pleasanton, that the mayor's office, in conjunction with the police department and the Border Patrol, is doing everything within its power to locate the perpetrators of these dastardly attacks and bring them to justice. We have reason to believe that at least two, and perhaps as many as a dozen, rogue zombies have breached our perimeter and are lurking within our community. In order to enable law enforcement to more effectively root out this cancer, I have instituted a mandatory curfew for all undead citizens. Effective immediately, all zombie residents are required to remain at home from 8pm until sunrise. If work arrangements preclude adherence to the curfew, special work permits are available at the Border Patrol office for seven hundred and fifty dollars apiece. I know this will be a hardship on some of you, but I beseech you to observe the curfew. Violators will be fined, and repeat offenders will be detained."

The mayor exhales deeply with somber, caring eyes. "The great town of Pleasanton prides itself on a history of tolerance. Former President Romero is one of my personal heroes. But in the interest of public safety and at the behest of town elders, this curfew reflects the bitter necessity of our times. I would hate to see any hardworking, taxpaying zombies mistakenly incarcerated – or worse – as our boys of the Border Patrol comb the streets in their singular mission of eradicating the flesh-craving threat. So in closing, my fair citizens, I implore you to do your part. Obey the curfew, and if you detect any suspicious zombie activity in your neighborhood, notify the Border Patrol immediately. Don't worry about false alarms; it's better to be safe than sorry in times like these. Additionally, a special excise tax on pork chops, cow tongue, and fast food will be instituted to help defray the cost of our search efforts. Thank you for your time. Goodnight and God bless."

The image of the mayor smiling lingers on the screen, as if his UV-saturated corpuscles have burned themselves into the glass, and I'm left with a sick feeling in my stomach. First it was a tax on zombie-owned property. Now it's a zombie-only curfew and a tax on zombie edibles. What's going to come next? Mr. Brumley, the history teacher who was mauled in front of the school, lectured last semester how governments sometimes scapegoat certain segments of the population in times of crisis as a means of consolidating power. They justify their actions by claiming that they advance the greater good. Unfortunately, those actions always seem to end the same way – badly.

Matlock comes on, and the eponymous attorney gets woken up in the middle of the night by a call from a guy who painted his house, claiming that he's been arrested for stealing a formula for curing baldness. The old litigator doesn't seem too pleased.

"What am I going to do?" Marvin mumbles, eyes locked on the screen. "I don't have seven hundred and fifty bucks for a work permit. I make eight bucks an hour for Christ's sake. Maybe ten, once you factor in the free food."

"Let's go to the game," I say.

"The game?" Ernest says.

"Yeah, the game. Let's get out of this basement for a while and get our minds off this crap."

"What's wrong with the basement?"

"It's starting to feel too much like a tomb."

9

Hundreds of kids are crammed into the bleachers of the Morbid High School gymnasium, screaming and chanting and drooling over corn dogs and the chance of a late foul. The Morbid Maulers are hosting the Harrison Hominids. My cousin Fred plays point guard for Harrison, and he's on the court now, digging for gold. Apparently he hasn't spotted the eight-by-twelve-foot jumbotron that Farmer Brown donated to the school back in '05 after discovering natural gas in a cornfield. My cousin's face is flashing on the screen every which way but airbrushed, finger in nose up to the wrist. The Maulers fans are exploding in a frenzy of laugher, launching aspersions that can't be repeated in commercially distributed literature. One of his teammates, the lanky center, finally smacks Fred in the back of the head and points to the screen. Instead of flushing crimson the way a normal person would, however, Fred hoists the booger-finger to the rafters for the entire gymnasium to see. As the bleachers fizzle into the silence of freeway-accident gawkers, he plunges the finger straight down his throat. Fans from both teams cheer. Fred takes a bow. The jumbotron lights up with the word *Score!*

In spite of my cousin's self-deprecation, Ernest's eyes are locked on the marching band. He's tried out for a spot three years in a row, failing each time to make the cut. It's a bit of a sensitive topic with him, so I don't bring it up much. He's peering like a hawk at Sissy Slupchek. Everyone has written her off as a zombie (even her parents, I've heard), but the rumor simply isn't true. She's alive, a little slow and a bit ripe, but definitely breathing, and Ernest has nurtured a Woodrow for her since the eighth grade. He's worse than I am at expressing his feelings though and can't even summon the courage to humiliate himself in a shameless ploy for attention. *Ask to see her sheet music*, I've suggested. *Trip in front of her with your clarinet case so she'll notice that you're a musician...and maybe take pity on you.* But he won't heed my advice. He's a deer in the headlights with only enough strength to mumble about her woodwind. He's infatuated with it. It's size. It's shimmer. The way she handles it.

The rest of the bleachers break down into a microcosm of the high school, with the jocks and popular kids on one side, nearest the team bench and cheerleaders; and the assorted nerds, dorks, and mutants on the other side, close to the visiting fans. From the corner of my eye, I can detect Fred's brothers – Jed and Little Ted – but I doubt they notice me. They're too enthralled by the drama of the game, waving umbrellas and shouting expletives. Besides, we adhere to an unwritten rule, my cousins and I, to ignore each other's existence. Ever since they pinned me down by the Christmas tree in the sixth grade and inflicted what Jed termed a Jules Verne wedgie, I'd so much as shoot them in the head with a nail gun as make small talk over Easter ham.

"I got us corn dogs," Marvin says, lugging a tray back from the vending booth. "Four for you. Six for me. And two for you, Ernest, from the trash, since I know you like aged meat."

"Very funny, Marvin. When are you going to take off that stupid paper hat?"

"When you change your underwear. Never."

Ernest, the chameleon, glows as orange as his hair and takes a double hit from his inhaler. He knows Marvin is right. We all do. The thing about being a zombie is that you don't lose your sense of smell. You don't complain about local stenches as much, on account of your own halitosis, but when a guy like Ernest is sitting right next to you, there's no ignoring it. I snort a slug of Oralcline from my travel bottle and swallow since there's nowhere to spit. Ernest wiggles on the bench, wrestling with a pesky itch.

In the front row, Chastity is talking with a group of Goth chicks, Super Gulp in hand. They resemble an Elvira convention, but Chastity is the only one of them with the headstones to back up the claim. She waves to me and smiles, and I wave back, and she shouts over the din of the cheering crowd. But I can't make out the words.

I feel like I'm in a dream.

And just like a dream, it's hard to tell what's real and what's not. I mean, Chastity and I have hung out at school a ton since our kiss in the basement. We've held hands and shared meatloaf. We've even exchanged phone numbers and sent texts. But we haven't joined lips again. I'm not sure why. Perhaps she's waiting for me to make the next move…you know…be a man and show some initiative. And like the paste eater that I can sometimes be, I've failed to do so. But I can't help it; the fear of rejection is still festering deep within my bowels. I want nothing more than our relationship to get to the next level, but I'm terrified that if I push too hard I might scare her off. It's crazy when you think about it. I risked (and lost) my life saving her from those falling shingles, but I can't work up the gumption to make her mine. It's a form of paralysis worse than rigor mortis. The fact that she's one of the hottest girls in class and I have a death certificate isn't enough to justify the madness.

Before I can invite Chastity to sit next to me though, our side of the bleachers erupts into a cacophony of cheers. Buddy Washington, the Hominids shooting guard, has just dunked on Doug Jerkins. Buddy is a zombie stud in the ancient Greek Olympian sense of the word – tall, muscular, agile as a fox. Normally zombies don't make the team on account of discrimination, but the Hominids coach made an exception in Buddy's case, since Buddy already played for the team before losing an ear (and part of his temporal lobe) to a meat slicer at his parents' delicatessen, and since his injuries in no way impede his vertical lift. He's got the ball again. And again he's gliding through the air, legs pumping an invisible bicycle. Two more on Doug Jerkins. *Score!* We're down by eleven now, and Doug is steaming.

"In your face," the visiting crowd cheers. "In your face, waste of space."

The Hominids cheerleaders burst out:

Go, Buddy. He's the man.
You can't catch him. No one can.
Built of steel and strong as brick.
He'll bust you up really quick.

"I bet he's dunked on a cheerleader or two," Marvin grins.

Amy and Wanda and the rest of Morbid's finest hoist their upturned hearts into the visitors' faces and respond:

Stupid crowd. Who needs you?
Your faces make us want to spew.
You're dumb and fat, no dignity.
You might as well all be zombies.

With nine seconds left in the second period, Buddy palms the ball again. He toys with Chad for a couple of seconds, hotdog-ging in circles around him, then drives to the basket, throwing an in-flight 360 over Doug and hanging on the rim as the buzzer sounds.

The Maulers are down by thirteen at the half.

Doug shouts something at Buddy, and Buddy laughs, shouting something in return. Doug motions for the zombie's headband (which he wears to cover the missing ear), but his teammates hold him back. Buddy dismisses Doug with a hand, the way a teacher's aide might wave off a loose-bowelled pre-schooler, and struts toward the visitors' bench.

Principal Dawson snatches the microphone from the announcer before the halftime routines can begin. She's wearing a Maulers sweatshirt and blue jeans. "Students and fans," she starts, stepping onto a milk crate. "Many of you had the opportunity to watch Mayor Shight's announcement on Channel 12 earlier today, and I trust you were as moved as I was by his heartfelt words. For those of you who couldn't watch, copies of his speech are available at the door for your reading pleasure. I suggest you take one after the game. In a nutshell, our good mayor spoke of hope in these trying times. Of action. And most importantly of the duty each one of us bears to monitor our streets and watch over each other's affairs. We are not alone in this threat. Not a single one of us. We have our families to depend on...our neighbors and our congregations. And I'd also like to think we have our schools. This is why, with great pride, I announce to you the Morbid High School Zombie Attack Fund."

On cue, Mrs. Hausenbaum, the school secretary, wheels out a blown-up portrait of Laundromom. It's identical to the one in the mayor's office, but at least four times as large. The picture was likely taken with a disposable camera, for it resembles a Seurat work in progress more than a snapshot of realism. From a distance though, the important details stand out – a mom with young children, the family trailer, a loving pit bull roaming free. There's no mistaking who it is. And in a situation like this, the details are probably extraneous anyway. She's a mother and a wife, trying her best to get by, crapped on by life and then ripped from it prematurely by the gnashing teeth of the undead hordes. And all she was trying to do was wash a pair of tighty whities. She's tragedy and inequity rolled into one. She's the symbol of our times.

Principal Dawson starts clapping; Mrs. Hausenbaum follows suit; and soon a trickle of applause hits forty on the decibel meter. Amy Fairchild, on cue, sprints into a quintuple backflip with a double twist and nails her landing on center court.

Laundromom!
Laundromom!
Laundromom!

Her words reverberate in the stands, transforming whispers into a war chant. I'm even tempted to join in, the way she's flashing her pom-poms.

"Laundromom," I mumble.

Marvin jams a corn dog stick into my leg.

Principle Dawson raises her arms, smiling, "Thank you, Amy. I'm glad to see you share your uncle's enthusiasm for the community. Now, as part of our school's commitment to the poor victims in need, the school board has approved this fund with an initial contribution of 2% of school carnival net revenues, after normal offsets for overhead, tax accruals, and interest amortization on the district's long-term debt obligation. But that's just the start. In their commitment to public service, the athletes and cheerleaders of Morbid High have taken it upon themselves to distribute Laundrocans at every game. If the school can do its part, so can you. Please contribute what you're comfortable with. A dollar. Five dollars. A hundred if you can endure that much joy. All of the proceeds will be distributed to the victims' families once program expenses and other modest administrative fees are deducted. Now, enough talk of generosity. Without further ado, I give you our very own Mauler Maidens."

Wanda Lopez and a bevy of bombshells blow out of the stands with pom-poms blaring. They join Amy at center court in a jumble of boobs and buttocks, bubbling and cheering, wiggling and thrusting, whipping the home crowd into a froth. Remarkably, they've managed to transform the girl wedgie into a seductive art form.

Go Maulers, Go Maulers.
We are the chosen few.
The rest of the county
Can't do the things we do.

Like zombies and losers
And lame kids God has trashed.
We hope that He remembers
To burn you all to ash.

They continue on for another five minutes, trashing rejects and zombies and everyone else in the world who isn't a Maulers jock or cheerleader, and I want to believe that when such a minority alienates the rest of society, common sense will prevail and send the hate mongers back under the rock whence they've slithered. But for some reason that doesn't happen. The crowd is screaming at the top of its lungs. *Burn to ash! Burn to ash!* Even some of the losers Amy is referring to are caught up in the frenzy. Lenny Stiles, for example, is waving the magic wand that he stole from me in the fifth grade, attempting, I imagine, to transform all of the zombies into talcum powder. I feel a thousand eyes bear down on me, and they're not compliment-ing my argyle sweater. Even Sissy Slupchek has stopped suck-ing on her clarinet reed long enough to stare my way. A corn dog pelts me in the back of the head, and it's only missing one bite, so I pick it up and ask Marvin to pass the mustard.

"That looks good," she says.

"What?"

"Can I have a bite?"

It's Chastity. "You snuck up behind me."

"Ninja training. Sorry."

"Cool."

"So what do you think about this pack of idiots? I tell you, at times like these, I'm embarrassed to be part of the human race."

"Amy seems to have a power over people."

Chastity frowns. "Whatever. She's nothing but a poser. Did you see that lame tumbling routine she threw down? She's get-ting old and tired. Her ass is bigger, too."

I double-check for myself and decide to take Chastity's word for it.

"It's bigger, trust me. I'm amazed she's managed to fit into her uniform this long with that weakness for Dong Dongs. The whole bulimia thing is so '18." Chastity jams a finger down her throat and pretends to gag. "Hey, I wanted to tell you some-thing. I really enjoyed lunch today. Meatloaf is one of my favor-ites. We should do it again sometime...soon. Maybe we could grab a bite at Artie's this weekend. I heard they got this four-course dinner special. And free drink refills."

"Yes."

"What's that?"

"Yes."

Ernest is pointing at Chastity. He's never been the most savvy individual in the world, given the physical, emotional, and psychological obstacles he's been forced to contend with, but pointing at someone is borderline rude. In fact his gesture is so obnoxious that it conjures images of Donald Sutherland from *Invasion of the Body Snatchers* when he rats out his girlfriend at the end, mouth hanging wide open. Marvin pulls the arm down, but it pops back up like Alfalfa's hair. I dislodge the corn dog stick from my leg and consider jamming it into Ernest's shoulder, to break his spell. But he's still alive and might not appreciate the sentiment.

"What's with him?" Chastity asks.

"He's never been so close to a girl."

She smiles a half-smile, unsure of how to respond.

Before we can delve back into the philosophical nuances of the herd mentality, the whistle blows and the third period begins. Doug Jerkins scores a layup on the Maulers' first possession and flips the bird in Buddy's face. Buddy shakes his head and laughs. Then he straightens his headband, and in a display of what has to be one of the most lopsided schoolings in the history of high school sports, performs a series of ten unfettered slam dunks over Doug Jerkins's head, springboarding off of the latter's shoulder for the final insult.

Doug is livid.

The referee calls a foul.

Doug misses his first free throw. Then he misses the second. Then he launches an elbow across Buddy's jaw with such force that it sounds like the crunch of Ruffles potato chips. Buddy stumbles back, holding his mouth. Then he lunges for Doug with a fist. The referees restrain Buddy, who struggles to shout something, but his lower jaw has completely unhinged, dangling by a wire of sinew or tendon.

Doug raises his arms in victory to the home crowd, and they explode into cheers. Amy Fairchild and crew incite them further with pom-poms ablaze.

Go Doug. He's our man.
If he can't do it, no one can.
Making shots in your face.
Putting zombies in their place.

The Hominids fans are booing at the tops of their lungs; a few are even pulling snow chains from their backpacks. My cousins, Jed and Little Ted, are brandishing umbrellas over their heads, chomping at the bit for retaliation. But for all of the commotion and impending melee, the person most enraged, at least as far as I can tell, is sitting right next to me. She crushes her Super Gulp in hand, dousing my khakis in Mountain Dew, then leaps onto the gymnasium floor.

"What's wrong with all of you?" Chastity screams. "What's wrong with all of you?"

No one is listening to her. They're too caught up in the moment.

She screams again and again, and when her screams have no effect, she demonstrates the power that cheerleaders, even former ones, have over adolescent males. With the grace and efficiency of a Vegas pole dancer, she rips her tank top clean off, exposing the twin peaks of her womanhood. They're held in place by black lace, but the depth of the cleavage could double as an Arizona landmark. In an instant, the silence of outer space bathes the gymnasium.

"Is this what it takes to put some sense into all of you? Boobs? What's wrong with you? Are you all a bunch of morons? This is a basketball game, for Christ's sake. A high school basketball game, not the Roman Colosseum. Doug Jerkins has been an a-hole since preschool, and it's totally uncool what he did to Buddy. Why are you cheering for him? Encouraging him? Are you total followers? Can't you see what Amy and Wanda are doing? They're brainwashing all of you into believing that they're somehow better than everyone else. Have some self-respect. Show some dignity. And stop scapegoating zombies."

"You're nothing but a skank," Amy shouts, charging onto half court.

"Takes one to know one."

"At least I don't strip in front of the whole school, like a slut."

"Yeah, you strip in the back seat of cars."

"You're such a loser," Amy shouts, tossing her hair. "You're not even relevant anymore."

"Oh yeah, well at least my ass isn't getting fat. Too many Dong Dongs, huh?"

The stands erupt into laugher, and Amy turns as red as Rudolph's nose. She's losing her grip on the crowd. Round one goes to Chastity.

"Oh yeah," Amy says, sneering.

"Yeah."

"Well, at least...at least I'm not a zombie lover."

Sighs echo throughout the gymnasium. Of all the insults she could have launched – Goth freak, meatloaf eater, A-list pariah – Amy chose the two words most adept at severing flesh. *Zombie Lover.* The phrase is practically an oxymoron in Pleasanton and likely illegal in Georgia and Mississippi. She's kicking below the belt, and Chastity has to respond fast and hard if she's going to win the bout. Round two goes to Amy.

Without a word, the Goth gladiatrix raises an arm to include the crowd in the final death blow. She saunters to the bleachers, grabs me by the hand, and leads me onto center court. I feel small and insignificant on the hardwood, a cracked piece of Tupperware floating in the North Atlantic. With a thousand eyes bearing down on us, she shouts. "I am a zombie lover, and you should be too!" Next thing I know her tongue is licking my tonsils. My instinct is to bite down and ingest the muscle, but I have the composure to realize that biting is a no-no, especially when you're a zombie. So I relax and even try to kiss back.

Twisting the blade further into Amy's heart, Chastity then guides my hand to her left dumpling and cups it. My fingers clamp down through instinct, the result of countless practice sessions with a Mystic Eight Ball, and I'm so overcome with joy that my tear ducts would cry if they still functioned. Chastity is using me to illustrate a point, but she's using me in such a mutually beneficial way that I want to pay her money.

Again, the vacuum of space blankets the gymnasium. The stands are wallpapered with the anesthetized faces of my peers – tongues dangling, drool dripping. Even Sissy Slupchek can't find her mouth with her woodwind instrument.

Amy is the first to speak. "But he peed his pants."

"It's Mountain Dew," I mumble proudly.

The crowd erupts. "Go, Paste Boy. Go, Chastity. Go, Paste Boy. Go, Chastity."

"That's my cousin," someone screams.

"His name is Chuck, I think," a different voice adds.

"Go, Chuck. Go, Chastity. Go, Chuck. Go, Chastity."

"No, I think his name is Chris."

"Go, Chris. Go, Chastity. Go, Chuck. Go, Chastity."

Amy is flabbergasted and for the first time in her life lacks a scathing retort. She's even struggling to breathe. Doug races to her side, gleaming in sweat, waiting for instructions that do not come. Acting on his own initiative, he belts me in the stomach, and a load of Beef 'n Cheese blasts my drawers. But the joke is on Doug tonight. I wore *three* pairs of tighty whities, just in case something like this happened.

Fans start flying out of the stands, drunk on the fumes of broken convention. Susie Monik, tennis champ, wrestles the Hominids center into a headlock, flexing the vise of her bicep around his reddening neck. Tad Wooster, off-track drag racer, swings a tire iron at a pack of Hominids motorheads. The steel shaft slips from his fingers and levels a band member, the second trombone. Even Ernest has gotten into the melee, joining a gang of chess club members in their valiant attempt to tear down the photo of Laundromom. The announcer is holding them off with a microphone, but they've latched onto his sweater vest and are dragging him to the floor.

Mauler Maidens are flailing in balls of hair and pom-poms with the Hominid Harem. Lenny Stiles, thief and two-bit magician, manages to steal a kiss from Principal Dawson. Before she can banish him to detention forever, he vanishes into the crowd in a puff of smoke. For all of the chaos and carnage though, surprisingly the only ones who are not acting like a bunch of crazies are Chastity, me, Amy Fairchild, and Doug Jerkins.

I look to Doug; he looks to me. Then he grabs me by the throat. Since I don't need to breathe anymore, I laugh, and this enrages him further. He raises an elbow, taking aim at my jaw, but before he can sever the speech tendons with a Pringles-crunching blow, Jed and Fred tackle him to the floor and start beating him with their umbrellas. Even Little Ted gets in on the action. He's gnawing through Doug's shoe, and Ted's not even a zombie.

Suddenly a familiar voice resonates through the gymnasium. It's more powerful than I remember, more ubiquitous. "Excuse me," it says. "Excuse me. Can I please have your attention."

The maelstrom subsides long enough to listen.

"Hi, it's Marvin. Remember me? I work at Artie's. First, I'd like to remind everyone of the new four-course dinner special we're advertising through the end of April. It includes your choice of premium sandwich, curly fries, shake or turnover, and bottomless fountain drink. All for $5.99."

"What about the mayor's excise tax?" someone screams.

"That includes the excise tax, but not the sales tax. Thanks for your clarifying question."

"Why is the fountain drink counted as a course?"

"Because it's bottomless."

"But wasn't it always bottomless?"

"Not with the collector's edition 48-ounce *Stellar Wars 17, Back to the Beginning* plastic cup."

"Oh, okay. Good deal."

"Of course it's a good deal. Now onto my second point. Why all the hatred? We're peaceful people, aren't we, deep down? Humans. Zombies. Band Members. We all have moms and dads and hopes and dreams, just trying to do our best in life and in death. We're not that dissimilar in the things that matter most to us. Sure, we zombies have been known to feast on human flesh from time to time, but those are the rogues. Don't let bad apples spoil the entire barrel. The world is big enough to accommodate us all, which is why I propose that we settle our differences amicably...in a style befitting our illustrious town."

A corn dog pelts Marvin in the head, knocking his paper hat askew, and he does what no zombie is able to resist. He picks it up and takes a bite. I expect the crowd to jeer and laugh and resume hostilities in the face of Marvin's shattered credibility. But they don't; they maintain attention. I guess Marvin's actions are considered a given for the state of his condition, like politicians lying to your face and reality television exposing the truth of human nature.

"I propose a contest," Marvin booms, "between Chris Kantra and Doug Jerkins to settle their differences once and for all. I propose a contest of such epic proportions that legends will be forged and songs will be sung. Next month, at the school carnival, I propose that man face off against zombie in the county hot dog eating contest!"

The crowd erupts. "Hot dog. Hot dog. Hot dog. Hot dog."

Doug crawls off the floor with a bruised cheek and bloodied eardrums, staggering a moment to regain his balance. Amy is shaking her head, pleading with him to blow the challenge off and ignore my existence. But Doug is too much of a man for that, too much of an intrinsic competitor. "Bring it on, paste boy," he gurgles.

Cheers.

"But one rule, seeing how you're a zombie and all. If your stomach bursts, I win."

"Agreed."

Buck (IQ=?), who's been shadowing me all week at school, materializes from thin air and yells at the top of his lungs. "No way you losers are going to break my record. Besides, it's five minutes to curfew."

He charges for me, but Little Ted bites into his ankle, toppling him like a Seattle redwood. Chastity grabs my hand and scrambles for the door. Marvin catches up, gripping three corn dog remnants. Even Ernest mans our six, pausing long enough to wink at Sissy Slupchek and toss her a new clarinet reed. We blow through the blue steel doors and into the parking lot, where an inch of snow has covered the ground. "Where to?" I ask.

"The black GTO."

"Cool."

The engine ignites, and Chastity blasts the heater so that Marvin and I don't freeze solid, and with nothing but a bra shielding her from the cold, she fishtails out of the parking lot. It's awesome, incredibly awesome. The speed, the flesh, and the roar of the 389 cubic inch V8 have unleashed a side of me I thought was nonexistent. Maybe it's courage, or perhaps it's desperation, or simply it's the primordial will to assert my existence to the world and declare that I will not decompose quietly. It's now or never time, my friend, and that guy named Kowalski's got nothing on me.

"Chastity," I say, squeezing her knee. "Will you go to prom with me?"

She chuckles, an omniscient gesture. "Of course I will. I was born to go to prom with you."

PART II

10

In space.

On a raft.

Floating in a sack of amniotic fluid.

Then an earthquake ruins the sensation.

Someone is screaming, too, in the distance. "Wake up," she says. "Chris, wake up."

When my eyes finally open, Mom is shaking the bejesus out of me, a look of horror across her face. The overhead bulbs are bearing down like interrogation lights, and even though I'm awake now the woman keeps trying to push me through the bed.

"I'm awake," I mumble.

"Wake up, Chris. Wake up."

"I'm awake. What's the problem?"

Mom's expression transforms to confusion, and her head cocks to one side. "Can't you hear the sirens?"

Now that she mentions it, I do hear something. It sounds like a tornado bearing down on Pleasanton, or maybe some kind of air raid. I've always been what you would call a sound sleeper, possessed of a clear conscience as Aunt Gertie likes to point out; but this is a little embarrassing. I guess when you're dead, you tend to sleep like it.

"What's going on?"

"Border Patrol."

I walk up the stairs and peer out the living room window, and sure enough half a dozen monster trucks are racing up and down the street, lights flashing and sirens blaring. A small army of border guards, dressed in the full regalia of black jumpsuits and baseball caps, start banging on the front doors across the street. A few of them already have their shotguns drawn.

"What the hell?"

"Hide," Mom says, trying to shove me into the closet. "It's just like '85. You need to hide."

Like any good teenager, I disregard Mom's parental advice and continue peering from the window. She turns off the light to make my profile less visible. Dad and Jimmy shuffle into the living room. Jimmy is clutching one of his darts.

"There's been another attack, over on Maple," Dad says. "At least that's what I heard one of the border guards screaming. "It sounds like it might have been Horace Billings."

"The crossing guard?"

"That's the one. The rogues ripped out his intestines and used them as a jump rope."

"Poor old guy."

"Cool," Jimmy mumbles.

"It's not cool," Mom snaps, shaking him by the shoulders. "Don't you understand? We're under attack, just like when I was a girl. Rogue zombies are on the loose, which means no one is safe. They could be lurking anywhere, hiding in the bushes, ready to pounce. Did you have your window open? Did you sleep with your window open?"

Jimmy nods his head, mouth unhinged.

"Let me see your fingers and toes. Let me see your fingers and toes." Mom wrestles him to the ground and rips off his socks. He writhes beneath her weight, but she's sitting right on top of his chest. She counts and recounts and then finally lets him up.

"It's okay," Dad says, hugging her. "The mayor said on the news that it's just a handful of rogues. That's not nearly as bad as the eighties. We just need to keep our wits about us and take precautions. No more walks under the moonlight. No more pup tents in the backyard."

"But we never do those things," I say.

"I said we need to take precautions."

Mom and Dad are obviously wigged out, and the infernal shriek of the sirens is enough to rile up even me. I mean I'm dead, so I don't really need to fear the gnashing teeth of the undead hordes, but all those border guards and guns and the way they're banging on the doors of private citizens have put me on edge. Two of them are at Mr. J's door right now. One is wielding a fire ax.

"Can I have a gun?" Jimmy squeaks.

Dad hesitates.

"No," Mom says.

"Why not? Tommy Parker's dad gave him a gun so that he won't get caught off guard by the undead hordes or by the inevitable squashing of civil liberties that will follow with the government's militant reaction. He showed it to me at recess. I think it's a thirty-eight."

Mom frowns and looks to Dad. Dad swallows dryly to find his words. "Guns are never the solution, son," he mumbles, unconvincingly. "People need to solve their problems through dialogue and compromise and even through a series of well-planned social programs, to better meet the needs of those who are likely to commit crimes on account of their limited economic prospects. Besides, we have the Border Patrol to protect us. Lord knows, we pay enough in taxes to support them."

Mom smiles and takes Dad's hand, but I'm not sure that Dad believes a word of what he's saying. I can't say that I blame the guy, either. I mean, we're under attack, by rogue zombies of all things. I think our situation warrants a little flexing of the Second Amendment. I still wouldn't give Jimmy a gun though simply because he's Jimmy; the kid is likely to shoot himself while goofing around...or worse... shoot me.

"What about a wall?" the little asswipe continues. "They built one on *Game of Thrones* to keep the White Walkers out. Why don't we build a wall around Pleasanton?"

Dad tries to bite down, but a chuckle leaks out. "That show is make-believe, son. Besides, everyone knows that walls don't keep people out. If folks want to get in, they'll always find a way. And who would pay for it? Do you want to pay more taxes to finance a wall? The rogue zombies certainly aren't going to pay for it."

A dumb look washes over Jimmy's face, which is nothing new, but this expression runs a little deeper than normal. I think it's going to take the kid a few more years to mature enough to appreciate the higher form of logic that my dad is wielding. Sometimes the right answer just isn't as simple as it might appear to be on the surface.

There's movement at Mr. J's place. He's answered his door. A large...and I mean humungous...border guard is talking to him. Mr. J keeps shaking his head.

"Move away from the window," Mom snaps.

"Wait a minute."

The border guard grabs Mr. J by the wrist, who slaps him across the face. But the border guard is too powerful for the retired ice cream parlor owner and soon has him handcuffed and crammed into the back of a monster truck.

I try to open the window, to scream out and help my neighbor, but Mom has me on the floor in a half nelson before I can crack my knuckles. She's pretty tough for an older woman, sort of like that chick from one of those *Terminator* movies... Sarah something.

"What's going on?"

"It's like '85. Hide in the closet."

"What do you mean?

Dad assumes a somber expression, the way he does when he thinks he's overpaid for something and wrestles with the notion of driving to the store to return it. "You're old enough to know the truth," he mutters, patting my shoulder. "The history books you read in school leave out a lot of the facts, son. They're watered down, even revisionist, probably as a means of brainwashing future generations into believing that humanity will always prevail in times of crisis. But in the years leading up to the Cleansing of '87, the zombie attacks were out of control. People were losing limbs and entrails left and right. A person couldn't walk down the street without hearing the screams of some poor victim in the distance. The town's economy was grinding to a halt as a result. People stopped going to work.

Even Artie's had to close its doors for fear that the rogues might ransack the meat locker."

"That's horrible."

Mom nods in concurrence.

"In an act of desperation, Mayor Arse declared martial law. He combined the police force and Border Patrol into one unified army and exterminated everything that even resembled a zombie. Innocent people were lost. Cats and dogs were caught in the crossfire. And if that wasn't bad enough, the mayor then herded all of the zombies' immediate relatives into internment camps to make sure the spread of the virus could be contained." Dad looks to his feet, searching for something that isn't there. "Not everyone made it back from those camps. My cousin Henry died of dysentery. Your mom's Aunt Bethany succumbed to a terrible bout of psoriasis. It was a completely treatable condition, but she just didn't receive the cream she needed in time."

Mom starts tearing up, and I feel the urge to give her a hug... you know, to offer comfort the way those families on TV do... but we've never really had that kind of relationship. It's probably not the best time to start.

"Why didn't they get injections?"

"This was before injections, Chris...two years before Dexapalm 87."

"That's right. But the mayor saved the town, didn't he?"

Dad swallows something dry. "But at what cost?"

Jimmy is glued to the window like one of those Garfield dolls, soaking in all of the action. Mrs. Mayweather across the street is giving the humungous border guard a piece of her mind, waving a black leather cat o' nine tails in his face; but the giant responds with an extension baton, quieting her down. She's dressed in negligee and a pair of knee-high leather boots, and her hair is rolled into one of those *I Dream of Jeannie* ponytails. Her fashion sense kind of stinks in my opinion, but I guess once you've retired, the brain has trouble matching outfits.

Mom starts. "Mayor Arse's methods were so effective that the President asked him to lead a special task force and adapt his process to a grander scale. Two years later the Cleansing of '87 rolled across the nation, and then across the globe. And a year after that, Mayor Arse won the general election by a landslide and claimed his spot in the Oval Office."

"I thought his name sounded familiar."

"He was something of a hero for a while, a candidate for a fifth head on Mount Rushmore, but like most men of power, he eventually went too far...something about illegal arms deals or shady real estate investments, or maybe it was that young, blonde deputy assistant press secretary with the huge best-white smile... I really can't remember. During his second term though, Congressman Romero led a coalition to impeach the man. President Arse resigned in disgrace before the Senate could try him. He lives in Florida now. I think he owns a golf course...either that or a roller rink."

I'm starting to remember some of this from eighth grade history class...at least the diluted version. "I think it's a roller rink, the kind that serves those little round pizzas."

"You're probably right."

"So why tell me all of this now? Do you think they're going to round us all up?"

Mom and Dad cock their heads to opposite sides, unsure of how to respond. They have those expressions they get when they're not sure if I'm joking or simply being dense. Dad is also counting with his lips, probably reviewing the chain of custody that links the moment I left the womb to the moment I left the hospital.

"You're the zombie, idiot," Jimmy chimes in.

The little asswipe is right.

Before Mom or Dad can elaborate, the doorbell rings. The temperature must drop about a hundred degrees because everyone freezes.

"Breathe," I tell them.

Mom is the first to suck in air. "In the closet, now. No more fooling around."

"But Mom, it's right next to the front door."

"That's the last place they'll look. Now hurry!"

I comply because I don't want the woman to drop dead of a coronary. One zombie in the family is already enough. The door to the closet is hollow, no better than tissue paper, so I can hear their voices leach through as plain as day.

"Should we answer it?" Mom says.

"I think we have to."

"Let's pretend we're not home. No one make a sound."

"They'll just break it down. You know how those gorillas can be."

"We'll let them break it down then."

"The city won't reimburse us. I'd hate to pay for a new door."

They debate for another minute or so as the pounding at the front door intensifies, but Dad's sense of economy eventually triumphs over Mom's instinct for caution. The sudden change in air pressure means our first line of defense has been breached.

Against Mom's better judgment, I crack open the closet door to get a better view of the action. Two border guards are standing in the doorway about five feet from me. The humungous one who accosted Mr. J must stand at least six-foot-six and weigh three hundred pounds. The top of his head is flush with the doorjamb and his chest protrudes like a fifty gallon rain barrel. He's covered in hair, too, or maybe it qualifies as fur. The other border guard is tall and sinewy with a lamb's bladder for a stomach and a silly-looking Village People moustache. It's Buck (IQ=?), Ernest's older brother.

"I'm Sergeant Barry, ma'am," the large one says. "And this is Officer Pratt. Our records indicate that you have a zombie living at this residence." He checks his notepad. "Goes by the name of Christopher Kantra. We need to take him to the station for routine questioning."

"What's this all about?" Mom snaps, arms crossed.

"A dozen zombie attacks occurred in this neighborhood over the course of the evening. We have ten confirmed reanimations and two total consumptions. Mayor Shight has authorized the Border Patrol to quarantine an eight block radius and bring every zombie found within that radius to the station for questioning. We need to verify that each posthuman is properly registered and up to date on his injections. Questionable cases will be detained longer until additional testing can be conducted. It's for your own safety."

"My son is fine."

"We'll be the judge of that, ma'am."

She looks to Buck for help, but all the idiot does is stare at his boots. Mom used to feed him cookies and milk when he was a kid, and she even treated him like he was equal to all of the other children in the neighborhood...and this is how the ingrate repays her.

Sergeant Barry steps into the foyer, nudging Mom to the side. I can smell the body odor emanating from his enormous frame. Mom's face flushes red, and she starts yelling at the top of her lungs. "Get out of my house! Get out of my house, right now!"

The border guard just ignores her, and when she goes to grab his arm, he turns with the look of impending damnation on his face. It's like kryptonite to Superman, and Mom goes silent mid-sentence. I didn't think anything from this planet was capable of producing that effect, especially when Mom gets mad, but the effect is undeniable.

Dad's blood starts boiling, and he enters the fray the only way he knows how. "This is an outrage. We didn't give you permission to enter our house. And you just assaulted my wife. Unless you leave right this instant, we're going to sue you and the Border Patrol and take our case all the way to the Supreme Court. I have the best lawyer in the county on retainer, at least of those that bill under $150 an hour."

"Do what you have to do, sir, but I suggest you get out of my way."

Dad steps to the side and Sergeant Barry starts searching the living room – opening cabinets and checking behind curtains. He then lumbers into the kitchen. The floorboards creak under his weight.

"I think the little rat sleeps in the basement," Buck adds.

"We'll, what are you waiting for, an invitation?"

Buck gets the hint and slithers down to the basement to fondle all of my stuff and probably steal my magazines. When Sergeant Barry finishes with the kitchen, he heads upstairs to the bedrooms. The racket he makes sends Mom over the edge.

"I just cleaned the house!"

He's up there a good five minutes, leaving me plenty of time to brood on the one possible tragedy that can come from all of this. I mean damaged property and bruised egos are one thing. And the trashing of civil liberties is never something to be taken lightly. But just days ago, in the chaos of a high school basketball game, Chastity Sky agreed to go to prom with me, making me the luckiest zombie in Pleasanton. I can't get detained at the station, not even for an hour. I need that time to figure out a way to take my relationship with Chastity to the next level. There's no room for distractions.

Sergeant Barry returns to the living room wearing a puzzled expression. He turns to Buck. "Did you find anything in the basement?"

"No, sir."

"Did you check under the bed...behind any couches?"

"Yes, sir."

"In the furnace room?"

"Yes, sir."

"Where is your son, Mrs. Kantra?"

Mom's face hardens like stone, the way it does when she's trying to bluff at poker. The expression rarely works. "Well, if you would have asked me at the beginning instead of ransacking my house, I would have told you. He's spending the night at a friend's house, Ernest Pratt. Why don't you go demolish their living room?"

Sergeant Barry looks to Buck. It takes the younger border guard a second to make the connection. "Hey, that's my little brother."

"Could her story be true?"

Buck shrugs his shoulders. "I guess so. They do hang out together."

Sergeant Barry's confusion intensifies. Mom has thrown him for a loop. He hovers for a moment in the foyer, eyes bouncing around like pinballs, then turns toward the front door. Mom has outdone herself, totally revising my assessment of her Texas hold 'em skills. But then something not entirely unexpected happens. My asswipe brother stabs me in the back with a lawn dart.

I'm not sure if he's doing it on purpose, or if all of the commotion has simply set his Tourette's into hyperdrive. But Jimmy keeps staring at the closet...won't take his eyes off of it. Buck is oblivious, of course, but Sergeant Barry quickly catches on. A ginormous grin spreads from ear to ear. With a dainty flick of the wrist, he opens the closet door and stares down at me.

"What's all the hubbub?" I try. "I must have fallen asleep in here."

My attempt at levity makes no headway, and within seconds the behemoth has me cuffed and out on the front lawn. Mr. J is nodding at me from the back of the monster truck. I think the old guy is relieved to have some company. He's always been a bit of a talker.

Mom pulls at Sergeant Barry's uniform.

Dad threatens to sue again.

Even Mrs. Mayweather across the street brandishes her cat o' nine tails.

And then the strangest thing happens. A familiar sound I never thought I'd be happy to hear spills out onto the street. It's the sound of a car without a muffler, you know, the kind that newspaper delivery guys like to drive. The distinct silhouette of a '92 Buick Regal rounds the corner, and the primer gray of its front quarter panel shimmers under the street lamp. You can still make out vestiges of the dent from the time Aunt Gertie rammed the drive-thru speaker at the Chicken Trough. The car pulls up to the curb. The passenger's side door swings open. Jed, Fred, and Little Ted pour out of the back seat. They're wielding umbrellas.

Sergeant Barry doesn't seem fazed one bit by them. His fists ball, and he pivots to face head-on whatever attack is about to come. But Jed, Fred, and Little Ted hold their position by the Buick, waiting. After about twenty seconds, the driver's side door swings open with the teeth-shattering screech of rusted metal. Aunt Gertie steps out and waddles up the driveway. Upon seeing her, Sergeant Barry's face turns ashen.

"What's going on here?" she asks.

"They're rounding up all the zombies for questioning," Mom blurts out. "Sergeant Barry ransacked our house and put Chris in handcuffs. It's terrible, Gertie, just terrible, like '85."

Aunt Gertie surveys the house and driveway, then turns to Buck and shakes her head. He can't meet her eyes and starts babbling some incomprehensible form of explanation, but she holds out her hand to make him stop. She then looks me up and down. "Did he hurt you, Chris?"

"I'm fine, Aunt Gertie. Just a little frazzled."

"I see." She then turns to Sergeant Barry, and it looks like the giant is using all of his power just to maintain eye contact with her. "What do you think you're doing?"

"Now wait a minute. This is official business...by order of Mayor Shight. I need to bring all zombies from an eight block radius down to the station for questioning, to make sure no rogues are hiding amongst their ranks. I can't let you interfere with this operation, ma'am...in the interest of public safety."

Aunt Gertie's eyebrow pops up, like Mr. Spock's. "Ma'am?"

"You know what I mean."

"I know you made a terrible mistake by putting my nephew in handcuffs; and I know you're going to let him go right this instant and apologize."

"I can't do that Gertie."

"I also know that you're going to clear all these trucks off the street."

Sergeant Barry is bright red now, a volcano ready to blow, but some otherworldly force is holding him back.

Aunt Gertie winks at me.

"Don't forget Mr. J," I say.

Aunt Gertie looks at the monster truck across the street. "And you're going to let that poor old ice cream parlor owner go as well. He's no rogue, and neither is my nephew, and if you just keep standing there, you know what I'm going to do."

"But Gertie..."

"I'd hate to let something like that slip out. It's the kind of thing a man of your stature won't be able to recover from."

Sergeant Barry turns ashen again...no...he turns Casper white. He looks to Buck; he looks to me; he looks up and down and side to side, in every direction of the compass except straight ahead where Aunt Gertie is standing. The man is on the verge of fainting.

"Now!"

Without further delay, Sergeant Barry instructs Buck to let Mr. J go. When the younger border guard protests, the sergeant swats him in the back of the head. He then removes my handcuffs and apologizes profusely to me and my family and whistles with his fingers to the rest of his squad. In less than two minutes, the monster trucks are rolling down the street in the direction whence they came. Their sirens are silent this time. It's totally anticlimactic.

When the purrs of their engines fade, Aunt Gertie lets out a big grin and snaps her fingers. Little Ted grabs a couple buckets of Major Trough's finest from the front passenger's seat of the Buick and walks up the driveway with his brothers.

They nod. I nod back.

And I can't help but ask the question. "What on earth made Sergeant Barry listen to you, Aunt Gertie? The man could tear a phone book in half with his bare hands."

She winks at me again, reaching for a greasy chicken thigh. "Well, Chris. I've known Sergeant Barry since before you were born. Let's just say he's not as big as he looks."

11

One of the challenges of being a zombie is that you don't generate internal body heat, on account of a lack of metabolism. That's why you don't see many zombie winter athletes flying off ski jumps or busting McTwists in the half pipe. We can freeze up, which slows our motor functions and inhibits our performance, and if we actually freeze solid, there's a very real risk of stuff breaking off. So Mom, in a deluge of relief after Sergeant Barry left our house, showered me with kisses in front of Jed and Fred – who snickered and posted a pic of the outburst online – and then sewed fifty small pouches into the liner of my coat to hold packets of liquid heat. Dad even spent real money on a hat he had embroidered with the words: *Curlers Rock the House*.

"Stop your loitering!" Clara shouts. "I want another twenty suicides."

Ernest and I skate back and forth across the rink, sliding to a stop in front of each hockey goal and then sprinting as fast as we can toward the opposite one. At number twelve, Ernest pukes on center ice – looks like he had chicken tenders and curly fries for lunch. At number eighteen, I do the same, but not because I feel nauseous. I just don't want Ernest to feel alone and embarrassed, and with half a dozen Beef 'n Cheeses sitting in my stomach, summoning the projectile vomit is an easy enough act of solidarity.

Ethyl immediately skates from the hack with her broom. "You poor boys, let me take care of that."

"What do you think you're doing?" Clara snaps, skating over. She's wearing spandex leggings and a sky blue winter coat with imitation fur around the hood, and for some reason has a pair of ski goggles propped up on her head.

"I'm just helping out the young ones."

"You're not their mother. You're not even their grand-mother. You know the rules." She points to a sign above the entrance. "Your vomit, your Comet."

That's Clara's way of telling us that we have to clean it up our-selves. Ethyl gives me a billowing smile, not unlike the kind that Grandma McGillicutty used to give every Thanksgiving when she served me extra mashed potatoes off her silver serving plat-ter. The thing is an heirloom, handed down from one gener-ation to next. Mom has it now.

Ethyl skates back to the hack and lets a stone go. Eunice sweeps like there's no tomorrow, and the stone glides wide of the house.

"You're over-sweeping!" Clara screams. "You need to go in bursts and watch the stone's path. Don't just sweep like a maid on parade."

"Sorry," Eunice squeaks.

"Do it again."

So she does, over and over.

"Man, Clara's got her panties in a ruffle today," Ernest says, skating over to the utility closet with me.

"It's the upcoming bonspiel in Urbana. Those bionic hip im-plants that the girls from Shady Meadows got over the winter have really got her worried. She's been watching old footage of Jaime Sommers to try to spot weakness."

"Who's that?"

"She was a bionic woman back in the last century...pretty hot."

Ernest's eyes click a few millions times, laboring through numerous calculations, but he doesn't ask for additional clari-fication. His mind is on another topic. "These zombie attacks are getting out of hand. There've been nearly twenty since that day we walked home from school and saw all that blood over on Chestnut Street. My mom barely lets me out of the house anymore. She even threw away my White Sox cap since the rogues' ringleader likes to wear one. It's such a waste. I don't look anything like a zombie."

Ernest takes a hit from his inhaler, and I can't help but study his face – skin almost as pale as the ice we're standing on; matted hair that looks like it might have some blood caked in it; eyes the color of a shallow, standing pond. And that smell.

"It's probably best she threw the cap away."

"Did you hear all those sirens the other night?"

I reach for a mop, refusing to justify his question with a response.

"Oh, that's right," he says, blushing. "Sorry. I'd almost forgotten. The Border Patrol had you in cuffs."

"Yeah, but Aunt Gertie saved the day."

"She's a tough old broad…likes fried chicken, too."

"One of the toughest."

He grabs a metal pail and a bottle of bleach but can't make eye contact with me. The white elephant is sitting on his larynx, crushing it. In a whisper, he finally mumbles, "Buck was just doing his job. He's not as bad as he seems."

"If you say so. What pisses me off though is that my mom used to give him milk and cookies, same as you. Oreos of all things, my favorite."

"I know."

"Lucky for him Jed, Fred, and Little Ted didn't have a chance to intervene. I know I've avoided them like the plague since that horrible Christmas morning, but they had my back on Thursday night. They were locked and loaded."

"What's with their umbrellas?"

"Don't ask."

We shuffle over the rubber mats to the utility tub and fill the pail with water. Clara glances over at us, probably wondering why we're taking so long, but Ethyl clips a stone with her skate while she's sweeping, sending the former Olympic alternate into a tizzy.

"I don't think you're supposed to use bleach on the ice," a

voice says. "Concrete and linoleum, sure. Even tile. But ice is probably a bad idea. I suggest cold water, that way it can freeze quickly and not disturb the surface of the rink too much."

We turn around to find Marvin, standing with two bags of Artie's finest in his hands. The grease is soaking through the bags, and my stomach reacts about as loudly as Niagara Falls. He's wearing his paper hat, slightly askew, and an orange extension cord is trailing out the back of his winter parka to an outlet by the front office.

"What's with the extension cord?" Ernest asks.

"Hot plate. What did you think?"

Marvin reaches into the bag and hands me a couple of Beef 'n Cheeses. I devour them in under a minute. A bag of curly fries follows suit, and then a third Beef 'n Cheese. Ernest licks his lips and reaches for a sandwich, but Marvin swats his hand.

"They're not for you," he snaps.

"What are you talking about?"

"Chris is in training, remember?"

"Oh, yeah."

And Marvin is right. For the past week, he's been sneaking me as many Beef 'n Cheeses from Artie's as he could manage – some from under the heat lamps, most from the dumpster behind the restaurant – as part of my training regimen for the upcoming hot dog eating contest. He has self-appointed himself as my manager, which is fine by me; that's why I don't have the heart to tell him that I just puked up the half dozen sandwiches he gave me for lunch.

"Ernest can have one," I say.

Marvin narrows his eyes but hands over a sandwich. It looks a little ripe, but Ernest doesn't seem to care. He sucks it down to fill the hole that the regurgitated chicken tenders left behind.

"Do you think he can beat Doug Jerkins?" Ernest asks, still eyeing the greasy bags.

Marvin chuckles. "That's not the right question. Of course he'll beat Doug Jerkins. He's a zombie. The real question is whether he'll make a legend of himself."

"A what?"

"A legend."

Legend. I like the sound of that word. It's the kind of word I grew up with reading Rick Riordan books and listening to Dad's Elvis tapes. But it's not the type of word I ever associated with my name, not even close, unless of course you venture into the realm of urban legend, where some idiot kid gets killed or maimed because he does something stupid...like eating Pop Rocks while drinking Pepsi.

"But he can't let his stomach burst," Ernest continues. "What is the advantage to being a zombie if he can't let his stomach burst?"

Marvin shakes his head, a schoolmaster at heart. "Zombies can roll their intestines."

"What?" Ernest says.

"What?" I say.

"Not now. You're not ready yet. When you're ready, I'll teach you."

"Cool."

We shoot the shitake for another minute or so until Clara gives us another dirty look. In response, we move onto the ice toward the puke stains. Marvin grabs the mop and pail and gets to work instinctively, almost as if he was hatched in a lab to thrive in the custodial arts. Ernest gives me a wink and cracks his knuckles, but I won't go for that. If Dad taught me anything in this life, he taught me that a man needs to pay his own way, even if that means clipping coupons and standing in line for the four o'clock buffet.

I snatch the mop from Marvin's hands and jam it into Ernest's ribs.

"Sorry," Marvin says. "It's a bad habit. When I see a mop, I can't help but use it. Randy runs a tight ship at Artie's."

"Don't worry about it. Ernest started this, so he can finish it."

Ernest gives me the evil eye, but I just ignore him. I have a burning question I've been meaning to ask. I hope it's not too insensitive.

"So how bad was it?"

"What?"

"Thursday night."

Marvin's smile diminishes a bit, and the white of his paper hat seems to yellow. He shifts the hot plate from his lower back to his lower abdomen; the orange extension cord is now running out the front of his coat like a long, skinny you-know-what.

"Ernest's stupid brother snatched me from the middle of a late shift," he says, glaring at the future astronaut. "Put me in cuffs and hauled me down to the station."

Ernest can't meet Marvin's eyes, and a look of desolation washes over his face – not remorse for being related to the ass-wipe border guard with the stupid moustache who harassed all of us, but anguish in the realization that his chances of scoring a second Beef 'n Cheese have just gone down the toilet. Tough luck.

"Buck and his cronies jammed me into a large holding cell in the subbasement with about fifty other zombies – mothers, fathers, sons, and daughters; even old Mr. Carpenter who lives on the bench in front of the church. We were pressed together like cattle...it was inhumane, not to mention downright un-comfortable. I don't think old Mr. Carpenter has used Oralcline in about twenty years. Night Train, sure, but that just adds to the halitosis."

"That guy's a zombie? I thought he was just some homeless wino."

"Unclear. I don't think the Border Patrol was being too picky."

"Wrong place at the wrong time," I mumble, remembering Frederick and the load of shingles that fell on my head.

"They shined a floodlight in our eyes, the kind the army used to use in World War II to spot enemy bombers. Then they sprayed us with some kind of disinfectant. It cut down on old Mr. Carpenter's aroma, but it blurred my vision."

"That's horrible."

"You're telling me. After about an hour...time they said they used to check our injection records...they performed another test. They grabbed some poor drifter from the drunk tank and threw him in the cell with us. He screamed in terror for about ten minutes, but they wouldn't let him out. When no one went for his jugular, they threw a bucket of blood on him. When still no one tried for an arm or a leg, they dragged him back to the drunk tank."

"No shower?"

"I couldn't see."

"That's so uncool. I mean, blood can be infectious."

"They were going to leave me there for the rest of the night, but Randy drove over to bail me out. Signed some sort of hardship waiver, claiming that he couldn't handle the drive-thru all by himself. I think he had to offer the border guards free food for a month."

"Including take out?" Ernest asks.

"No, dine-in only. Randy's a pretty tough negotiator."

Marvin downs two of my Beef 'n Cheeses nervously before realizing what he's doing. "Oh, sorry. I'll get you some more later. You're lucky your aunt stood up for you. It wasn't a pleasant experience. The rest of my family didn't get back home until morning. They were held in a different cell but suffered a similar experience. My mom and sister were pretty shaken up, but my dad seemed no worse for wear. He claims that working at the DMV helped prepare him for large crowds and long waits, not to mention uncertainty in the process."

"I guess that's a kind of fringe benefit."

"I guess."

Ernest has done a piss-poor job of mopping up our vomit. Chunks of chicken tender and roast beef are spread across the ice, bound together by a web of light brown gravy streaks. The montage almost resembles an atom cloud, something dense like plutonium.

"Give me that," I say, snatching the mop.

When I can't do much better, Marvin stares me down with imploring eyes. I hand over the mop, and the fast food worker makes quick work of the mess. "You have to go over one patch at a time. You can't try for the whole enchilada at once; that just spreads everything around. You need to have patience, as with most things in life."

As usual, the zombie is right. It's a shame that Marvin is chained to the drive-thru window. If he hadn't died from that spoiled can of tuna and been relegated to a world of menial labor, he might have been destined for greater things – an engineering degree from MIT, maybe even a PhD in philosophy from Harvard. I can picture him now, imparting his vast wisdom onto young, eager minds, wearing a paper hat not because he has to, but because it connects him to what he might have been.

"I've got to go," he says, handing me the greasy bags. "I have a shift starting in twenty minutes. Eat the rest of those sandwiches as quickly as you can. I'll bring more over tonight. Maybe we can watch another episode of *Matlock,* that is if you're not too busy." He winks, and I think I blush.

Ernest rolls his eyes.

"You're a lucky zombie, Chris. Make sure you don't blow it."

"Sure thing."

He leaves the ice arena, trailing an orange extension cord behind him.

"Where is Chastity, by the way?" Ernest asks.

"She's at her dojo, working out. She's going to swing by after practice to pick me up."

"Are you going to be *preoccupied* all afternoon?" he says, not winking like Marvin, but despondent like a neglected puppy.

"Come over at five. We can get in a few rounds of Blockbuilder."

"Cool."

Clara finally shrieks at us, unable to contain her displeasure any longer. I mean, we just paused to chat for a couple of minutes, and she's already blowing a gasket. If I didn't know any better, I'd say she woke up on the wrong side of the bed.

"Another twenty suicides!"

"Damn it."

"This is insane."

"How are we supposed to beat the ladies from Shady Meadows if we never get to practice throwing stones?"

Clara waves her broom, and we get to sprinting between the hockey goals. No one vomits this time, although Ernest is turning green. The contrast with his reddish hair makes me think of a backwards tomato. As we skate back to Eunice and Ethyl, I can feel my legs tightening up. It's not the sensation of lactic acid burning through the muscles. It's the sensation of temperature-induced rigor mortis. It takes me awhile to get to the hack, and Clara shakes her head.

"You're going to have to fix that."

"I know, sorry. I'll ask my mom to buy extra packets of liquid heat. I think she can get them by the pallet at Pam's Club. A hot plate probably wouldn't work, since the extension cord might be a tripping hazard."

"What?"

"Never mind."

The Canadian taskmaster blows her whistle in my ear, signifying the end of another curling practice. Ernest and I grab our bags and head toward the exit. Chastity is standing in the doorway, waving. I wave back. Per usual, she's wearing black jeans and black combat boots, and the black leather of her jacket complements the oil spill mascara surrounding her eyes. She's the most gorgeous girl in the world.

"Why doesn't she come in to watch us practice?" Ernest asks.

"I'm not sure. She mentioned that she gets cold easily, something about having only 1% body fat."

"But she ran out into the snow after the basketball game with only a bra on."

"That was only for a minute, remember. Then she cranked up the car heater."

"I guess that's one of the downsides to being so hot," Ernest murmurs.

"You can say that again."

When he tries to, I sock him in the arm.

12

"I thought I'd find you two here," she says, blushing.

Chastity rolls off of me and tries to rub the black lipstick from my face. "Ms. Twid," she chirps, almost as a question.

"Oh, I remember what it is to be young. You wouldn't think it now, the way I've let myself go; but I used to be a bit of a looker in my day. I'm no stranger to the bushes beside the grounds-keeper's shed, either. Even had a rendezvous with Willie Shight before he grew too big for his britches."

"Mayor Shight?"

"He wasn't the mayor back then, just a handsome tight end with a bright future and romance in his eyes."

As a zombie, I no longer experience nausea, not even after eating week-old Beef 'n Cheeses, but the Squid is pushing me beyond the realm of gastrointestinal tolerance.

"Sorry to interrupt you two love birds, but I wanted to tell you something." She looks over her shoulder, searching for phantoms. "I'm not sure I should be telling you this, but...have you two seen Mr. Pratt around?"

Again, a glance over both shoulders.

"Buck? No. Why?"

"Never mind. Anyway, I want you two to know that I've been watching you. I have to admit, at first I didn't approve of your relationship. I'm not a big fan of zombies. No offense, Mr. Kantra."

"None taken."

"You see, a rogue took my Nigel back in '93.

"We didn't know you were married."

"Engaged. I was a kindergarten teacher, and he was a line cook, and we made plans to experience the world's wonders together. We were the proverbial match made in heaven until that vicious rogue tore out his heart."

"I'm so sorry," Chastity says. "Was it total consumption?"

"No, he came back, but things were never the same without his heart. No flowers. No candy. No mid-morning phone calls to the teacher's lounge. Nigel became obsessed with the notion of his mortality and construed death as an absence of a future. He barricaded himself in the linen closet for weeks and wouldn't even come out for bangers and mash. And this was before Golift and Likapro became household names, and long before the FDA approved any variants for undead consumption. So we slowly drifted apart, postponing the wedding until it became clear there would be no wedding; and Nigel inevitably decided one morning over French toast that he had to leave. *We're no longer compatible*, he said. There were no kisses or goodbyes. No long-winded explanations. Just an understanding that death is a mighty obstacle to the living and that the loss of a heart can affect the outcome of any romance. I often think about Nigel on rainy nights when *The Wheel of Life* is a rerun and the trash can in the kitchen begins to smolder, but I never learned what became of him."

The Squid pauses, sifting through the clouds of her memory. "Anyway, enough of old Ms. Twid's Greek tragedy. I just wanted to say that the two of you have inspired me by your willingness to make a go of it. Not everyone has the courage to engage in a necromantic relationship. Society will scoff at you, even turn its back, but try not to let the narrow minds get you down. Take it from a woman who once tried to bridge the gap between life and death and failed – the only perspective worth a damn is your own. As long as you have each other, you have enough."

Chastity stares at me blankly and shrugs her shoulders, and I can't help but notice that the Squid is wearing a bit of meatloaf on her chin. She has cat hair on her smock, too, calico I think. She's glancing over her shoulder again, still searching for some ethereal nemesis – a shark or killer whale perhaps – but nothing seems out of the ordinary.

"I'm not sure I should be telling you this, but I made a commitment to myself that I would. As you might know, I am a member of the Pleasanton City Council...have been since '99. I do my best to represent the interests of the school and the local arts community. I have to admit though, my main reason for joining the council was to stay close to Willie Shight. The man hasn't lost his charm after all these years, and when he decks himself out in a new suit and musky cologne...well, he can sure spark the heat flashes."

Chastity and I exchange a bit of telepathy. The message is a bit hazy and muddled, but there's no denying the word *run*.

"The point I'm trying to make is that last night, in a debate over how to quell the growing zombie scourge, that self-serving, self-righteous, gorgeous bastard went too far. I mean, pulling law-abiding zombies out of their homes for questioning in the middle of the night is one thing; there's precedent for that, especially given the recent spate of rogue attacks. But what he proposed last night takes everything to a whole new level. He proposed that we segregate Pleasanton's zombie population through a mandatory relocation effort. All zombies would be transported to the dead zone and offered basic undead services for as long as it takes to ferret out the rogue assailants. He dubbed his proposal the *kill-two-birds-with-one-stone* strategy, on account of its two-pronged goal – shielding the human population from what experts claim are attacks from within, and providing the Border Patrol with the flexibility it desires to conduct a proper investigation. Apparently the 28th Amendment and local ordinances suspend due process for zombies residing in the dead zone."

"That's so uncool," Chastity blurts out.

"He can't do that, can he?"

"I'm afraid he can. He even proposed that we build a wall."

The shock of the news is making it hard for me to breathe, even more so than being dead. I mean, pulling me out of the house in the middle of the night and cuffing me like some loser from a *COPS* episode was bad enough, but forcing me to live in a squalid tent city in the dead zone...behind a wall...away from Chasity. I can't think of any worse fate. It must be obvious that I'm having trouble breathing, because Chastity presses her thumb knuckle between my shoulder blades. The gesture loosens up my airways.

"How'd you do that?"

"I'm a third degree black belt, remember?"

"Oh, yeah." I turn my attentions back to the Squid. "But everyone knows that walls never work."

"I know," the teacher concedes, shaking her head.

"Who's going to pay for it?" Chastity asks.

"Tax on zombie businesses...something about correcting a long-standing trade imbalance. I don't really understand the economics behind the proposal...no one on the City Council does...but Willie Shight seems sure of himself. He kept saying how great it's going to be."

Chastity leaps to her feet and starts roundhousing the groundskeeper's shed. The boards creak under the pressure of her blows. "But you implied that the relocation was temporary, until the rogues could be captured. Why do we need a wall then? Walls are permanent fixtures. And what will that mean for Chris and me? If he gets relocated to the dead zone, will I get to visit him? Could I relocate voluntarily if I wanted to?"

"No communication or contact whatsoever would be allowed across the border. As to voluntary relocation, I have to say that's not a very good idea, dear. An attractive young woman with red blood still pumping through her arteries has no business living in the dead zone...even for love. Although I must admire you for your chutzpah."

Chastity lets a bombshell fly, and one of the two-by-eights of the shed cracks in half.

"It's okay," I say, hugging her. "We'll find a way around this. We're not going to let the mayor tear us apart."

The Squid's eyes grow misty, reminiscing about her lost Nigel, I imagine, and a subtle breeze seems to drop the temperature about ten degrees. A montage of my post-death experiences assemble themselves in a Technicolor flash, reminding me of all that I have to lose. A few months ago, I wouldn't have cared less about the mayor's proposal, trapped in my basement with Ernest and his lame Blockbuilder skills; but now... with Chastity at my side and the tightness of her glutes giving me hope that my death, far more than my miserable life, might usher in an age of discovery...I can't stomach the thought of spending one moment without her.

"The mayor's proposal goes up for vote at the City Council next week," the Squid continues, "and if we approve it by a sixty percent supermajority, eight votes out of twelve, it will go to public referendum. In the current climate, with twenty-one attacks in five weeks, I'm afraid the *kill-two-birds-with-one-stone* strategy would pass."

Chastity cocks her leg again, ready to level the grounds-keeper's shed, but the Squid places a hand on her shoulder and attempts a smile. "No worries, dear. It's not over until the proverbial fat lady sings. Willie requires eight votes to push the proposal to referendum, and he's only secured seven so far. Martin Ayers, the token zombie on the council, will never vote for it. *Not over my dead body*, he gurgled. And Ethyl Bernstein grew up in Europe, witnessing the horrors of mass hysteria."

"Hey, she's on my curling team."

"I don't think Sanjay Weathers or Jerry Rogers will vote for the proposal either. They're businessmen and appreciate the value of cheap labor. So that leaves me, the eighth vote, and I can say with certitude that old Willie will never get me to concede, not even with chocolates or flowers or promises of nature walks behind the school. He's gone too far this time. If we allow him to trample justice now, there's no telling what he'll try next. We need to nip his bud while we still can."

Chastity hugs the Squid, and the woman turns flush, as if ready to spawn.

"I thought of resigning in protest, until the ombudsman informed me that with eleven active council members, seven votes would represent a supermajority. So I'm staying put and holding firm. I just thought you two should know about the proposal, on account of your relationship, so that you might prepare for the outcome." A shadowy figure in the parking lot catches her attention, and she stares at it a long while before lowering into a whisper. "Something has been nagging at me though, even more than the proposal...something about Willie's eyes, the way they roll back like a shark's when he's trying to convince me to vote his way. He wore that look before, amidst the bushes of yesteryear, when three words he didn't mean flowed from his lips. He's up to something. I know it. He's up to something devious. Once I find out what it is, I'll fill you kids in. Ms. Twid still has the power to turn a man's head."

The bell rings, and the Squid swims off, and Chastity and I are left with a sense of impending doom – the doom of a romance cleft in two, the doom of the Squid flaunting her womanly wiles to extract information from a sixty-year-old mayor.

"Oh, my God," Chastity says. "Like I needed to learn the details of Ms. Twid's love life. And that Nigel guy, what a loser."

"Funny name, too."

"Do you think the vote will pass?"

"Not if the Squid sticks to her word. She has it out for Mayor Shight, and it sounds like she'll vote against him out of spite, no matter how she feels about zombies. What a bastard he is, trying to tear us apart. The thought of not being able to see you... I mean, we can't let that happen. I don't know what I would do if..."

Chastity places a finger to my lips, followed by her own, and kisses me with the delicacy of gossamer. Then she gropes my backside, and I return the favor, pressing my corpse against her flesh and drawing comfort from its texture.

"It'll be all right," she says omnisciently. "I won't let you go over there alone."

"But you can't come to the dead zone...you're not a zombie. I couldn't let you do that."

She pauses, mulling over my words. "It's my decision, Chris."

"But Chastity..."

"Let's just get to class."

13

Seniors, at least the cool ones, perceive the bell as a guideline rather than a hard-and-fast rule. They tend to loiter in the halls, clinging to freedom for as long as possible before the teacher slams the door shut. They're like death row inmates in a sense, savoring every minute in the yard. Today is no exception.

"Hi, guys," Reggie Matheson, the varsity running back, says, offering me a high five.

"How's it shaking, Chuck?" Marty Garcia pats my shoulder near the lockers. He's captain of the lacrosse team and stands six-foot-six.

"Hey, Chaz, don't do anything I wouldn't do." Bruce Barber is undressing Chastity with his eyes and reeks like Suds Beer and breath mints, but he pitched a no hitter in last year's state championship and receives a bit of leeway from the faculty.

Greetings and salutations are not uncommon now. Ever since Chastity's exhibition in the gymnasium, an aura of coolness has washed over me. I know it's a halo effect, and I'm not self-delusional enough to believe that if Chastity ever ditched me, the popular kids would continue to acknowledge my existence; but I have to admit, acceptance by the ruling class is a boost to the ego. Just yesterday, for example, Jenny Jennison, a mat maid for the wrestling team, asked for my phone number at lunch. Chastity wrenched her into a half nelson and slammed her head into the lockers before I could decline the request, and the poor girl had to crawl to the nurse's office for a splint; but when you really think about it, a month ago Jenny would have spit in my face rather than sit next to me on the bus. That's quite a shift...virtually tectonic.

Chastity hasn't really responded to the attention though. In fact, she couldn't care less about it. I guess once a person has sauntered through the halls as part of the ruling elite, a simple *hello* by smelly jocks doesn't carry a lot of horsepower. She *was* once a cheerleader after all; she's got nothing left to prove.

But I'm smart enough not to get cocky. I can't afford to. I'm still Chris Kantra, the paste eater whose mom guzzled Tab soda and inhaled Twinkies while she was pregnant and broke her water rocking out at a Hemloch reunion. I know who my real friends are. They serve curly fries and play chess and like to see how many days they can go without changing underwear. Besides, the ruling elite could turn on me in an instant if the wind were to change direction. That's just the nature of high school.

Speaking of which, Amy Fairchild and Wanda Lopez are standing by the lockers right now under a banner that reads: *No Zombies at Prom. It's Not Safe or Sanitary With Them Around.* To get back at Chastity, the two of them circulated a petition to ban all zombies from the aforementioned dance. Principal Dawson approved of the idea, but required them to gather one hundred signatures as a prerequisite for submitting the petition to the student council. I don't think they're making much progress in their canvassing efforts, however. The middle ranks of the school (folks between cool and loser status) seem uninterested in what they have to say, and it doesn't help Amy's cause that every time she manages to assemble an audience by her poster of Laundromom, Chastity French kisses me and performs a bit of a striptease.

"You're never going to get those one hundred signatures," Chastity growls. "Nothing is going to stop Chris and me from going to prom."

Amy puts a hand to her ear and turns to Doug Jerkins. "What's that? Is someone talking to me? It's hard to tell. My ears aren't very good at detecting the sound of irrelevance."

"That's a big word for you, tramp."

"I wouldn't talk if I were you. You're giving it up to a zombie for Christ's sake. I can't think of anything more pathetic than that. Hold on...correction notice. If you were dating a zombie Brad Pitt or something, back when he was young, you know from the *Thelma & Louise* years, then maybe it wouldn't be quite as gross. But a zombie Chris Kantra? A zombie paste boy?" She starts to laugh. "How the mighty have fallen."

That's the first time I can remember Amy getting my name right. And she thinks I'm getting some, which means the other kids probably think I'm getting some, which means in spite of her enmity and poisoned inner soul, the cheerleading captain just inadvertently raised my social stock. As onlookers start to gather around us, I can't help but hold my head up higher.

"And look at that stupid hat he's wearing."

"I like his hat," Chastity says. "He's on the curling team and proud of it. It's no different than any other team you losers play on." She stares down Doug Jerkins and Chad Parker. They seem mildly amused. "You should know something about teams, Amy. You've been friendly with more than one."

The cheerleading captain turns a little flush. "You don't know what you're talking about."

"Don't I?"

"Well at least I have the common sense to stay within city limits. I'm not an idiot like you, exposing myself in the dead zone. Of all the stupid things."

"That wasn't my idea."

"Well, that's not what I heard."

"It wasn't my idea."

"And now look out you, dressed like Elvira. What are you trying to hide?"

Chastity is livid now, and her weight is shifting to her left leg. Any moment, Amy is going to get a roundhouse to the head. I can almost hear her vertebrae crack. If Chastity loses her cool and breaks the cheerleader's neck, our prom date is going to be put in serious jeopardy. I mean, there's no way Principal Dawson would let her attend the dance, especially not when Amy is the mayor's niece. Cutting class and dealing crack might be pardonable offenses, but second-degree murder? That's a long shot, even at Morbid High.

As to Chastity exposing herself in the dead zone, that's news to my ears. I'm getting the sense it has something to do with Amy's and Chastity's falling out. I want to ask Chastity all about it, to empathize and offer my support...and of course learn if any guy was involved...but now doesn't seem like the right time.

"She's not worth it," I mumble.

Chastity doesn't hear me. The battle rage has consumed her.

"Amy's not worth it, babe. Don't let her get to you. The best way for us to fight back is to make sure we attend prom. Amy doesn't matter anymore. I don't think she ever did."

Amy turns to me with a look of death upon her face, and I can't help but feel like a piece of fecal matter under a microscope. Wanda Lopez's mouth comes unhinged. Doug Jerkins balls his fists, primed to pummel me.

"Did you just talk about me?"

"I mean...I meant to say..."

"Oh, my God. The loser did just talk about me." Amy puts her hands over her ears like one of those stupid monkey figurines. "What is this world coming to, people? Paste boy just said that I don't matter. I've never heard anything so absurd in all of my life. I'm not sure if I should laugh at what he said or just plain puke. It must be the rogue zombie attacks. They've made this town hysterical. The next thing you know the marching band will start demanding a seat on the student council. And then the chess club. These are dangerous times, people, dangerous times. Life as we know it hangs in the balance. That's exactly why you need to honor the memory of Laundromom; that's exactly why you need to sign my petition to ban zombies from prom. We can't afford to fall asleep at the wheel...not on our watch. If today a paste eater can insult a cheerleading captain, then tomorrow a stinking zombie might run for President. And then where would that leave us? The line has to be drawn here, today. The battle needs to be fought now. Anything less is just plain surrender. Are you with me?"

A few of the popular kids groan their acknowledgments. Most just stand there with open mouths. I'm not sure Amy's words are having an effect. Either that or the onlookers are just disappointed at not seeing a cat fight.

Chastity claps. "Nice try, but no one cares. Chris was right. You don't matter anymore."

"Shut up."

"It's undeniable."

Amy turns to Doug Jerkins and points a finger in his face. "You better beat this loser in the hot dog eating contest. Do you hear me? You'd better be willing to sacrifice your life in the name of our cause or don't bother trying to get me in the back seat of your Charger anymore."

Doug grins awkwardly, caught off guard.

"See what I mean," Chastity continues. "All Amy can talk about is the back seat of a car. That's so junior year."

Without warning, Amy charges Chastity, who steps to the side, tripping her. The cheerleader tumbles face first into my groin. It's a strange sensation and something I can't truthfully say I've never imagined before, but the encounter is so brief that I have little time to react. Without wasting a breath, Chastity heads straight for the *No Zombies at Prom* banner and starts to tear it down. But Amy has some pep left in her step and grabs onto Chastity's legs, pulling her away.

I look to Doug. He looks to me. And for an instant we share a moment of camaraderie that we haven't exchanged since the seventh grade. I guess deep down every guy likes a good cat fight. But the moment of male bonding is ephemeral, and Doug quickly regains his composure. He makes a gesture at me with hand and mouth, already practicing for our upcoming contest.

Before Chastity has a chance to levy a deathblow to Amy's spine, a gun goes off...not the kind with bullets or blanks, but something a lot more juvenile. It kind of sounds like the cap guns that Ernest and I used to play with when we were kids and imagined we'd grow up to be cowboys.

Holding the plastic six-shooter in the air behind us stands Buck (IQ=?). He's wearing a black jumpsuit and a black baseball cap and is even sporting a pair of mirrored sunglasses. The words *Border Patrol* are stenciled on the hat. "Okay, kiddos. That's enough. Now get back to class. There's a time and a place for a good cat fight, but that time ain't now."

No one moves, so Buck squeezes off a couple more caps. When still no one moves, he pulls out his Glock 17 and points it at my head. That gets people scurrying back to their lockers. The asswipe grins, stretching his Village People moustache into an irregular parallelogram.

"What's with the cap gun, dude?" Doug Jerkins asks.

"Crowd control."

Doug shakes his head and walks off. Amy gives Chastity the look of death and follows him. Buck studies the pendular motions of Amy's backside for a good twenty seconds, until she turns a corner. Then he refocuses his attention on me.

"So you think you're hot stuff now?" he says, whacking my gut with the handle of his Glock 17.

I sense movement in my bowels but no extrusion. "Leave me alone."

"You got lucky the other night, punk, hiding behind your aunt. If my boss hadn't been such a coward, we would have hauled you to the station and discovered the truth."

"What truth?"

"You know."

"No, I don't."

"Stop trying to talk in circles." Buck whacks me in the gut again, and this time I can feel a bit of Beef 'n Cheese find its way to my inner pair of undies.

"Leave him alone," Chastity snaps.

"Was I talking to you, missy? Why don't you go wrap yourself around a pole or something while the men are talking."

Chastity clenches two fists and repositions her stance for a strike, but I wave her off. Buck simply isn't worth the effort. If Chastity were to break his neck, she still might miss prom. The odds are less likely than if she broke Amy's neck, given Buck's relative unimportance to the community, but murder is murder, even in a town once named Morbid. Although if push came to shove, I'm sure Chastity and I could concoct a feasible self-defense story.

"Move out of the way," I say. "We have to get to class."

Buck pulls a lighter from his pocket and starts flicking it near my face. "You better watch your step. Your chicken-fried aunt isn't here to protect you."

"Put that away," Chastity says.

"I know about Dexapalm 90...took a course at the community college. Get too close to an open flame and poof! You'll save Larry, the cremator, the trouble."

"That's not funny, Buck," Chastity says. "Be careful with that lighter."

He steps closer, and the flames reach for me, fluttering on a breeze. "And you'll never beat my hot dog eating record. You shouldn't even try."

"That's enough," Chastity snaps.

She pivots into a roundhouse, and in a fraction of a second the lighter explodes in Buck's hand, dousing his arm in flames. The appendage ignites like a mummy's corpse, on account of the forest of gorilla hair, and the stench of roasting follicles summons memories of my last night at Cub Scouts (never mind the details). Buck screams and flails. Chastity sweeps his feet out from under him. As he hits the ground, she stamps out his arm with the heel of her boot. It's red and patchy, but no worse for wear.

"You burned my arm off," he shrieks.

"Stop being a sissy," Chastity says, collecting her backpack. "You just singed a little bit of hair."

"But you broke my wrist."

"You'd better leave Chris alone, or I'll break your head next time."

14

Our nation is filled with national treasures. Yellowstone. The Grand Canyon. The Declaration of Independence. Just ask any of the twenty-three million visitors that descend upon Washington DC each year, and they'll tell you that the catalogue of attractions is impressive. Twenty distinct Smithsonian museums. The Washington Monument. The Lincoln Memorial. The World War II Memorial. The Korean War Veterans Memorial. The Vietnam Veterans Memorial. The FDR Memorial. Even a national zoo. And on the east side of the second floor of the National Museum of American History, a permanent display of the zombie scourge (part of the *American Stories* exhibit).

Encased in glass (just like the Hope Diamond), stands a replica of Corpse One. He was an insurance salesman from Pennsylvania credited with becoming the first zombie of the modern age – back in '68. The display depicts him in a black burial suit and matching tie, with matted gray hair and a puzzled, bloodthirsty expression across his face. Next to him on a patch of artificial turf lies a replica of Victim One. He's a younger man with thick plastic glasses, also dressed in a suit, and his skull is split open where it struck a gravestone. His entrails are tangled about his legs, giving the exhibit a realistic flare. A placard on the front of the display recounts the spread of the zombie scourge from rural Pennsylvania, by way of airplane cabins and gas station restrooms, to every corner of the globe. The placard goes on to describe sightings as far north as Greenland, where some Inuit tribes have purportedly used frozen undead relatives as totem poles, and as far south as McMurdo Station, where back in '79 a glaciologist got killed in a freak drilling accident and came back to eat half the station before a helicopter pilot incinerated him with gasoline and a signal flare. A movie based loosely on this incident stars Kurt Russell, but most of the facts have been changed, blaming the carnage on space aliens and Norwegians.

The point to all of this is that people take great pride in the artifacts that define their lineage. They look to them for continuity and inspiration. Pleasanton is no exception. We have our treasures, too. There's the giant ball of yarn on Route 57, for example, which Farmer Brown assembled over a lifetime from his wife's botched crochet projects, and the Lincoln Arch, which boasts three actual stones from Abe Lincoln's great aunt's fireplace, and the À La Mode, a condemned ice cream parlor at the fringe of the dead zone where a group of fraternity brothers mistakenly surmised they could make a killing selling smoothies to the undead market. They held out for three days, the legend goes, engaging in vicious hand-to-hand combat with ice cream scoopers and Popsicle sticks, sending over a hundred corpses back to the grave before the gnashing teeth of the moaning hordes reduced them to sprinkles.

Among Pleasanton's monuments of civic pride, however, the most awe-inspiring has to be the mausoleum of Colonel Morbid. It's really a granite bust situated next to a toolshed, which houses the lawnmower that the caretaker uses to maintain the cemetery grounds, but from a distance it looms against the horizon like a beacon of time. A placard celebrates the colonel's many accomplishments, including the thousand Yankee soldiers he killed with cavalry saber and pearl-handled Walker .44; and a small rectangular case constructed from bulletproof glass displays the ivory peg leg that General Lee awarded the colonel in 1864 for his sacrifice and bravery. The epitaph reads: *A Straight Shooter, a Man of Action, and a Staunch Proponent of Indoor Plumbing.* The town website boasts that nearly three hundred visitors frequent the colonel's tomb each year and inject into the local economy (once motel stays, restaurant tabs, and related souvenirs are factored in) nearly fourteen thousand dollars – more than enough to pay the caretaker six bucks an hour (cash) to cut the grass and wipe the bird poop off of the colonel's head.

The small bluff upon which the colonel's tomb resides overlooks a pond that local residents dug in '94 as a retention reservoir for runoff during heavy rains. Most folks stay out of the water, on account of the high pesticide content, but during the lazy days of summer, you can always find a stalwart soul or two atop inflatable rafts, daring one another to dive into the phosphorous depths. Walter's World of Water, the local aqua park, considers the pond to be its biggest competition, and for years Walter has petitioned the City Council to condemn the site for safety reasons. But the council has repeatedly rejected his requests, citing a provision in the city code that protects the pond as part of the Colonel Morbid Memorial.

It's Chastity's favorite place.

We're here now, lying on the grass in each other's arms, watching a mallard corpse bob up and down with the breeze. It's drifting toward a patch of reeds, where it will likely get stuck and slowly decompose. A dozen or so of its brethren are tangled in the reeds already, at various stages of decay, forming a garden of putrefaction.

"Isn't this place serene?" Chastity says.

"Yeah."

"There's so much history locked in the ground for everyone to enjoy. Lives and loves from across the generations, lying at rest for eternity and slowly decomposing. It's a community, Chris, a cross section of society coming together for a common purpose. You don't see much of that anymore, with the crematorium and all. People are in such a hurry nowadays to flash fry at eighteen hundred degrees, just to avoid a little reanimation. If you ask my opinion, cremation is a lot less romantic...a lot less natural. Although the ash does make for pretty sunsets."

"That's what my mom says."

"I come here a lot by myself, to think. It's usually pretty quiet."

I look around. There's not a soul to be seen, at least not above ground. "Did you pick out your dress yet?"

"I did. It's going to be blue. Blue to match this beautiful world."

"And your beautiful eyes."

She kisses me on the lips.

I manage to unclasp her bra in under three minutes – a new record for me – and I'm working my hands up and down her tender flesh. She feels a bit cool to the touch, and I hope she's not coming down with something. Prom is not far off, and I want her to be healthy. I offer her my *Curlers Rock the House* hat, but she declines, content to let the breeze rifle through her jet black hair. Although we're kissing, she seems distracted, beside me and beyond me simultaneously, as if commuting between two worlds, unsure of where to park. She stops my hand when I try to remove one of her combat boots. I've yet to see her bare feet.

"What's bothering you? Is it my breath?"

"No, of course not," she winces. "The Oralcline takes enough of the edge off."

"Are my hands too cold?"

"Not really."

"Is it...is it because I'm dead?"

She frowns, annoyed even. "Is that what you think? Do you think I'm holding back because you're dead?"

"I don't know. I mean, most people might have an issue with it. I'm the kind of guy that looks forward to week-old Beef 'n Cheeses. And my hair and nails keep growing like weeds."

"I'm not most people."

"I know," I say, flushing as close to red as one can get with burnt motor oil in his veins. "I'm sorry. I just don't have a lot of experience with, well, you know. You're the first girl to pay attention to me, the first to make me feel alive. I don't want to screw things up. I want to make sure everything goes right."

Chastity takes my hand and presses it to her heart. Due to her world-class conditioning, I can't even feel it beating. "I'm only going to say this once, so listen well. It's not whether a boy is alive or dead that matters to me, Chris. It's who he is inside that counts. I'd rather spend the rest of my life in the arms of a sensitive, rotting corpse than spend five minutes in the back seat of a Camaro with a jerkwad jock. You listen so much better than the other boys I've dated. I don't know if that's because you're dead or because you're a natural listener, but I feel comfortable being myself around you. I don't have to hide my feelings or pretend to be someone I'm not."

I squeeze her tightly.

"You're my Zombie Sven," she whispers, teary-eyed. "And I've finally found you."

For those of you who've never been compared to a plastic doll that little girls play with to learn the nuances of social apartheid, it's not as bad as you might think. In fact, it's a bit of a compliment. Sven is a stud in a *don't-have-to-do-a-damned-thing-to-get-the-girl* kind of way, and he and I share a number of characteristics. For starters, we're both inanimate and don't talk much. We're handsome, in an expressionless sort of way, and we're both preserved by petroleum-based compounds. We're also inflexible, jobless, and if either one of us were to lose an arm to a farm combine or a rabid collie, our contribution to the social fabric would remain unchanged. And...I can't emphasize this point enough...we both love to watch Darbie change outfits.

"I don't care what you call me," I whisper. "Sven, Chuck, it makes no difference."

Chastity regains her composure and wipes her raccoon eyes. "I'm still a virgin, too."

"Too? I never said I was a virgin."

She grimaces, as though I'm recounting the time I saved Christmas by helping Santa repair the runner on his sleigh.

"Okay, you got me."

"There's something else I have to tell you. I've never shared this with anyone before. It's really personal and kind of embarrassing, but I feel that I can trust you. Zombies are good at keeping secrets, right? I can trust you, right Chris?"

"Of course you can trust me."

She smiles. "As you know, I cheered my freshman year and was best friends with Amy and Wanda. The three of us were inseparable back then – cutting class, cruising the mall, exchanging tips on nail polish. We owned the school and knew we were hot stuff, and...I'm embarrassed to admit this now...thought we were superior to everyone else. What a jerk I was. I mean, I never really believed that I was better than the rest of the world. Sure, boys buzzed around me like bees at a picnic, and Mr. Ericson from gym class always picked me to demonstrate a new wrestling move, but I allowed Amy and Wanda to suck me into their fiction and then played my part like a pathetic little conformist. I mean, back then I was so caught up in the vacuous image of being a cheerleader that I doubt I would have talked to you. Not because you're a zombie, but for the stupid reason that you're not a jock."

"I'm learning to curl."

"That's right, sorry. I meant to say you're not a football player."

"Oh."

"Anyway, in case you didn't realize this, cheerleading is hard work. In addition to the endless dieting and grooming, a girl has to practice – and I mean practice hard. Tumbles. Flips. Twists. Not to mention the complex cheers and ever-changing choreographies. It's simply not possible to learn all the moves in September in time for the first game. So cheerleaders attend summer training camp, just like the players. It's tons of work, but a lot of fun, too, bonding with the girls and engaging in the occasional pillow fight after long sessions in the sauna. Unfortunately, I learned that camp wasn't all fun and games. During the second week, the older girls informed the returning sophomores that the most sacred of traditions of cheerleading camp was to hook up with a football player by the end of the session. Amy and Wanda had already met their quota, making it with Doug and Chad on the fifty-yard line, so they received their golden pom-poms immediately. But I was the lone holdout... laggard...loser. Even that cow, Betty Turnbaum, who wouldn't have made the squad if it weren't for the fact she was Wanda's cousin, scored with the team's equipment manager. Apparently, a loophole in the team charter included him as an inactive kicker. The stress was horrible. Real *Heathers* type peer pressure. It's not that I didn't have offers. God knows I had offers.

Doug and Chad tried to pull me into more than one huddle, and even Coach Parsons intonated his willingness to show me the ropes in order to preserve *the team's most venerable tradition.* But I had always envisioned my first time as being special, you know, like here in nature, by the pond with Colonel Morbid watching over me."

I look to the bust of the colonel and can't say that I share the same warm and fuzzy feeling. The man has a stern look in his eyes, the kind that makes me feel like I've done something wrong. In fact, he's kind of creeping me out. I want to throw a blanket over his head, but I'm positive that would extinguish Chastity's mojo.

"When I wouldn't go for any of the smelly football players, Amy and Wanda introduced me to William. He was tall and handsome and strong and muscular and acted so much more maturely than all of the other boys. He wore a sweater vest and combed his hair and even drove a vintage Corvette. As it turned out, he'd graduated from Morbid High a few years earlier and had played quarterback, which qualified him for golden pom-pom credit. He was taking some time off from college to work for his father, the mayor. William Shight, Jr. was his name, and of all things, he treated me like a lady."

"You did it with the mayor's son?"

Chastity glares at me. "Aren't you listening to me? I told you I was a virgin."

"Oh, sorry."

The thought of Chastity kissing someone as hideous as Mayor Shight's son, even if he was tall and handsome and played quarterback and drove a vintage Corvette, is making my stomach turn. I don't think my reaction is what Marvin meant by rolling the intestine, but it has to be close.

"At the time, I thought it was fate. I mean, I was young and naïve and let my heart get the best of me. After a week of nighttime strolls near the dead zone and candlelit dinners at the Taco Tower, the impending golden pom-pom deadline bore down on me. I finally conceded to William's not-so-subtle assertions. Over burritos and orange soda, we decided on a time and a place – right here, by the colonel, the last night of cheerleading camp. I was so excited that I could have danced on air. I felt like a princess about to be kissed by Prince Charming in a forest of diamonds and candy canes. When the night came, William brought champagne, and I brought protection. It was going to be glorious, everything that I had hoped a first time would be. But then it happened. My world turned upside down. Beside the mallard garden, William transformed into a frog."

Chastity stares off into the assemblage of mallard corpses, ensnared by the barbed wire of memory, and all I can think of doing is tearing out William's throat.

"He changed his mind," she continues.

"He didn't want to make it with you anymore?"

"No, he didn't want to make it near the bust of Colonel Morbid."

The guy sounds like an ass, but I don't think I can blame him for shying away from the brooding stone bust of a one-legged Confederate colonel – especially when he's about to get his mojo on. "What do you mean?"

"He wanted to do it in the dead zone, near the ruins of the À la Mode."

"That's kind of creepy."

"I know. I resisted, but he broke open the champagne, and it went straight to my head. I think he might have spiked it with something stronger. Before I knew what was happening, I went along with his stupid idea."

"You mean you made it with him in the dead zone?"

"Aren't you listening to me?"

"Sorry."

Chastity's head is hanging low now, and she can't look me in the eyes. I hate to see her this way. I've gotten so used to her tempered Goth cheerfulness, laced with a dose of brooding self-reflection, that to witness her now on the verge of tears is nothing short of alarming. What makes it even worse is that I'm not sure why she's so shaken up. I mean, she went to the dead zone with some loser frat boy. In the history of our great nation, plenty of teenage girls have made far worse decisions.

I take her hand. It's limp. "He shouldn't have spiked your drink."

"When we got there, everything seemed fine. The sun was setting, and the breeze was rustling through the trees. We spread out a blanket and started kissing beneath the remnants of the À la Mode sign."

I inspect *our* blanket, hoping to God that it's not the same one.

"And then it happened. He had me down to my underwear, and I was searching through my purse for the protection, when a twig snapped. It startled the hell out of us, and William jumped to his feet. Before I had a chance to stand though, three rogue zombies charged straight for us from the trees. I wasn't too alarmed at first, knowing that I had a handsome former quarterback to protect me, but then the biggest disappointment in my life occurred." Chastity swallows sand, barely able to continue. "William ran. He ran as fast as he could back to safety leaving me to fend for myself."

"What a jerk," I say, remembering the words of wisdom that Grandpa McGillicutty once shared that time he took Jimmy and me on an overnight camping trip. *If a bear ever chases you, Chris, you don't have to outrun it. You just have to outrun whoever else is with you.*

I guess the same wisdom applies to zombies.

"What a jerk," I repeat.

"Fortunately, even then I knew a little something about self-defense. I don't know if I've mentioned this to you, but my dad is a former MMA fighter. He taught me how to punch and kick ever since I could walk. So I was able to keep the rogues at bay. Unfortunately, when I cracked one of them in the head with a rock, its blood sprayed all over my face. I got zombie goo in my eyes. That's what I meant when I told you before that I've already been exposed to the virus. I'm going to be a zombie someday, Chris. There's no getting around it."

She goes silent for a good minute and a half, and despite the million and one questions that are peppering my mind, I find the good judgment to keep my trap shut. A breeze kicks up, sending another mallard corpse into the reeds to join its brethren. I twist open one of Chastity's Mountain Dews and take a big swig.

"I never saw William after that. Last I heard, he went back

to college. I still hold Amy personally responsible for what happened. William was her cousin, and she's the idiot who set me up with him."

Chastity stares into the distance toward a place I cannot follow, and I get the sense there's more to the story. But this is all she seems willing to share at this point, and I need to respect her boundaries. Despite all of my own insecurities and the bite of the green monster in my belly, I need to respect her boundaries.

"Thank you for confiding in me," I say. "It sounds like this William was a total creep and put you in jeopardy. He didn't deserve to be with you. I'm glad you didn't make it with him."

"Chris…"

"Yes?"

"Never mind."

15

"You should leak the scheme to the Gazette," Marvin says, pulling a pack of Dependables out of a SlowMart bag. "That might sway public opinion before the mayor gets a chance to take his *kill-two-birds-with-one-stone* proposal to vote before the City Council. Like most media outlets, the Gazette has liberal leanings, so the story might help folks sympathize with the zombie cause. The good citizens of Pleasanton might even surprise us and put pressure on the council members to vote the proposal down."

"What's with the Dependables?" Ernest asks, gnawing on one of my Beef 'n Cheeses.

"I don't know if there's time," I say, ignoring the future astronaut. "I think the proposal goes up for vote in a couple of days."

"So what do you suggest we do then, nothing?"

"That's not what I'm saying. I told you guys that the Squid went undercover. If we leak the story now, we might expose her as an informant and torpedo any progress she's making. I think we should just sit tight and have a little faith in our English teacher's abilities."

Marvin grins. "Do you think she really went *undercover*?"

"Don't put that image back in my head."

"She's not *that* bad, Chris. I mean if you were like a hundred years old or something...with one eye and a terrible case of psoriasis, she'd make a pretty good catch."

"You're such a pervert."

"I'm a zombie who makes eight bucks an hour. Cut me some slack."

"I don't know how much faith we can put in Ms. Twid," Ernest adds. "She gave me an F on my last composition. That doesn't reflect well on her judgment."

"But you wrote about flying to Mars and mooning the camera."

"So?"

"The topic was *what makes our nation great*."

"That's a matter of opinion," Ernest says, grabbing a handful of my curly fries.

Marvin unwraps the package of Dependables. "He's got you there, Chris."

"I do?"

"He does?" I say.

"It's all about the First Amendment. The cornerstone of our great democracy is the freedom of expression. A free press. The freedom to congregate and exchange ideas. Even the freedom to produce one crappy reality TV show after another, which do nothing for society but continually rub our noses in the rotten underbelly of what it means to be human. You don't see that kind of freedom in Russia or China. I doubt you even see it in the UK. I mean, the Brits have a free press and everything, but with a queen and those classy accents, I don't think they have as much tolerance for so many weight-loss shows. I guess what I'm trying to say is that the quintessence of what makes our nation great is the freedom to say what's on our minds, even if it's offensive or untrue. Just read a few social media feeds, and you'll see what I'm talking about. So if Ernest wants to express himself on Mars by waving his fanny to the camera...more power to him. I doubt I could think of anything more American."

The weight of Marvin's words weigh heavily upon Ernest's and my mind. Once again, the zombie fast food worker has given us much to ponder.

"See," Ernest finally says, "I should have gotten an A, for defending our freedom of expression."

"Hold on there," Marvin adds. "Spelling and grammar still

count for something. Why don't we just call it a B- to be safe? I mean Chris and I might be zombies, but we don't live in fairy-land."

"Cool. My best grade yet."

Without missing a step, Marvin spreads a couple of Dependables across the coffee table and inspects them for imperfections. When he satisfies himself that the manufacturing process has maintained a consistent level of quality, he grabs a pair and hands it to me.

"What do you want me to do with that?"

"Put it on."

"What for?"

"So I can show you how to roll your intestine."

I throw the adult diaper on the ground and kick it away. "You're kidding, right? You want me to wear a diaper? I know I'm a zombie and eat food from a dumpster and go through a bottle of Oralcline every day just to keep people from flinching when I talk to them, but I still have a little dignity left. I'm not some eighty-year-old grandmother with an overactive bladder. Besides, my three pairs of tighty whities have been working just fine."

"Pick it up."

"No."

"Pick it up."

"No."

"If you want me to be your manager, then you'd better pick that diaper up and put it on."

Marvin's eyes narrow and his paper hat assumes an air of ferocity, with a crease that could cut through a variety of soft woods...pine, balsa, and the like. Ernest takes a step back, just in case the fast food worker is turning rogue.

"Take it easy, Marvin."

He reaches for a Beef 'n Cheese and devours it in one bite. The greasy sandwich seems to take the edge off.

"Sorry. I don't usually lose my cool. If being a zombie has taught me anything, it's taught me that keeping a low profile is the way to go. The undead can't afford to give humans any excuse to round them up and ship them off to the crematorium, especially not in today's climate."

I look to Ernest, who shrugs his shoulders. "That doesn't sound like the Marvin I know...the drive-thru philosopher with the positive attitude who's always coming up with big ideas. What's bothering you?"

"Nothing."

"Come on. You can tell us. You're amongst friends."

Marvin peels his eyes away from his feet and makes contact with mine. If his tear ducts still functioned, he'd probably be crying. "I'll be fine. Don't worry about me. You have more important things to focus on, like training for the contest."

"Tell us, Marvin."

He takes a deep breath. "Well...I mean...I guess the best way for me to put it is that sometimes even zombies get the blues."

"That sounds like a song," Ernest says.

"Yeah, or a Diana Rowland novel."

No one has ever accused me of being the sensitive type; and certainly no one has ever suspected me of being perceptive. But I have to say, something has got Marvin really bummed out. I mean his entire family turned into zombies, and he had to drop out of school to work for minimum wage so that he could afford his injections and keep from going rogue, but other than those minor setbacks, he's got a lot going for him. He's my hot dog eating contest manager for one thing, and he gets to wear a paper hat, and he has a couple of friends that hang around him for reasons in addition to his ability to score them free Beef 'n Cheeses.

Although the free Beef 'n Cheeses do carry a lot of weight.

Crap...when I put it that way, his life does kind of suck.

"I'm so tired of being a second-class citizen," Marvin starts, reading my mind. "Don't you think I want to finish high school, maybe even go on to community college? As a kid, I always thought I'd so something special with my life. I mean, I didn't have any delusions like Ernest of flying to Mars, but I always figured I'd make more than minimum wage...maybe even get a job with one of those fancy 401(k) plans. But no, I punch a clock, and I pick food out of a dumpster, and that cute assistant manager at the Wienerworld doesn't even remember my name. Hell, look at my car. I drive a '76 Toyota pickup for Christ's sake."

"That's a classic."

"It has a lawnmower engine. I might as well weld a blade to the fender and cut grass for a living." He takes another deep breath, then presses on. "But I ate that can of spoiled tuna with the rest of my family and came back as one of the undead. Those were the cards that the Lord dealt me, and I've tried to come to terms with my situation. But sometimes, especially when Randy starts barking orders down my neck and when punk junior high schoolers take laxatives as a gag so they can spray diarrhea in the restroom, knowing I'll have to clean it up, I can't help but wonder what might have been. How my life might have turned out differently if I'd just gone for the Hamburger Helper."

"I like Hamburger Helper," Ernest tries.

I sock him in the shoulder.

"There's still time. Your life's not over yet."

Marvin grins.

"You know what I mean."

"I do, and thank you for the sentiment. But don't you see, Chris? Haven't you figured it out yet? The hot dog eating contest isn't just some stupid carnival sideshow where folks can watch idiots stuff their faces to the point of explosion. It's not just a way of getting back at Amy Fairchild or Doug Jerkins or all of the other mindless conformists who hold the reins of power. It's much more than that. It's an opportunity for us to prove to the world that zombies are still people, with rights and feelings and the ability to do great things. That's why you can't just beat Doug. You have to destroy him. You have to erase any iota of doubt in anyone's mind that he even stood a chance. For at the end of the day, that's the only way to accomplish the one true purpose to all of this...to create a legend...so that twenty years from now, when a young zombie boy or girl feels the weight of a hostile world crashing down upon his shoulders, he can look at your picture on the cafeteria wall for inspiration and realize without equivocation that zombies still have the right to dream."

I take a deep breath. Marvin is my friend and manager, but

more than anything else he is a zombie's zombie. I know this wasn't his intention, but his words have shrunken me to the size of a sea monkey. Without further hesitation, I pick up the diaper and place a hand on his shoulder. "I'll have it on in a jiffy."

The thing is a loose fit, but I get the sense that's part of the plan. When I come back from the bathroom, Marvin and Ernest are in stitches about something.

"What's so funny?"

"Our job can't be that tough," Ernest says. "The mayor must have a screw loose."

"What do you mean?"

"His proposal to build a wall...everyone knows that walls don't keep people out."

"Yeah," Marvin adds. "And who does he think is going to pay for it? The zombies?"

I shrug my shoulders. "Silly, isn't it? But what does it say about Pleasanton that our parents voted him into office?"

My friends have no answer. The crickets outside start screaming.

A wave of seriousness washes over Marvin's face as he switches gears. "Enough of that travesty for now. Today, I'm going to show you a practice that not many folks from the developed world know about. I call it rolling the intestine. I learned it a few years back on a trip to the Amazon with my Bible study group. I wasn't a zombie back then and still felt like my one-dimensional view of the world was the only correct one; so as you can imagine, I was eager to spread the word. But I can tell you this: I learned a heck of a lot more from those indigenous tribes than they ever learned from me. One tribe in particular, buried deep in the thickest part of the jungle, developed the practice of revering zombies as gods. They don't have Dexapalm 90, of course, so whenever a member of their tribe comes back from the dead, the tribesmen tie him to a tree until he turns rogue. Then to celebrate the essence of their would-be god, they feed him a constant supply of food. I'm talking 24/7...fish, bananas, wild boars, even some kind of roots they dig up from the ground...cartloads of the stuff. Of course the zombie just eats without stopping, and when the ceremony was first developed, the zombie's stomach would burst, creating a mess and bringing dishonor to the tribe. So the clever tribesmen came up with a solution. They figured out a way to push down and twist on the rogue's intestines to create a manually-induced and *controllable* form of peristalsis. When done right, the food just comes out the back end, in a constant stream. You can actually achieve a state of equilibrium. The tribesmen use a reed basket to catch the effluence, and when times are tough, they reuse some of the food, like a form of recycling. Since we don't have a basket and since I have absolutely no desire to see your butt, we're going to try this with Dependables. Besides, during the contest we can't let the judges see what we're up to. The rules are unclear on this matter, and I don't want to take any chances on some conservative interpretation."

I look to Ernest. He looks to me. In unison we say, "Cool."

"How long do they perform the ceremony?"

"A week."

"Then what happens?"

"They cut off the rogue's head and burn it on a funeral pyre."

Again, in unison, "Cool."

"Now come on. You need to bend over the coffee table and try to relax."

For the next hour or so we practice the mysterious technique, and since Marvin only brought over two dozen Beef 'n Cheeses, we need to resort to a bit of recycling. I won't go into the gory details, but it's not as bad as you might think. To take our minds off the messy business though, Ernest flips on the TV and starts searching for another dog show.

"Find *Matlock*," Marvin says.

"That show is stupid."

"It's better than watching a bunch of poodles prance around."

"It's not just poodles."

Ernest can't find anything remotely resembling a dog show, so he finally concedes and flips on Channel 12. A stripper in black lace and a perm is wiggling her fanny on stage while a bunch of drunken patrons hoot. Afterwards, she checks on her young son, who's reading a book in the dressing room. Her ex-husband barges through the door and serves her papers, claiming that he's going to sue for custody. The stripper threatens that she'll do whatever it takes to stop him. In the next scene, a shadowy figure in high heels and a perm breaks into the guy's house and shoots him dead with a snub-nosed .38.

"Oh, this is going to be a good one," Marvin yelps.

Matlock then gets hijacked by a special news bulletin.

"Damn it!"

It's Kirk Karson, the local news anchor. He's away from his desk, out on location. A gusty breeze is flapping through his windbreaker, but not a single follicle on his full head of hair is moving. He's standing in front of Mystery Mel's Sandwich Shoppe, and the blue and white lights of police cars and Border Patrol trucks are reflecting off the building like strobes off a disco ball. About a dozen law enforcement personnel are taping off the scene and scouring the bushes with a pack of German shepherds. The sounds of walkie-talkies obscure bits of Kirk's report.

"Ladies and gentleman. Tragedy has struck Pleasanton once again. Early reports indicate that another rogue zombie attack has occurred...this time right outside of Mystery Mel's Sandwich Shoppe. My sources inside law enforcement are telling me that the victim is Eloise Twid, a beloved high school English teacher. The coroner has confirmed a rash of bite marks across the corpse's arms and back, but what's even more disturbing is that the poor teacher's head is missing. Law enforcement officials are busy searching the vicinity as we speak. DNA samples have been sent to the lab in Urbana to confirm Ms. Twid's identity, but according to the coroner, a tattoo in an undisclosed location of the woman's body professing eternal love for someone named Nigel leaves little room for doubt. Ms. Twid's sister, who lives in Champaign, saw artist's sketches of the tattoo on an earlier broadcast and contacted the Pleasanton Police Department."

Kirk Karson pauses for a moment as the cameras zoom in on a body bag in the middle of the sandwich shop's parking lot. Mystery Mel, the shop's proprietor, is holding what's left of one of the Squid's hands. He's wearing the mask he's come to be known for (as part of his branding identity) and is thrusting his free fist up to the heavens. Either he knew the Squid or is pissed off beyond belief about how this tragedy is going to affect his sandwich sales. Whatever his motivations are, the man is creating a scene and won't let go of the Squid's hand. Sergeant Barry tries to drag him away, but the sandwich shop owner resists, so Sergeant Barry pulls hard. The Squid's hand eventually rips off at the wrist, and the cameras pan to the left toward the German shepherds. After about ten seconds, the cameras zoom back in on the sandwich shop, where a couple of female border guards are leading Mel to a picnic table. It's hard to make out, but I'd swear that a hand is bulging from his front pocket.

"Maybe I'll pass now," is the first thing out of Ernest's mouth. "Substitute teachers tend to go easier on kids."

"That's all you can think about? The Squid was our best chance to stop the mayor. She went undercover to expose the truth and lost her head. I'm not sure we can count on her to figure things out anymore."

Ernest blinks a few hundred times, still stuck on his grade prospects.

I just rearrange my diaper. It's full to the brim and must weigh at least twenty pounds.

But Marvin straightens his paper hat and even mutes the next scene from *Matlock*. A subtle grin overtakes his face. "Don't be so hasty, Chris. Don't be so hasty."

16

Mr. J is tilling the soil in his garden, dressed in Bermuda shorts and a Fruit of the Loom tank top. A pile of fresh tomatoes is sitting in a large wicker basket next to a pair of shears, and all I can think to say is, "Hi, Mr. J. Do you think I might be able to borrow your basket someday?"

"Why sure, Chris. What do you need it for?"

"A little recycling."

That seems to be a good enough answer for the retired ice cream parlor owner, and he pauses from his work to look my way. He seems a lot older to me now, even for a rotting corpse, with bags under his eyes and a suit of skin that might actually be shedding. I mean, the old guy probably has a good ten years left on account of the Dexapalm 90 in his system, but to see him now you'd think he was one step away from sharing a grave with that creepy Crypt Keeper character. I think the pressure is getting to him.

"How are you doing, Mr. J?"

"As well as can be expected, Chris."

"Aunt Gertie sure saved our butts last week, didn't she?"

"That she did. I never got to thank her for standing up to that gorilla. I still remember when she and your mother were little girls and would tumble into my ice cream parlor like a couple of tornadoes. Your mom was always very polite and would order a single scoop of French vanilla, no sprinkles, while little Gertie would demand a triple scoop of rocky road. She liked extra peanuts on it, too. Every now and then I went out of my way to throw in a chicken thigh. She liked fried chicken almost as much as she liked ice cream. Said they made a great combination."

"I can't say that I've ever tried that."

"I don't think anyone else has. Make sure you thank your aunt for me next time you see her."

"Will do."

Mr. J gets back to tilling, and if I wanted to, I could march right off without having to make up an excuse for leaving. As I mentioned before, the old guy is a talker, the kind that Dad says you never want to sit next to on a plane, so the few sentences he just exchanged with me are a record low for him. Something must be bothering him.

"What's wrong, Mr. J?"

"How do you mean, Chris?"

"You look a little blue. I have a friend named Marvin who was blue the other day, but we talked about what was bothering him, and it made him feel better. A few Beef 'n Cheeses didn't hurt either. I thought that maybe a little talk might cheer you up as well."

Mr. J relinquishes a warm smile, the kind that has come to define him. He pats me on the shoulder, staining my shirt with topsoil. "Did you read the newspaper this morning?"

"Not today. I was running late for school."

"Well the Gazette broke a story about a vote the City Council had last night. They voted for some proposal that the mayor is calling the *kill-two-birds-with-one-stone* strategy. He wants to relocate all of the zombies to the dead zone until the rogue assailants can be apprehended. He even wants to build a wall."

"But those never keep people out."

"I know, but the vote passed, seven votes to four. Now the proposal goes to referendum in a couple of weeks. The townspeople will get their chance to vote yea or nay. I have this nagging feeling that the *yeas* might triumph."

"Maybe not. Didn't you say the other day that human decency would prevail?"

"That was the other day."

Before he can get another word in, a Honda Odyssey shrieks around the corner. As it cruises by, one of the tinted windows slides down and a wad of poop flies straight for Mr. J's chest. It splatters across his tank top. The Fudgies inside the minivan giggle to kingdom come as their troop leader peels away.

"That's the third time this week," he says, mixing the poop with his topsoil. "Things are getting bad, Chris, perhaps even worse than the days leading up to the zombie riots of '74." He sniffs a wad of the excrement. "It's not human poop yet, thank Jesus, just canine…almost as good of a fertilizer as the ash from the crematorium."

"You don't have to take this, Mr. J. You don't have to sit there and accept what those little cheerleaders in training throw at you."

"I'm not accepting anything, Chris. I'm just putting the free fertilizer to good use and biding my time. When voting day arrives, I'll slip into my best suit and porkpie hat and walk down to the polling station. I'll be the first in line to cast my ballot. In spite of everything, Chris, I still have faith in the system. I won't let those little banshees diminish my belief in the democratic process. The power of a single vote can sometimes move mountains."

"But votes can be manipulated."

"Not in this country."

I've always thought of Mr. J as one of the wisest men I know, and I still do, but something about his faith in the system just feels a little antiquated. I mean, the system is only as good as the people that participate in it. Fear and ignorance in, fear and ignorance out. If the only people who turn up to vote are the Laundromom supporters, then the zombies in this town don't stand a chance. We need the reasonable, hardworking citizens of Pleasanton to turn up and vote their conscience, the ones who've pondered the issues, and especially the ones who can read. That has to be part of our plan – voter turnout.

A second minivan screeches around the corner, and a ballet troupe hurls about a dozen wads of poop our way. The majority of them strike Mr. J in the chest and face because he can't dodge too well, but one of them hits me in the mouth. It doesn't taste very good. I mean, it's not terrible, but it's not what I would call appealing either. It smells a bit like broccoli beef.

"That was Coach Fawcett's wife driving the minivan," I yell, dumbfounded. "She teaches up at the University. I think she has a PhD in urban studies. My mom says she was a Rhodes scholar." I pause for a moment, blinking. "Shit, I think we're in trouble."

"Looks that way."

"Don't worry, Mr. J. My friends and I are working on a plan."

"What is it?"

"A plan, but we're still working on it."

"Well, that's great to hear, Chris. It's good to see young people getting involved. Our nation needs more of that, young minds thinking outside the box. Without new blood and new ideas, society tends to grow stale. That's when the mold takes over."

Mr. J returns to his tilling, but this time I don't disturb him. Another set of screeching tires grabs my attention. It's Chastity in her black GTO. She fishtails in the middle of the street, pulling a one-eighty up to the curb. Bauhaus is blaring on the stereo.

"Hi, Chris," she shouts from the behind the wheel.

"Hi, Chastity."

She struts up the driveway and plants a ginormous kiss on my lips. As usual, her oil spill mascara is thick and cakey, and her black-on-black ensemble stretches from shoulder to toe. She's wearing a low-cut T-shirt though, the one she was sporting that day in class when she told me to drop dead by the lockers. A bit of cleavage is spilling through, capturing my eyes and my attention.

"What's got you in such a chipper mood?" I ask.

"I'm glad we're finally putting our heads together to come up with a plan. We're running out of time. Without the Squid to stonewall, the stupid City Council approved the mayor's *kill-two-birds-with-one-stone* proposal. It goes to referendum in a couple of weeks."

"Mr. J told me."

She waves to the old guy. "We need to do something fast,

Chris. We can't just keep sitting around. I was thinking about using my ninja stars the next time the mayor leaves City Hall for his Porsche, but then I realized that probably wouldn't set the best example for all the little girls out there. Besides, it might get me banned from prom."

"We don't want that happening." I lean in to kiss her again, and her full lips press against mine. I can smell the remnants of her lunch – sloppy joes from the school cafeteria. "I invited a couple other folks to help us."

"Who?"

Before I can respond, the sound of a lawnmower on steroids buzzes up the street. It's Marvin in his '76 Toyota pickup. He parks behind Chastity's GTO and shuffles up the driveway with four or five greasy paper bags under his arms. He's still wearing his Artie's uniform.

"Hi, guys. I brought a couple dozen Beef 'n Cheeses and about ten orders of curly fries. That should tide us over for an hour or so."

Chastity nods without saying anything. She confided in me the other day that Marvin gives her a bit of the creeps, and I'm not sure she likes him too much. I mean, he's a zombie and smells like a deep fryer and never takes off his paper hat, but what's not to like? He tends to have a way of thinking outside the box, which is good, since we're going to need all the help we can get if we're going to bring down the mayor's plan. So I don't know what to do about Chastity's feelings toward him. I mean, having more than one friend at a time and balancing their competing concerns is really not something I have a lot of experience with.

He's eyeballing Chastity right now, a bit too long. She takes a step back.

"Thanks for the food, Marvin," I say.

"No problem. You get most of it, since you're still in training."

"Is that it?" Chastity asks. "Can we start planning now?"

"One more."

The clink and grind of a rusty bike chain turns the corner. It's Ernest on his Schwinn. He lets the bicycle drop on my front lawn near the mailbox as if he were still eight years old and takes two hits from his inhaler.

"Don't you have a kickstand?"

"It takes too much time."

"My dad is going to get pissed when he comes home. He hates bikes on the lawn."

"I'll move it if he says anything."

"Enough socializing," Chastity snaps. "This isn't a country club. We have work to do. Let's get started."

Instinctively, we fall in line and march through my front door. I think the three of us have all been yelled at by women for most of our lives – mothers, teachers, cheerleaders – and can't help but react when a strong female voice delivers a command.

My mom beams like a starburst when she sees Chastity but quickly loses the luster when Marvin and Ernest follow behind. Although she'd never admit it, I think she's a bit prejudiced against zombies; and even though her son is one of the undead now, she still doesn't want me hanging around them. As for the future astronaut, well, I don't think my mom has ever liked him. She's mentioned more than once that he's a bad influence, enabling my addiction to Blockbuilder.

"Are you kids hungry?"

"I brought Artie's," Marvin says.

"Oh, you can't live on fast food your whole life. How about some nice home-cooked pork chops? Extra rare? There was a sale at Pam's Club, on account of the expiration date."

"Thank you, Mrs. Kantra," Chastity says, licking her lips.

"Sounds good, Mom. We'll be in the basement hanging out. Just give us a little privacy, okay?"

"Of course, dear. Do you think I'm in the habit of eavesdropping?"

I take the Fifth on that question and lead the gang into the basement, where we spend the next hour racking our brains about what to do. Chastity wants to confront the mayor directly at his house, early in the morning when she has the element of surprise on her side. Ernest wants to develop a software virus so that we can hack into the voting booths. I keep reminding him that he doesn't know how to code, but he seems stuck on the notion that he can do it with emojis. Marvin is just sitting on my bed quietly studying Chastity. I should probably say something, seeing how she's my girlfriend and all, but usually when a guy overreaches with his eyes or hands, Chastity just lashes out with a roundhouse. I keep waiting for the bomb to drop on Marvin's head, but something about him has put her on the defensive. She won't look him in the eye or confront him about his stares. It's totally weird and out of character for her.

"Why so much makeup?" Marvin asks.

"Excuse me?"

"Why do you wear so much black mascara?"

I look to Chastity, but she's avoiding eye contact.

"Because she's a Goth, you idiot," I say. "Why do you care?"

Marvin ignores me. "Chris has a bonspiel in Urbana coming up next month. Are you going to go? I know you pick him up from curling practice on Saturdays, but you haven't ever watched him. Are you going to watch the bonspiel? It's a big deal to him...almost as important as the hot dog eating contest."

"Shut up, Marvin. What's gotten into you?"

"It's a simple question."

"No, it's not. You've been eyeing Chastity all night. What's the deal? Are you a pervert or something? Have you inhaled too many grease fumes at Artie's?"

Marvin ignores me again. "I know it gets a little chilly in the arena, but you can always wear an extra sweater. That leather jacket looks pretty warm, too."

"Stop harassing my girlfriend," I say. "Manager or no manager, keep it up and you're going to be sorry."

"Settle down, guys," Ernest tries, taking a hit from his inhaler. "I know we're totally stressed out, but we shouldn't take our frustrations out on each other."

We both ignore him.

And then Marvin crosses the line. He walks up to Chastity and starts sniffing her, like a dog. His nose isn't near her butt or anything, but the advance is obviously unwanted. It's like that time I visited Aunt Gertie at the trailer park when I was nine and her pit bull, Jasper, knocked me to the ground. She claimed he was just happy to see me, but his happiness still landed me in the ER with five stitches to the scalp.

"Get away."

But he doesn't, and before I realize what's happening, my fist is flying toward his head. Marvin has pretty good reflexes though, and he ducks to avoid my knuckles. He doesn't duck low enough to save his paper hat though. I connect straight-on with the thing and send it flying across the room. It crashes against the wall and slithers down the paneling like a KO'd boxer.

"My hat!" Marvin scurries to the crumpled wad of paper and desperately tries to work out the wrinkles. The thing looks like it might be a goner.

"I'm sorry, Marvin. I didn't mean to kill your hat. I was trying to hit you."

He takes a deep breath, broken from his spell. "I know, Chris. It's not your fault. I shouldn't have ducked."

"I'll buy you a new one."

"I get them for free."

"So what's the big deal?" Ernest asks.

"This one has sentimental value. I was wearing it the day Randy promoted me from fry cook to drive-thru attendant."

Before I can process the relative importance of such a senti-ment, Chastity presses her lips to mine. She even reaches for my backside and gives it a little tussle. "You stood up for me," she says.

"I died for you, baby."

All eyes turn to Marvin. He squirms beneath their weight. "I'm sorry, Chastity. I didn't mean to make you feel uncomfort-able. It's just that sometimes when a question pops into my head, I can't stop researching it until I find an answer. It's like a compulsion."

"What question?" I ask.

"It was stupid. I can't even remember now."

"That happens to me sometimes," Ernest adds. "I think it might have something to do with all the mosquito repellant my mom makes me wear."

I know that Marvin didn't forget the question. He's too quick-witted and deliberate for such a lapse. But now is not the time to press him. We have bigger fish to fry.

"No hard feelings," Marvin says, extending his hand.

"None taken," I say, shaking it.

"We still need to figure out a way to thwart the mayor's proposal," Chastity says, impatient again. "We can't waste any more time fooling around."

Ernest inadvertently drops a Mentos into his Mountain Dew and gets sprayed from head to toe.

"Brilliant," Marvin says.

"What?"

"Ernest just reminded me of what the Squid's carotid artery must have done when the rogues tore off her head."

"So?"

"I don't think it's a coincidence that she got attacked. I think there's a conspiracy afoot in the state of Denmark. She must have gotten too close to the mayor and found something out that he didn't want her repeating. At least that's what Matlock would deduce."

"And what would Matlock suggest?"

The fast food worker puts on the wrinkled paper hat and straightens it as best as he can. Then he stares into our eyes with his amber-colored beacons. They're virtually on fire. "We need to find the Squid's head."

17

"A chupacabra got her," Sissy Slupchek says, drooling all over her clarinet reed. "They've been known to tear off the heads of cattle."

Ernest can't take his eyes off the girl; he can't speak in intelligible sentences either. The two of them are sitting by the Tilt-A-Whirl, exchanging the vibe that Barry White often alluded to in his lyrical observations of the human condition. I keep telling Ernest to ask her out, to spring for Pepsis and corn dogs and take a walk over by the bumblebee ride where it's less crowded, but the idiot ran out of money trying to win a BB gun at the ring toss. He knows as well as I do that the carnies rig these games, but he got addicted, and I wasn't there to intervene until it was too late.

"Here," I say, handing him my last ten-spot. "Put it to good use."

"Thanks, Chris. You know I'll pay you back."

"Sure thing," I lie.

Despite the carnage that has struck Pleasanton in recent weeks, including the decapitation of Morbid High's favorite English teacher, Principal Dawson decided to start the school carnival on schedule – seeing how revenues hang in the balance. That's where I am now, on the third day of the festivities, waiting patiently by the stage for my shot at glory. The smell of boiling weenies is wafting through the air, and the crowd is growing restless for the competition to begin. This is the first year that a zombie is taking part in a head-to-head hot dog eating contest – making me something of a novelty – and as such, Dr. Thurgood has been called in to monitor my performance. The rules of engagement are clear: if my stomach ruptures, I loose. That's the only way the officials could think to keep the playing field level with a zombie competing against a Neanderthal in a meat-eating contest.

Buck (IQ=?) is already sitting on stage next to an eight-by-twelve-foot poster of Laundromom. He's the guest of honor, being the only surviving record holder who resides in Illinois, the rest having succumbed to bouts of arteriosclerosis and mad cow disease. He's dressed in a suit and tie, which he likely bought for $12.95 at Larry's gently used fire sale (held behind the crematorium on Friday nights), and a lapel pin in the shape of the number 64 that signifies his status as the all-time record holder. His arm is bandaged, on account of Chastity's act of good samaritanism, but his spirits seem high. I can tell he's nervous though by the way he keeps picking his nose. The record is the only shot a guy like him has at immortality – and it's about to get stamped out.

But the ladies from the curling club are taking forever to boil the weenies in a vat over by the porta potties. We're behind schedule, and Principal Dawson is starting to fume. She's way too smart though to try to hurry the ladies along, especially when they're wielding knives and ladles. They've forgone reruns of *Barnaby Jones* to help Mrs. Marshall, the lunch lady, whose rheumatoid arthritis has started to interfere with her ability to stir a cauldron. She knows Clara back from the days of the Johnson administration, and the two of them are laughing it up, intoxicated no doubt by the fumes leaching out of the mystery meat. In fact, the ladies are taking so long that Eunice and Ethyl even found the time to knit me a sweater. It's purple with red letters across the front that read: *Curlers Like to Sweep Around.*

Unfortunately, Marvin has me wearing the official Wiener-world T-shirt instead. He's spent the entire morning hitting on the assistant manager from that hot dog chain, which sponsored the contest by donating a vanload of weenies. He doesn't want me rocking the boat with unapproved clothing and blowing his chances with her.

"Are you ready?" he asks.

"Yeah."

"Don't get nervous, and remember to breathe. Are you wearing our secret weapon?"

"Of course."

"A loose pair."

"Yes."

"Remember what we practiced."

"Of course I'll remember. I just don't see how the bulge in my ass won't be obvious once I start sucking those weenies down. I mean the Dependables are a miracle garment, preserving the dignity of countless seniors around the globe, but they can't possibly hold the volume of a wicker basket."

"That's why I loaned you my Adidas track suit. It's made for fat guys. No one will notice the diaper under those baggie pants."

I take a deep breath, but I'm starting to hyperventilate. I'm sure it's all in my mind, since I'm dead and shouldn't give a rat's ass about the CO_2 levels in my blood; but the effect seems real enough. I take a seat on the grass and attempt to meditate, the way Chastity has been trying to teach me; but it's hard to concentrate with so much going on.

Before I can get three Oms in, Jimmy bolts by with a humungous stuffed elephant clutched between his arms. A one-eyed carnie is chasing him in hot pursuit. He's wearing an eye patch, and the patch has a dart sticking out of it. From what I can tell, that means Jimmy missed his mark and doesn't deserve the furry prize. He must have thieved it.

In his panic, the little asswipe knocks over the deep-fried Snickers bar vendor's stand, spilling molten chocolate all over Aunt Gertie's gently used suede skirt. She got it at the thrift store on sale and claims that it highlights her curves. I wouldn't know anything about that, but I can tell you that she won't need a dry cleaner the way she's licking off the sweet goo. Jimmy latches onto the skirt, and the carnie stops dead in his tracks when he confronts my aunt's imposing figure. The two of them exchange a few words. The carnie then starts waving his arms. Aunt Gertie just shakes her head slowly, and when the moment is right she jams a finger into the carnie's chest. That knocks him back a few steps and deflates his mojo. He's about to walk away, completely dejected, but she motions for him to stop. She then pulls Jimmy by the ear and swats him on the behind – something Mom and Dad should have done a long time ago. The little asswipe resists, so she swats him again; and when he tries to run off, Jed, Fred, and Little Ted block his escape with their umbrellas. Cornered, my brother finally relents and hands the stuffed elephant back to the carnie. In a true act of good sportsmanship, the carnie pulls the dart out of his eye patch and hands it to Jimmy.

Aunt Gertie sees me watching her and waves, and I wave back. She mouths the words *good luck*, and I mouth back the words *thank you*.

"Are you ready, dear?" Mom says, startling the bejesus out of me.

"Yeah. Where did you sneak up on me from?"

"The balloon toss. Your tightwad father cut me off after a measly forty dollars. I was just getting the hang of the game. A few more tries and I would have won that cute little *Trolls* pencil eraser."

"For forty dollars, I could buy you five dozen of those things, honey."

"That's beside the point. I wouldn't have won those."

My dad rolls his eyes and takes a deep breath. He then peeks into his wallet slowly, as if the thing might explode if its contents are exposed to too much sunlight. "We only have enough left for a couple of Swigmont Colas...small. No cotton candy for us today. We're on a budget after all."

"See what I mean," Mom says, winking at me.

"Dad sure knows the value of a dollar."

"That's right, son. And I've tried to instill the valuable skill of frugality in you and your brother. A penny saved is a penny earned. That's what Grandpa Kantra always used to say."

My grandpa is buried in a pine box in virtually what amounts to an unmarked grave. He died of old age, so wasn't at risk of turning into a zombie, and since he'd already prepaid his funeral plot in the cheapest section of the cemetery – the part usually reserved for paupers and other vagrants – my dad honored his wishes and didn't cremate him. Every now and then when he's had a few whiskeys, my dad mumbles about visiting Grandpa Kantra's grave, but the crime rates in that part of the cemetery have gotten pretty bad. It's not safe there anymore.

"Good luck, sweetie," Mom says, planting a kiss on my cheek. "We're all rooting for you. Remember though, it's not whether you win or lose that matters, it's whether you try your best."

"Thanks, Mom."

Dad rolls his eyes again and shakes my hand. It's the first time I can remember him sharing the gesture with me. "Good luck, son. I know you'll make us proud. And if there's any prize money, I'd be happy to invest it for you in a money market account."

Mom pulls his hand toward the balloon toss, but Dad resists, steering her toward the refreshment stand. The contest should begin any minute, so I better get back to my meditation. Chastity has been teaching me how to visualize an outcome. She says that if you can clearly visualize what you want to accomplish, then you're more than half way toward actualizing it. She got the notion from her sensei and claims that it helped her break cinder blocks with her head. I don't know about cinder blocks, but I can picture those weenies sliding down my throat – salty, fatty goodness. I roll my intestine a bit, to keep it warmed up, and it responds by depositing a little surprise in my Dependables. It's probably the four Beef 'n Cheeses that I had for breakfast. I'm not sure if I should have eaten anything this morning, but I was feeling kind of hungry.

"Are you ready?" Chastity asks, stretching her hamstrings.

"As ready as I'll ever be. Why are you stretching?"

"This is more than a contest, Chris. This is an outright battle...us against Amy, her drones, and those stupid lemmings who keep chanting *Laundromom*. When you destroy Doug at the weenie table, things could get ugly. I want to make sure I'm prepared."

"Smart."

"More like retarded," Amy quips, standing behind us with Wanda Lopez and Doug Jerkins in tow. She's glowering like she has pine mouth, and Doug seems a little drunk. Wanda is just holding a big sign that reads *No Zombies at Prom*.

"Get out of here, skank."

"Takes one to know one. Besides, I just wanted to let you two losers know that I got the hundred signatures. My petition to ban zombies from prom goes up for vote at the student council week after next. I don't think it will have any trouble passing. So when Doug and I accept our crowns as prom king and queen, you two can hang out in paste boy's basement playing video games…or whatever it is the socially irrelevant do nowadays."

"Blockbuilder is harder than you think, Amy."

She scowls at me. "Was I talking to you?"

"Yeah, you were."

She rolls her eyes and points her finger in Chastity's face. I can tell that my girlfriend wants to bite the digit off, but she's using every ounce of her martial arts training to keep cool.

"Get that finger out of my face before you lose it."

"Game over, dear."

Amy tosses her hair and saunters off with pendular hips in motion. Her Rod of Asclepius tattoo hisses at us from the small of her back.

"What a bitch," Chastity says. "Don't worry about them. They're just trying to psyche you out. That means they're scared. We have them right where we want them."

"As long as we don't get disqualified."

"Don't worry about that," Marvin says, also sneaking up on us. "The rules clearly state that any contestant who vomits during the competition will lose. They're silent, however, on what happens when a contestant craps his pants. I know we're pushing the envelope on our interpretation with the whole rolling the intestine thing, but if we get caught, at least we have a good faith argument."

"Don't get caught," Chastity says.

I rearrange my Dependables to make room for the weenies.

The master of ceremonies is finally taking the stage to kick off the competition. The honor is usually reserved for Mayor Shight or for one of the Illinois governors making his rounds upon release from prison, but this year the school board has made another choice in its never-ending pursuit of securing supplier discounts. He's walking up to the microphone now, mask on face, double-M stenciled on his shirt. His chest appears to be caved in a bit on the left side, probably a result of the disappointment he experienced at being beat out by the Wienerworld for the chance to donate a vanload of week-old hot dogs. Little Tiffany Tucker, a girl with a lisp who's featured on the library's Little Literates web page, is busy working the front row, handing out two-for-one sandwich coupons.

Mystery Mel opens his mouth, revealing a set of medieval teeth, and begins to speak in one of those east coast dialects. "Oi! Hallo, hallo. Good townsfolk of Pleasanton, I'd like to thank you from the bottom of my...from the bottom of my soul for this magnificent honor. Today is a wonderful time on the shire, for today we will bear witness as two competitors engage on the field of battle. Not with swords or lances, mind you, but with steaming weenies they will test each other's metal. And through their struggle for immortality, they will honor the memory of my sweet Eloise, who was taken from us seven days erstwhile. Now, it's hard to hide the fact that I wasn't born in Pleasanton, and I know my true identity eludes many of you, but please be assured that I knew Eloise long ago, when the breeze was sweet and the night was young. I was never a prince to her. In fact, I was a bit of a knave, unaware of the beauty that pulsed in my hands until I had crushed it asunder, lost on the moors of my own self-pity. I didn't deserve her; she didn't deserve such harshness. I can only pray now that she's watching us from on high, correcting grammar and still yearning for a plate of bangers and mash. Forgive me, Eloise, forgive my insensitivity. I never meant to be heartless." He pauses for a moment, but then regains his composure. "Anyway, enough about my loss. Today is a day for these strapping lads. Good luck, gentlemen. Pack in the weenies and make your mums proud. To mark the occasion, I'm giving out specials all week long at my sandwich shop – two for the price of one. God save the Queen."

The crowd cheers, despite its confusion. Game time has arrived.

Chastity slips me a bit of tongue and massages my shoulders before walking me on stage. "Don't be nervous," she says, looking fairly anxious herself. "This is your time to shine and show this town what you're made of. Just remember what we talked about. Eye of the tiger, Chris. Eye of the tiger."

"Eye of the tiger," I say.

"That's right. Eye of the tiger. You're my man."

Suffice it to say, that song by Survivor is now stuck in my head and won't come unstuck until I hear the *Macarena* or shoot myself in the brain with a .357 Magnum. I lean forward in my chair, as pumped on adrenaline as any dead person could hope to be, and stare into the ocean of weenies. I don't bother glancing over at Doug. He's irrelevant. It's between me and the frankfurters now.

The gun goes off, and the .45 caliber hollow-point barely misses Marvin's wrinkled paper hat.

One weenie, two weenies, three weenies, four. Five weenies, six weenies, save room for more. Seven weenies. Eight weenies. Nine weenies. Ten. Roll the intestine, just like Zombie Sven. Eleven. Twelve. Two plus six. That makes twenty magic tricks. Thirty. Forty. Another score. The Dependables are filling, but I want more. Seventy. Eighty. Oh my, God. Buck is crying. What a rod. Just keep going. Don't you stop. Not until you hear a plop. Space is bending. Time is still. Down the wormhole. Up the hill. Floating in the depths of space. My senses warped. My girlfriend's face. I'm losing track. Can't count this high. Another tray. Another try. Just keep eating. Enjoy the taste. Of greasy cardboard and human waste. Note to self. Zombie snacks. Port-a-dogs. Or pottie-packs. Just one thing, to make them great. A little spice. It cannot wait.

I come to a halt, just for a moment, figuring that I'm ahead by at least ten or twelve weenies, and stand up to stretch. The mouths of the crowd have come unhinged, and Doug Jerkins is glowing the color of split pea soup. I'm not sure he's breathing.

"Do you have any mustard?" I ask.

The lead judge, Mr. Zantack, who works as the town pharmacist during the week, holds out his hand, instructing me to stop. He asks Doug if he can go on. Doug is as purple as an eggplant now, and blood is dripping from his nostrils. He grunts his desire to continue, but Mr. Zantack is skeptical. He motions to Dr. Thurgood, who then shines a penlight into Doug's pupils and shakes his head. "They're fully dilated. That's not a good sign."

"He can continue," Amy Fairchild screams at the top of her lungs. "You keep going, Doug."

He moans.

"Are you a man or a twit? Are you going to let a zombie win? Now suck it up like a real man and fight through the pain."

Doug grabs a dog, but his hand is trembling. Sweat is pouring down his face. Mr. Zantack requests a count, to determine how close the race is. Mrs. Marshall walks on stage with a clipboard in hand and a pencil behind her ear. She spends a couple of minutes calculating with fingers and pantomime.

"Doug Jerkins...eighty-seven," she says. "Chris Kantra...let me just double-check...yeah, that's right...my Lord...Chris Kantra...two hundred and seventy-three."

Sweet victory. I slip a couple extra weenies into my mouth and ingest them whole, just to rub it in, daring Doug to follow suit. He takes a bite. One more. A third. And then the most beautiful and yet most disturbing thing I've ever witnessed happens. He turns Casper white and vomits right into Amy Fairchild's open mouth. Then onto her *No Zombies at Prom* sign. Then onto Buck. Then onto Amy again. I swear to God his intestines have come to life, a creature from that Kurt Russell movie.

The crowd cheers. Doug keels over, unconscious. Amy swallows by reflex and then vomits herself. Chastity runs back onto the stage to hug me. My diaper is bulging about the size of a beach ball, but no one seems to care. They're too caught up in the moment.

"Go, Chuck. Go, Chast. Go, Chuck. Go, Chast."

"Go, Chuck. Go, Chast. Go, Chuck. Go, Chast."

Then Lenny Stiles, the magic wand thief and secret admirer of Principal Dawson, materializes beside me and shouts something that I thought I would never hear in all of my life...and which I didn't, actually. So I guess it's only fitting that I'm hearing it during my death.

"Chris and Chastity for Prom King and Queen!"

The crowd pauses, thinking, then erupts. "Chuck and Chast. King and Queen."

"Chuck and Chast. King and Queen."

I French kiss Chastity until she gags and hoist my arms in victory. *Eye of the Tiger* is still blaring in my head. In the audience, Mom is pressing her hands together over her heart, and tears of joy are streaming down her face. Even life itself can't get much better than this.

"Let's go to Artie's," I say. "I could use a few curly fries."

18

Aunt Gertie is singing like a lark in the kitchen right now, helping Mom prepare a batch of country-fried chicken. The deep-fried Snickers bar vendor is coming over for dinner, to meet the family. She's more excited than I've ever seen her, even more than the time she thought she'd won the lottery.

Last year, a week before Thanksgiving, Aunt Gertie was watching *Hunk of Love* reruns with Mom, debating as they always do about whether or not Burt Mitchel is going bald, when she flipped to the lotto channel a minute before the hour (annoying the hell out of Mom, who was dying to find out which tramp got voted out of bed next), and the images of six ping pong balls burned themselves into her retinas. *It was like slow motion*, she later said. *The story of my life just popped out of a little plastic air machine.*

3 – number of kids she knows about.

4 – number of failed marriages.

13 – months spent on probation on trumped up charges.

18 – number of favorite chicken parts.

29 – age she wishes she could be again.

39 – a lady never tells.

In less than a minute, Aunt Gertie went from trailer park lifer to partial winner of three hundred twenty-seven million dollars. The woman exploded off the couch and bounced off the walls and consumed every Hi Di Ho in sight before yelling at the top of her lungs and dancing the *Macarena*. Mom bumped and grinded with her. Dad recommended annuities. Asswipe Jimmy even requested a vintage '87 IROC-Z. The entire family was on cloud nine, suddenly launched from the realm of pond scum to the place where eagles soar.

But then a terrible thing happened – nothing unpredictable if you know my family, but certainly the seed for a minor Greek tragedy. Aunt Gertie remembered that she didn't buy the ticket. She'd siphoned the funds, for sure, from her Chicken Trough and Taco Tower budgets, but she'd given the money to Jed and asked him to buy the ticket. Dad fainted. Mom ruined the couch with a bout of colitis. Jimmy cut off the head of another G.I. Joe. And Aunt Gertie's face dropped like an anchor. In the blast of a single synapse, her dreams of new curtains and community college sank into the depths, leaving behind the bitter reality of SMEAT and chicken noodle soup. Her fear wasn't so much that Jed had forgotten to buy the ticket as it was that he'd run off with it. It must have been the worst feeling that any loving mother could have possibly experienced – betrayal by your firstborn. I could tell by her eyes that she was already rationalizing the horror, convincing herself that Jed's stripper girlfriend was the mastermind behind the caper, intoxicating her poor, helpless boy with sweet talk and tender promises. But Aunt Gertie is a fighter. Always was. And she wasn't about to lose her little boy to the forces of nature. So the entire family spent the entire night scouring the town for my genius cousin, searching every bar and back alley where he'd been known to carouse, until Jimmy found him loitering in front of Preetap's Liquors drinking a forty-ounce and smoking a menthol.

What transpired next is the stuff of legends. Aunt Gertie asked him where the ticket was, and when he admitted to blowing the ticket money on booze and pork rinds, Aunt Gertie wept tears of joy. Now to normal people, I mean folks who reside outside of the Pleasanton, IL greater metropolitan area, the loss of millions of dollars at the hands of an imbecile son would justify Congress to legalize murder. But Aunt Gertie is a pillar of the community and the embodiment of its family values, so she simply smothered Jed's face in her bosom and thanked the

Lord that he'd only gotten drunk and not forsaken his mother's trust. She later told me that family is all we have, and that family is more important than all the money in the world.

That theme has stuck with me, and for all of my complaints and mildly amusing tirades, I have to admit that I love my family. Most of them at least – addictions, mental illnesses, and all. And I don't know what I would do without them. I'm scared, you see. Really scared. The vote on Mayor Shight's *kill-two-birds-with-one-stone* proposal is fast approaching – less than two weeks away now – and the only image that keeps flashing through my mind is one from that movie, *District 9*, where a bunch of refugee space aliens cower in a crappy, third-world slum in the outskirts of Johannesburg. I mean, I don't need food or sanitation to survive. I'm a zombie for Christ's sake. But just like space aliens, I do need love...especially from a girl like Chastity. The thought of being separated from her is too much to bear.

Our plan to thwart the mayor is coming together, and I'll talk a little more about that later. But even the best of plans is still subject to countless unforeseen variables. Earthquakes. Tidal waves. Six-mile wide asteroids hurling down from space. I mean, I'm a hot dog eating legend now, and when the judges asked me to say a few words onstage after my victory, I tried my best to appeal to the crowd's finer sensibilities, getting a bit political (which is out of character for me) and asking them to vote down the proposal on humanitarian grounds. They cheered, of course, but they were high on the fumes of boiling weenies. Now that a few days have passed and heads have cooled, I'm beginning to wonder if my speech made an impact. It's so frustrating. The fate of my existence hangs in the balance of a group of townspeople who enshrined the ivory peg leg of a Confederate colonel – and I'm not even old enough to vote.

Enough of this depressing talk though. It's putting a crimp in my mood. This is my big night after all, the night I become a man. I've prepared as best as I could, drinking Oralcline to freshen the length of my digestive tract. Doing a few push-ups to look buffed. Even spraying down the rest of my body with an entire can of Axe. The rest is up to nature.

And so here I am, gnawing on a rare pork chop to calm my nerves, listening to Aunt Gertie sing *Like a Virgin*, feeling a little light-headed. Life really is a laugh riot. In death I'm about to go where no living man has gone before. Getting my mojo on with the hottest girl in school. That's right. Hottest. Move over Amy Fairchild.

The horn blares outside.

"Sorry I'm going to miss your dinner, Aunt Gertie. But I have to go."

"Go where?" Mom asks.

"I understand," Aunt Gertie says, winking. "Good luck. And be safe."

"You, too. And make sure to share the chicken."

* * *

The purr of a finely tuned GTO is like nothing else on the planet. Tough yet silky. Visceral while transcendent. A chainsaw cutting through lingerie in a warm bubble bath. It simply reeks sexy. If Barry White were to reincarnate as a car, and no Escalades were available, he'd definitely come back as a bitchin' GTO.

The black paint is reflecting the rays of the setting sun, creating the illusion of a burning pool of Iraqi oil. And behind the wheel, dressed in black jeans and a black leather jacket, Chastity is smiling with one of the biggest best-white smiles I've ever seen.

"What's that?" she asks, gripping the wheel.

"Supplies for our special night. A six-pack of Swigmont Cola, romance candles, and a vintage Madonna CD."

"Where'd you get the Swigmont?"

"Mr. J. The CD is from my own collection."

"Cool. I brought protection and a two-liter bottle of Mountain Dew."

"Yes."

"Get in."

The wheels screech, and the stench of burning rubber floods the air, and the GTO catapults down the road like a bat out of hell. Mrs. Walsh's calico, the one that keeps pooping in Mom's hostas, bolts into the street at exactly the right time. You can barely feel the bump.

"So much for nine lives," Chastity whispers.

At eighty miles an hour, the ride to the cemetery takes less than five minutes. Houses, pedestrians, and tombstones smear by in a puree of time's different phases. Chastity hits the brakes and fishtails into the handicapped spot and stares silently into the glare of the setting sun. The orb shimmers like Betelgeuse, on account of the crematorium ash, and ignites her eyes into lava lamps. Her smile suddenly disappears.

"Is something wrong?" I ask. "You seem a little tense."

"I don't want to talk about it."

"Are you sure? I'm here for you."

"I'm sure," she whispers.

This isn't exactly how I envisioned the start of our special night. I expected frivolity and laughter and the muted snarls of a self-reflective Goth. But instead, I find myself faced with a distraught hottie (which is kind of sexy in its own way). Something has gotten Chastity upset, and there's no way for me to help her if I can't diagnose the problem. This feeling of helplessness is maddening, especially when I'm dangling on the precipice of becoming a man, so I say something I've been meaning to say for quite some time but haven't had the guts to make audible.

"I love you,"

"I love you, too," she responds, without hesitation. "Hold me tight."

"What's wrong, baby. You can talk to me."

She sighs and grips my hand. "Okay, I might as well. My brother Benson read through my diary. But that's not the worst part. The ass muncher showed it to my dad."

I swallow. "The MMA fighter?"

"Former MMA fighter. Let's just say Dad blew his top. He hates zombies. After throwing a few chairs and denting the refrigerator with his head, he flat out forbade me from going to prom with you. *Over my dead body*, he said. I thought about using the three-knuckle delayed heart explosion technique, but Dad's still pretty fit. I don't think I could take him by myself."

"It'll be all right," I say, doubtful.

"Don't worry though. He doesn't know it's you. I've been using the code name Sven in my diary, just in case that rat, Benson, got to it."

"That was good thinking."

"It's only a matter of time though before he figures it out... before he figures everything out. The man doesn't have a racist bone is his body, but when it comes to the undead, for some reason he displays zero tolerance. He once told me that if Benson or I were ever stupid enough to come back from the dead, he would disown us."

Images of Chris Kantra locked in a cage with Chastity's dad flash on the screen. Fists, elbows, and ankles...flying everywhere...sticking to the wire mesh. Unfortunately, those body parts are mine. Even if I were to go rogue and lunge for the man's throat, he would simply tear my jaw off before I could bite down. He's big and strong and bald. A mild-mannered zombie is just no match for a former heavyweight contender, especially in a cage without a gun. Let's just hope it doesn't come to that. I'd like to think that deep down in his heart, the man wants what's best for his daughter; and despite the scar tissue and cauliflower ears possesses a sensitive side, one which responds to reason. My sugar tongue still works. Maybe I could talk some sense into him.

"I could say something. Once your dad gets to know me, he'll realize that I'm not so bad."

Chastity shakes her head violently. "That's not a good idea."

"I'm not afraid of him."

"Oh, Chris. I know you're brave."

She crushes me in a bear hug and nuzzles her head beneath my chin. She smells a little like Zesty Mint Oralcline. Either that or a box of Tic Tacs.

"Should we wait?" I offer, nearly biting off my tongue.

"No, tonight is our special night. I won't let my dad stand in our way."

"Whatever works best for you," I say, nearly biting off my tongue again. "This is your night as much as it is mine."

"Come on. Follow me."

Chastity leads me by the hand along the pond, gulping a

Swigmont Cola. When we reach the statue of Colonel Morbid, she spreads a blanket over the grass and lights the romance candles (since I'm not allowed to touch open flames). I load the Madonna CD into a boom box and embrace Chastity to the sweetness of *Papa Don't Preach*. The moment is what I dreamed it would be. Breathtaking. The sun is liquefying into night along the horizon, and in the subtle glow of its dissolution, the mallard garden bobbles in the breeze.

"No one will tear us apart," she says.

"No one."

"To the colonel," she says, raising her can. "May he always watch over us."

"To the colonel and his peg leg."

"I love you, Chris."

"I love you, too, Chast. You're better than I deserve."

And without further ado, I set a new record for unclasping her bra: one minute, thirty-seven seconds. She does not disappoint. Her flesh is soft and supple, inviting me to immerse myself in it completely.

One dumpling.

A second.

McMurdo Station.

Chastity is purring on the blanket, eyes closed, as vulnerable and as receptive as any third-degree black belt could hope to be. She trusts me, and I trust her, and as I try to untie her black leather combat boots, she sits up and stares into my eyes.

"Wait," she whispers, breathing heavily. "I need to tell you something first."

"Something else?"

"Yes. It's really important. I've been meaning to tell you for quite some time, but I haven't found the right opportunity. I wanted to tell you that night in your basement after you stood up to Marvin for me, but I chickened out."

"What is it?"

"Chris, I'm…what I mean to say is…I guess…"

"Go on."

"Only one other person knows."

"What is it?"

She sighs, and then her eyes stretch wide, and for some mysterious reason she leaps to her feet. "Watch out!"

"Watch out for what?"

But Chastity is too busy engaging in hand-to-hand combat with a couple of rogue zombies to answer my question. She roundhouses one to the head, sending him into the phosphorous pond. She then thrusts both palms into the other's abdomen, shattering his ribs like dried twigs. He crumples over, holding his intestines.

"Chris, run!"

"Why?"

"They're not trying to eat us. They're trying to kill us."

Chastity must be getting her terms confused, probably a side effect of her battle lust. I'm already dead, so what would the rogues want with me? Chastity is the live one, and therefore the person in real jeopardy. Besides, what kind of boyfriend would I be if I were to run off to safety while she's fighting for her life? I'm not like that loser frat boy, Willie Shight, Jr.

A third rogue bolts out of the bushes straight for me, but I trip over a rock just as he lunges at my head. Without my corpse to stop his momentum, he sails to the ground. Chastity stomps his face in with the heel of her boot.

"Good move," she says.

"Thanks."

But the three assailants aren't dead – or what I mean to say is destroyed – they're merely maimed, so they regroup over by a patch of reeds in some kind of huddle.

"What do you want with us?" Chastity screams.

The middle one, who's wearing one of those stupid propeller hats, flips her the bird. "Nice boobs, tramp. Don't you know what a bra is?"

Chastity goes berserk and charges all three. She punches and kicks and flips and twirls, and I swear she even performs a triple back with a twist; but the rogues are pretty hearty, former football players I imagine, and absorb most of her blows. One grabs her by the arm and gnashes with his teeth, but she stomps on his foot and maneuvers away in time.

"Chris, run!"

But I'm no coward, at least not really. I charge the rogue who's wearing a rugby shirt and bounce off of his chest. He laughs and swats me across the face with a backhand. The blow knocks out a few of my teeth, a serious injury for a zombie.

"You jerk!"

I charge again, and he lifts me from the ground and slams my back over his knee. I hear my spine crack. That's going to wreak havoc on my posture.

Chastity sees me in trouble and sweeps the legs out from under the other two rogues. They drop to the ground like felled redwoods. She then pummels the giant in the rugby shirt, backing him off of me. He grabs her arms and lunges for her throat, but she doesn't scream, so he must have missed. In response, she drops to a split and thrusts her fist straight up into his marble sack. He grunts and falls to his knees. Before she can split his head open with her boot though, he crawls to his pals, and the three of them limp toward a large maple tree in the distance.

Standing under the tree watching the action is the rogue with the White Sox baseball cap. I can't make out his face; he's keeping to the shadows. I doubt I would recognize him anyway.

"Can you see his face?" I shout to Chastity.

"No, he's too far away."

"Why did they attack us?"

"I'm not sure."

I want to charge after the rogues and finish the job, but I'm waiting for Chastity to lead the way. She's the third-degree black belt after all and has better instinct for this sort of thing. When she doesn't pursue them, I figure our best move is to stay put.

The rogues pile into a black Suburban and peel away.

"I didn't think rogues from the dead zone drove Suburbans."

Chastity shrugs her shoulders. "They don't." She's clutching the right side of her neck.

"Chastity!"

I try to inspect the wound, but she won't remove her hand.

"Let me see! Oh, my God. Did that asshole bite your neck? Oh, my God. Did he get the artery? But where's the blood? Maybe it's not too bad. Let me see. We need to get you to a hospital. Dr.

Thurgood can stitch you up. We can't let you die. We can't let you die. Come on, hurry. Let's get to the GTO. Should I carry you? I'll drive. Where are the keys? How do I work the clutch?"

"I'm not going to die."

"What do you mean?" I say, dumbfounded.

She lowers her hand, and a slow trickle of burnt motor oil flows down the side of her neck. "Just hand me a napkin, okay."

"I don't understand. What's going on? We need to hurry. We can't let you die."

"I said I'm not going to die."

"You're in shock. You don't know what you're saying."

"Chris, calm down. This is what I've been meaning to tell you. I'm not going to die because I'm already dead."

PART III

19

When I was a kid, around eight or nine years old, a recurring nightmare plagued me. I was chained by the ankle to a cannonball that was shot into space, and while it dragged me into the depths of the abyss, my screams amounted to silence, on account of the vacuum. The sense of hopelessness that the nightmare instilled was terrifying, as was the impact on my self-esteem. For two years, I moped around the house and school not expecting people to hear me when I spoke. I mean, why would I? My life emulated the nightmare. Amy Fairchild ignored me when she wasn't daring me into reckless behavior. Dad browsed the business section instead of teaching me how to toss the pigskin. Even Mom spent all of her time grooming Jimmy when she wasn't sipping Tab soda or watching *Oprah*. So imagine how surprised I was when I asked Mom to take down her Iron Maiden poster from my wall – and she actually complied. *I think it might be contributing to my nightmares*, I said. *I think you might be right*, she agreed. Eventually I outgrew the bad dream and regained limited use of my self-confidence, and with REM restored, I was able to find solace in my stamp collections and video games. I also developed a valuable skill, which has served me well to this day. I learned to talk to myself and engage in extensive monologues.

Perhaps Chastity telling me that she was already dead was just a nightmare, too. I mean, I have nothing against zombies.

I'm one of them for Christ's sake. And when you look at my best friends – Marvin and Ernest – the former is a zombie and the latter might as well be. Holding Chastity's undead status against her would make me a total hypocrite. It's just that something got stuck in my craw when she told me. I don't know if the effect was the result of a bruised ego, realizing that a "live" girl was still beyond my reach, or if the fact that she didn't trust me enough to tell me sooner exposed a schism between us that I didn't realize existed. Whatever the reason, I guess it really doesn't matter. I still think she's the hottest girl in school, and she's super nice, and I'd be a liar if I told you that I wasn't jonesing to get my mojo on with her. Perhaps in a not-so-weird way, our relationship makes more sense now.

"I love you," I say. "I don't care if you're a rotting corpse."

"Oh, Chris, that's so romantic. I love you, too." Chastity grins, and the tendons on her face pull at the flap of skin over her carotid artery. The wound has stopped dripping, and a lump of black gore has started to clot around it, sort of like summer asphalt. It's quite the contrast to the whitewashed walls of Dr. Thurgood's waiting room.

"Why didn't you tell me?"

"I wanted to. Lord knows I did. And I was just about to tell you before those frat boy losers jumped us. I'm so sorry I didn't tell you sooner, Chris. I should have. The way that you handled yourself out there leaves no doubt in my mind that I can count on you when the chips are down. You didn't run off like William did. You fought by my side with your heart and soul."

"I tried."

"I still can't get over that move you made when you fell to your back just as that palooka in the rugby shirt was diving for your head."

"I tripped."

"But you tripped at the right time. That takes warrior instinct."

"Cool."

"I owe you an explanation." She takes my hand and places it over her cheek. "As you probably figured out by now, I didn't survive that attack in the dead zone the last night of cheerleading camp. Rogues kept coming out of the woodwork like cockroaches in the school cafeteria. I must have put down seven of those bastards beneath the moonlight – shattering spines and crushing skulls – but just as I was climbing a fence to make a break for town limits, one of them took a chunk out of my ankle...hit an artery. I didn't feel much pain, and I was able to decapitate him with a longneck Suds bottle before he could feed on my insides. But the blood kept flowing and my head got light, and fortunately for me the other rogues sensed that I was turning and lost interest. So as I lay in the grass beneath the rusted-out sign of the À La Mode, bleeding out like a gutted farm animal, my last thought as a living, breathing cheerleader was: *how am I going to tell my dad?*

"How did you?"

Chastity cocks her head, the way Mom and Dad do when I fail to get their jokes. "I didn't."

"Oh."

"That's why I turned Goth, to conceal the bags under my eyes. And that's why I wouldn't let you take off my combat boots." Her wedge of a nose crinkles into a frown. "You didn't really think I enjoy dressing up like Elvira and moping around the halls, did you?"

"Of course not."

"This black-on-black routine is a cover, and it's really starting to take a toll."

"I can imagine."

"I like pink, too, you know. Even Zombie Darbie got to accessorize."

I take her hand and kiss her lips and only now do I realize that her flesh is room temperature, just like mine. It's weird. I should have noticed such an obvious detail long before; but I guess my other senses were just so overwhelmed by Chastity's hotness aura that my temperature gauge got thrown out of whack.

"But why haven't you turned rogue?"

"Dr. Thurgood has been giving me free injections. Other than you, he's the only person who knows my secret."

"Why didn't he report you? He's a stickler for the rules."

"He's my great uncle."

I perform a few calculations in my head, multiplying a brother by a sister and carrying the cousin, but my family tree arithmetic is a little rusty. Chastity must sense my confusion, on account of her ninja training.

"He's my mother's uncle."

"You've only mentioned your mother once," I say, before I can shut my stupid mouth. "I mean...that didn't come out the right way."

Chastity walks to a picture of the Louvre that's hanging near the magazine rack and traces her figure along the glass pyramids. "These look so out of place, wouldn't you say? The glass and metal juxtaposed to the stone and mortar?"

"I guess."

"And yet somehow they blend together in an uneasy harmony, almost like the convergence of the ancient and the modern, the forgotten and the remembered." She turns to me before I can respond. "I haven't seen my mother in a long time, Chris. She died in a car accident when I was eight...over on Route 57. She dozed off at the wheel coming home from a Yahtzee tournament and crashed into Farmer Brown's giant ball of yarn. It took three hours before another car came along and reported the incident. By that time, my mom had turned. Like any good zombie, she got her injections and lined up a job at the car wash, but something about her just wasn't the same. The luster in her eyes diminished; the *joie de vivre* that once embodied her personality became less *joie* and no *vivre*."

"That stuff's pretty good for dipping Beef 'n Cheeses."

"My dad tried to adjust and be supportive. He even went down to the car wash and put the manager in a choke hold. After that, my mom got twenty minutes for her lunch break instead of the standard ten required by the 28th Amendment. But it wasn't enough."

"She wanted a half hour?"

"No, washing cars and wringing out shammies just wasn't enough to fulfill her. I guess the work she had done at the lab, with lasers and colliders and what not, had been a lot more stimulating. She was always pretty good with numbers...got

173

her PhD in quantum physics at MIT."

"That's a decent school."

Chastity lowers her head, and her lip starts trembling, but no tears flow. I'm not sure what to do, so I try to hug her, but she holds out her hand. "I guess Benson and I weren't enough for her either. So one day she just up and left. She placed a short note on the kitchen table saying how much she loved us and how painful it was for her to leave...yada, yada, yada...but in the end she couldn't resist the drive to find herself and her new place in the world. She went to the dead zone, Chris. She packed her rollaway and walked straight into the dead zone."

"I'm so sorry, Chastity."

"My dad went searching for her, hoping he could convince her to come back. He even lined up a new job for her at his gym mopping blood off the mats. But he never found her. After engaging in hand-to-hand combat for two weeks with four hundred rogues, the poor man just lost his steam. I think that's the day he starting hating zombies. I'm no Freud, but I think his hatred stems from some kind of pent up frustration with my mom."

"I think Jung would agree."

"I also think that's really why I consented to go with William that night to the dead zone. I mean, the spiked champagne didn't hurt, but deep down I think I was hoping to find my mom."

"Come here, baby." This time I get her in a hug, and she feels strangely feeble for a third-degree black belt, ninja-star-throwing ex-cheerleader. That's got to be tough to have a mother just run off like that, leaving you with a former MMA fighter as your only parental role model. I mean, I've wished for years that my parents would move to Greenland and take Jimmy with them, leaving me on my own to look after the house and the family's other related business interests; but of course that will never happen. And of course, I don't really mean it deep down (although sending Jimmy to boarding school in Greenland is something I've suggested multiple times). My family is here for me, good or bad, and I'm stuck with them no matter how much they get under my skin or embarrass me in front of my friends and teachers. In a weird sort of way, that makes me pretty lucky.

"Do you think she's…?"

"What?"

"Never mind. Forget I said anything. My lips are moving again before my brain can stop them."

"Out with it, Chris."

"Well, I mean…she's gone for years without Dexapalm 90 injections. Do you think she's turned rogue?"

Chastity releases a weak, anemic grin, but it's a grin nonetheless. "I've asked Dr. Thurgood that same question at least a million times."

"And what did he say?"

"He said that if anyone could figure out a way to beat this stupid virus it would be my mom."

As if flexing his Spidey sense, Dr. Thurgood opens the door to the examination room on cue. Another patient walks out, some old woman I don't recognize with a mole the size of a walnut on her neck. Chastity hides her face in her leather jacket just to be safe.

"My favorite grandniece," he says, "and Pleasanton's very own hot dog eating champion."

"Hello, doc," I say.

"How's the stomach?"

Before I can answer, he jams a light probe down my pie hole. "The lining is a little worn but still intact. I can see you had Beef 'n Cheeses for breakfast; curly fries, too, and some peanuts and pork chops and wait…what's that…it looks like a Pez dispenser."

"It got caught in the mix."

"Do you want me to fish it out?"

"I'll be fine."

The old country doctor studies me for a couple of seconds with a wry grin on his face. "Well, I guess you know what you're doing, seeing how you've mastered the art of rolling the intestine."

"What?"

"Don't worry, son, your secret is safe with me. I ventured into the Amazon once myself when I was young and in search of adventure. I learned many things from the native tribesmen about philosophy, economics, and even medicine. You should see their remedy for erectile dysfunction. My goodness, it feels like medieval torture but works like a charm."

I think I'm starting to blush.

Dr. Thurgood blinks a couple times. "You didn't really think a trained physician would believe that a seventeen-year-old zombie could hold two hundred seventy-three weenies in his stomach all at once, did you?"

"Two hundred seventy-five," I smile. "Don't forget the extra two that I ate to rub my victory in Doug Jerkins's face."

"What did you use, Dependables?"

"Yeah."

"Good choice."

Chastity clears her throat to break up the doctor-patient love fest. "Chris knows, Uncle Desmond."

"Knows what, dear?"

"About me."

A somber cloud washes over Dr. Thurgood's face, displacing the frivolity of our superficial banter, and he scans me from head to toe with the probing eyes of an overly protective father figure. "How did he find out?"

"We were hanging out together in the mallard garden when some rogues jumped us. Chris fought valiantly by my side, but a big son of a gun in a rugby shirt managed to get a bite out of my jugular." She lowers the collar of her jacket to expose the wound. "I need a little stitching up. Chris needs a steel rod for his spine, too."

The doctor eyes me again. "I noticed you were slouching, but I figured it was just bad posture. You know kids nowadays, hunched over their laptops all day playing Pac Man."

Without another word, the physician gets down to business, rummaging through utility closets and cabinets, checking drawers and peeking behind curtains. Finally, in a dark corner of his examination room, behind a faded plastic palm tree, he finds an aerosol can.

"Magic Seal," he blurts out. "It was developed by NASA back in the eighties to seal holes in the space shuttle. It was so versatile and easy to use that astronauts out on spacewalks could simply find the damage, point the can, and shoot. The rest was chemistry." He shakes the can vigorously. It sounds half full. "But after the space shuttle program was mothballed and NASA's budget was cut, the space agency had to sell off some of its intellectual property rights to cover overhead expenses for their food court. Magic Seal was conveyed unceremoniously to a Japanese conglomerate. Now a watered-down retail version is pitched in late-night infomercials by some bearded guy with an Australian accent. He likes to drone on and on about its long list of uses... sealing rain gutters, fixing leaky sinks, even plugging holes in the bottoms of fishing pontoons."

"I've seen those," I say.

Dr. Thurgood releases a wily grin. "What he hasn't figured out yet is its countless medical applications...off-label of course. I use it now and then for reconstructive surgery." He sprays the stuff on Chastity's wound and molds it to the contours of her neck with a wooden tongue depressor. Then he blows it down with a hair dryer for about two minutes. It smells like burning glue. "Voilà. Good as new."

And Chastity's neck does looks as good as new. The lines and symmetry are perfect, and the sinewy ridge that Dr. Thurgood sculpted even makes it look like she still has an artery running underneath the skin. There's only one hitch.

"The stuff is as black as tar."

"It only comes in one color. I've written the company numerous times requesting a line of various skin tones, but they're a little wary of promoting off-label applications that haven't been FDA approved. I guess they don't feel comfortable competing in the pharmaceutical space. I'm not sure why. They'd fit right in. They have a product made from chemicals that no one can pronounce with a list of possible side effects longer than my arm."

"I can cover it with my jacket," Chastity says, "maybe even draw a tattoo around it."

"No need for that, dear. The stuff is spray-paintable. All you kids need to do is go down to the hardware store and pick out a matching color. I think eggshell might be a good fit, or maybe ivory."

Chastity hugs her great uncle, and the man runs his hand

across the length of her jet black hair. "Have you considered returning to your natural hair color?" he whispers. "And washing some of that mascara off your face?"

"You know I can't do that, Uncle Desmond."

"Of course you can, child. There's nothing to be ashamed about. Plenty of great people have had the misfortune of transforming into zombies through no fault of their own. It's just like any other medical condition...leprosy or psoriasis or herpes, for example. Now you don't see society shunning those folks, do you?

"I guess not."

"Maybe Chris finding out about your secret is a sign. Maybe it's time to come clean. You've been carrying this weight around much too long."

"But my dad."

The cotton balls above Dr. Thurgood's eyes collide in a determined frown. "If that father of yours can't take the fact that his darling girl has become a zombie, you tell him to come talk to me. I have a few tricks up my sleeve. I could cut off his corticosteroid injections for starters, and if that doesn't make him relent, I could move onto his arthritis medication. Let's see him try to get out of bed in the morning without that."

"I love you, Uncle Desmond," Chastity says, hugging the man, "but I'm not ready."

"Are you sure?"

"Uh-huh."

"Well, what about this one? Can we trust him?" Sometime during their discussion, Dr. Thurgood managed to pick up a scalpel. I don't think he needs it for Chastity's procedure, but then again I'm no doctor. The way he's holding it though, as if ready to slash, is making me feel a little uncomfortable.

"Can I count on you to keep my secret, Chris?"

"Of course you can, baby."

"I knew I could." Chastity hugs me, and Dr. Thurgood coincidentally puts the scalpel back on the tray.

"I think Marvin suspects," she continues. "That's why he was asking me all of those questions in your basement the other day, about my makeup and attending your bonspiel."

"Don't worry about him. He's a good zombie."

"That might be, but if he keeps asking, I might need to take action."

"Let me worry about Marvin. I know how to handle him."

"Are you sure?"

"Of course I'm sure."

"Wonderful," Dr. Thurgood says. "I'd love to keep chatting with you young people. It keeps me in synch with the times. But I do have other patients on the docket for today. With the way the insurance companies try to squeeze us doctors, I need to fit in at least twenty examinations an hour to turn a profit. After you two, I have one hundred and twenty-seven more to go."

"What about Chris's back?"

"I haven't forgotten. I don't have any steel rods on hand at the moment, so we'll have to improvise." He searches the examination room again, finding what he needs in one of the utility closets. He grabs a mop and breaks it over his knee.

"Bend over," he says. "I can use this mop handle for now."

"Is it going to hurt?"

"Of course not. But I can't say it's going to be comfortable."

20

"This is the best we could come up with?" Chastity snaps, irate.

"It's a good plan."

"Yeah, maybe if we were still in the third grade. There's no way I can mention this to my sensei. He'd ban me from the dojo for a lack of military creativity."

"This isn't a military operation. It's a reconnaissance mission. There's a big difference. We have to be subtle about this... and convincing. All those years my mom made me attend Baby Thespians are finally going to pay off."

Reluctantly, my girlfriend fires up the GTO and peels out of my driveway. She's wearing a pair of sky-blue polyester slacks and a yellow and white blouse with carnations on it that we bought from Targette. I tried to get her to wear a pair of vinyl shoes with Velcro straps, too, but she patently refused. The black combat boots totally clash with the rest of her outfit, but I guess they'll have to do.

"This pillow is uncomfortable."

"Try a broom handle stuck up your you-know-what."

"Don't exaggerate, Chris."

Well, bolted to my vertebrae is the next worst thing. I feel like one of those aristocratic teenage girls from the eighteenth century – locked in my training corset while my suitor's mom inspects my posture with a level and a tape measure.

"You need to look like you've had a few kids," I say. "Marvin said that his mom is a size twelve."

"I don't think this pillow is big enough to bring me up to a size twelve."

"It will have to do. And put your wig on. Marvin said that his mom is a dyed blonde."

Chastity slams on the brakes and fishtails to the curb in front of Ernest's house. He's waiting on the lawn dressed in the same Halloween costume that he's worn for the past three years – the victim of an ax murderer. I'm sure psychologists from Seattle to Miami would have a field day with that one. I mean, the kid opts to be the victim of a murderer instead of the murderer himself. Talk about low self-esteem.

"Did I put enough blood on?" he asks.

"Get in the car."

"You'd better stay on that drop cloth," Chastity snaps, "or you might end up looking like that for real."

"You did a great job with your makeup," Ernest responds. "You look just like a zombie."

Chastity snarls and gives me the evil eye. I mean, what can I say? If we're going to pose as Marvin's parents, we have to look like zombies. They did all die from that same can of spoiled tuna. Little does Ernest know that Chastity took makeup off instead of putting more on. She's really going out on a limb on this one, but that's the kind of warrior princess I fell in love with. I readjust my short sleeve dress shirt and clip-on tie and add a couple of red pens to my pocket protector.

"And you look just like that guy at the DMV who failed me when I took my driving test," Ernest continues. "You two should be in show business."

Chastity peels out again, venting her frustration, and heads toward the south side of town. When we come to the railroad tracks, she slams on the brakes to protect her alignment. As we inch across to the other side, it sort of feels like we've slipped into another dimension. The road contains more potholes than asphalt; large brick tenements covered in soot and graffiti block out the sun; four or five liquor stores line every block with winos and hookers buzzing around them like busy bees. I swear

I can hear gunfire.

"Are you sure we're in the right place?" Ernest asks, paler than usual.

"Marvin said his family had to move to Zombietown."

"I thought this place was just a legend, you know, made up by our parents to make sure we minded our fingers and toes. My mom used to tell me that if I was ever a bad kid and got turned into a zombie, she would make me go live in Zombietown with some maggot-infested cousin I'm supposed to have."

"My dad just threatened cremation."

In case you're wondering, Zombietown is a sixteen square block area on the outskirts of Pleasanton where many of the town's zombies choose to reside. The rents are cheap, and the rats are ginormous. Technically, Zombietown isn't even part of Pleasanton. It's part of the dead zone; but in a never-ending effort to boost revenues, the mayor annexed the neighborhood a couple of years ago and made it an official territory. In exchange for basic social services, Pleasanton now gets to tax all of Zombietown's residents. Not surprisingly, the biggest social service that the residents of Zombietown receive is protection by the Border Patrol. A border guard in mirrored sunglasses is busy protecting the crap out of a teenage zombie right now. The teenager keeps mouthing back though, which makes the border guard protect him even harder.

"Leave him alone," Chastity screams from her window.

The border guard turns his head but seems uninterested in the three of us. Before he can continue serving the teenager though, Chastity whips out her phone and starts recording. That gets the lawman's attention, and he runs up to our car.

"Give me that phone."

Chasity burns rubber and ducks down an alley before he can get back to his monster truck. With the 389 cubic inch V8 purring and the radio turned off, we sit quietly in the alley for a good ten minutes. The monster truck cruises up and down the street about a dozen times but doesn't spot us in the alley. Eventually, the border guard loses interest and crosses back over the tracks to the better part of town. The teenage zombie scurries from behind a dumpster and crawls through a broken window on the far side of what once might have been a park.

"This place sucks," Ernest says,

"The conditions suck," I clarify.

"Come on," Chastity snaps. "Let's find Marvin and get out of here."

It takes us about another twenty minutes to distinguish Zombie Lane from Zombie Street, and Zombie Boulevard from Zombie Avenue...and my navigation app isn't much help. It keeps confusing the locations, directing us to a burned-out lot called Zombie Court. But we finally find our way out of the maze with a piece of paper called a *map* and pull up to 357 Zombie Terrace, where Marvin is sitting on the stoop, whistling. I think the tune is *We Are the Champions* by Queen.

"You guys are late," he says.

"We had a little run-in with a border guard."

"Yeah, they sure like to protect this neighborhood. Sorry for making you drive all the way out here, but my Toyota pickup finally broke down. The guy at the hardware store tells me he can install a new lawnmower engine, but it's going to cost me a hundred and fifty-seven simoleons, not including tax. So I'm stuck taking the bus to work until I can save up."

"It's no problem, Marvin. Why are you still wearing your Artie's uniform?"

"It's part of my costume."

"You were supposed to dress like a rogue."

"Well, what's a rogue supposed to dress like?"

The crickets start singing as we unravel the onion of that riddle. As a kid, I always envisioned rogues as bloodthirsty creatures, dressed in rags and rolling around in their own gore. But as I've recently learned, sometimes they can dress like frat boys and drive Suburbans. So I guess it's no stretch of the imagination to picture a rogue decked out in the full regalia of an Artie's uniform. After all, Marvin's paper hat is still pretty wrinkled.

"Did you bring your injection record?"

"Of course. Here."

I fold up the piece of paper and tuck it behind my pocket protector.

Chastity burns rubber again, only to slam on the brakes as we approach the tracks.

"Why don't you just drive up to the tracks slowly if you're so concerned about your alignment?" Ernest snaps. "You made me drop my frozen burrito."

"That's not how GTOs work."

"Oh."

"I still don't know why you're convinced that the Squid's head will be at the station," she says to Marvin.

"Where else would it be?"

"In a gutter or down a well, maybe."

"Great possibilities, but unlikely. If the mayor is up to no good, as we all suspect, and if he and the Squid used to be sweet on each other, as you two mentioned, then the only logical conclusion is that Mayor Shight took her head into custody. On the one hand, he can still be close to her. On the other hand, she can't reveal to the world whatever it is that got her killed."

"But maybe he's keeping her at his mansion."

"Possibly, but the security there can't be as strong as at the station."

"But the station has witnesses."

"Not in holding cell number nine."

A cold blanket smothers us at the mention of those words. *Holding cell number nine.* When Marvin and his family were detained during the mayor's zombie round up, they got put in holding cells number one and two. And of all the memoirs ever to make it to bookstores that told of the atrocities that allegedly occurred in the subterranean caverns of the Border Patrol station, the deepest level witnessed was level five. But number nine, which most kids believe is just another legend (the town has a lot of them), is the place where people get *disappeared.* Spies and traitors. Terrorists and political prisoners. Even those brave news anchors who dared to insist that their stories were true and not fake. If holding cell number nine actually exists, and I hope that it doesn't, it will be a place immersed in complete coldness, on account of the absence of God.

"Do you think that place is for real?" I ask.

"I do."

"Well, if no one ever returns from there, how on earth are we supposed to get you out, let alone the Squid?"

"Let me worry about that," Marvin says. "As with all good plans, I'll need to make some of it up as I go. You know, improvise, just like MacGyver."

"Good grief," Ernest says.

* * *

"Make it look real."

"We've got this, Chris. We must have rehearsed at least two or three times. Now you and Chastity get to your places." Marvin winks at my girlfriend. "You look pretty convincing as a zombie by the way."

"I noticed the same thing," Ernest adds. "She's got real talent."

"Shut up, losers," Chastity says. "Keep your mind on the plan and try not to screw anything up."

Marvin stretches out his arms and starts moaning.

"This isn't *Night of the Living Dead*."

"I'm just warming up."

"You need to act more like *28 Days Later*."

"Those weren't real zombies. They were more like rabies victims or something. Anyway, do *you* guys want to do this? I'd be happy to let you put your butts on the line when officers Larry, Curly, and Moe come running out of the station." Marvin pauses for a moment, but we have no response. "Okay then, please let an actor do his thing."

Chastity roundhouses a mosquito to stay lose, and I climb back into the GTO. It's parked across the street near a telephone pole, giving me a good vantage point of the action.

Marvin takes a deep breath and straightens his paper hat and finally starts howling at the Moon.

Ernest moans in anguish.

Chastity screams in her best horror flick shower-scene voice. "Help! Help! It's a rogue! It's a rouge! A rogue zombie is attacking that poor boy!"

When she pauses to take a breath, the crickets are echoing back.

She screams the same line again and again, and Marvin ratchets his growling up a few notches, but nobody comes out of the station. I thought this town was supposed to be on high alert, which is why the four of us are staging a zombie attack right in front of the building. But there's no response, not even a subtle peek through the blinds. I look at my watch, but it's only four in the afternoon. The station should still be open, even with banker's hours. I glance down the street, just in case a doughnut convention is in full throttle, but there's nothing going on, just old Mr. Carpenter lying on his bench and a few dozen tumbleweeds rolling by.

"Louder," I yell from the window.

Marvin and Ernest and Chastity scream and scream for another fifteen minutes until their vocal cords are shot. Then they walk back to the car to take a break. I hand them a few cold cuts and lemonade. Each person also gets two Oreos.

"No Beef 'n Cheeses?" Ernest quips.

"Marvin's car broke down, remember? He can't carry as much food with him on the bus."

Ernest looks to Marvin, flabbergasted.

Marvin shrugs his shoulders. "Sorry."

"What's wrong with these people?" Chastity yells. "Are they freaking deaf or something?"

"Maybe they're all out on patrol."

"Yeah, right. They're probably just playing cards down in one of the holding cells. Either that or sleeping on the job."

"My brother doesn't sleep on the job," Ernest says.

"He doesn't need to. He's barely awake as it is."

Ernest tries to respond, but his lips quickly realize that his brain hasn't come up with anything. So they remain silent.

"Everybody just calm down," I say. "We'll figure something out."

"We don't have time to calm down," Chastity says. "Besides, I have an idea."

"What?"

"Everybody just get back to your positions."

"Let me finish my cookies."

"Hurry up."

It takes Ernest awhile to finish because he likes to lick out the creamy center of each Oreo before nibbling the crispy cookie part. But he finally gets them down, and he and Marvin walk back to the front of the station. They don't look too happy. I think they were expecting twenty minutes for their break.

"Well, what's your idea?" Marvin asks.

Chastity picks up a brick and hurls it through the front window.

An alarm sounds off.

She runs back to the GTO.

A few seconds later, half a dozen border guards pour out of the station. Their moustaches look to be covered in flour, so I guess they were busy baking pizzas or pies or something. I know that firemen like to cook. It's not a stretch to imagine border guards flexing their own culinary muscles.

On cue, Marvin pretends to tear out Ernest's throat.

Sergeant Barry wipes the flour off his moustache and starts beating Marvin across the back with his baton. The fast food worker tries to claw the man, which makes him whack harder. Ernest falls to the ground, writhing. "Oh, I'm dead. That rogue zombie killed me. That rogue zombie needs to be locked up in holding cell number nine."

The border guards don't pay any attention to Ernest though and keep pummeling Marvin. He's on the ground now, covering his head, and his paper hat is in shambles.

"They're going to kill him," Chastity says. "This has gone too far. We need to do something now."

"Hold on," I say. "Marvin is a tough kid."

The border guards beat Marvin for another five minutes until they get winded; then a calm ensues, as with any storm. Marvin is lying face down on the asphalt now, not moving. His paper hat is in tatters at his side.

"Shoot, I think we waited too long."

Chastity glares at me.

"Let's kill this one before he turns," Sergeant Barry says.

Ernest springs up and grabs Marvin's hat. "It was just a gag. It was just a gag." He scurries to the GTO and dives into the back seat. Chastity hits the gas and fishtails down the street. In the side mirror, I watch the border guards scrape Marvin off the asphalt and carry his corpse into the station.

21

"You idiot," Chastity yells. "You let them kill Marvin. We should have saved him while we had the chance, but we just sat there like losers."

"He's a zombie, Chastity," Ernest says, gnawing on a Beef 'n Cheese. "They can't kill him. He's already dead."

"That's not what I mean."

Our foolproof plan hasn't exactly been foolproof. No one anticipated the level of ferocity that the border guards would unleash upon Marvin. That flour they were cooking with must have been bleached flour; that's the kind that Mom says can spike a person's blood sugar.

"I'm sorry. I let Marvin down." But what I really mean to say is that I let Chastity down. She was never keen on our plan, but I pushed it, and now poor Marvin might be in a million pieces.

"It's not over yet," she snarls. "Maybe he's not dead."

"Of course he's dead," Ernest says. "He's a zombie."

"Just eat your sandwich, Ernest."

The three of us sit in the Artie's parking lot for another half hour, not saying much, and the silence works its insidious poison into our bloodstreams. When he can't take the tension anymore, Ernest walks to the restaurant to refill his drink. The idiot still has his Halloween costume on. Chastity retrieves her grip strengtheners from the glove box and starts cranking down on them. I shuffle over to the dumpster and dive in head first. Dozens of stale and festering sandwiches succumb to my gnashing teeth, but they do little to assuage my guilt. I keep eating though because it's the closest I can come to Marvin without actually letting him roll my intestine from behind. So in his honor, I roll my own intestine, the way he taught me, and a big plop resonates against the dumpster's steel bottom.

"That load is for you, Marvin. I just wish I had a wicker basket."

The GTO's horn blares.

"It's seven o'clock," Chastity yells. "Come on."

I pull up my pants and take my place at shotgun. Ernest is in the back, rubbing a bruise on the side of his cheek.

"What happened to you?"

"I got jumped by some kindergarteners. They saw all the blood on me and figured I was a zombie piñata. Randy had to scare them off with a broom before asking me to leave the restaurant. He gave me this twenty-dollar gift card though in exchange for signing some waiver. It was a pretty good deal, except I didn't get to refill my drink."

"Are you guys ready?" Chastity says.

"Do you think it really matters now?"

"It always matters, Chris. We have to try." She stares into my eyes, deeper than ever before. "I'm so sorry that I called you an idiot. You know I didn't mean it. You're one of the smartest zombies I know. I just let my anger get the best of me and ran off at the mouth. I hope you can forgive me."

"Come here, baby. There's nothing to be sorry about."

She reaches for my backside, and I grab one of her dumplings, and as she maneuvers onto my lap, one of her elbows rubs against the horn.

"Get a room, guys," Ernest says.

"Sorry."

Chastity jumps back into the driver's seat and fixes her wig. Then she burns rubber out of the parking lot, nearly pancaking Mildred Manning. She's the chairwoman of the Laundromom Action Committee and a vocal supporter of the mayor's *kill-two-birds-with-one-stone* proposal.

"You missed her."

"There's always tomorrow."

"How do we know this plan can still work?" the future astronaut continues. "I mean, what if the Border Patrol contacted Marvin's real parents already?"

"Marvin said that his parents would be at Bingo all night. And that his little sister would be working at the cotton gin."

"That's delicate work."

"She has small fingers."

Within a couple of minutes, we're back at the station. Chastity pulls a one-eighty into the spot near the telephone pole, the same spot where we witnessed Marvin get beaten to a pulp. I have to say, the nostalgia is not pleasant.

"Are you ready?"

"Yeah."

She straightens my pocket protector and then rearranges the pillow down the front of her pants. "There's no way I'm going to pass for a size twelve. Size ten maybe, but not a size twelve."

"Don't worry. I don't think guys notice that sort of thing."

We leave Ernest waiting in the car and walk hand-in-hand into the station. The air inside is thick and hazy with a thin scent of something burning. Overhead fluorescent lights shine with the brightness of a small sun, and the faint murmurings of faceless whispers echo in the background. No one is at the front desk, so Chastity dings the bell. When no one comes, she dings it about a dozen more times. Finally, the desk sergeant emerges from a room behind frosted glass and stares down at us. He's about my parents' age, with the healthy beginnings of a chrome dome.

"Can I help you, ma'am?"

"Yes, we're here about our son, Marvin Reynolds. He and his friends were involved in some prank in front of the station, and you detained him. We got a message on our answering machine. We're here to pay the fine and take him home."

Sergeant Whitaker flips through a clipboard but doesn't seem to find anything.

"What did you say his name was again?"

"Marvin Reynolds?"

"And you are?"

"His mother and father, Mr. and Mrs. Reynolds."

The border guard looks us both up and down, spending most of his time somewhere between Chastity's neck and waistline. "Do you have your zombie identification papers?"

Chastity hands him a card, which Marvin swiped from his mom. Sergeant Whitaker studies the identification for a moment with flickering eyes. "This says here that you're a size twelve." He scans Chastity's torso once more. "You don't look like a size twelve to me. Size ten maybe, or a healthy size eight."

"I've been on a diet. A girl's got to watch her figure."

The line makes no sense, since zombies don't have any metabolism, but it seems to be enough to fill the void in the inquisitive border guard's mind. He relinquishes a subdued smile and hands back her card.

"And you?"

"I hand him Marvin's dad's card, and the man scans me like a laser printer. "The photo on your identification card shows four red pens in your pocket protector. I only see three."

"One of them ran out of ink."

He narrows his eyes and starts shaking his head.

"My husband can be a little inattentive at times," Chastity interrupts, batting her eyelashes. "You know how civil servants are, especially when the five o'clock hour approaches."

Sergeant Whitaker smiles wholeheartedly this time and hands back my card. "Don't I know it. You should replace that pen as soon as possible, sir. You never know when you might run into a stickler."

"Will do. And here is my son's injection record. He's no threat to the community. He's just a dumb teenager. You know what they can be like."

Sergeant Whitaker studies the piece of paper for a moment and then flips through his clipboard again. "I'm not seeing him, folks. Are you sure you were contacted by this station? We have checkpoints all along the border. Perhaps someone from one of those satellite locations called you."

"We got a call from your headquarters. We're sure of it."

The sergeant tightens his shoulders, the way that guy from the dry cleaner did that time Dad demanded to be reimbursed for a dress shirt that got torn. It's the *there's no freaking way you're going to get anything out of me* look. Of course the shirt had already been torn before Dad got it cleaned, but the dry cleaner did make the tear worse. The clerk probably should have given Dad something.

Chastity pivots her rear leg, and I can sense the potential energy gathering. Before she can crush Sergeant Whitaker's larynx with her shin bone though, we spot Marvin in the back room. He's covered in Band-Aids and is being led in cuffs by Buck (IQ=?).

"Marvin, my son," Chastity yells.

Marvin looks over. He seems to be in a chipper mood. "Hi, Mom. Hi, Dad."

"That's your son?" Sergeant Whitaker asks, lighthearted again. "Of course I know that boy. What a pistol he is. Some *moron* must have forgotten to put him on the list." The sergeant stares down Buck, who can't make eye contact.

"Apologize to Mr. and Mrs. Reynolds. I almost took them into custody for making me check the clipboard twice, and it would have been your fault."

"Sorry, Mr. and Mrs. Reynolds," he mumbles, clueless as to our true identities.

"That's okay, Buck," I say. "You can't help but be the way God made you."

"We were going to send your son straight to the crematorium and burn him into a pile of ash, but the rascal started telling jokes...damn good ones, with priests and strippers and water guns. He's quite the whip...had us all in stitches for over twenty minutes. But then a few pieces started falling off, on account of our protection services, so we had Nurse Patty patch him up. Except for the three hundred stitches, he's as good as new. I got to hand it to that boy. He's a stand-up kid, took a punch and didn't threaten to sue us like all those other peckerwoods. That kind of leadership commands respect around here. If he hadn't impersonated a rogue and interrupted our pizza party, we might have let him go."

"Well, we're here to take him home now," Chastity says. "How much is the fine? And how much do you recommend for the unofficial donation?" She digs into her purse, searching for the wad of hundreds that she "borrowed" from her dad, but Sergeant Whitaker takes her wrist and directs her to stop.

"That's awfully kind of you, ma'am. Not many customers volunteer their donations at first. It usually takes a bit of convincing. But keep your money. Your son can't go home with you tonight."

"Why not?"

"Well, that's the thing. If the boy had actually been a rogue, we might have worked out a deal to give him probation and deport him to the dead zone. I mean, a rogue can't help what he is…sort of like what you said about Buck, Mr. Reynolds. But the law is the law. Unfortunately for your son, the punishment for impersonating a rogue is the harshest punishment we can offer our customers – holding cell number nine."

"No."

"Since you're good people, I felt you should know." He winks. "But don't let anyone in on our little secret, okay? We're supposed to keep that place under wraps…adds to the mystique."

"Well, when can we bail him out? A day? A week? We can mortgage our house and raise a more sizable donation."

"That's very generous of you, ma'am, but I don't have an answer for you. The terms and conditions of his stay with us are above my pay grade." Sergeant Whitaker breaks eye contact with Chastity's torso, a little embarrassed. "I need to ask you to sign here, so that we have a record that your son's next of kin were notified."

"What's all the fine print?"

"Don't concern yourself with that. It's just lawyer speak. Something about forfeiting due process rights in exchange for bread and water. The district attorney says it's legit, so it's okay for you to sign."

"Well, if you already had a lawyer review it." Chastity signs Mrs. Reynolds's name, and I follow suit on behalf of Mr. Reynolds.

"Could you please give him this?" Chastity asks, batting her eyelashes again.

"I'm not supposed to give our customers anything, ma'am,

especially not from family members."

In a stroke of luck, the top buttons of Chastity's polyester blouse come undone and soften Sergeant Whitaker's stance. He blushes and looks to me, as if asking for permission. "Well, for a lovely lady like you, with such a snappy fashion sense, I can make an exception just this once."

Chastity strokes the man's arm and hands him Marvin's tattered paper hat.

"I'll make sure he gets it, ma'am. I can relate to the sanctity of a uniform."

"I know I can count on you."

Sergeant Whitaker barks at Buck to take Marvin down to the holding cells, but before the asswipe can process the order, Marvin shakes his head back and forth the way some folks from the far east do to signify the word *yes*. That's the sign. It means the fast food worker/superspy has found something.

The moment we leave the building, Chastity throws her wig to the ground and stomps it into dust. Then she tears the artificial down out of the pillow that's stuck in the front of her pants. It's like warm, fluffy snow. "I told you I wouldn't pass for a size twelve," she yells.

"You were right."

"This plan just keeps getting worse. How are we supposed to get Marvin out now?"

"I have no clue," I say, shrugging my shoulders. "I have no clue."

22

"Laundromom! Build a wall!"

"Laundromom! Build a wall!"

Amy and the other cheerleaders are leading a chant at a pep rally that Principal Dawson called to help raise awareness for the upcoming referendum. The girls are twirling and tumbling and flipping and twisting, and for some reason the red undies they usually wear beneath their skirts have narrowed to the size of dental floss. I'm not complaining; I mean, if the cheerleaders find that the new underpants improve their performance, who am I to question their fashion sense? It's part of a larger trend across other female sports, beach volleyball being a great example.

Principal Dawson announced that the pep rally would be an unbiased venue for objective debate. In fact, there's actually going to be a debate – between Chad Parker, the three-letter athlete who supports the mayor's plan, and our very own Ernest Pratt, who was handpicked by the principal herself to represent the zombie's side. The educator said that she selected Ernest on account of his razor-sharp wit and recent improvement in grades. I don't know about his wit, but his grades have certainly improved, especially since he got placed in the *tap into your potential* studies curriculum.

The future astronaut has taken the responsibility seriously and spent the past three days holed up in his room researching the issues. Chastity and I offered to help him, but he turned our offer down, claiming that it was his one opportunity to prove to the world and the doctors that they were wrong about him. What was I supposed to say? I mean, I had my moment on stage with over two hundred undigested weenies crammed into my Dependables...and it was glorious. I guess Ernest deserves his shot at stardom, too.

He's fidgeting in the bleachers next to me right now, nervous as hell, almost as nervous as Chastity and me.

"Look at all those signs," Chastity snaps, dressed in black from head to toe. "I thought this was supposed to be an unbiased debate."

About fifty signs and posters adorn the walls of the school gymnasium, and they all say *Laundromom*, *Build a Wall*, or *Ban Zombies from Prom*.

"I guess Principal Dawson meant that the First Amendment is alive and well," Ernest responds. "Maybe it was up to each side's supporters to mobilize their grassroots efforts. Amy and her gang were obviously pretty busy. Why didn't you guys put up any posters?"

I look to Chastity, and she looks to me. I mutter the first thing that comes to mind. "I hope Marvin is okay. You need to do well for Marvin's sake."

"You're changing the subject."

"No, I'm not. I'm just trying to keep you focused on the important issues."

"Yeah, Ernest, don't be so insensitive," Chastity says.

"Sorry, guys. I don't know what came over me."

"That's okay."

Principal Dawson struts across the gymnasium floor, clapping her hands, and the cheers of the crowd slowly subside to a simmer. She's wearing a new mink coat and diamond earrings and a gold chain that would make any '80s rapper proud. The school carnival must have done pretty well this year.

On cue, Lenny Stiles, the magic wand thief, runs onto the court with a microphone in hand. He adjusts the sound equipment to its lowest position and then places a milk crate beneath it so that the diminutive educator can reach the mouthpiece.

There's some kind of writing on the crate that I can't make out.

"Can you see what that crate says?"

Chastity squints her hawk eyes. "It's Cyrillic. It says beluga caviar."

"Oh."

"Ladies and gentlemen," the principal says, raising her arms to quell the vestigial murmurings. "I am so happy that all of you could attend our mandatory pep rally this fine spring morning. I've been an educator for over twenty-five years, and I have to say that I've never had the privilege of speaking to a finer crowd than this." Lenny Stiles holds up a sign that reads *Applause*, and the bleachers respond with lukewarm clapping. "Thank you. You are too kind. But enough about me. The true reason we are here to today is to celebrate the spirit of democracy and engage in a healthy debate that might very well determine the fate of our lives." She pauses for a moment to let the full weight of her words percolate through the clay of our young minds. "As you must have heard by now, our beautiful city is under siege. Over the past six weeks, fifty-three of Pleasanton's citizens have fallen to the gnashing teeth of the rogue zombie horde. Mayor Shight, in his vast wisdom, has put forth a proposal to relocate our law-abiding zombie friends and colleagues to the dead zone until these rogues can be flushed out and brought to justice. Most of the town is already in favor of the plan, and I for one will vote in the affirmative in next week's referendum. I hope and pray that your parents will do the same and that those of you who have reached that magical age of draft eligibility will also follow suit. It's a good proposal. It is fair and just. And it harkens back to the legendary leadership of former President Arse, before that B-movie director turned politician led a witch hunt to bring the great man down." Again Principal Dawson pauses to let the gravity of her words sink in. Ernest starts picking his nose.

"This is crap," Chastity whispers.

Amy Fairchild coughs in the background a few times to make sure the principal can hear her.

"And just like peaches and cream, our very own cheerleading captain has worked hard to do her part, collecting the requisite number of signatures to put before the student council a proposal banning all zombies from prom. The vote is next week, the day after the referendum. I urge all of the student council members to vote with their conscience and vote in the affirmative for the ban. I also beseech the greater student populace to exercise their democratic muscles and put pressure on the student council members to vote for the ban. In the spirit of democracy, aggressive exercising of your liberties will not be a punishable offense."

The five-foot educator strokes her solid gold chain and readjusts her diamond earrings. "As you also know, Morbid High School takes great pride in its commitment to vanquishing ignorance. Our communal test scores are strong. In fact, the state superintendent of education recently informed me that Morbid High has moved to the top of the lowest quartile in overall achievement. Do you hear that people? The *top* of the lowest quartile. If that's not cause for celebration, I don't know what is."

Again, Lenny Stiles holds up the *Applause* sign, and this time the crowd responds with a little more enthusiasm – forty decibels worth, maybe.

"That means at least half of you can read. The other half can just take my word for it. Great work...and I mean that. You all deserve a round of applause." Lenny's sign goes up again, and the crowd hits fifty decibels. "But high performance, ladies and gentlemen, requires high responsibility. And a great learning institution such as ours must do its damnedest to continuously exercise the tenets that make this country great – education, healthy debate, and tolerance. That is why today's debate must remain objective and unbiased. Do you hear me? Although the issue has already been decided, each side will get equal time to be heard."

"She doesn't sound unbiased to me," I say.

Chastity rolls her eyes.

"We have two of Morbid's finest representing each side of the debate today. On the pro side we have our beloved Chad Parker, star wide receiver, all-state basketball guard, and future NFL first-round draft pick."

The crowd blares out this time.

"And representing the con side we have Ernest Pruitt, chess club member, clarinet player, and what does it say here? Oh yeah, avid curler."

No one cheers, except for the crickets.

"You go, Ernest!" Chastity screams, reaching for her blouse.

But Sissy Slupchek beats her to the punch and tears off her shirt, screaming Ernest's name as best as she can through her orthodontic headgear. Her bra looks a lot different than Chastity's, like it has cones or small lampshades tucked inside of it.

"Finally," Chastity says, "someone else with spirit."

Chad takes his place behind a lectern. Chastity and I push Ernest out of the bleachers so hard that he face plants on the hardwood floor. He looks a little dazed at first but quickly recovers. The adrenaline rush will do his brain some good.

"I approached Pleasanton's very own Kirk Karson, the news anchor, to be the moderator for today's debate, but the arrogant man insisted on compiling his own independent questions. That seemed like a big waste of time to me, since we already know the correct answers. So I decided to moderate today's debate myself, keeping it within the family."

Ernest finally makes it behind his lectern, greener than he gets after eating week-old Beef 'n Cheeses. He looks as nervous as hell, and I hope for the sake of his credibility that he doesn't vomit.

"The rules are simple. I will ask a question, and each side will have two minutes to respond." Principal Dawson flips a coin onto the back of her hand and reads the result. "Chad Parker will start with the first question. Let's begin."

"Mr. Parker, tell me how the mayor's *kill-two-birds-with-one-stone* plan could possibly be wrong. Everyone in town already seems to support it, so why would some naysayer have the gall to waste people's time and claim that it's bad policy?"

Chad furrows his brow, exhibiting an attempt at introspection. I get the sense that his posturing was rehearsed. "The mayor's plan can't be wrong; that's the whole point to this debate, and anybody who speaks out against it simply doesn't know the facts. Mayor Shight, in his great wisdom, put together a strategy to save our lives. The least that we can do is help the man do the job that our parents elected him to do."

"Very good, Mr. Parker. That answer is correct. Now Mr. Pruitt, could you possibly have anything intelligent to say in response to such a compelling argument?"

Ernest is dead silent and hasn't stopped picking his nose. Swaths of the crowd are snickering, and my friend's credibility is plummeting off a cliff the way the stock market did back in '08. His hue is red now, and it looks like he can't breathe.

"Is he choking?" Chastity asks.

I look around our seats and spot his inhaler lying next to a Beef 'n Cheese wrapper. "Ernest, here!" I scream, tossing the albuterol toward him.

It tumbles over and over through the air, almost in slow motion, and Ernest extends his arm straight up and jumps, catching the tiny canister with his fingertips. He takes two hits, then inhales a gulp of air. His color returns to the usual chalk water.

"A closer reading of the mayor's proposal suggests that his plan violates Section 3, paragraph 12 of the 28th Amendment. Although it is true that due process is suspended for zombies residing in the dead zone, the 28th Amendment certainly does not suspend due process for zombies residing anywhere else, unless a probable and specific cause can be shown for each zombie in question that he or she poses a grave threat to the health, well-being, or economic viability of his or her family, neighbors, or community. Since the zombies that Mayor Shight wants to relocate currently reside within Pleasanton city limits, this due process protection is currently in effect. According to Section 27, subparagraph 16b of the aforementioned amendment, the mayor therefore must demonstrate with incontrovertible proof that each individual zombie he wants to relocate has failed the above-mentioned test, and he must prove it in a public hearing, where each defendant is entitled to competent legal counsel provided to him at the city's expense." Ernest scans the crowd, his head held high. "The mayor simply cannot enforce an overly broad policy across a general population. That clearly violates due process."

Chad's face assumes that moronic expression it gets when a

substitute teacher is unaware of his exempt athletic status and asks him an academic question in class. Principal Dawson stares desperately at Amy, as if the cheerleader forgot to plant a bucket of pig's blood in the rafters above Ernest's head. The rest of the crowd is just listening to the crickets sing.

"Mr. Pruitt, I will ask you politely not to confound the issue by throwing a bunch of legalese at the student body. This is a place of learning, not ambulance chasing." Principal Dawson turns to the crowd. "I will remind all of you what Pleasanton's very own Sergeant Barry once told us during one of our very popular lunch 'n learns: *if you're innocent, then you don't need a lawyer.* I hope to God you're not trying to hide something, Mr. Pruitt, with all of that fancy legal talk."

Ernest just shrugs his shoulders.

"Now onto our next question. Mr. Pruitt, if you are so convinced that the Border Patrol can effectively apprehend the rouge zombies in our midst without relocating the law-abiding zombies to the dead zone, then please tell us the identities of those rogues. Instead of playing games, you could save everyone a lot of time and money."

"How am I supposed to know that?"

"Exactly. Now what do you have to say on this topic, Mr. Parker?"

"I've never been one to maintain airs, fellow classmates. I'm a straight shooter and call things the way I see them. Of course I don't know who the rogue zombie assailants are, and unlike Mr. Pruitt, I would never pretend to know. That's why we need to implement the mayor's plan; so that we can bring those filthy rogues to justice and save our town."

A few cheers ring out. The crowd seems to be responding to Chad's straight talk.

"Correct again, Mr. Parker," the principal says. "Now, Mr. Parker, wouldn't you say that the temporary relocation of Pleasanton's zombies to the dead zone will have absolutely no detrimental effect on the town's economy? After all, we all know that zombies contribute little to our society, don't pay their taxes, and commit all kinds of heinous crimes. So isn't it safe to say that relocating the zombies is a positive thing?"

"Yes," Chad says, unsure of what else to say. He starts sniffing his nose, as if experiencing an allergy attack; then he takes a big gulp of water. I think Principal Dawson accidentally stole his line. She narrows her eyes at him, coaxing him to keep talking. "Yes, the temporary relocation of Pleasanton's zombies to the dead zone will have absolutely no detrimental effect on the town's economy. After all, we all know that zombies contribute little to our society, don't pay their taxes, and commit all kinds of heinous crimes. So isn't it safe to say that relocating the zombies is a positive thing?"

The crowd doesn't cheer this time, more confused than anything else.

"Mr. Pruitt, do you have any additional exaggerations to share with us today?"

"Ernest Pratt. My name is Ernest Pratt, not Pruitt."

"Whatever," the principal says. "I hope you realize that you're using your two minutes."

Ernest clears his throat. "Relocating the zombies would levy a devastating blow to Pleasanton's economy. According to recent Department of Labor statistics and the town's own biannual *Survey of Economic and Urban Commerce*, zombies contribute 37% of Pleasanton's gross domestic product and 49% of its tax base. That number rises to 54% once you factor in property taxes and additional zombie-specific surcharges. As to compliance, over the past ten years zombies on average have paid their taxes 99.97% of the time, while humans have only achieved an 88.52% compliance rate over the same time period. As far as crime rates go, a recent report commissioned by the sheriff's office and titled *Incidents of Violence, The Human/Zombie Benchmark Study*, clearly states that violent crimes perpetrated by zombies within town limits have averaged 3 in every ten thousand of the population over the past twenty years, while violent crimes perpetuated by humans have averaged 347 in every ten thousand over the same time period. As you can plainly see, the facts speak for themselves. Zombies are not only a safe, law-abiding, and valuable addition to our community, they are essential for its health and well-being."

A few folks in the audience start clapping, then a few more.

"Mr. Pruitt," Principal Dawson snaps, visibly flustered. "Chad Parker would be the first to tell you that the website ZombieHaters.com clearly states that zombies commit more crimes and contribute less to the economy than their average human counterparts."

"What statistics does that website list?"

"Let's not confuse details with the main point, Mr. Pruitt. Let's stick to straight talk. What's important to note is that zombies contribute less, and there's a reputable website out there that has the facts."

"Have you corroborated those facts with independent, government-sponsored sources?"

"I don't need to."

"Why not?"

"Because if it's on the internet we know it's true."

A few chuckles erupt in the stands, and Principal Dawson turns as red as a tomato. She must realize that my man Ernest has outmaneuvered her. She takes a deep breath and turns her back to the audience, releasing a loud snorting sound with her nose. The tension must have triggered her allergies, too.

"My facts come from reputable, governmental sources that anyone can look up and verify," Ernest continues. "I'm not sure why you keep insisting that zombies are a drag on our community when the facts simply tell the opposite story."

"Let's just say that Mr. Parker has alternative facts," the Principal says, not making eye contact. "Alternative facts are part of any healthy, democratic debate. They're the fundamental indicator of opens minds. You're not suggesting that we all act like mindless robots and accept the same set of facts as you, are you Mr. Pruitt?"

Ernest looks to me and Chastity in the stands, completely astonished.

"Exactly. Now let's move on. The next question is yours, Mr. Pruitt." The pint-sized educator pulls a calculator out of her mink coat. "What is the square root of 5,678?"

"75.3525."

"What is the cube root of 1,678,232?"

"118.83672."

"What is the capital of Botswana?"

"Gaborone."

"Wait a second." Principal Dawson taps the screen of her cell phone for about twenty seconds. "Damn. Lucky guess."

Chatter is sweeping through the crowd like plague through medieval Europe...one in every three or two, depending on what source you cite, is making noise. The commotion-wave slams into Chastity and me and froths into a crescendo. We can't help but chant in unison with the mob. "Go, Ernest. Go, Ernest. Go, Ernest. Go, Ernest."

"Man," Chastity says, "Ernest sure prepared for this debate."

"That boy definitely knows how to surf the web."

"Hold it down," Principal Dawson screams. "Hold it down."

The crowd doesn't respond to her, so Amy Fairchild yells into a megaphone. "Shut up, you losers. The debate isn't over yet." When the crowd doesn't respond to her either, she winks at Wanda Lopez, and the two of them perform a series of twenty-seven backflips which somehow manage to wedge their red dental floss undies even deeper into their goldmines.

The crowd settles down, confused by their own competing motivations – an underdog overcoming the odds stacked against him, or cheerleaders' skimpy underwear.

"Give me a question, Principal Dawson," Chads yells, capitalizing on the vacuum.

"Mr. Parker, how many state championships have you helped lead the team to?"

"Three."

"Why do you like Wanda Lopez so much?"

"She has a huge best-white smile."

"Why do you think that Ernest Pruitt is weaving a basket of lies?"

Chad smiles, at home within his element. "Well, I can tell you this. In the third grade, he made me slug him in the stomach. The little rat wouldn't turn over his lunch money and left me no other choice. The point is, he crapped his pants. And since Nurse Cindy wouldn't let him use her phone to call his mom because he smelled so bad, he had to finish off the school day reeking like poop. That's why we used to call him Stinky Ernest.

I mean, how can you believe the word of someone who walked around all day smelling like poop? I know I sure don't. I could never believe the made-up facts of someone named Stinky Ernest."

On cue, Amy and the other cheerleaders start a chant. "Stinky Ernest! Throw Him Out! Stinky Ernest! Throw Him Out!"

The crowd wastes no time joining the frenzy. "Stinky Ernest! Throw Him Out! Stinky Ernest! Throw Him Out!"

Ernest is green again, a bug pinned to a Petri dish. He tries to step away from the lectern, but Doug Jerkins blocks his path.

"This is ridiculous," Chastity screams, reaching for her blouse.

But once again Sissy Slupchek beats her to the punch. "Leave him alone," she slurps. "Ernest is smarter than the rest of you combined, smart enough even to find Sasquatch someday. This isn't a debate. This is a three-ring circus. I know you good people don't mean to behave this way. That horrible ringmaster has just whipped you into a frenzy, feeding on the hatred of society's underlying prejudices. Don't be tricked. Don't be manipulated. You're too smart for that. Grab ahold of reason and put an end to this madness."

Principal Dawson grins like the Big Bad Wolf and looks to Chad. "I'm just trying to moderate an open debate here," she says. "And these hecklers, not very attractive ones I must add, just can't help but interrupt. I guess they feel bad about themselves for being poor and stupid and want to get their fifteen seconds of fame. Well, we won't fall for their tricks. We're on a mission, you see; we're on a mission to make this city great again."

"Make this city great again!" Amy cheers. "Make this city great again!"

The crowd follows suit once more. "Make this city great again! Make this city great again!"

Principal Dawson scans the gym with narrow, beady eyes. "I wouldn't be surprised or offended in any way if someone were to beat the crap out of such a rude person like that heckler. I might even look the other way and tear up any reprimands."

The crowd takes a few moments to process what the principal said, then closes in on Sissy. She whips out her clarinet and starts swinging, but the mob is too thick with bloodthirsty patriots, and they're coming at her from all sides.

Without missing a beat, Ernest stomps on Doug Jerkins's foot and races for the bleachers. I toss his clarinet through the air, and just as with the inhaler, the future astronaut leaps with an outstretched hand and grasps the woodwind with his fingertips. He joins Sissy, pressing his back to hers, and together they swing at the mob with everything they have.

"We need to help them," Chastity says.

"Come on."

Chastity starts punching and kicking, cutting a path to our friends; and something called inspiration swats me in the back of the head. I whip out the bottle of ketchup that I keep in my coat pocket (you never know when it will come in handy) and smear the zesty sauce across my face and neck. Then I stretch out my arms and start growling. The kids in my immediate vicinity step away in horror, so I start gnashing my teeth at them for added effect. Soon my ploy goes viral.

"It's a rogue, run!"

"Watch out, it's a rogue. Don't let it bite you."

"It killed Principal Dawson, ripped out her throat."

"Get her gold chain. She doesn't need it anymore."

The mob dissolves into chaos. Arms and legs flail everywhere, while shrieks and screams echo off the rafters. And somewhere in the melee, a bit of hysteria overcomes me, too. The gnashing and biting and clawing and growling somehow feel natural, a power buried deep within my soul that has ventured to the surface for the first time. I actually want to rip the throat out of one of these idiots and transform his flesh into fodder for my Dependables. But I realize such a lapse would be stupid. Consuming human flesh is the quickest way for a zombie to turn rogue, and once rogue, there's no coming back. But the sensation is so powerful that I snap my teeth within inches of Wanda Lopez's jugular. The cheerleader shrieks and kicks me in the walnuts.

"Brilliant idea!" Chastity yells. "You can stop now."

But I don't.

"Chris, stop."

I run after Cherry Kwan, the captain of the gymnastics team, and just as I have the pipsqueak's ponytail in my hand, Chastity puts me in a choke hold.

"Calm down. We need to get out of here."

"Okay," I gurgle.

"When are you due for your next injection?"

"The tenth."

"Of May?"

"Yeah."

"It's the thirteenth, you idiot."

"My bad."

"Let's get you to Uncle Desmond. He'll set you straight."

And with that, Chastity, Ernest, Sissy, and I bolt for the GTO. Chastity hits the gas, and torrents of burning rubber fill the air. It's the first time in my life that I've ever cut class.

23

"Why do we have to do this at night?"

"Because that's when the full moon is out."

"I thought that was for werewolves."

"Don't be silly. Werewolves don't exist."

We raced straight to Dr. Thurgood's office at over one hundred miles an hour, where the wily physician jammed a syringe deep into my arm, hitting bone. The Dexapalm 90 injection took, but just barely. I feel normal again, thank God, dead and numb. Since I'm dating his grandniece, Dr. Thurgood held off on reporting me to the Border Patrol. While waiting in his office, Chastity was struck by a bolt of inspiration.

"Are you sure this will work?"

"No, but the *Book of the Dead* that I checked out of the library suggested that it might. We have a full moon; now we just need a little blood from a virgin."

We all turn to Sissy Slupchek, waiting. "Don't look at me," she says, practically offended.

"What do you mean?"

"Band camp."

Ernest seems crestfallen. "What are we going to do now?"

We all scratch our heads, falling into the trap of that ugly monster called *stereotype*. Sissy and Ernest just assume that Chastity isn't a virgin because she's superhot and was once a cheerleader. All of us assume that a virgin, in the context of any kind of supernatural ritual, has to be female.

Sissy is the first to open her mind. "What about you, Ernest?"

"What about me?"

The woodwind aficionado raises her eyebrow.

"What about Chris?" Ernest tries.

"He's got zombie blood," she responds. "That won't work. Plus, he's dating Chastity. There's no way he could still be a virgin."

I want to correct her, to let her know that despite my not-so-subtle hints and innuendo, Chastity has been too preoccupied with saving Marvin and the town to finish what we started that night in the mallard garden. But I don't. That's Chastity's and my personal business. Besides, I kind of like the idea of having a rep.

"Come on, Ernest," Chastity says.

The future astronaut holds out his finger and looks away. Chastity pulls a bowie knife from her leather jacket and gently places it beside the bust of Colonel Morbid. Then she takes a sewing needle and pricks Ernest's finger. "We just need a drop. Hold still." She squeezes the finger until it turns bright red and lets a drop of blood fall onto the face of the casket. Then she hands Ernest an alcohol wipe. "Wipe thoroughly. You don't want that to get infected."

"The grave wasn't as deep as I thought it would be," I say.

"What would you say, two feet?"

"Barely."

"I still got a blister," Ernest says.

Chastity rolls her eyes and opens the *Book of the Dead*, flipping through the skin parchment to her place on page 87. I shine a flashlight on the text so she can read it. It's in the original Latin, so I'll translate as she goes.

"By the power of all that is dead in the universe and according to the covenant forged in ancient times, I command you to rise, son of the dead, and embrace the miserable fate that destiny has pinched you with."

"Pinched?" Ernest says.

"That doesn't make any sense," Sissy slurps.

Chastity and I confer a bit over ancient Latin inflections. The best that we can come up with is that the text predates the empire. "My bad," she says. "I command you to rise, son of the dead, and embrace the miserable fate that destiny has *cursed* you with."

We wait for a few seconds, but nothing happens, so Chastity raises her arms and repeats the incantation. This time, a cacophony of thunder and lightning fills the sky, despite the lack of clouds, and a gust of wind blows leaves across our faces like a sandblaster. But still nothing happens, so she tries a third time.

When still nothing happens with the casket, Chastity gets pissed off and hurls the *Book of the Dead* into the same bush where Ernest relieved his bladder a few minutes ago. "Screw this," she says, grabbing an ax. She strikes the face of the casket, and the zip of a broken vacuum seal whistles out. She then strikes the casket about a dozen more times and uses one of our shovels to pry away the pieces. The rest of us help her.

Lying there with arms crossed, dressed in the full regalia of his Confederate uniform, is Colonel Morbid. His eyes are closed, and his beard is disheveled, but his skin tone and tautness resemble those of any run-of-the-mill zombie his age. The hermetic seal of his casket must have kept him from rotting.

"Check out that sword," Ernest says, reaching for it.

"Don't do that?"

"Why not?"

"Because in all the movies, that's exactly what the dumbass teenager does before getting eaten alive."

"Good point. What do we do now then?"

"We wait," Chastity says.

"But what makes you think he was infected before he died?" Sissy asks. "The first reported case of the zombie virus raising the dead was in '68, with that insurance salesman. You all learned about that in class. You can't get infected after you're dead."

"That insurance guy was the first reported case of the modern era, whatever that means. I think the virus has been around a lot longer."

"What makes you say that?"

"Because there's a two-thousand-year-old, pissed-stained

book that I just checked out of the library that talks about the undead hordes."

"But the incantation didn't work."

"You can't throw out the baby with the bathwater."

We all mull over Chastity's words for a minute, and even if everything that she said is true, a minor detail keeps clawing at the back of my throat. "I hate to spoil the party, but if he was infected with the virus before he died, he might come back as a rogue. It's been like a hundred plus years since he blew out his own heart with a shotgun."

Chastity bites her lip, annoyed. "We'll just have to take that chance."

So we sit and wait...forever it seems. Now I don't know if you've ever been in a cemetery at night beside a pond filled with rotting mallard carcasses, waiting for the corpse of a Confederate colonel to reanimate and help you save your town, but if you have, then you'd know how slowly time can move. Tick-tock, tick-tock, like a crippled slug. It's maddening.

"Stop it," Chastity snaps.

"What?"

"Stop saying tick-tock."

"Sorry, I must be thinking out loud."

"I do that sometimes," Sissy says. "Usually in class when I'm developing my strategies to track down Sasquatch or catch a chupacabra. Can you imagine how much money a zoo would pay for one of those things? Millions. I'd be set for life...we're talking private jets, a house in Malibu, even an unlimited supply of clarinet reeds so that I don't have to keep using the same one. I'm not as crazy as everyone says. I'm an entrepreneur, just like that dead guy who invented the smartphone."

"I don't think you're crazy," Ernest says, taking her hand. "We all have dreams, Sissy. Mine is to fly to Mars and moon the camera."

"That's so cool."

"Thanks. If I've learned anything in this life, I've learned that you can't ever let anyone poop on your dream. They'll try, out of envy or just plain narrow-mindedness, and even call into question your sanity when they don't have the brainpower to fully understand your vision; but you can't let them discourage you. You can't let them shame you. Because if you do, then you're letting them diminish all of us, stifling a ray of sunshine before it has the chance to kiss the morning dew."

"Oh, Ernest. I think you might be a genius."

"And I think you might be the prettiest girl in all of Pleasanton."

The two kiss and then roll into the bushes sucking on each other's tonsils. Sissy's orthodontic headgear nearly puts out one of Ernest's eyes, but she undoes the fifteen straps holding the gear in place and flings it onto one of the mallard corpses. Then she takes the future astronaut's hand and brings it to her best-white smile.

The feeling of amore is in the air.

I press my lips to Chastity's, and they're a bit more lukewarm than usual, so I walk her to the edge of the pond, where the moonlight shines like a waterfall of diamonds on a dozen mallard corpses. It only takes a minute for the ambience to work its magic. She grabs my backside, and I go for her bra, and this time I have it undone in fifty-seven seconds flat. A bashful girl, she leads me by the hand behind a tree where Ernest and Sissy can't see us.

"I love you, Chris."

"I love you, too, Chastity."

"I don't know what's come over me, but the moonlight and the stench of the rotting ducks and the sight of Colonel Morbid lying in an open casket…it's too much for a girl to resist. I want you to take me. I want you to take me now."

She hands me protection…I'm not sure why…and I struggle with the wrapper for a few seconds. When I pause to look for the instructions, she helps me put it on, and it takes all of my visualization skills not to get ahead of myself. Sorry, Grandma McGillicutty.

"Go ahead," she says. "I'm ready."

And I do what no other boy, alive or dead, has ever done before. I remove Chastity Sky's black leather combat boots.

She coos when I do it, on account of the soothing breeze, and I stroke the tips of her toes and the arches of her feet. When

I get to the massive bite mark above her left Achilles tendon, I tease it with my tongue before showering it with tender kisses. That gets her cooing some more, and she closes her eyes, waiting for me. The moment is everything that I've always dreamed about and then some, because in my fantasies I never got to remove a Goth chick's footwear. The rest of the act almost seems anticlimactic. But I like to finish what I start, so I position myself on top of Chastity and lean toward her secret chamber.

"That's not it, baby," she whispers.

So I try again.

"That's still not it."

Before I can try a third time, a series of grunts leaks out of the bushes.

"What's that?" she says, sitting up.

"Nothing, baby. Lie back down."

"I heard something."

"It's just Ernest or Sissy. Don't worry about them."

"Are you sure?"

"Of course, I'm sure. Just relax and let a hot dog eating legend work his magic on you."

Chastity lies back down, but I can tell she's been knocked out of the mood. Her eyes are wide open, struggling to help her ears scan the environs, and her legs are clamped shut like a bear trap. I'm not kidding about that either. My girlfriend has third-degree black belt legs, capable of snapping small trees.

"Relax, baby. You just need to relax."

"Someone get my leg," a low, gravelly voice reverberates.

Chastity jumps into her combat boots and refastens her bra. The jeans and sweater come next.

Damn it.

"It's the colonel," she says, running toward his casket. "It's the colonel."

She nearly knocks the man over when she barrels into him with a hug, but the veteran of countless bloody campaigns steadies himself against his own granite likeness. If I didn't know any better, I'd say that Chastity just reunited with a long lost grandfather.

"Why hello there, little lady. Where's the funeral? And does your husband know you're out here unaccompanied?"

"I'm not married. This is my boyfriend, Chris."

The colonel looks me up and down without emotion. "You need a little sunshine, boy. Maybe a dose of arsenic, too, to help get the blood flowing."

Ernest and Sissy scurry out of the bushes, sucking wind and wearing each other's shirts. A feather is sticking out of Sissy's orthodontic headgear.

The colonel flinches when he notices her. "You need to see my surgeon, young lady, right away. That shrapnel will cause infection if you don't have it removed."

"Huh?"

"Where am I?"

"Pleasanton, IL."

"Where's that?"

"It's about a hundred and some odd miles southwest of Chicago."

The colonel blinks his eyes and furrows his impressive brow. "That sounds like where Morbid, IL is, son. How can two towns be in the same place at once?"

Chastity and I exchange glances. She seems happy to take the lead on that question. "Well, Colonel, it's a long story. Why don't you take a seat, and I'll fill you in. A lot has happened since you blew out your heart with a shotgun."

Colonel Morbid reaches for his heart through instinct. The medals on his chest clang like wind chimes. "Do you mean to say I'm dead?"

"Well, sort of."

"Damn it. I knew I shouldn't have reached into that beehive. I just needed a bit of honey for my afternoon tea." He winks at Chastity. "This old war dog succumbs to a bit of the sweet tooth now and again."

"A beehive?"

"Yes, ma'am. I'm allergic to bees. Have been since I was a little boy. I think one of those buggers might have stung me. Last thing I remember was not being able to breathe."

I don't think the rest of us are breathing, either. Of course Chastity and I don't need air to survive since we're rotting corpses, but Ernest and Sissy do, and they're looking a little blue right now. It might the moonlight, but I suspect it's the shock of learning that the legend we've heard since birth about the town's founder blasting his own heart out with a shotgun is nothing more than a load of crap.

Chastity shares the legend with the colonel.

He begins to chuckle. "Who kills himself by shooting out his own heart? If you're going to do it, do it right and aim for the head. It must have been Captain Townsend, spinning a yarn. He always was the dramatic type." The colonel's eyes narrow. "He was always a bit light in the britches, too, if you know what I mean. Shied away from violence. Can you imagine that? That's probably why he said I only killed a thousand Yankees. The number is closer to ten thousand. But who's counting?"

Ernest is struggling to say something, and the word finally breaks loose. "Wow."

"Never a woman or child," the colonel continues. "And never a man who surrendered. Although I have to admit, I didn't give folks much time to raise a white flag before I came in shooting."

Colonel Morbid spins the cylinder of his pearl-handled Walker .44 and blows through the barrel. "Needs some oil. Now would one of you good young people please hand me my leg. It was given to me by General Lee himself."

Without hesitation, Chastity roundhouses the bulletproof glass holding the colonel's ivory peg leg and hands it to him.

The soldier pops it in place and stands tall...a towering five foot eight. "You must take ballet, young lady."

"Something like that."

"Now what's this about me being sort of dead? Obviously, I'm talking to you, so that means those Godless heathens didn't know their kerchiefs from their britches. The afterlife is not total blackness. Is this the Lord's kingdom then? Are you his angels sent to bring me through the Pearly Gates?"

Sissy bursts into laughter.

"What's so funny?"

"Angels are fictional."

The colonel blinks a few dozen times, unable to compute Sissy's strange tongue.

"Please sit down, Colonel," Chasity says, glaring at Sissy. "I have a lot to tell you. A lot has changed since you savaged these lands."

Chastity spends a good twenty minutes bringing the colonel up to speed on all that has transpired over the past hundred and forty years – the assembly line and mass production, Wilbur and Orville Wright, the First and Second World Wars, even the Korean police action. The zombie virus, of course, and man walking on the Moon. Vietnam, Disco, Iraq. A little on the Berlin Wall. She even gets sidetracked on Chuck Norris for a couple of minutes before Ernest interjects about the Chicken Trough, Wienerworld, and Artie's. Chastity then regroups and talks about how Morbid was renamed Pleasanton and the Cleansing of '87 and the need for Dexapalm 90 injections. She ends with recent developments, reciting the mayor's proposal and making an impassioned plea to the colonel to flex his military genius to help us free Marvin and save the town.

None of it seems to intrigue the man, except one minor detail. "So you say every house has indoor plumbing now, even on the second floor? That must mean someone finally figured out the gravity problem."

"That's right."

"Amazing."

When Sissy lets her guard down, Chastity accidentally shoves her into the colonel' arms. When she tries to get away, Chastity accidentally holds her there.

"What are you doing?" she yelps.

"Just testing something. We really should get you over to my great uncle's office for your Dexapalm 90 injection, Colonel. It's better to be safe than sorry."

"I feel fine. If I was one of those rogue creatures you were talking about, wouldn't I have torn out this poor girl's throat when she tripped into my arms?"

"I imagine so."

Sissy sneers at Chastity.

"Now tell me more about this mayor of yours."

Chastity spends another ten minutes describing every gory detail. The colonel winces and grimaces and even has to chop down a few small trees with his saber to let off a little steam. He finally settles down though and assumes the genteel stoicism that defines a country gentleman.

"So the man wants to relocate all the zombies to this dead zone?"

"That's right."

"Will they have running water?"

"No. Running water isn't a basic zombie service."

The colonel scowls.

"Neither is healthcare."

"Health who?"

"Healthcare."

"And he wants to build a wall?"

"I'm afraid so."

"But everybody knows that walls don't keep people out. Is this man an imbecile?"

Chastity shrugs her shoulders. "I don't think so. He's always on TV talking about the good brain he has."

The colonel adjusts his collar and sheathes his sword. He then takes Chastity by the shoulders and looks up into her eyes. "I will help you, young lady, because it's the right thing to do. It's the honorable thing. And I cannot in good conscience stand idly by as justice gets trodden underfoot. And if you'd allow me to be so bold, I'll let you in on a little secret. In all of my battles and conquests and horrors and victories, leading men through the gates of Hell, sometimes bringing them back and other times sacrificing them to the gods of war, I've learned one thing about a man's character. And it's this: if a man has to keep repeating himself about how good he is at something, you can bet the farm that he's not."

24

"What's an alarm?" Colonel Morbid asks.

Ernest tries his best to explain the technology, starting with Tesla and the famous AC vs. DC electricity debate, leading up to integrated circuitry and infrared lasers. "Some of the same technology will help me get to Mars," the future astronaut concludes.

The colonel looks Ernest up and down like he's two eggs short of a dozen, the way the rest of us used to look at him before we witnessed his talent for absorbing knowledge off the internet.

"So you mean we can't just break down the door?"

"No, the police would descend on us like locusts?"

"My good Lord, what has this world come to when a soldier can't just break down a door in the middle of the night?"

"Some say it's the end of days," Sissy slurps. "Others just call it due process."

The colonel limps around the building a few dozen times, searching for another means of access. The man just doesn't understand that every nook and cranny is wired to prevent the very thing that we're contemplating.

"Can't you magicians turn this alarm thingy off?"

Chastity shrugs her shoulders. "My sensei hasn't taught me that yet. Telepathic circuit manipulation isn't until the fifth degree."

"I have an idea," I say, reaching for my phone. It takes me about a minute to work up the gumption to dial the number, but with one big gulp, I swallow what's left of my pride. "Aunt Gertie, hi, it's Chris. Is Jed around?"

About twenty minutes later, the sound of a car without a muffler rounds the corner, and Aunt Gertie's '92 Buick Regal pulls up to the curb. Jed, Fred, and Little Ted pour out of the back seat, wielding their umbrellas. Their mother follows next, chicken thigh in hand.

"I didn't mean to get you involved, Aunt Gertie," I say, scowling at my cousins. "Jed was supposed to come by himself."

"Suspended license. The genius got caught doing doughnuts in the police station parking lot. Don't worry yourself though. Aunt Gertie is happy to pitch in for such a noble cause. Besides, there wasn't anything good on TV."

She walks up to Colonel Morbid and pats the bob of her hair. "Now who is this fine-looking gentleman?"

I make the introductions.

"Well, Chris," she says, straightening her muumuu and burning me with laser eyes, "if you would have warned me that I was going to meet such a legend, I would have put my face on, maybe even my girdle. You know I gained a few pounds recently, on account of all the stress in my life."

The colonel grins as widely as the Cheshire Cat. "Nonsense. A woman with curves is a healthy woman indeed."

"Oh, Colonel, you devil."

Chastity rolls her eyes, and Ernest turns green, but I think the future astronaut's condition might stem from that frozen burrito he forgot to heat up.

"The clock is ticking," Chastity says.

"Hush, dear," Aunt Gertie responds, grabbing the colonel's hand.

So while my two-hundred-forty-pound aunt and the reanimated Confederate colonel acquaint themselves for a couple of minutes beneath the leaves of a weeping willow, I'm left staring down my three psycho cousins.

"Good job at the hot dog eating contest," Jed finally says. "You made the family proud. No one's ever been a champion before."

"Thank you."

"Yeah, and congratulations on landing such a superhot piece of ...I mean girlfriend," Fred says. He's staring straight at Chastity's cleavage, and her left leg is winding up for a spine-snapping strike. Before she can let loose though, Fred shifts his gaze to Sissy's cleavage.

"Hi, cousin Chris," Little Ted says, as cute as a button. "I killed a squirrel today. I was trying to do my homework afterschool, and the furry guy just wouldn't shut up. He kept asking me to play the piano; said he wanted to dance a waltz."

"How rude of him."

"Yeah, it turns out he couldn't breathe underwater. What a loser squirrel."

A couple more minutes of silence ensue, and Fred's eyes are still locked on Sissy's cleavage. I realize that my cousin is trying his best to be respectful, diverting his attention away from *my* girlfriend's cleavage, but Ernest is getting pissed. His face is a mixture of green and red now, like bloody head-cold snot.

"Stop staring at my girlfriend," he finally says.

Fred's expression remains stone, but there's movement in his umbrella.

I step in between them. "Guys, let's remember that we're on the same side. Let's save it for the enemy, okay?"

Ernest takes two hits from his inhaler and leads Sissy to a large Dutch elm. Fred just studies their movements, making mental notes. He has a bad habit of doing that, especially when people cross him. I've been meaning to conduct an informal survey, you know, to see if other people have gotten the same stalker vibe, but I haven't been able to locate any of his rivals. I think they all moved away.

Aunt Gertie claps her hands, shattering a few eardrums. "Well, don't just loiter around like you're waiting in the cheese line, folks. Man your positions. Colonel Morbid has a battle to wage." She turns to Jed. "Now do it the way I taught you, son. I know you can. Your mama has always been proud of you."

Jed swallows the lump of pressure in his throat that only a mother's love can generate. He looks like he might be choking. "I won't let you down, mom."

And he doesn't. He picks the door lock and disables the alarm in less time than it takes me to unfasten Chastity's bra. A couple minutes later, we're all standing at the back of the Pleasanton Museum, in the military history section.

"There she is," the colonel smiles. "Old Betsy. I left her to the museum in my will."

"It's so big," Aunt Gertie coos.

"Fires a twelve pound load."

"Just one?"

"Multiple."

If you haven't figured it out yet, Old Betsy is a Civil War era field cannon, complete with cast iron barrel and wooden wheels for mobility. The plaque says that a trained crew could load, prime, and fire off a shot every twenty-five seconds. That's pretty good. They must have all been teenagers.

"Hitch up the horses, men."

"We don't have any horses," Ernest says.

"What, no horses? My God, what planet do I live on?"

Our group stares at one another with unhinged mouths. It's an instance that recovering alcoholics sometimes refer to as a moment of clarity. I like to call it a pig without lipstick. "Don't worry, sir," Chastity finally says. "We have 360 horses."

She bolts from the museum with the grace and speed of a third-degree black belt Goth, and Jed, Fred, and I follow in hot pursuit. We help her drag the chains that she keeps for emergencies in the trunk of her GTO. She only has about two hundred feet worth, but it's enough to reach the cannon. Jed and Fred make the necessary attachments, and Chastity slowly eases the cannon into the street. Ernest and Sissy use an old wooden wheelbarrow to load the trunk of the GTO with twelve pound cannonballs. Standing beside Old Betsy, the colonel removes his hat and scratches his gray head of hair.

"By Jiminy. We don't have any gunpowder. I didn't see any in the museum."

"Can't we go to the gunpowder store?" Ernest asks.

"It doesn't open until seven in the morning," Sissy replies.

Aunt Gertie winks at me and opens the trunk of her Buick, revealing a few wooden kegs. "We got you covered there, Colonel."

"What are you doing with gunpowder in your trunk, Aunt Gertie?"

"In this day and age, a woman needs to stay prepared."

* * *

"Fire!"

The turbulence from the first shot nearly blows my *Curlers Rock the House* hat off, so I take a few steps away from the tip of the barrel. The next shot is a bullseye and transforms the front door of the Border Patrol station into a pile of kindling. Border guards start swarming out of the wreckage like ants out of a rain-soaked nest. They're choking on the smoke and struggling in vain to cover their eyes.

"Fire!"

The third shot takes out a large section of the roof. About a hundred shingles fall on top of Sergeant Barry, but the giant shrugs the impact off. He reaches for his Glock 17, but a cannonball strips it from his hand. Then he reaches for his baton, but another twelve pound ball snaps it into a million toothpicks. And then for some strange reason, the border guard reaches for his crotch. I don't know if he suffers from jock itch or something, but you'd think the man would put two and two together and see a pattern.

"Fire!"

Sergeant Barry dives into a pool of broken glass just in time to avoid castration; then he scurries away as fast as a field mouse. Most of his unit follows closely behind.

"Fire!"

Jed, Fred, and Little Ted are manning Old Betsy like a well-oiled pit crew, with Jed ramming the gunpowder, Fred feeding her cannonballs, and Little Ted lighting the fuse. The colonel only explained to them once how to man the cannon, but to watch them in action, you'd think they'd been doing it for years. By the tenth volley, the station is a pile of rubble.

"I think we did it, Colonel," Chastity says.

"Nonsense. I didn't see any white flags."

Another twenty volleys later, the pile of rubble has given birth to a litter of baby piles of rubble. Several adjacent buildings have suffered the same fate, too – the Dunk-It Donuts, the

Spiffy Lube, and Moe's Neighborhood Pawn Shop. I experience mixed emotions about that last casualty. It's the place where Dad bought Mom's engagement ring when they found out she was pregnant with me.

"Whose Porsche was that in the Spiffy Lube?" Ernest asks.

"I think it was the mayor's."

"May she rest in peace."

"You mean pieces."

The firing finally stops, but only because we've run out of cannonballs. Colonel Morbid scans the remaining buildings, searching for something. "Is there a sundries store around here?"

"Yeah, on the next block. Why?"

"I need someone to get down there pronto and fetch us a barrel of nails...the rustier the better."

"What for?"

"I still haven't seen any white flags."

Chastity looks to me, and I look to Ernest; Ernest looks to Sissy; and she turns back to Chastity. We continue this dance for about twelve circuits, like a cat chasing its own tail. It's a really inefficient way of making decisions.

"Colonel, sir," Aunt Gertie finally says, taking the man's hand. "I think we won."

It takes a few seconds, but the colonel's bloodlust eventually recedes. "I think you might be right, ma'am. Except for that big fellow, those cowards didn't even turn to fight. The whole affair was a tad disappointing if you ask me, a downright travesty to warmongering."

"They don't make men the way they used to."

"That might be, ma'am, but I have to say you have three fine sons there...born to take up arms. They set a new field record for loading Old Betsy."

"I tried my best to raise them, but it was difficult without their fathers around."

"Off to war?"

"Off to the strip club."

The colonel shakes his head and pats the dust off his uniform. "Some men just don't have their priorities straight."

Movement in the rubble disturbs their conversation, and the colonel unsheathes his saber. The tip glistens in the moonlight. "Who goes there?"

"It's just me," Buck (IQ=?) squeals. He emerges from behind a mangled Frigidaire, holding one of his tube socks on the end of a broom handle. "I surrender."

"Well, it's about time, son. I nearly started using nails."

"Sorry."

"No need to apologize. Someone always loses in war. Now come over here so we can take you prisoner. I run a pretty decent POW camp. Bread and water at least once a day... and separate latrines for those men with dysentery."

Little Ted is shaking his head, livid. He runs up to Buck and starts beating the crap out of him with his umbrella. "Bad squirrel," he shouts. "Bad squirrel."

Buck retreats to his monster truck, but it swallowed our first cannonball, the one that missed the station and nearly knocked my hat off. There's not much left of the hood or engine block. There's not much left of the cab for that matter.

"Damn it!"

So Buck runs down the street, dragging one leg behind him. Little Ted follows in hot pursuit. "Bad squirrel," he shouts. "We don't take prisoners."

Aunt Gertie blushes red. "I'm so sorry, Colonel. My son disobeyed your order."

The old war dog chuckles. "No worries, ma'am. Battle tends to bring out the spirit in a boy, especially the young ones. He's just having a little fun. He earned it."

"It's good to see him get exercise."

After about five minutes, the dust finally settles and my ears stop ringing, and I start to remember why we're here. "Let's get Marvin and the Squid's head before someone wakes up. We made a lot of noise."

So we do.

Chastity and I take the lead with Ernest and Sissy in the rear. Colonel Morbid, Aunt Gertie, and my three cousins stay behind to secure our perimeter. The four of us manage to locate what's left of the staircase and slowly descend into the bowels of the station. The first couple of levels contain holding cells with a few run-of-the-mill zombies and protestors. One of them is Father Delaney.

"Hi, Chris," he says. "I haven't seen you in church recently."

"Sorry, father. I've been a little busy."

"No one is too busy for the Lord."

"So what do they have you in here for?"

The clergyman furls his brow. "I wouldn't turn over ten percent of the church's annual tithings. I kept telling the mayor's administration that the church is a tax-exempt organization under federal law, but they wouldn't listen. It's crazy. I even tried to explain to them that if they insisted on taxing the church's tax on parishioners that that would amount to double taxation. I mean, the mayor's cronies are supply-siders. Double taxation should be a taboo. But no luck there. They seized the church's assets anyway and stuck me in this filthy cell."

Chastity flips the handle that opens the holding cells. "Well, God works in mysterious ways, father," she says. "I was raised a Protestant."

"God bless you, my child. And let me know if you need any nails. The church stores a few rusty barrels full in the basement."

The next level is empty, but level four houses a bunch of Hollywood movie directors with leftist leanings. I think one of them might be the guy who directed that heart-wrenching story about the World War II concentration camp, but it could also be the guy who allowed that space opera franchise to piss on itself. It's hard to tell. They both wear glasses and sport beards.

Level five houses what you would expect level five to house – a bunch of homicidal maniacs, mostly guys but not all, strapped in straitjackets, gnawing at their own tongues. One of them looks like Anthony Hopkins. Chastity and I aren't sure what to do because I think the real actor (not his look-alike) might have been knighted, so we take the conservative approach and flip the handle.

"You're free now," Chastity says.

The Anthony Hopkins look-alike just smiles.

Level six houses a few Russian poets who fled to the U.S. seeking asylum.

Level seven houses a few Russian novelists who fled to the U.S. seeking asylum.

Level eight gets interesting. I can barely believe my own eyes. Growling and howling and shrieking and slithering are a bevy of fictional characters. We're talking vampires and werewolves and Sasquatches and Grim Reapers. There's even a cute little acid-washed dog/cat thing with fangs the size of shark's teeth. I'm not sure what to call it.

"That's a chupacabra," Sissy cheers. "I knew it was real. Come here little guy." She pets the creature's head, and Ernest pulls her hand away before she loses it.

And finally, in the bowels of the earth, we reach the infamous holding cell number nine. The four of us pause by the fire door, uncertain if we should proceed.

"Do you think we were right to let all of those folks out?" I ask. "I mean the poets and novelists, sure, and some of the directors. But does the world need more psycho killers, or vampires and yetis for that matter?"

Chastity shrugs her shoulders. "Who are we to judge? I'm only second-guessing myself about one guy. And he'd better not let that space opera franchise sink even deeper into the toilet. I mean, think up an original plotline for Christ's sake. You can't keep rehashing the same old story, even if you do keep jumping back and forth in time."

"As crazy as it sounds, I think some people really liked the last installment."

"Yeah, right. That's why it only took a few months to hit Netbuster streaming."

"Maybe we can still find him. He couldn't have gotten far."

"Tempting, but we need to focus on the task at hand."

And with that, we flip the handle to holding cell number nine. The whistle of a broken vacuum seal leaks out. The room is bright, like a doctor's office, and soothing elevator music is trickling from overhead speakers at just the right volume. I think the tune is *Danke Schoen* by Wayne Newton. A half dozen plush sofas line the walls, and sitting on one of them is Marvin

Reynolds, nibbling on what looks to be a cucumber sandwich. He's still in his Artie's uniform, and it seems like he ironed out his paper hat. Sitting next to him on a coffee table is the Squid's head. Her eyes are yellow and the tentacles of what's left of her throat are slithering about. Marvin politely pops a cucumber sandwich into her mouth. The English teacher chews and swallows, and the sandwich empties out the bottom of her neck. So Marvin repeats the motion. It's recycling at its best.

Sitting across from them on a comfy-looking Barcalounger is a guy that bears a strong resemblance to Mr. Rogers. He's even wearing slippers and a sky blue sweater vest.

"What the hell?" I say.

Marvin turns to us and smiles. "Hi, guys. What took you so long?"

"We had to do a little remodeling."

"Well, Ms. Twid has quite the story to tell. Let's get going."

"Where?"

"Your house."

25

"Oh my," Mom says, dressed in a faded pink bathrobe and matching hair rollers.

"Sorry, Mom, but we need to use the house for an emergency meeting. We just rescued Marvin and Ms. Twid's head from holding cell number nine. She's going to help us bring down Mayor Shight and his plan to relocate the zombies."

My mom blinks a few dozen times, struggling in vain to translate the gobbledygook that just leaked from her son's mouth. "That's nice, honey. Good for you. I'll make everyone some sandwiches."

Dad shuffles into the living room next, wearing a Culture Club T-shirt and a pair of orange parachute pants – they're his pajamas. A large wet spot adorns his left thigh. I hope it's from a cold beer or a can of lemonade.

"What's going on?" he blurts out.

"Emergency meeting, Dad, to save the town."

He scans the room and its ragtag band of crusaders. They return the gesture, focusing on his wet spot. "Why do I recognize you?" he asks.

"Colonel Morbid, sir. Pleased to make your acquaintance."

"Sorry we changed the name of the town," Dad says, shaking his hand. "It was done for revenue purposes."

The colonel grins. "I'm a military man first, but a business-man second. If you recall, I prospered in dry goods for a spell after the war. I know as well as the next man how a little re-branding can help a person unload the same old bag of manure. Tell you what, when we're done here, why don't you just show me one of those newfangled toilets that Miss Gertrude keeps telling me about. I'd like to see it in action. She says it delivers the refuse to a contained underground system that empties into a centralized facility for decontamination and reprocessing."

"That's right."

"And it only backs up into your house during heavy rain-storms?"

"Right again."

"Amazing."

Mom brings out a tray of bologna sandwiches, and Dad pours Colonel Morbid a whiskey. I then make all the formal introduc-tions that an important event like this requires. I also make a few phone calls to strengthen our numbers.

Mr. J knocks on the front door first, with Mrs. Mayweather in tow. The retired ice cream parlor owner is wearing a tank top and Bermuda shorts, and old Mrs. Mayweather is clad in her black leather boots and matching negligee again. Her cat o' nine tails is strapped securely to her thigh with one of those garter belts. They both look like they've been doing aerobics.

"Hello, Mr. J."

"Why hello, Chris. Now what's this all about?"

"You'll see in a few minutes."

Dr. Thurgood knocks on the door next, wielding a stetho-scope in one hand and a syringe in the other. Chastity imme-diately envelops her great uncle in a bear hug. "Where's my pa-tient?" he asks. Chastity points to our old English teacher.

"I'm okay," the Squid says. She's resting on the coffee table. "Willie Shight injected me with Dexapalm 90 while he held me captive so that I wouldn't turn rogue. He was trying to bore me to death with all of his confessions and figured I needed a clear mind to absolve him."

"But he doesn't have a license to practice medicine."

"He doesn't have a license to drive, either, but that's never stopped him."

The old country doctor shakes his head. "You'd better let me administer this injection just to be safe."

"You're the doctor." The Squid closes her eyes and winces as the needle enters her carotid artery.

Mom, a former school nurse, is always on the lookout for ways to ease a patient's suffering, unless of course you fall into one of the exemptions, like being related to her. "Here, maybe this will make you feel more comfortable." She lifts the Squid by the hair and places her on Grandma McGillicutty's Thanksgiving serving platter. It's quite an honor, and I think the Squid is perceptive enough to realize that fact.

"Thank you, dear. This is such a lovely platter. Please excuse my wretched appearance."

"Don't be so hard on yourself. You look wonderful. Did you lose some weight?"

"A little."

"It shows."

"And what about you?" Dr. Thurgood says, pulling another syringe from his lab coat.

Colonel Morbid takes a step back, startled. "I'm fine. No rogue here."

"But how could that be?"

"He died from a bee sting, Uncle Desmond. Could that be the reason?"

Dr. Thurgood nods his head and chuckles to himself. "Well, I'll be damned. I've always suspected that anaphylaxis had the potential to inhibit the T17 connector. You might be onto something, sir. You might have finally figured out a way to undercut those greedy pharmaceutical companies with a solution that's completely green...and free. Would you mind very much if I dissected you a bit when this referendum nonsense is all over?"

"I'd be glad to help."

"Okay, let's get started," I say. "We have a lot to cover." But no one listens to me. They're too busy stuffing their faces with bologna sandwiches and making small talk about politics and the weather. I clap my hands, but still no one acknowledges me. It's like one of those business meetings that Dad tells me about when a subordinate tries to command the attention of more senior employees – it just never works. It's only when the senior partner walks into the room that the so-called professionals snap to attention.

"Do you want me to break something?" Chastity asks.

"No, let them talk. Besides, you don't know what my mom had to go through to get my dad to cough up the dough for this furniture."

So they talk, and they talk, and when the third round of bologna sandwiches is nearly depleted, a bit of a scuffle breaks out.

"You fought on the wrong side, sir," Mr. J shouts. "You fought on the side that supported slavery."

Colonel Morbid reaches for his saber, but Aunt Gertie holds his hand back.

"I fought for state sovereignty, sir, against the imperialistic tendencies of a Yankee central government. Those bureaucrats in Washington wanted to destroy an entire way of life and rip from a whole swath of the country its ability to support itself."

"That may be, but when a way of life is based upon the enslavement of others, it needs to be ripped out...like a cancer."

Everyone turns to Dr. Thurgood, since he's a doctor and the word cancer was mentioned. The old physician clears his throat and straightens his back. "Mr. Jorgensen was using a metaphor."

"Oh."

Everyone turns back to Colonel Morbid. His eyes are narrowing and his fist is balling up, and I think poor Mr. J might have met his end; but like usual, Aunt Gertie steps in to save the day. "We talked about this, Horatio, on the car ride over here."

The colonel lowers his head and takes a breath. Then he tosses his Confederate regimental commander's hat on the sofa. Standing tall at the full length of his towering five-eight frame, the old war dog says, "I stand corrected, sir. I did fight on the wrong side. Thanks to the beauty and insight of this lovely woman here, I've finally come around to see the error of my ways. Enslaving one's fellow man is about the most dastardly action a person can take. It cannot be condoned...ever."

"Good show," Mr. J says.

"The last thing I want to do is wake up on the wrong side of history."

"But you already did," Sissy Slupchek slurps.

"Well, I aim to do something about that and make amends."

The room cheers.

In the lull that ensues, I enlist Jed's and Fred's help to get everyone's attention. A few well-placed umbrellas prove to be quite persuasive. "Ms. Twid has an announcement to make. If you recall, people, that's the whole reason we're here. So please give her your undivided attention."

The Squid clears what's left of her throat. "Thank you, Chris, for that lovely introduction. And thank you, Mr. and Mrs. Kantra, for hosting this gathering and making us all feel welcome."

Mom smiles and takes Dad's hand.

"I'd also like to thank each of you for taking time out of your busy schedules to listen to the musings of an old woman. I trust you will find my story disturbing enough to warrant your attention. As some of you might be aware, I had the displeasure of dating Willie Shight in high school. Our relationship was casual and nothing for the memoirs, but let's just say I learned a little something about him...how he thinks, the lengths to which he will go. From the start of this whole *kill-two-birds-with-one-stone* nonsense, I sensed the stench of subterfuge. If you know Willie the way I know Willie, then you'd know he always plays an ulterior motive. Padded expense accounts. Offshore tax shelters. Voting districts that wiggle like electrified worms. You get the picture. Six months ago, I might have turned a cheek and let his shenanigans pass. He's done a reasonable job of managing this town, and honestly, I've never been a great supporter of the zombie horde, bearing scars from my own experience with one of them. But when I witnessed the love that a real girl and a zombie boy could share (she smiles at Chastity and me), all of the old emotions came rushing back and I wanted to feel what it was like to love again."

She pauses, eyes misty.

Dr. Thurgood stares down his grandniece. I think the man is still concerned that she refuses to come clean about her undead status. She can't meet the old physician's eyes and tries to hide behind me.

"I realized at that moment that if I were ever going to love again, I first needed to be able to look myself in the mirror. I couldn't stand idly by while the mayor cleaved this young couple in two. So I vowed to do the right thing. I went undercover. *Deep* undercover. Now given my experience with Willie Shight, I knew he had a weak spot, and I knew what that weak spot was. So I exploited it with all my magic, as if we were teenagers again, and pumped all the gory details right out of him."

The Squid pauses, markedly distressed, and Marvin feeds her a bit of the bologna sandwich that she's already swallowed. "It's almost too dastardly to speak aloud, but I'll give it the old college try. His plan is to relocate all of the zombies to the dead zone so that he can seize their assets. Of course he's hiding behind a pretext – that the relocation will protect Pleasanton's citizens while the Border Patrol isolates the rogues. And that once the rogues are found, the zombies will be allowed to return to their homes. But the real mechanism of his deceit hinges on a dusty old provision of the health code, which gives him the power to seize zombie property that has remained uninhabited for six months. As each day passes, he'll shake the hands of babies and kiss their mothers' cheeks and declare with a straight face to the camera that the Border Patrol is on the verge of cracking the case. But in reality he'll just bide his time, smug in the knowledge that the rogues will never be found. You see, the truly despicable thing is that he commissioned the rogues himself, to stir up trouble and make the relocation possible. At last count, over ninety people have died horrible deaths, and the mayor sanctioned them all."

"It's a hundred and twenty-seven now," Ernest corrects.

Sighs and gurgles fill the room.

"And if that weren't enough to keep you from sitting comfortably on a hard surface, the rogues are Willie Jr. and his fraternity buddies."

"No way. Are they zombies?"

"Of course they're zombies. They were mauled last year in Fort Lauderdale in some botched spring break prank. Willie has kept his son under wraps, fearful that the boy's undead status might jeopardize his reelection chances. Unfortunately, Willie

Jr. was allergic to Dexapalm 90, so he broke out of the cellar and ate the maid. She was the first victim of this sordid affair but never made the news. Instead, her gruesome death gave the mayor an idea and the tool to make it happen. He claims that he hatched the scheme to save his son by funneling funds to Scotland for Dolly cake research. But I think that's another load of balderdash, one which he can't even admit to himself."

"Oh, my God, William," Chastity says. "*He's* the one in the White Sox cap."

"I'm afraid so, dear."

"But...but...but I always thought he was a Cubs fan."

Silence. Shock. Disbelief. So many emotions to choose from. The depravity of the scheme is almost impossible to comprehend – like some self-indulgent horror novel that relies on gore and poop jokes to compensate for a lack of suspense.

"What's a Dolly cake?" Ernest asks.

"Cloned human flesh that may someday tame the Craving in rogue zombies."

"Who's Dolly."

"A singer from Tennessee."

"Were the fraternity brothers in the cellar, too?" Dad asks.

"No. They roam the dead zone. The mayor keeps border guards on the payroll who let them through when they're needed. The rogue that was caught eating Bill Jefferson was later set free for the mere price of a pizza."

"A large?"

"No. A medium with three toppings."

"But why didn't they kill you?" Aunt Gertie asks. "I mean in all the gangster movies...except the James Bond series, of course... the crooks never let a witness live."

The Squid takes the question in stride, a trooper through and through. "Technically, I'm not alive, but I guess I'm not entirely dead either. Once the blood rushed back to Willie's head, he realized that he'd revealed too much. He couldn't afford to let me live, no matter how strong the pull of nostalgia, so he ordered his rogues to devour me. He also demanded my head as a souvenir, for old time's sake. The man can be sentimental when he lets his hair down. He planned on mounting me to the wall, next to his other trophies – deer and moose heads, a twenty pound bass – but I used my silver tongue to talk my way out of it...eventually became a shoulder for him to cry on."

I can tell that Ernest is itching to tell the Squid that she no longer has a shoulder, but the future astronaut manages to keep his mouth shut. He takes two hits from his inhaler to deal with the resulting stress.

"What should we do?" Mom asks.

"We need to spread the word, and fast. Willie's propaganda machine is rolling ahead at full steam, and the referendum is in a couple of days. Unless we expose his scheme tout suite, my death will have been in vain."

While the shock of the mayor's insidious plan continues to sink in, someone else knocks on the door. The adults are too preoccupied to respond, so asswipe Jimmy crawls out of his hiding spot behind the grandfather clock and opens it. He has a couple of plastic darts clenched in his hand.

"Oi! Hallo, hallo," Mystery Mel says, holding Buck (IQ=?) in an armlock. Little Ted is glued to the border guard's leg, beating on him with an umbrella.

"There you are," Aunt Gertie says.

"Bad Squirrel! Bad Squirrel!"

Aunt Gertie stretches the sides of her mouth with her pinkies and whistles in a pitch so high that every dog on the block starts barking. Little Ted runs to her side and latches onto her thigh. She's got him better trained than I thought.

"That's what I call discipline," Colonel Morbid says.

"What are you doing here?" Dad asks.

Mystery Mel shoves Buck onto the floor and clears his throat. "I caught this Peeping Tom outside in the bushes. He tried to flash his badge and say he was on official business, but I know that's a load of crap. First, no border guard on official business is going to have a nine-year-old beating the bejesus out of his cobblers with an umbrella. Second, we live in a world of laws, people. Real border guards are required to knock on your door twice before kicking it in. They don't hide in the bushes."

Everyone nods. The law is still the law.

"I was delivering sandwiches next door when I spotted this

bugger. It's part of my new business model, delivery that is, a desperate attempt to guard my turf from the Fatbelly's that just opened up on Main."

Colonel Morbid glares at Buck and draws his saber. "Aren't you supposed to be my prisoner, son?"

"Yes, sir. That's why I was outside, trying to find you."

Yeah, right.

"Good man. Now go sit in the corner and don't talk until you're spoken to."

Buck grins a sigh of relief. The order must bring back fond memories of high school.

"Are you folks having a party?" Mystery Mel asks. "I could bring back some sandwiches. A deli platter for twelve is only $49.95."

The Squid clears what's left of her throat, visibly annoyed. "Ladies and gentleman, let's not forget why we're here."

Upon hearing her lovely aquatic voice, Mystery Mel stops his sales pitch mid-sentence. I don't think he noticed her head before. It's partially obscured by Mom's favorite lampshade, and the glare from the light is making the Squid's skin look kind of artificial, like papier-mâché.

"Eloise?" he says, removing his mask.

"Nigel?"

Without warning, the theme song from *The Sound of Music* leaks from my phone as Mel races to the Squid's head. The former lovers press their lips together and engage in a kiss that would make Melanie Melonson, the oil worker from Texas with the best-white smile, blush. The tip of something starts wiggling at the base of the Squid's throat, and I think it might be Mel's tongue. After about a minute, Mom covers Jimmy's eyes.

"I missed you," the sandwich maker finally says.

"It was horrible, Nigel. One of those rascals that captured me kept eating chili all day while standing next to my nose."

Mel unsheathes a spatula from his apron. The edge of it looks like it could cut diamonds. "Chili, you say? I'll prune the bloke's cobblers."

"Oh, Nigel."

Squid love is not exactly the healthiest thing for a teenage mind to absorb. I think the image is going to give me more nightmares than Mom's old Iron Maiden poster ever did. Chastity has her head buried in my shoulder and keeps mumbling how she's going to gouge out her own eyes. I believe she's exaggerating, which is a common trait of my generation, but she does have a ninja throwing star in hand. I try to wrest the thing from her for safety reasons, but somehow it ends up wedged in my arm. Fortunately, another knock on the door clears the haze of amore from the room.

It's the assistant manager from the Wienerworld. She's still wearing her red, yellow, and blue striped uniform, with a matching top hat and name tag. A bit of mustard is crusted on the side of her cheek, but she's smiling up a storm and doesn't seem to care.

"Your name is Floyd?" I ask.

"Oh, no. I spilled relish all over *my* uniform and had to change into this spare one that was hanging in the storage locker. It's a little vintage, but I think Floyd used to be a fry cook back in the day. I forgot to switch name tags."

"I don't remember calling you. Why are you here?"

"Marvin texted me. He said there was a bologna party."

I look to the zombie fast food worker, and he gives me a devilish wink. He then straightens his paper hat and hands the would-be Floyd the last of the bologna sandwiches. She sucks it down in one bite, which is pretty impressive. I don't think she's a zombie since she's in management, but I have to be honest, it's not entirely clear.

"Yummy," she says. "Bologna is the same as a wiener rolled out flat."

"I always suspected that."

"Are you expecting more company?"

"What do you mean?"

"There's a bunch of rowdy-looking guys outside in a black Suburban."

26

Before we can even peek through the blinds, a gang of rogue zombies bursts through the window. Colonel Morbid immediately swings his saber and cuts one in half, but the torso crawls after Aunt Gertie, growling and gnashing its teeth. She jumps onto a chair, screeching like a '50s housewife confronting a mouse, until Jed and Fred beat the thing silly with their umbrellas.

A second rogue, the one wearing a propeller cap, rushes past Chastity and gooses her in the backside. "Hey, babe. I see you figured out how to wear a bra."

I throw a punch, but the bastard bobs and weaves like a professional boxer. A few jabs connect with my nose – lucky shots – and then a hook sets my ear ringing. Without knowing how I got there, my ass is glued to the floor. My warrior instincts must have kicked in again.

"Uncool, dude," I scream. "You're acting just like that politician who got caught on camera bragging about how he gropes women."

"Yeah, well, he got elected, didn't he?"

The asswipe makes a second pass, but this time my girlfriend is ready. In a rage, Chastity whips out her bowie knife and starts flailing like a helicopter rotor, kicking and slicing and biting and screaming. Pieces of a propeller cap fly through the air, along with fingers and toes and kidneys and ribs. Another chunk of anatomy sticks to Mrs. Mayweather's hair. It resembles a thumb, but it's thicker and less rigid. She screams and throws it into Mom's fern. Unwilling to take chances, Mr. J grabs her cat o' nine tails and whips the appendage raw. He then tosses it on the floor and grinds it to dust with his heel. You can see the hope dissolve in the rogue's eyes. "Little Buddy," he cries, as Chastity stomps his brain with her combat boot. What a way to go.

She's doused in oily goo – zombie blood – but Chastity won't slow down. She's jumping and sliding and tumbling and kicking, breaking everything in her path, including Mom's Shaun Cassidy flowerpot. But then something punches her three times in the back, and she crashes into the coffee table, knocking the Squid's head onto the floor. Buck (IQ=?) has shot her. Chastity rolls over, dazed. "You moron," she screams.

"My bad. Why aren't you dead?"

"None of your business."

"I wasn't aiming for you. I was aiming for Chris."

"What the hell?"

The rogue in the White Sox cap leaps off the couch and onto my foot. I can hear the bones crack. "I'll deal with you later, paste boy."

"How did you know my nickname?"

"Word travels, loser."

He then charges Buck, who shoots him three times in the chest, but the hot lead passes right through the desiccated flesh. One shatters Mom's second favorite mirror. A second knocks off Marvin's paper hat. The third strikes me in the leg. This simply isn't a good day.

"Aim for his brain, you idiot!"

But Buck's Glock 17 is empty, and he clicks it futilely in Willie Jr.'s face. The frat boy laughs and tears out the border guard's throat – one artery at a time. It's more disturbing than I imagined it would be to watch a grown man with a Village People moustache shriek like a little girl. The curtains flutter as Darwin's ghost passes overhead.

Ernest is too busy fighting off another rogue to mourn his brother's death. This zombie is huge, maybe six-eight, with a crew cut and acne and a grass-stained rugby shirt. He's got

Sissy by the arm, and Ernest keeps stabbing at him with his clarinet. He manages to sever the zombie's hand, but the rogue grabs the clarinet with his other hand and starts beating Ernest over the head with it. In the nick of time, Sissy rams her woodwind through the monster's heart and kicks him in the walnuts, breaking him down to size. Dr. Thurgood then jams a syringe into his neck, but the rogue flings the doctor into Mom's China cabinet and bites Ernest on the leg, tearing open the femoral artery. A torrent of blood sprays onto Mom's ceiling, tracing a portrait of three flies caught in a cobweb eating an order of curly fries. With his last breath, Ernest jams his clarinet into the rogue's temple and pierces the brain. Oily goo oozes through the woodwind, but the rogue insists on gnawing at Ernest's arm, so Sissy rips her clarinet from the monster's heart and jams it into his face, obliterating the cerebellum. He stops moving, but Sissy stabs him again and again, just to be safe. Then she takes Ernest into her arms and howls to the Moon. I want to tell her that the Band-Aid she's putting on his leg won't stop the bleeding in time, but it's their final moment. Their last duet.

Meanwhile, the torso that went after Aunt Gertie is at it again. Somehow the thing survived the beating that my cousins gave it and flung itself onto her thigh. Before it can sink its teeth into her fleshy goodness though, Colonel Morbid kicks it in the ribs. The torso plops to the ground, none too pleased by the interruption, and bites into the colonel's ankle. The old war dog laughs at the pathetic, futile assault. "Men," he says. "He's all yours."

Jed and Fred charge the abomination once more with their umbrellas, but this time it springs from the ground (using its arms for propulsion) and latches onto Fred's neck. He tries to pry it off, but it's glued to him like one of those pods in the movie *Alien*. Jed jabs at the thing with the razor sharp point of his umbrella, but its fangs rip open Fred's carotid artery. Blood gushes everywhere, ruining Mom's curtains. As my psycho cousin topples to the ground, Jed beats the torso with everything he has left, breaking his beloved umbrella in half. Then he grabs the piece with the point and pins the creature to the ground. Aunt Gertie immediately plunges a chicken bone straight through the top of its head. Little Ted even starts gnawing off its ear.

"My son," the woman wails.

"Bad squirrel!"

Across the room, Willie Jr. has Jimmy by the arm, and I consider helping my poor brother before he gets torn limb from limb; but then I remember that Jimmy is the kind of kid that can take care of himself. He values his independence more than anything else.

A crash blares out next. Mom's chandelier. Another rogue, dressed in a letterman sweater and a pair of khakis, flings the Diamique projectiles in all directions, pummeling people with faux diamond shrapnel. One knocks Marvin's paper hat off for a second time, and you can see the steam rise off of his head. Another strikes Mr. J in the face, severing an ear. A third cracks me in the mouth and shatters my tooth. Chastity crushes the rogue's sternum with a flying roundhouse, but she's gathered so much momentum in her rage that she can't slow down in time. She barrels right through the window and onto the front lawn. A few neighbors have gathered in the street, straining to get a better look at all the hubbub. Mrs. Walsh from next door turns up her nose and threatens to sue if the damage encroaches upon her property. Mrs. Epstein from across the street asks Chastity if she needs any hot cocoa. My girlfriend politely declines and leaps back through the window, where Mom has taken matters into her own hands.

"I got that chandelier on sale," she screams, brandishing a thermometer in either hand. "Do you know how hard it is to find quality knockoffs on sale? You inconsiderate little twit. Who's your mother? I have half a mind to tell her what mischief you've been up to."

"Don't do that, ma'am," the rogue says. "I'm sorry about the chandelier. It was an accident."

"It's too late for apologies, buster."

And with that Mom leaps with the agility she once demonstrated when snatching Burt Mitchel's bandana from midair at a Hemloch concert and jams the thermometers into the rogue's head. Oral in the front. Rectal in the rear. He stumbles around a bit, disoriented, and lunges for her throat, but Dad grabs him from behind in a choke hold. "We saved over two hundred dollars on that purchase," he screams. The rogue is too strong for Dad, however, and wrestles himself free, snapping Dad's arm for fun. Dad bellows in anguish, and in a spate of desperation performs a feat I would have never considered possible. He pulls a Benjamin Franklin from his pocket and tears it in half.

"Dude," the rogue blurts out. "What are you doing? That's a hundred dollar bill."

Famous last words. Before the rogue knows what hits him, Dr. Thurgood jams a syringe the size of a turkey baster into his skull, and Mr. J follows suit with a razor sharp ice cream scooper. The aged men exchange high fives as the rogue crumbles to the ground, and then they help Dad to his feet. He immediately gathers the halves of the hundred dollar bill with his good arm.

"Quick, honey," he screams. "Get the tape."

Mom's couch – the one she bought from CJ Nickel's when Dad was away at an accounting convention – is the next victim. A rogue dressed in flip-flops and a muscle-man tank top urinates all over the faux leather upholstery. Marvin breaks a lamp over his head, but the rogue slashes Marvin across the face with the yellow stream, temporarily blinding him. The rouge then tries to decapitate him with Grandma McGillicutty's Thanksgiving serving platter, but the assistant manager from the Wiener-world dives into the path and takes the brunt of the blow to her chest. Her sternum cracks open like a patient undergoing open-heart surgery, and a torrent of blood drenches Mom's couch. Marvin scrambles to stem the blood loss with his paper hat, screaming to the gods of fast food for help, but his efforts are futile. With her last dying breath, the assistant manager whispers into Marvin's ear, and he nods in agreement. Then he bites her on the lip and spits.

As the assistant manager passes into whatever comes next, rage consumes Marvin's face – something out of the Old Testament. His eyes ignite into flaming heat lamps, and he pulls the bloody paper hat back over his head. Then he scrapes his

Pumas across the carpet like a bull about to charge and impales the rogue's chest with his cranium. He reemerges with heart in mouth, and spits the organ into the rogue's face, and gnaws off the rogue's arm at the shoulder, and jams the humerus straight into its eye. A grapefruit-sized chunk of gray matter blasts out the back of the frat boy's skull.

Marvin then collapses to his knees, weighted by grief, and Mystery Mel walks up to the rogue's twitching corpse with a spatula in one hand and the Squid's head in the other.

"He was the worst," the Squid says, almost too horrified to look. "He was the one who ate the chili."

Mystery Mel slaps the rogue a couple of times to get his attention, then makes quick work of the brute's anatomy with his spatula – starting, as promised, with the cobblers.

The carnage rivals any straight-to-DVD slasher flick. Mosaics of blood and gore adorn the walls and ceiling. Chunks of liver and pancreas drip from the curtains and Mrs. Mayweather's hair. Carcasses quiver and twitch in a Stonehenge of nerve impulses and muscle spasms. Some of my friends are dead, for the first time, and their courage is seeping through the upholstery. But the fight isn't over. One rogue remains – the nastiest of all. Willie Jr. stumbles toward me with darts sticking from both eyes, swinging Colonel Morbid's saber. He inadvertently lops off Mystery Mel's legs.

"Bloody hell!"

"That little ass muncher put out my eyes!" Willie Jr. screams. "I don't want to work at the freaking library with Sylvester Carnsworth!"

"Great job, Jimmy," I say.

Jimmy takes a bow, wielding another dart.

"How did he get the colonel's sword?"

"He pulled it out of his you-know-what."

"Get over here, paste boy."

Before I can charge him, Chastity glides up to Willie Jr., ducking and weaving to avoid the sword strikes, and grabs him by the shoulders. "You hurt me, William. You hurt me more than I thought I could be hurt. How could you have run off when I needed you?"

"Chastity? What the hell? Why are you dating this loser?"

"He's not a loser. He's a talented poet and the county hot dog eating champion and a future Olympic curler. And he has the courage to stand and fight for the woman he loves."

"That's right, jerkwad," I say.

"Chris, please."

"Whatever," Willie Jr. says. "If you want to go slumming with losers, that's your problem. You had your shot at the big league. Now get out of the way."

"Put the sword down, William. For once in your life do the right thing. Show some integrity. It's not too late. You don't have to follow in your father's footsteps."

"You're starting to get on my nerves, necrophile. I have work to do. Now step aside."

"I can't."

"Well then shut the hell up and go paint your nails or something."

"No one talks to my girlfriend like that," I say, jumping in. "Let me handle this."

"Oh, Chris. My Zombie Lancelot. Are you sure?"

"I'm sure."

"Your funeral," Willie Jr. laughs, and with his first strike cuts off two of my fingers.

Then an ear.

Finally the tip of my nose. And the bastard can't even see!

"Do you think maybe I can have a turn now?" Chastity asks. "You were so brave to stand up for me, especially against a blind zombie. You can press on if you like, but given the way William left me in the lurch, I'd sure like a chance to make him pay."

"I was just about to finish him off."

"I can see that. But please, let me have a turn."

"Well, okay. If you insist. But I was just warming up. Sometimes the warrior instinct needs a little priming."

"I know. And thank you for understanding."

And with that Chastity wrests the sword from Willie Jr.'s hand and reduces him to a pile of quivering parts. It's like that game Speed Slice on Wii Sports Resort, and the artistry of her motions summons in me an urge to eat at a Japanese steakhouse. With the final blow, she cleaves Willie Jr.'s head in two, and his eyeballs pop out, still impaled by Jimmy's darts. I crush them underfoot to add a finishing touch.

It takes a couple of minutes for the blood clouds to settle and for the reality of what just transpired to sink in. But slowly and with the steadfast solidarity of a family that has massacred a gang of zombies together, we marshal our forces and drag our fallen brethren onto the front lawn. Ernest. The assistant manager from the Wienerworld. My psycho cousin, Fred. Sissy has to remind us nine times to get Buck (IQ=0). We try to ignore her, but she's relentless, and we finally concede to shut her up. As we finish the heavy lifting and start spraying Bactine on our wounds, Little Ted, as cute as a button, makes a poignant observation.

"Where's the talking head?"

And as if to accentuate his point, my beloved house, with all of its fond memories and crushing heartbreaks, bursts into flames. Something must have ruptured a gas line.

"What the hell!" Mom screams, racing for the door. "My Burt Mitchel bandana."

But Dad holds her back before she can put herself in harm's way. He rubs zombie blood out of his eyes, then releases a warm, reassuring smile. "Don't worry, honey. The homeowner's policy is paid up."

Mom nods her head, but tears are still streaming down her cheeks.

Aunt Gertie is kneeling beside her with Fred's corpse in her arms. Her lip is quivering and her eyes are glass, but she still has the presence of mind to reach for his billfold. As she once told me at Grandma McGillicutty's Easter Sunday funeral ceremony: *Why wait for probate court? The government doesn't deserve a cut.*

The dance of flames is completely hypnotic and slowly draws us under its spell. Fortunately, Marvin somehow remains immune. He reminds us all of Little Ted's observation. "The Squid is the only witness."

"Eloise!" Mystery Mel screams, crawling toward the house.

Chastity motions for the door, but I hold her back. "I've got this, baby."

"But the open flames."

"You and me both," I whisper. "Besides, I think Marvin and some of the others saw you get shot three times. The last thing we need now is for you to walk out of that house burned to a crisp and smiling. That would be a little hard to explain."

Chastity lowers her head and closes her eyes.

"Wish me luck," I say, adjusting my Dependables.

"Chris, you're the bravest zombie I know. I love you so much."

"I love you, too."

And with that I race toward the flames screaming, "Cojones!"

27

The sun is slowly setting on the horizon, and if I weren't so damned famished, the image would almost be romantic. I nudge Marvin in the ribs, and he pulls the last of the Beef 'n Cheeses out of our rollaway cooler. We had fifty sandwiches at the start of the morning, courtesy of the dumpster behind Artie's, but walking around town all day knocking on doors works up one hell of an appetite – especially when you're dead. Chastity has reached her limit though (old cheerleader instincts), and Ernest is too preoccupied with Sissy Slupchek's orthodontic headgear to notice, so Marvin and I engage in a quick three rounds of rock-paper-scissors. I win two out of three but still have the class to tear the sandwich in half. Marvin seems relieved.

"Your spray paint looks good," he says.

"Thanks."

"I tried to get him to try jamocha fudge," Chastity adds, "but he didn't want to experiment...stuck with run-of-the-mill eggshell."

"Whatever the color, you did a great job on him. A person with good eyesight has to be within twenty yards to even tell that it's not real skin."

"I've had practice with makeup."

There's a new trust between Marvin and my girlfriend, probably due to the heroic beating the former took when he went undercover to find the Squid's head. I know Chastity well enough to know that she respects that kind of warrior spirit in a person. In return, Marvin has stopped prying about her excessive makeup and aversion to the cold. I think he knows that she's a zombie, and I think Chastity knows that he knows, and they've both found comfort in the fact that some understandings are better left unsaid – which means I got burned to a crisp for no reason. Well, that's not entirely true. I did save the Squid's head.

"You'd better keep it under wraps," I say.

Marvin nods and straightens his paper hat.

"Keep what under wraps?"

"Shut up, Ernest."

The future astronaut is limping pretty badly now, on account of the damage his leg sustained in the attack, but it hasn't seemed to slow him down much. He keeps bragging to Sissy how he's going to fly to Mars and moon the camera and then leverage his fame to open up a chain of restaurants. *Elegant but cheap*, he keeps saying, *for the fine diner who's on a budget*. I don't know about the viability of his business model, but one bonus to him joining the ranks of the undead is that he doesn't need his inhaler anymore. The other is that Marvin and I no longer have to worry about him getting food poisoning from the dumpster. There's a third bonus, too, which I'd never admit to his face; and that's the fact that I still have my friend and curling partner. I guess I can thank fate for that. I mean, what are the odds that another ambulance would crash on the way to the hospital before Ernest's cremation clause could be enforced?

"This is the last house," Ernest says, ringing the doorbell. "The polls close in less than an hour."

Mansion is a better word to describe the place. Humongous white columns anchor a front wrap-around porch, and the landscaping looks like it came straight out of one of those fancy magazines my mom likes to drool over. A middle-aged woman wearing a skimpy black party dress opens the door. She's kind of hot in what my dad once called a mature *Linda Evans* sort of way and for some strange reason looks very familiar. The blonde hair, the ice blue eyes, the way she's peering down on us like we're pond scum – it's almost déjà vu.

"The sign says no solicitors," she snaps.

"We're not lawyers, ma'am. We're here to make sure that you were aware of the referendum that's going on today and exercised your God-given, American right to vote. If not, there's still time."

"Of course I voted, you imbecile. I'm not some trailer trash slum dog that lies on the couch all day eating Dong Dongs, unaware of this town's dire state of affairs."

"That's great to hear, ma'am. So did the Colonel Morbid interview sway your vote at all?"

The door slams in Ernest's face. Then it opens a crack and slams again.

"No way," Chastity says, finally making the connection. She's not angry in the least bit, just amused. "The road apple doesn't fall too far from the horse's ass."

"What do you mean?"

"That was Amy's mom."

"No way."

We all start laughing, except for Marvin. He walks over to the mailbox and unclasps his belt. Then he straightens his paper hat and puts his hand around his stomach.

"What are you doing?"

"What does it look like I'm doing? You folks might want to turn away."

The boy is a genius.

"Gross," Sissy Slupchek slurps, smacking Ernest in the back of the head. "Why didn't you think of rolling your intestine?"

The interview that Ernest was referencing happened yesterday morning, the day after the attack. Colonel Morbid walked down to the local news station and asked Kirk Karson to put him on the *magic picture box* so that he could appeal to the citizenry and sway their vote. The news anchor was hesitant at first, given his inherent Yankee proclivities, but the tip of the colonel's sword helped him realize that it was the right thing to do. So Colonel Morbid, Aunt Gertie, and the Squid went on Channel 12 and spilled the beans on the mayor's plot. They also urged people to get out and vote. Kirk Karson tried to end the interview early, jealous that the colonel was stealing the spot-light; but the colonel cocked his pearl-handled Walker .44 and placed it on his lap. The business end of the revolver happened to be pointed at Kirk's family jewels, so the colonel got a little extra airtime. He droned on for a while about the wonders of indoor plumbing and the marvels of modern sanitation, but then with a little help from my aunt got back on point. He called Mayor Shight the lowest form of bottom feeder that he'd ever encountered, unfit to peel potatoes in even the Union army. He then challenged the mayor to a duel.

About thirty minutes later, the mayor's spokeswoman came on the air denying all of the charges and threatened to sue for defamation of character. She was wearing a baseball cap that read *Make Our City Great Again* and a T-shirt that read *Build a Wall*, and somehow she managed to spend half of her time pitching a line of steaks and other meat products from a company the mayor had recently invested in. At no point did she mention the mayor's response to the colonel's challenge. We're still waiting to see how things turn out.

"Let's head on over," I say.

"About time," Marvin says. "I'm famished."

We pile into Chastity's GTO and burn rubber in front of Amy's house, and within ten minutes we get to the entrance of Aunt Gertie's trailer park. It's pretty classy as far as trailer parks go, with a rusted jungle gym at the center where the kids can play hide-and-seek with tetanus, and a big rod iron arch that reads *Rothschild Estates*. The *R* in Rothschild is missing, but everyone who's anyone knows what it's supposed to be. On a clear night, when the smoke from the crematorium isn't too thick, you can see the burning garbage cans down in Zombietown.

Unfortunately for Mom and Dad, the fire department got our address wrong, and our house burned to the ground. I was never all that attached to the place, given the mixed bag of emotions it summoned, and part of me can't help but say good riddance. True to form though, Aunt Gertie opened her big, charitable heart and invited Mom, Dad, Jimmy, and me to stay with her. There's no room inside her trailer, of course, since Jed, Undead Fred, and Little Ted share one room, and the colonel is bunking in the other. But we have a couple of tents set up on the patch of artificial turf in the front, and when Jasper 2, Aunt Gertie's new pit bull, isn't busy humping every bitch within a two mile radius, the soothing sounds of crickets and alcohol-fueled tirades make for a refreshing slumber.

Aunt Gertie and Mom are manning both burners of the hot plate now. The crackle of the deep fryer has captured Marvin's attention. He walks over to it, mesmerized, and submerges his hand into the sizzling depths. He then pulls out an oily, coagulated wad of chicken skin.

"Go on," Aunt Gertie says. "That's the best part."

"Are you sure?"

"You're my guest. I might not have much to show for my life, but I've never been short on hospitality."

Marvin slurps it down, grinning from ear to ear. "You reuse the oil?"

"Of course I do, sonny...that's the only way to unlock the full potential of the flavor."

"You make me reconsider religion, ma'am. Now how can I be of assistance?"

While Marvin gets stuck setting the picnic table that Jed and Undead Fred borrowed from the kiddy park, Chastity and I check on the ladies from the curling club. Clara has Eunice and Ethyl running suicides over by the porta potties. Eunice looks like she might be having a coronary, and poor Ethyl is down with an injured hip. I'm beginning to question Aunt Gertie's decision to invite them.

"Stand up and shake it off," Clara snaps. "There's no time to get bionics implanted. The bonspiel is in a couple of weeks."

"But it hurts," Ethyl cries. "I've fallen and I can't get up."

"No pain, no gain. I thought you understood that by now." Clara whips out a syringe from her faux mink fanny pack and jams it into Ethyl's hip. Within seconds, the pangs of anguish melt off the woman's face. "What was that?"

"Magic. Now give me ten more suicides. And if you hear a grinding sound in your hip, disregard it. That's just your body's way of trying to be weak."

Ethyl gets back to her workout, and Clara turns her sights on

Chastity and me. "Why are you two just loitering around? This isn't a breadline. Now get over there and give me twenty."

Chastity laughs the order off. "I'm not on the curling team, ma'am."

"What's your excuse, Kantra?"

"I'm still recovering from my injuries." I show her my hand, which is missing two fingers. Then I show her my spray paint. She seems unimpressed, probably agreeing with Chastity that my color choice was too mundane.

"I've seen curlers put four stones in the house with only six fingers and one eye. It's a question of attitude, Kantra, not body parts. I expect you back at practice on Saturday...you and that other corpse. What was his name again?"

"Ernest."

"Yeah, you and Ernest. Don't think I haven't noticed how many suicides you two have missed. Being dead is no excuse for shirking your responsibilities." She turns to Chastity. "So are you going to cheer Chris on at the bonspiel, missy? That's what you do, right, cheer?"

"I'm certainly considering it."

"Consider nonsense. What kind of girlfriend doesn't support her man at a bonspiel? When I was a girl, we lined up for miles to watch our favorite sweepers. I even had a poster of Jacque Beaucoup right above my bed. Broom, skates, skintight polyester slacks. He was a dreamboat, and I had fantasies of marrying the man until it leaked out that he preferred a different kind of hack."

"Dinnertime," Aunt Gertie screams, saving us from Clara. She claps her massive, meaty hands together, signaling everyone to gather around the table. We try to squeeze onto the benches, turning sideways and sucking in our guts, but there's simply not enough room. Unfortunately, the kiddy park only had one picnic table. So the younger folks get stuck sitting on cinder blocks, myself included, and Jed's stripper girlfriend wiggles onto his lap to conserve space.

Aunt Gertie has never been one for speeches, but she says a few words about family and how proud she is about the effort we all put in to get people to vote. She also announces without equivocation how she and the deep-fried Snickers bar vendor are kaput, to assuage any appearance of impropriety given the colonel's new sleeping arrangements. Then she does what she does best – serve food. Mounds of mashed potatoes. A bevy of breasts and thighs. The biggest, longest corncobs you've ever seen, doused in hot, creamy butter. It's a feast to end all feasts, an epicure's wet dream.

There's not much talk, save for the requisite requests for salt and pepper and a little hot sauce. Our mouths are too full to be concerned with words. But when we hit the wall and come up for air, the white elephant in the room finds its vocal cords.

"How do you think we'll do?"

Aunt Gertie nearly chokes on a chicken bone. "Who said that?"

We all stare at each other, searching our minds for phantom voices. Little Ted is the first to notice. "Good squirrel," he says, pointing at the ground. Lying on her ear under the table is the Squid's head. I think I might have accidentally kicked her a few times.

"Ms. Twid," I say. "How'd you get down there?"

"I got bumped by a bowl of mashed potatoes. Then I had an unpleasant run-in with a pair of stinky feet. Without Nigel here to keep me anchored, I'm afraid I just got lost in the shuffle."

Nigel (aka Mystery Mel) is recuperating right now in the back of his sandwich shop. Dr. Thurgood spent twelve hours in surgery, reattaching an assortment of different legs from the morgue (yes, it still exists; not everyone has the zombie virus). The ones that his body didn't reject belonged to a somewhat famous semipro basketball player named Frank Stein. I have an appointment next week to get new fingers.

"You poor dear," Mom says, placing the Squid's head at the center of the table. "How could we be so callous?"

"No worries. I've been tossed around before. Now back to my question, do you think we're going to win?"

"Resoundingly," Dad says. "It'll be a landslide. The good people of Pleasanton won't let us down, especially not with the real facts at their disposal."

"We did expose the mayor for the piece of slime that he is,"

Aunt Gertie says. "He'd be in jail already if he didn't have the police chief in his pocket."

"Justice always prevails," Little Ted squeaks, "despite the bad squirrels."

"It's on now," Chastity says, running toward the portable TV. She turns up the volume, and Allison Fisher, the local beat reporter, is standing outside of City Hall next to the mayor. A small mole of a man with a gray suit and glasses as thick as the Palomar telescope is sitting at a table next to them, tapping at a laptop.

"That man is an accountant," Dad says.

The mole of a man hands Allison Fisher a slip of paper, and she reads the results to the camera. She looks uncomfortable at first but manages to maintain her composure, a true newswoman. "Ladies and gentleman and other citizens of Pleasanton, we have the official, audited results of today's referendum. It's hard to believe, but we have a tie. I repeat, we have a tie. According to the accounting firm of Smoke, Mirror, and Monty, of Pleasanton's 12,135 residents, 7,324 are of voting age. Of those, 1,242 are registered to vote. Of those, 424 cast their ballots today...212 in favor of the mayor's proposal and 212 opposed. There was one write-in vote to elect Neil deGrasse Tyson as President, but that ballot had to be discarded due to poor penmanship."

Aunt Gertie immediately turns to Jed with eyes that could burn through granite. My psycho cousin has a Christmas morning grin on his face, the kind you get before the disappointment of opening your presents.

"What did you do?" Aunt Gertie screams.

"You know about my penchant for cosmology, Mom. Neil deGrasse Tyson is a visionary. He could really get this country back on track."

"Yes, honey, I agree, but today was not the time or place. Once we save the money for MIT, then maybe we can revisit this topic." A mist forms in her eyes. "I don't want to discourage your passion for discovery, honey, but your love of the stars cost us this election."

Jed loses his grin, and Undead Fred whacks him over the head with an umbrella.

Allison Fisher continues her report. "According to city by-laws, in the case of a tie vote, the mayor gets to decide the final outcome."

Our jaws drop.

Corn kernels and chicken gravy slide down the sides of our faces.

The only sound is Jasper 2 romancing the neighbor's poodle.

"Get my horse!" the colonel finally orders. "All 360 of them."

"Yes, sir," Chastity says. "Where are we going?"

"To set things right, the way we should have done a long time ago."

28

"Come out, you coward!" the colonel screams.

A huge crowd, practically the entire town, has formed in front of City Hall. Even a six-foot-nine Mystery Mel has limped from his sandwich shop on crutches to get a better view. The cameras are rolling live, broadcasting every deliciously gory detail to half the state. It's reality TV at its finest, which explains the huge turnout.

"Come out here now and face me like a man."

Mayor Shight is holed up in the building with the door barricaded. An army of border guards has formed a human shield on the steps. The mayor is peering through a second-floor window, continually running a hand through his hair. It must be a nervous twitch.

"I'm not armed," he whines.

"I just want to talk and settle this like reasonable men."

Amy Fairchild and her mom push their way to the front of the crowd. The younger woman scowls at me and Chastity, as if these hostilities were somehow our fault, and flips us the bird. Chastity responds with a strange kind of mouth gesture – probably a secret cheerleader signal. Doug Jerkins just waves his fist, but there's really nothing for me to fear. I'm wearing a fresh pair of Dependables.

"Come out and face this relic," Mrs. Fairchild screams. "You're the leader of this town for Christ's sake. Don't be intimidated by this zombie's good looks, commanding presence, and towering five-eight frame."

"But he's got a sword."

"And you have your ambition. Don't throw away everything you've schemed for. Don't run into the closet and hide like you did when we were kids and Dad came after us in a drunken stupor."

The mayor thinks for a few seconds, eyes blinking rapidly, but remains paralyzed.

"Go fetch me Old Betsy," Colonel Morbid commands.

Jed, Undead Fred, and Little Ted pile into the back of Chastity's GTO, and the four of them burn rubber. Within minutes, they return with the Civil War era cannon in tow.

"Aim her at the door."

Undead Fred maneuvers the artillery piece with the precision of a rocket engineer, and I finally have to admit that it's a good thing Aunt Gertie didn't have the funds to buy the psycho a cremation clause.

"This is my first and last warning, which is one more warning than I usually give."

The border guards look to Sergeant Barry for direction, but the moustached giant remains immobile. He's peering at Colonel Morbid with fists balled.

"We're out of cannonballs, sir," Jed whispers.

"I've got you covered there," Father Delaney says. He's carrying a bucket of rusty nails. "I saw all the commotion on TV and figured the church should offer its assistance."

"Good man," the colonel says. "God favors the bold."

At the colonel's order, Jed packs the gunpowder, and Undead Fred pours the bucket of rusty nails down its muzzle. Little Ted stands at attention with a lighted punk.

The border guards scatter, even Sergeant Barry.

The only one brave or stupid enough to remain on the steps is Zombie Buck (IQ=N/A). His mouth is open, and drool is mixing with the coagulated blood that still clings to what's left of his neck.

"Well, son. Make up your mind. You can die for good this time for a cause that no one cares about, or you can face cold reality and surrender again. There's no dishonor in surrender when you're woefully outgunned. This isn't the Orient for Christ's sake."

Zombie Buck looks to the crowd in search of divine providence, or maybe an order from one of his old high school teachers. He meets Ernest's eyes instead. The future astronaut approaches the steps. "For once in your life, do the right thing, Buck. I know you have it in you. In case you haven't noticed, I've always looked up to you...your strength and intelligence, your good looks and way with the women. Ever since I was a little kid I wanted to be just like you...I wanted to *be* you. But God made me short and asthmatic and pale and redheaded, and I'm beginning to suspect that Mom might have had one too many glasses of wine at the Blue Lobster and mistook another guy for Dad. But that's beside the point. The point is that despite all of the wedgies and insults and backhands and misery you've doled out over the years, I've always loved you. Don't throw my love away. Do the right thing and earn my admiration."

Sissy Slupchek runs to Ernest and jams her tongue down his throat.

Zombie Buck hovers on the steps with his mouth completely unhinged now. It's an expression of deep thought, practically Einsteinian. He finally pulls a soiled tissue from his pocket and waves it to be clear about his intentions. He then walks over to Ernest and gives him a big hug. Little Ted runs over to them and starts beating the bejesus out of the border guard with his umbrella. "Bad squirrel! Bad squirrel!"

Colonel Morbid pries the bugger off. "Whoa, son. Take it easy. I appreciate your enthusiasm, but don't throw the baby out with the bathwater. 99.9% of border guards are hardworking men and women, doing the best they can at a very difficult job... risking their lives every day to keep the citizens of this town safe. We can't let a few rotten apples and failed leadership spoil the whole barrel. Buck is sorry for what he did, and we must look within our hearts to forgive him. The real problem stems from the top, from that man up there." The colonel points at the mayor, and Little Ted aims his umbrella. "Very bad squirrel," he squeaks.

"Fire!"

Old Betsy clears her throat, and a wave of rusty nails travels at supersonic speed into the wooden door. What's left is sawdust and splinters. Zombie Buck doesn't have quite enough time to get out of the way and loses an arm. But with Dr. Thurgood's new experimental surgery techniques he should be no worse for wear.

"Don't make me go up there," the colonel shouts.

"I'm coming down," Mayor Shight says, waving a handful of copy paper. "Hold your fire. We can talk this through."

He emerges from the rubble of the front door, using his lawyer as a human shield. The ambulance chaser doesn't look too pleased, but I don't think he has much choice in the matter. He's probably on retainer. Colonel Morbid immediately draws his saber and rams the lawyer through the heart. Then he cleaves his head in two.

"But he wasn't a zombie," the mayor says.

"Worse. He was a bloodsucker."

The tip of the sword then finds the soft spot beneath Mayor Shight's chin. The pressure of the blade raises him to his tippy-toes.

"I thought you said we could settle this like reasonable men."

"I am being reasonable, sir, and I'm certainly settling things."

"Tell me what you want. Cars? Women? Backstage passes to *Hamilton*? I'm willing to offer you thirty percent of unappropriated city funds."

The saber draws blood.

"Okay, forty percent, but that's my final offer."

The saber finds an ear.

"Forty-five, damn it. Forty-five."

The colonel scowls at the mayor the way a person might look at a pile of horse manure that's stuck to the bottom of his boot. "This isn't about money, Yankee. This is about honor. Now tell these good townsfolk what you did, and maybe I'll let you live."

The mayor shakes his head, so the colonel's sword finds another ear.

"Keep your mouth shut, Willie," Mrs. Fairchild yells. "Think about the rest of us."

But no one is running to the mayor's rescue, least of all the Border Patrol. Without any lawyers to hide behind or ivory towers to lock himself away in, Mayor Shight is about as exposed as a cockroach in seventh grade science lab. The only difference is that the poor cockroach deserves sympathy.

"Okay, okay." With a deep breath Mayor Shight straightens his tie and strokes his hair and confesses to all of his crimes. His sister faints into Doug Jerkins's arms, devastated that the family gravy train has come off the tracks. Amy Fairchild simply starts crying.

"She's crying," is all I can say.

"It's an act," Chastity responds.

"Those tears look real to me."

"Of course the tears are real, but she's not broken up. A person needs to have a heart to get broken up. She's just trying to manipulate the people around her, same as usual. She's always been a better actress than a cheerleader. I wouldn't pay much attention to her."

"But what if she really is devastated, Chastity? Are you saying that we should check our humanity at the door?"

The third-degree black belt Goth takes a deep breath and straightens her leather jacket. Then she kisses my forehead in a way that a red belt grandmaster might to reassure a promising young protégé. "I'm saying that sometimes even pyros get burned."

Words to live by.

"You said you would let me live," the mayor whines.

Colonel Morbid lowers his sword and spits on the slimeball's feet. "I'm a man of my word. I'm not going to kill you."

The mayor steps back, visibly relieved.

"Where do you think you're going?"

"You said you weren't going to kill me."

"I did, but I didn't say you were free to go. I have other plans for you."

"What plans?"

To answer his question, Colonel Morbid backhands Mayor Shight across the face. Then he slaps him again. He repeats the motion a couple dozen times until the mayor drops to all fours and begs the old war dog to stop.

The colonel then turns to me and winks. "We used to have a term for this back in my day, even before the Yankees sought to impose their imperialistic ideals on us. We called it bitch slapping, Chris. I think I'll make the mayor my bitch."

The crowd cheers.

"Now go fetch me one of those outfits I saw in that play your aunt showed me on the magic picture box. What was that fella's name again? The Pimp?"

"The Gimp," Aunt Gertie clarifies.

"Yeah, the Gimp. Go fetch me one of those gimp outfits."

I'm at too much of a loss for words to even think, let alone meet the colonel's request. But my psycho cousins, as usual, have come prepared. Undead Fred opens the trunk of his mother's '92 Buick Regal and grabs a genuine black leather gimp outfit. It's still in the original packaging, unopened. He hands it to me, and I hand it to Colonel Morbid.

"Good man."

Before Mayor Shight can strip completely nude, Marvin Reynolds climbs up the steps of City Hall. He then straightens his paper hat and raises his arms to settle the crowd. When he has their attention, he says, "In light of the new facts, I think there should be a new vote. Now I see no reason why we can't get a show of hands...the whole town is here. We can emulate the ancient Greek city-states and the venerable tradition of pure democracy."

The pesky crickets are singing again.

"All those against the relocation of zombies, raise your hand."

A clear majority do, so Marvin motions to the mole of a man behind the laptop to record the result. The accountant complies.

"All those in favor of Colonel Morbid becoming our new mayor, raise your hand."

A clear majority do, so the accountant records that result, too.

Marvin then thanks the crowd for their time and commitment to democracy and starts walking down the steps, but Chastity runs up and joins him. "I have one," she says. "I have one."

"Go ahead."

"All those in favor of renaming our town Morbid, IL, raise your hand."

A few folks do, including my friends and family members, but that's about it. The colonel doesn't look too pleased by the result. "Men," he says, "reload Old Betsy."

My psycho cousins load and prime a fresh bucket of rusty nails, courtesy of the church and Father Delaney, and point the old cannon in the crowd's direction.

"I guess you didn't hear me clearly," Chastity repeats. "All those in favor of renaming our town Morbid, IL, raise your hand."

The result is unanimous this time.

The spirit of democracy is intoxicating, and before my brain can even register what my feet are doing, I find myself standing on the steps of City Hall next to the zombie I love and the best drive-thru worker that Artie's has ever known. The way I see it, why risk a closed-door vote of the student council, where kids can say one thing to your face and then take out their passive-aggressive tantrums in the ballot box? An issue as big as who gets to attend senior prom needs to be settled in a public forum. Besides, Old Betsy has a strange power to help people vote the right way. We shouldn't waste it.

"All those in favor of banning zombies from prom, raise your hand."

Amy raises her hand, as does her mom. So do Principal Dawson, Wanda Lopez, and Chad Parker. Amy punches Doug Jerkins in his gut to get his hand up. But that's about it. Even the other jocks and cheerleaders have come to see the light.

Little Ted unsheathes his umbrella and screams out, "Bad squirrels!"

"It's settled then. The ban is defeated. Zombies are free to go to prom."

Marvin gives me a high five. Chastity gives me a French kiss. And Little Ted, as cute as a button, gives me a military salute. I return the gesture, and he grins from ear to ear. Then he chases Doug Jerkins around City Hall with a loaded umbrella in one hand and Colonel Morbid's pearl-handled Walker .44 in the other.

"Cute boy," the colonel says. "Full of piss and vinegar."

29

666 Sunnyside Lane – that's an appropriate address for a gorgeous third-degree black belt zombie. The limo pulls up to the curb, engine purring. Ernest and Sissy Slupchek are conjoined at the mouths like Siamese twins. Ernest is wearing a Miami Vice era pastel blue tuxedo, and Sissy has on a white and yellow dress that accentuates her cone-shaped bra. She left her orthodontic headgear at home, and both of them have switched from glasses to contact lenses. I can't say that they're the cutest couple that Morbid High has ever known, but I can say that they're cute in their own way, which kind of sounds like what a mother would say when she can't think up a real compliment. But I don't mean it like that.

Sitting across from them in the back of our limo, Marvin Reynolds is wearing black slacks and one of those tuxedo T-shirts. He still has a paper hat on his head, but somehow the fast food worker just makes the ensemble work. He re-enrolled in school, since Colonel Morbid's first act as mayor was to abolish the excise tax imposed on zombie families. Now his folks don't need him to work anymore to help pay the rent for their three-room Zombietown hovel. He still decided to stay on at Artie's part-time though, for the free food. Things are looking up.

He's holding hands with the assistant manager from the Wienerworld, whose skintight blue, red, and yellow Lycra dress would probably ball up to the size of a jawbreaker. It turns out she was human, so Marvin's heroic effort to bite her lip and spit out any flesh (so he wouldn't turn rogue) enabled her to rise from the dead. She's showing plenty of cleavage right now, unfazed by the gnarly zipper scar she got from Grandma McGillicutty's Thanksgiving serving platter. Dr. Thurgood used thirty-pound test to sew her chest cavity closed, and I have to admit, the scar is kind of hot in a walking dead sort of way. Marvin claims he gets to untie it at night, but I think he's just pulling my chain.

As for me, I'm wearing a standard black tuxedo with a clip-on bowtie and a fresh coat of eggshell spray paint. Mom made me drink an entire bottle of Oralcline to control the halitosis, and Dad insisted that I clip my eight fingernails. Add to that my *Curlers Rock the House* hat, and I must admit, I'm looking pretty damn suave right about now. Move over George Clooney.

I swallow deeply and ring the doorbell. Chastity and I rehearsed this moment about a hundred times yesterday, and I'm using every dead cell in my body to visualize being brave and holding my ground. Her dad is a former MMA heavyweight and hates zombies, and when he realizes that a member of the undead is taking his precious daughter to prom, he's going to blow a gasket. But I'm prepared for the inevitable. I studied the menu at Dr. Thurgood's office and feel confident that the physician can replace any body parts the ex-fighter might tear off of me. Besides, I'm more than willing to take whatever the bald-headed Mr. Clean can dish out. No one stands between me and my girlfriend. No one.

The door opens, and I close my eyes, and when I raise my eyelids, a radiant young zombie, dressed in a white silk dress, with hair that can only be described as Reykjavik blonde, is standing there smiling. There's a small red spot near her shoulder that looks like blood, but it's probably just tomato juice. I step back and check the address three times; then I look in the bushes for some reason that doesn't even register. "Excuse me, miss. I'm sorry if I got the wrong house, but is Chastity Sky here?"

"It's me, Chris."

The lights reflecting off of her dress and hair are nearly blinding. "What's going on?"

"I told my dad."

"What?"

"I told my dad that I'm a zombie."

"But I didn't need you to do that. I was ready to stand up to your dad. I was ready to fight for the woman I love."

She presses her lips to mine, and I can smell the Zesty Mint Oralcline. "I didn't tell him just for you, Chris. I told him for myself and for all the other zombies out there, especially for my mom. After everything we went through these past few weeks, fighting for our existence and saving the town, I finally came to realize how important it is for each person to be true to herself. The world takes all kinds, Chris, and there's room for everyone – gays, lesbians, transgenders, even chess club members and clarinet players. And most of all, there's room for zombies, too. I just got so tired of hiding, and the more I thought about it, the more I came to realize that hiding is the worst thing a person can do. Because if you hide from yourself, then how could you ever expect anyone else to truly love you for who you are?"

"I'm so proud of you," I say, hugging her. "And I'm sure your mom, wherever she is, would be proud of you, too."

I can tell that Chastity is crying, even though her tear ducts no longer function. But her moistless tears are not tears of sadness or pain. They're tears of relief and freedom and the promise of a new world where everyone is judged on his merits and opportunity is apportioned in equal servings no matter what your zip code or favorite TV show. It's what philosophers and science fiction writers once called *utopia*, but I don't mean it in a bad way.

"He wants to meet you."

"Who?"

"My dad, silly."

My feet won't move, so Chastity drags me by the arm to the living room. Sitting in a La-Z-Boy with both arms broken and a leg that's bent at a geometrically impossible angle is Chastity's dad. His face and chrome dome have pretty deep lacerations, and one of the bones in his arm is sticking about three inches out of the skin; but for the most part he seems rather chipper. I can tell that he's been crying, but I imagine those tears are tears of reconciliation, not pain.

"Daddy, this is my boyfriend, Chris Kantra. He's a zombie, just like me."

The man tries to stand, but his shattered leg gives way, refusing to take any weight; so I walk to the chair and shake one of his fingers in order to save him the embarrassment of appearing crippled.

"Nice to meet you, Chris. I expect you to treat my daughter with honor and respect. Can you do that?"

"Daddy! You said you weren't going to grill my boyfriend. That's why I let you out of the choke hold."

The former MMA fighter motions with his head that he has everything under control. "Can you do that?" he repeats.

"Of course I can, sir. I love your daughter with all my heart."

"Good, because bones heal, son. Just remember that."

We then engage in a bit of parlor talk, and I provide some background on myself, starting, as requested, with the day I was conceived. Then I pin a white orchid to Chastity's dress, right below her best-white smile. Somehow her dad manages to snap a few pics, grunting every time he has to touch the screen. But the former MMA fighter mans up and captures this special moment for posterity.

"I'm so proud of you, baby," he says, tearing up. "I'm so sorry I made you hide who you really are. I never intended for that to happen. I was just so overcome with grief after losing your mother to the dead zone that I became blind to all the beauty that I still had left in my life. Please forgive me, baby. Please find it in your heart to forgive me."

"I forgive you, Daddy," Chastity says, smothering the man in an embrace. He grunts at the pressure, and more blood finds its way to Chastity's dress; but she's a zombie, just like me, so a little blood somehow seems appropriate.

"Thank you, baby, for beating the crap out of me and helping me see things clearly again."

"You're welcome, Daddy. You're so, so welcome."

They spend another moment entwined, and I imagine what Chastity must have been like as a little towheaded girl, bouncing on her father's lap while practicing new heart explosion techniques on his chest. The image is adorable.

"Well, you two better head out," the man says, wiping his eyes on his shoulders. "You don't want to be late for your own prom. And don't forget, baby, you're my daughter...so you hold your head up high."

I shake the man's finger again, and Chastity and I head for the door, and when it closes, I can't help but ask a question. "Shouldn't you call an ambulance for your dad? I mean, there's only a one-in-eight chance that it will crash."

Chastity giggles. "No need for that. I called my sensei. He's going to drive over later and inspect the damage that I inflicted upon my dad. If it passes muster, I might get my fourth degree. Can you believe that, Chris? My fourth degree."

I open the limo door and lead Chastity in by the hand. We sit next to our friends and toast over a bit of sparkling cider. Sissy compliments Chastity's hair and dress, and Chastity reciprocates with a genuine comment about Sissy's contact lenses. Marvin, Ernest, and I share omniscient nods, the kind a hundred years ago we might have exchanged over brandies and cigars. I always imagined I would go to prom, but I never envisioned it would be quite like this. So to answer Chastity's question, I guess I am willing to believe just about anything right now.

* * *

Every senior at Morbid High must be in attendance tonight. The gymnasium is packed to the brim with jocks and cheerleaders, band and chess club members, even an assorted smattering of mutants (of which the zombies are a subcategory). Under the glitter of the disco ball and amidst the thick soup of swirling pheromones, the social castes have joined together to set aside their petty differences for one night and celebrate the common strand that bonds us all: the inevitability of adulthood. I'm not sure if we're all ready for it, but what I've learned over the past few months is that nature has a way of forcing her agenda, whether a person is ready for it or not.

Marvin and the assistant manager from the Wienerworld waste no time running out onto the dance floor. They start bumping and grinding to the sounds of Katy Perry, and Marvin keeps placing his hand on his paper hat and twirling in circles like some zombie Fred Astaire. The assistant manager is holding her own, shoving cleavage in and out of his face. The gnarly zipper scar is flexing beneath the strobe lights and might burst open if she doesn't slow down.

Ernest is trying to dance, too, but his interpretation of the act is better suited to that '83 Styx hit, *Mr. Roboto*. Sissy Slupchek keeps trying to speed up the tempo, and he keeps using his bum leg as a pretext for a lack of rhythm. With Ernest's pumpkin hair (now matted with dried blood) and Sissy's cone-shaped bra, the two of them resemble that monster movie in which Godzilla battled Gigan and destroyed half of Tokyo. But they're laughing and having fun, taking turns at stepping on each other's feet, and at the end of the day that's what matters most.

And they're not alone. Romance is in the air, and it reeks of methane and sulfur. Tennis champ, Susie Monik, is swaying her redwood frame alongside Tad Wooster. The outline of her Adidas shirt is peeking through the lace of her dress, but her pit stains aren't visible. The tattoo of Count Chocula is popping and locking (Tad is wearing a sleeveless tuxedo shirt, similar to Marvin's, and is waving a socket wrench in the air). He reminds me of those banditos in the old westerns who fire pistols overhead whenever they find gold or get drunk. Reggie Matheson is grooving next to Tad with his dates, moving slower than the music, almost between the beats. The fluidity of his motions transcends the laws of Newtonian physics, as if he's tapped into another dimension where the god of funk has blessed him with the knowledge of cool. Behind him, Frederick, the janitor, is getting into the groove, too, sneaking a nip or two from his beloved flask in synch with the baseline. He's doing his best to clean up the vomit, but the crowd is too worked up, and he's falling behind.

As *Roar* ends and the herd storms the tables for the spiked Hawaiian Punch (courtesy of Chad Parker), Amy Fairchild can't help but approach us. She's wearing a tight pink satin dress, low-cut, to flaunt her perfect cleavage. "I'm so sorry to see what happened to you, Chastity," she smiles. "You were an okay friend once, with average cheerleading skills, so I have to admit it's refreshing to see your natural hair color again. But the rest of your body, well, that's a different story. I guess you got what you deserved. I think we're all going to miss you."

"I'm still here."

"Not really."

Chastity reaches for a cup of punch, and I can already envision it splashing in Amy's face, but my girlfriend manages to exercise restraint, the hallmark of a fourth-degree black belt.

"Besides, now that you're a zombie, you don't have to labor under the false expectation of becoming prom queen. The only reason you ever had a chance is because you used to be a cheerleader, but now look at you. You're a corpse for goodness sake… and a stinky one at that."

The smirk on Amy's face would make me hurl if it didn't reveal such stunningly white teeth. They're enough to make any zombie take notice. She's gloating in that *Seventeen* magazine sort of pose she has, the way she did when she made me eat that jar of Elmer's.

"We're beyond you now, Amy," I say. "You and your gimp uncle."

The smirk vanishes. "Don't talk about my uncle, paste boy."

"He's going to make a cute pet for the colonel."

Before Amy can spew any more venom our way, Mystery Mel (who was good enough to act as an usher) limps on stage with his new forty-five inch inseam. He's carrying the head of our new principal – the Squid. He places her on the podium in front of the microphone and slices open an envelope with his razor-sharp spatula. Principal Squid clears her throat.

"Ladies and gentleman, it's the moment we've all been waiting for. The tally is in. With great pleasure I present to you Morbid High School's prom king and prom queen. Chris Kantra and Chastity Sky!"

The crowd erupts. Chastity tries to cry. Marvin even offers me a high five. As I limp on stage with my arm wrapped around the woman I love, a sensation of thankfulness overcomes me. Not thankfulness for being dead or discovering that spray paint can double as skin; not even thankfulness for rising to the height of teenage popularity on the back of tragedy, fear, and death. But thankfulness for sharing one of the most important moments of my existence with the most important person in my life. Chastity Sky. And as if to honor us with a gesture of congratulations, one she knows we couldn't help but appreciate, Amy Fairchild vomits all over Doug Jerkins's tuxedo. He tries to push her away, but she clings to him and empties the contents of her stomach onto his chest. The dark, mulchy consistency hints of Dong Dongs.

I place Chastity's crown on her head and she places my crown on mine, and we join tongues in a passionate French kiss. Then we saunter onto the dance floor for our featured dance. The DJ blares *Monster* by Lady Gaga, and we start to move. Chastity wants to lead (being the better dancer) and so do I (being the king), and as we debate and struggle for control of the dance, I begin to moan and flail around the dance floor. But the crowd doesn't scream and run for their lives. Neither do they rush at us with fire axes and flamethrowers. Instead they cheer. Louder than at any basketball game. It's deafening actually.

"Go, Chast. Go, Chuck."

"Go, Chast. Go, Chuck."

Amidst the fervor of their support, Chastity and I finally settle into a slow teeter, the kind preferred by frat boys who clutch red plastic beer cups, and when Lady Gaga sings: *he ate my heart...and then he ate my brain*, Chastity and I start laughing. We know it's a metaphor, but somehow the song just seems appropriate.

"I love you, Chris. You'll always be my prom king."

"I love you, too, Chastity. You're the only girl for me."

As we start to make out, the rest of the senior class flows onto the dance floor and fills me with a sense of warmth. I won't bore you with the technical explanation of how their combined body heat and the gymnasium's lack of circulation act in concert to raise the ambient temperature, warming every inanimate object contained within, including zombies. Let's just say it's the feeling of camaraderie. And the feeling is so strong that even Doug Jerkins is trying his best to dance with a ruptured stomach lining and Dong-Dong-stained shirt. Wanda Lopez is helping him, the consummate cheerleader, rubbing her chest in his face for encouragement; and Chad Parker, who's always possessed a munificent heart, seems to be a good sport about sharing his date. But Amy Fairchild, cantankerous banshee to the end, will have none of it. She slaps Doug across the face and kicks him in the walnuts.

"You're such a moron," she yells. "Don't you even realize that paste boy and his slut girlfriend just took our rightful place as prom king and queen?"

"Being prom king and queen isn't everything," Doug stutters.

"Did that hot dog eating contest damage your brain, too?" Amy yells, marching off.

Doug straightens his back with Wanda's support. "Maybe, but at least my ass isn't getting fat."

"Amen, brother," Chastity whispers.

When *Monster* ends, I realize that I've ingested at least a gallon of punch and better take a leak before I start to leak. Given the formality of the occasion, I risked not wearing my Dependables. So I leave the gymnasium and limp down the hall and discuss with Chastity (who needs to use the restroom, too) whether we should head out to the mallard garden now for our little rendezvous. Before she can assuage my fears that she's decided to wait until marriage, someone pushes me from behind.

"You're such a loser," Amy Fairchild blares out. "Both of you. And what's with the bright white dress? There's no way in hell you're still a virgin, slut."

"Screw you, bulimia bitch."

"I wouldn't talk, necrophile. That's my crown."

Amy reaches for Chastity's crown, but Chastity twists Amy's arm behind her back and smashes her face into the wall. She then grabs Amy's chin and twists, fixing to sever the spinal cord, but I place my good hand (the one with all its fingers) on her wrist and gently pull it away.

"What are you doing? Why are you defending her?"

"I'm not defending her, Chastity. I'm defending you. You're not a murderer. You're a prom queen. You can't just go around killing people whenever you disagree with their philosophical frameworks...even if you do reside in Morbid, IL."

Chastity takes a deep breath and counts to ten. I think she's using her visualization technique to calm down. Amy keeps writhing and kicking, but there's no chance of her wrestling free of Chastity's arm bar.

"You're absolutely right, Chris. I'm not a murderer. I'm a zombie. And just like my mom, I need to be myself." And with that, she tears a big chunk out of Amy's neck.

The cheerleading captain screeches to high heaven as blood erupts from her jugular, but the music inside the gymnasium is too loud for anyone to hear. Chastity continues with her feast, biting off one of Amy's ears. She chews it slowly, savoring the subtle nuance of its elfin flavor. She moves onto the second ear next, and then to the wedge of Amy's nose. The cheerleader is whimpering now, the way young children do when they realize that everything is not going to be okay.

"Chastity, no! You're going to turn rogue!"

But my girlfriend just smiles and continues to gnaw on Amy. She takes little bites, to prolong the cheerleader's agony, and spits out a couple of finger bones. "This tastes a lot better than I thought it would, Chris. I never would have figured that a skank like Amy could taste so sweet."

"Stop it, Chastity. You're a prom queen for Christ's sake."

"I've gone all-in now, Chris. I know I'm going to turn rogue, but I was planning on venturing into the dead zone anyway. My mom is out there, and I need to find her. I've always known that I'd go searching for her someday, and your love and support have finally helped me realize that that day is now. I mean, I was going to wait until tomorrow, after our special night at the mallard garden, but Amy just made it too hard to resist. I guess I don't deserve my fourth degree after all."

"Weren't you going to tell me?"

"Of course I was...after our special night. And I was going to ask you to join me."

Amy squirms, so Chastity rams her fist through the cheerleader's back, yanking out a short rib. She starts gnawing on it without breaking eye contact with me.

"But what about school? What about our friends? There's no coming back from turning rogue."

Chastity drops the polished bone to the ground and reaches into Amy's carcass for another rib. "I'm not so sure about that. Remember what Uncle Desmond said? If anyone could find a cure, it would be my mom."

"That's right. She got her PhD from MIT."

"And that's a fairly decent school."

I can appreciate my girlfriend's need to reunite with her long, lost mother. I mean, what child unrelated to me could bear to live without her mom, but the decision to turn rogue and roam the dead zone is so sudden and extreme that my limited synaptic activity is having trouble getting ahold of it. I mean, I'm prom king now and was looking forward to all of the rights and privileges associated with the title. And Mr. Broomfield, the school counselor, told me that if I work really hard on my grades this semester, I might have a real shot at getting into community college. And the bonspiel. Ernest and the ladies from the curling club are really counting on me.

"Please come with me," Chastity asks, batting her blonde, bloodstained eyelashes. "I don't know if I can do this without you. We're a team now, like the *A-Team*."

"Well, I guess I could ask Marvin to step in for me at the bonspiel. The boy is a natural athlete and a quick learner, and Clara might like him better anyway."

"I'm sure Marvin would be happy to help out."

"And I could always defer community college for a year. I've read that rich kids like to do that so they can go travel the world and learn from the richness of experience. I guess the dead zone kind of fits into the definition of experience."

"Of course it does."

"And there really isn't enough room for me at Aunt Gertie's trailer. Jimmy is old enough to have his own tent now. Besides, I'm sick of listening to him read my copy of *Big Smiles* in the middle of the night."

"Exactly."

"So what should I do?"

Chastity looks to Amy's quivering carcass. The cheerleader is still clinging to life, but just barely. "The meat tastes best while it's warm."

I lick my lips, and my stomach gurgles, and I realize for the first time since kindergarten that I never really liked the flavor of paste. I know that a great philosopher once taught us that when we're wronged by somebody, instead of lashing back we should just turn the other cheek, but I can't imagine he was referring to zombies (even though he supposedly came back from the dead, too). So I'm left in a bit of a quandary. Should I do the right thing, or should I go with my instincts? Or in this whole new paradigm in which the dead walk the earth, are my instincts the new right thing? The loop of logic is enough to make any young zombie's head explode.

But Amy's twitching, hemorrhaging body is just looking so damn tasty right now, and if I don't act soon, Chastity is going to hog all the good parts. So I lean toward the small of Amy's back and lick the outline of her Rod of Asclepius tattoo. Then I sink my teeth into her flesh with the gentleness it deserves. Her carcass cringes, and she tries to call for help with her last breath, but Chastity gets to her vocal cords first; so the cheerleader merely releases a gurgle before falling silent. I feel like I should say something profound to commemorate the moment; it's not so often that a person gets to facilitate the passing of a mortal enemy. But Amy's exposed pancreas finally rams home the realization that she was only human, same as me – no better or worse, perhaps just a bit more misdirected – and in the grand scheme of things she probably doesn't warrant another single thought.

But words are coming to my lips anyway through a will of their own, so I relax my jaw and set them free. "Hey Chastity, you wouldn't happen to have any hot sauce, would you?"

EPILOGUE

The roar of the engine knocks me out of a deep sleep, the kind without dreams or even the urge to urinate. My movements summon Chastity from her slumber, too. She's lying beside me, half nude.

That's right, people: *half nude*. I'll let you read into that what you will.

She barely has enough time to put her Bananarama shirt on before the door to our hovel gets kicked down. Two border guards rush in, dressed in black Kevlar vests and black baseball caps. One of them is Chad Parker. The other is Ernest Pratt.

"Chris?" he says. "Chastity?"

"Ernest?"

I run to hug him, and he reciprocates, and after about twenty seconds of intimate boy love, we remember that others are standing in the room. So we take a step back from one another.

"Damn glad to see you again," I say, forcing my voice into the bass register.

"Likewise," Ernest says, shaking my hand.

"Why did you kick down our door?"

"We got reports that two rogues were lurking around the building. Now that Zombietown is officially part of the dead zone again, I got stationed out here. Colonel Morbid took a case all the way to the Supreme Court, arguing that the Border Patrol isn't technically law enforcement, given its long history of ignoring the law, and as such can't hide behind the exemption to the integration laws of '96."

"So he won?"

"Just barely. Everyone thought the court was going to throw out the case, but during oral arguments, the colonel worked his magic and won over a couple of the female justices; one of the gay ones, too. The decision was five-four."

"That's fantastic."

"Yeah, it opens up a lot of possibilities for hardworking zombies everywhere. The benefits are good and the hours are tolerable, and to be perfectly honest, we mingle in better with the natives. Buck even got promoted to station chief...long overdue if you ask me. The colonel said that my brother was a natural for management – smart enough to get the job done but not clever enough to get his own ideas."

"You look great in that uniform, Ernest," Chastity says. "And you washed the blood out of your hair, too. How's Sissy?"

"She's fine. Thanks for asking. She's majoring in cryptozoology at the community college...wants to set up an expedition to find that chupacabra we set free from holding cell number eight. She thinks it'll be worth millions."

"Could be. People have always liked to be entertained by freaks and oddities. We'll let you know if we spot it."

"Cool."

I look my former Blockbuilder partner up and down and have to admit, the uniform does give him an aura of authority. But he's still the same concave-chested, spindly-armed gamer I grew up with, and the thought of him wrestling rogue zombies to the ground with his bare hands doesn't really add up. I know he wanted to be like Zombie Buck and drive a monster truck, but I can't see him doing this job for the rest of his death.

"I thought you wanted to be an astronaut."

Ernest straightens his back and lights up like a Rockefeller Center Christmas tree. "That's the beauty of it. The colonel pulled some strings and got me enrolled in the Border Patrol's Astronaut Training Program. It's a new joint venture with NASA. The administrators over at Cape Canaveral figure that shiny new colonies on Mars will attract undesirable elements.

They want to make sure they have a plan in place to keep those elements at bay."

"Good for you."

He scans our room and then peers from the window, still searching.

"*These* are the rogues," Chad Parker says, growing impatient. "These are the rogues that ate Amy."

"Shut up, Chad, unless you want to walk back to the station." Ernest points to the stripes on his arm. He then turns to me. "It's hard to find good help these days. The desk sergeant insisted that I bring this rookie along for a ride, you know, to show him the ropes. The beauty of the arrangement is that I get to decide whether or not he's Border Patrol material."

Chastity erupts into laughter.

Chad shrugs his shoulders. "I blew out my knee during the first practice at SC. They took away my scholarship and made me reimburse them for the plane ticket."

"What makes you think we ate Amy?" I ask.

"She told us."

I can feel my jaw drop, almost to the ground, but being the consummate gentleman that I am, I help press Chastity's mandible back into place before working on my own. We both figured that Amy was a goner. I mean, we tied what was left of her up in chains and stuffed her down a septic tank. It seemed like the appropriate thing to do at the time.

"She came back?"

"Oh yeah," Ernest says. "Pissed as hell. She's been gurgling about how it takes more than six months at the bottom of a septic tank to get rid of a cheerleader."

"How...how is she?" Chasity asks.

"She looks like crap, but somehow the fecal matter kept her from turning rogue. She's been looking for you guys. I'd watch my back if I were you."

"Let her look," Chastity says, fists balled.

Ernest searches the closet. Then he peeks under the bed. When he reaches the kitchen, he sniffs a bag of month-old Oreos. "Can I have one?"

"Help yourself. How's Marvin?"

"He led our curling team to victory over Shady Meadows. Randy was so impressed by the influx of senior customers that the win generated that he promoted Marvin to assistant manager. He's training Doug Jerkins to work the drive-thru now. Doug isn't exactly what you would call a quick learner. I had to start getting my lunch inside because he kept screwing up the drink order."

"What a pain."

"With the extra fifty cents an hour though, Marvin finally got a new lawnmower engine for his '76 Toyota pickup."

"Yeah, I can hear him buzzing by at night sometimes on the way home from a late shift. We haven't approached him though...we don't want to implicate him or his family in any way. Besides, we've spent nearly ninety percent of our time deep in the dead zone. We only come back to Zombietown for showers and a bit of dumpster diving."

"Any luck?" Ernest asks, turning to Chastity.

"Not yet," she says, shaking her head.

"But we'll keep trying," I say, "for as long as it takes. It's a big, raw world out there, and we've only scratched the surface. You should come with us sometime, Ernest. You'd be amazed by all the kooky characters."

The border guard strokes the moss on his chin. It kind of resembles a goatee.

"Maybe someday. For now, I need to focus on keeping our borders safe and training for a Mars mission. It was good seeing you guys again though. We really had one hell of a senior year, didn't we?"

Chastity nods, as do I, and I can't help but acknowledge how far I've come from playing Blockbuilder in my mom's basement every Friday night. Death can be good to a person sometimes, as crazy as that sounds.

"Well, I'd better get going," Ernest says, winking. "You two let me know if you come across those rogues, okay?"

"Will do."

He then pulls out his baton and whacks Chad in his bad knee. The former football star crumbles like a sack of horse manure and tries to crawl away. Before Chastity and I pounce on him, we look to Ernest, as if for permission.

The future astronaut just shrugs his shoulders. "He wasn't Border Patrol material."

ABOUT THE AUTHOR

Joe Arzac has been a fan of zombie films and literature since he first saw *Night of the Living Dead* on TV as a kid. He was probably too young to be watching, which is one reason why the movie left such an indelible impression on him. *DROP DEAD, LOSER* is his attempt to pay homage to the genre by taking a somewhat humorous approach.

A graduate of Stanford University and The University of Chicago, Joe lives with his family in Illinois and hopes that zombies, along with their vampire and werewolf cousins, stay fictional for the foreseeable future.

73073171R00171

Made in the USA
Columbia, SC
06 September 2019